...the

husband and their three children. In addition to devoting herself full-time to writing, Cristina also works for the family beekeeping business, dealing with the care of queen bees, and enjoys cultivating a variety of roses. The world of perfumes and natural essences has been a passion of Cristina's for many years. Her debut novel, *The Secret Ways of Perfume*, is a tribute to the connection between scent, memory and emotion. Due to be published in twenty-six countries, *The Secret Ways of Perfume* has already been a bestseller in Italy, Germany, Holland, Spain and Portugal.

THE SECRET WAYS OF PERFUME

Cristina Caboni

BLACK SWAN

TRANSWORLD PUBLISHERS
61–63 Uxbridge Road, London W5 5SA
www.penguin.co.uk

Transworld is part of the Penguin Random House group of companies
whose addresses can be found at global.penguinrandomhouse.com

Penguin
Random House
UK

First published in Great Britain in 2016 by Black Swan
an imprint of Transworld Publishers

A CIP catalogue record for this book
is available from the British Library.

ISBN
9781784160500

Typeset in 11/13.5pt Bembo by Falcon Oast Graphic Art Ltd.
Printed and bound by Clays Ltd, Bungay, Suffolk.

Penguin Random House is committed to a sustainable
future for our business, our readers and our planet. This book is
made from Forest Stewardship Council® certified paper.

1 3 5 7 9 10 8 6 4 2

Tell me woman where you hide your mystery
woman waters deep volume transparent
more secret the more you undress
what is the strength of your unarmed splendour
your dazzling armour of beauty

Tomás Segovia (1927–2011),
translated by Ruth Clarke

To all the women in my life
my mother, my sisters,
my daughters, my friends.
This book is for you.

'Happiness is nothing more than the scent of our soul.'

Coco Chanel

Prologue

*Rosewood: movement. Sweet and fruity with a hint of spice,
obtained from tropical trees.*
The fragrance of trust and serenity.
Evokes the sweet pain of longing and hope.

Florence, twenty years ago

'Close your eyes, little one.'

'Like this, Grandma?'

'Yes, Elena, like that. Now do what I taught you.'

In the semi-darkness of the room, with her hands resting on the table, the little girl closes her eyes tight. Her slender fingers sweep across the surface and catch hold of the smooth edge in front of her. But it's not the essences in the jars covering the walls that she can smell. It's her grandmother's impatience. It's the scent of her own fear.

'Well?'

'I'm trying.'

The old lady purses her lips. The smell of her anger is bitter, like the last puff of smoke a piece of wood exudes before it turns to ash. In a minute Grandma will hit her, and then she'll storm out. Elena knows she just has to hold out a little longer; just a little . . .

'Come on, concentrate! And close your eyes like I told you!'

The slap barely puts a hair out of place on Elena's head. It's not a real slap, but fake, just like everything else. Like the lies her grandmother tells, and the lies Elena tells her in return.

'So – tell me what it is.' Tired of waiting, Lucia Rossini waves a vial full of essences under the child's nose. But she's not looking for a simple answer from the girl. She wants something else – something Elena has no intention of giving her.

'Rosemary, thyme, verbena.'

Another slap.

Tears sting her eyes. But she doesn't give in, and to steel herself she starts to hum a little tune.

'No, no. You won't find the Perfect Perfume like that. Don't stay outside it. Go in – *look* for it! It's part of you – you have to feel what it's saying to you, you have to understand it, you have to love it. Try again, and this time try harder!'

But Elena doesn't love perfume any more. She doesn't want to see the meadows along the riverbank where her mother took her when she was little, just outside the village. She doesn't want to hear the sound of the tender grass as it grows, or the water as it trickles by. She doesn't want to feel the frogs' eyes staring out at her from the reeds.

She squeezes her eyelids shut and grits her teeth, deter-mined to block everything out. But in that darkness, a spark suddenly ignites.

'The rosemary is white.'

Her grandmother's eyes widen. 'Yes,' she murmurs, her face

lighting up with hope. 'Why? Tell me all about it.'

Elena lets the feelings drift into her, filling her mind and her heart.

The rosemary is a colour now. She can feel it on the tip of her tongue, coursing under her skin, making her shiver. The bare white becomes red, then purple.

The girl's eyes narrow in fright.

'No, I don't want to! I don't want to!'

Frowning, her grandmother watches as she runs out of the room. Then, after a long sigh, she goes over to the window and opens the shutters. The tired evening light yawns its way into the laboratory that has belonged to the Rossini family for over three centuries.

Lucia takes a key from her apron pocket, reaches up and unlocks the wooden cupboard that spans the entire wall. As she opens the door, the gentle aroma of wild herbs emerges, followed by a fresh citrus perfume, blending into the scent of vanilla in the room.

Enveloped in this symphony of contrasting smells, the woman strokes the meticulously ordered volumes in front of her and then calmly selects one. She holds it against her chest for a moment. Then, sitting at the polished wood table, she opens it with care, running her fingers over the time-yellowed pages, as she has done countless times before, in search of the Perfect Perfume.

In that moment, it seems as if Lucia is looking for something else, too. But there's nothing in the neat handwriting that can help her explain to her granddaughter that perfume is not something you choose.

Perfume is the way. And following it means finding your own heart.

1

Oak moss: lightness of heart. Intense, penetrating, ancestral.
The fragrance of perseverance and strength.
Drives away thoughts of our own mistakes. Lessens nostalgia
*   for what might have been.*

The present day

There was a dry smell rising up from the river Arno. The smell of mouldy flour, nauseating like the disappointment churning her stomach.

Elena Rossini stood on the Ponte Vecchio and wrapped her arms around her chest. In front of her, the river trickled by, parched by a dry summer that had barely seen rain.

'There aren't even any stars,' she murmured to herself, staring up at the sky.

Yet from time to time a shaft of light illuminated the warm September evening and sparkled on the metallic surfaces of the 'love locks' – lovers' padlocks that were clustered together on the bridge railing, like the thoughts jostling for space in her mind.

She stretched out her hand and touched one. For lovers, the objects represented promises of eternal commitment. Matteo had chosen a big, sturdy padlock; he had fastened it in front of her and then thrown the key into the river. Elena could still remember the taste of the kiss he gave her afterwards, right before he asked her to move in with him.

She froze.

Now he was her ex-boyfriend, ex-business partner, ex- so many things.

She wrapped her arms around her chest more tightly, staving off a shiver, and started walking, heading for Piazzale Michelangelo. But just before she set off, Elena cast one last glance at the string of romantic hopes. Matteo would soon be placing a new padlock there, she was willing to bet. A shiny gold one, if she knew her ex-boyfriend.

Matteo and Alessia – that was the name of the new chef, the woman who'd taken her place. The woman who, for a while, Elena had foolishly considered a friend. There was a time when they would giggle, huddled together, telling one another the things it seemed nobody else in the world could understand.

It was her own stupid fault, Elena told herself. She should have guessed there was something wrong, but Matteo had given nothing away – he'd never acted differently around Alessia. The thought filled her with anger. It wasn't fair. He'd given her no choice.

She picked up her pace, as though she wanted to leave the scene she'd witnessed that morning behind her. But it was no use; the images kept playing over and over in her mind, like a scene from a film on a loop.

★ ★ ★

Elena had gone into the little restaurant she ran with Matteo. Normally, at that time of day, he'd be in the kitchen, sorting out the day's menu. But when she opened the door she was greeted by a sight that stopped her in her tracks. She had to grab hold of the doorframe as her knees gave way with the shock.

Alessia and Matteo sprang up, trying to cover themselves any way they could.

The three of them looked at one another, stunned, the silence broken only by the laboured breathing of the two lovers.

Elena stood speechless, immobile, trying to comprehend exactly what she'd just witnessed. Then, slowly, her thoughts managed to push their way through the confusion in her mind.

'What on earth are you doing?' Elena shouted.

Later, she wished she'd said a lot more and done something completely different, regretting such a pointless question: the answer was glaringly obvious. If the blood hadn't drained entirely from her head, taking her sense of humour with it, Elena would have laughed at the grotesque scene in front of her. Instead, she just stood there, with her fists clenched and her heart beating furiously against her ribs – insulted, indignant, waiting for Matteo to explain himself.

But Matteo didn't even bother to deny it. There was no 'Darling, it's not what it looks like'. Instead, he went on the attack.

'What are you doing here? Shouldn't you be in Milan?' he snarled at her.

This reaction bewildered her – as if she were the one who needed to justify herself. She hadn't been feeling well so she'd come back. She hadn't let him know, though, because she hadn't thought it was necessary.

'How could you do something like this to me?'

The wrong phrase again.

Silence, embarrassment, helplessness, and – finally – anger. Words had never been her forte, and in that moment they deserted her completely. So she turned her gaze from him to Alessia, as if *she* could explain the obvious. Elena wanted to hit her, stamp on her 'friend' with all her might. Didn't she realize what she'd just done?

Elena had been going out with Matteo for over two years. They were supposed to get married one day. Not that he'd asked her in so many words – but weren't they living together? Hadn't Elena invested the best part of her savings in his damned restaurant?

And now, her dreams, her plans . . . gone. It was all over.

'There's no point getting upset. These things happen,' Matteo said.

These things happen?

That was the point her indignation reached its peak and, rather than falling to her knees, broken by the betrayal, she felt a fierce anger flow through her – and suddenly explode.

Seconds later, a pan was flying through the air straight towards the couple, who ran for cover behind the table. The clatter of metal hitting the floor marked the end of the whole affair.

Then Elena turned around and walked away from everything that, until just a few moments earlier, she had believed represented her future.

Nearby laughter tore her from her thoughts, making way for a bittersweet reflection, a thought that was barely even a memory but gave her a stab of satisfaction nonetheless: her grandmother, Lucia, had never liked Matteo Ferrari.

18

Elena, on the other hand, had adored him from the very beginning. She'd spoiled him and supported him. Yes, she'd helped him the way she thought a good partner should. She had never compromised their relationship by seeing other men – pointless dates and one-night stands simply didn't interest her. Matteo was what she needed. He wanted a family, he liked children. And that was essential for her. It was, in the end, the reason she'd chosen him and done everything she could to keep him happy and fulfil his needs.

But he'd betrayed her anyway.

That was what stung the most. Her reward for making a commitment, for putting herself out there, had been more than disappointing: it had been a complete disaster.

There were so many people out that night. The picturesque, historic centre of Florence didn't go to sleep until dawn: the piazzas were full of artists, students and tourists, stopping to chat under the streetlamps, or in darker corners perfect for more intimate encounters.

Elena walked on, letting her memories drift away, immersing herself in the familiar smells of the Santa Croce district. She knew every little crack in those streets, every cobblestone smoothed by centuries of footsteps. The outlines of houses soothed her tired eyes. Shop signs glimmered in the dark. The area never seemed to change; Elena was surprised by the strange pleasure she took from seeing these places again.

A year, she thought. It was over a year since she'd been back to her grandmother's place. After Lucia's death, she hadn't set foot in the house again.

Yet for so long it had been her world. She'd been to junior school and then high school with the nuns in via della Colonna, just a stone's throw from the Rossini family home.

She used to watch the other children playing from those same windows.

None of them had understood about perfume. They'd never even seen an alembic still, had no idea, for instance, that fat absorbed smells. *Essence, concrete, absolute* and *blend* were just random words to them.

But they all had a mother and father.

At first, she'd ignored the other children. But then she found herself envying their cosy, conventional world, wanting to be part of it, wanting to be like them.

Her classmates' parents were always very nice to her: there were presents, invitations . . . She was never not included. But their smiles never reached their eyes. Their glances would flicker over her, as if she were a duty that had to be taken care of, a chore to be performed and forgotten.

And then she understood.

The bitter taste of shame had distanced her from even those friends who seemed not to mind the strange house she lived in, or the fact that it was her grandmother who went to school concerts and parents' evenings. There were other orphaned children, of course. The point was, though, that Elena did actually have a mother.

Angrily, she pushed down that memory, which had lain dormant for years. Feeling sorry for herself . . . that was all she needed!

Swallowing back the bitterness, she picked up her pace again. She was almost there now. The high stone palazzo walls all around her felt welcoming and comforting. The air had turned cool, and the pavement gave off an acrid scent of humidity. Elena breathed it in, waiting for the moment it would meet the smell coming from the river. The smell of the past, the smell of loss.

She stopped in front of a huge door, put an old key into the lock and turned it. Closing her eyes for just a moment, she immediately felt better.

She was back.

Even though returning to her grandmother's house was the only sensible thing to do, the young woman couldn't ignore the deep sense of defeat. She'd left determined to change her life, and instead she was back here, in the house she'd left behind when she was so full of dreams for the future.

Elena almost ran up the stairs, trying not to look down the two dark corridors that led to what had once been the laboratory and Lucia Rossini's workshop. She went into the bathroom, took a quick shower, then changed the sheets and got into bed.

Lavender, bergamot and sage. Their perfume drifted through the whole house: it was penetrating, like the loneliness crushing her heart. A moment before she surrendered to exhaustion, she thought she felt a soft hand stroking her hair.

The following morning she woke up early, as usual. She lay still for a moment, staring at the ceiling. She'd left the shutters open, that's why it was so bright. The floor and the bed were bathed in sunlight. But it was the perfume of the house that fought its way through her lethargy and wrapped itself around her.

She got up, because she didn't know what else to do. Downstairs, she took a seat in the same place she'd always sat since she was a little girl. After a moment she looked at the polished wood table and noticed just how big it was. She fidgeted awkwardly in her chair. There was a gloomy, oppressive silence.

'I could put the TV on,' she mumbled aloud. But her grandmother didn't have one; she'd always hated television. And Elena wasn't a huge fan either; she much preferred reading.

But all her books were still at Matteo's place.

An overwhelming pain stirred in the pit of her stomach. Her life had fallen apart . . . what on earth was she going to do?

She looked around, bewildered. Every single thing in the house was familiar to her, and she loved all those strange, old objects: the plates hanging on the wall, the glazed terracotta pots her grandmother kept pasta in, the furniture she'd so often had to polish, no matter how much she complained. She should have felt less lonely surrounded by these things, but instead she felt empty, so empty and alone.

She stood up, and with her head bowed, went straight back to her bedroom. She thought about calling her friend Monie and telling her everything. About that snake Matteo, and about Alessia. They made a fine couple. She bit back a swear word. Then, realizing she was alone and there was no one to shock, she rattled off a whole stream of profanities. She said them all, every single bad word she knew. She started quietly, then her voice grew stronger until she was shouting. She carried on yelling until she felt ridiculous, and only then did she stop.

A moment later, sitting on the bed, she dialled Monie's number, wiping away her tears as she did so. She mustn't cry – Monie would be able to tell. Her friend had no time for cry-babies, Elena reminded herself. She took a couple of deep breaths, counting the rings.

How long was it since she'd spoken to Monique? A month, maybe two? She'd been so busy managing the restaurant, and coping with all Matteo's demands.

'*Oui?*'

'Monie, is that you?'

'Elena? *Chérie*, how are you? Do you know, I was just thinking about you! How's it going?'

Elena didn't answer – she couldn't. Cluching her mobile tight, she burst into tears.

Myrtle: forgiveness. Beautiful, magical, evergreen. Intense and
*   deeply aromatic.*
The fragrance of serenity, the very essence of the soul.
Soothes the spirit, relieves anger and resentment.

'Perfume is emotion, it's a vision that you have to transform into a fragrance.'

'Yes, Grandma.'

'This is what we do. This is our job, my girl. It's our duty, and a privilege.'

Elena looks down. Lucia's words dart through the air like delicate notes of jasmine; first lightly, seemingly innocuous, then intense, hypnotic and compelling. She doesn't want to listen to them, she doesn't want to lose herself in the dreams they evoke, she doesn't want to follow them. Her heart starts to race, and colours run through her. Now they're scents, but they turn into a sky full of shining stars.

It's easy to lose herself in them, it's fun. They make her

smile, they make her happy. There's no reality, no responsibilities. Nothing matters now; only the colours, only the perfume.

'Perfume is a language – it's how we speak. Remember, Elena, perfume is the truth – the only thing that really counts. You can't lie to perfume. Perfume is what we are. It's our true essence.'

A loud buzz interrupted Elena's dream and she sat up with a start, bewildered. As the last threads of sleep dissolved, she took in the familiar objects and realized where she was. The weight of her memories was heavy, and relentless. There had been one second of detachment from reality, a moment when time and space didn't exist. Then she heard her mobile vibrate again.

She jumped out of bed, tripping over the sheets tangled around her legs, and, kneeling on the polished floorboards, she fumbled in her handbag.

'Where are you, for God's sake? Where have you got to?' she wailed as the contents of her shoulder bag scattered across the floor, rolling in all directions. She finally got hold of her mobile and opened it. When she saw the name on the screen, she closed her eyes, pressing the device to her lips.

'Monie?' she said, still half-asleep.

'Elena, what are you doing? I've been here nearly an hour. I can't believe you forgot we were meeting this morning.'

'Sorry, you're right. It's just ...' Elena paused and sighed. 'Listen, do you mind if we cancel? I really don't feel like going out today.'

'If you're going to carry on like this, you might as well ring the priest and ask him to bury you now, Elena. I've got half a mind to call my mum and tell her what's going on.'

'No! You promised you wouldn't, remember?'

'No, I don't remember. It must be the Florence air, the same thing that made you forget we were meeting this morning.'

Elena felt guilty. 'Look, I'll get over it, Monie. I just need some time.'

'Pff! I'm not leaving you to wallow in self-pity. That's not going to help. Anyway, going out might be just what you need.'

Silence, then Elena tried again. 'Another time, maybe. OK?'

'No, we can't do it another time,' Monique replied. 'My flight to Paris is tonight, as well you know. I need you, Elena. You promised you'd come with me. And,' she continued, 'it can only do you good. At least it'll stop you dragging yourself around like a ghost hunting for its tomb. Where are you now?'

'At my grandmother's house.'

'*Parfait!* It'll take you less than twenty minutes to get to Leopolda station. I'll be waiting for you outside the gates.' And Monique hung up.

Elena looked at her mobile, then turned to the window where she could almost count the thousand different rays making up the stream of sunlight.

Maybe Monie was right, maybe it was time to start living again. Going out was as good an attempt as any, and besides, shutting herself away in the house wouldn't make this go away. Not that she wanted to go back to the relationship. Now she could see clearly, she realized it had existed only because she had convinced herself it did. No, what was really devastating was suddenly finding herself with nothing. No plans, no ambition, no thoughts, no certainty.

Yes, she decided, going out with Monique wasn't such a bad idea after all.

'You've handled worse, Elena,' she muttered, standing up and heading to the bathroom.

Half an hour later, she was making her way through the courtyard of the old Florentine station that was home to Pitti Fragranze, the most important event in international artistic perfumery. It was a long time since she'd visited this kingdom of essences.

Monique walked towards her, kissed her three times on the cheeks and dragged her inside. She was wearing a very simple black silk dress, which she had paired with red patent stilettos. Tall, slim and exotic, Monique's quick, sinewy movements revealed her past as a model; but her beauty was all in her caramel skin and the mass of tight black curls spilling halfway down her back. To say she was beautiful was an understatement.

As they walked side by side, Elena looked down at her own flip-flops, denim skirt and pink floral shirt, and gave a glum shake of her head.

'I've already picked up the tickets. Put this on,' Monique said, handing her a badge.

'Narcissus?' Elena asked, staring at the name tag.

'*Oui*. Now you're my . . . what shall we call you? Assistant, that's it.'

Right, of course. To look at her, nobody would have thought she had anything to do with Narcissus, one of the most prestigious artistic perfume houses in Paris. Monique had worked there for almost a year now, and she loved the place. The most chic store in all of Paris, she said.

Chic, indeed. It wasn't somewhere Elena would ever have felt comfortable. Her style was simple, and not at all sophisticated. She was twenty-eight, but still as slender as a teenager, with big green eyes shining out from her perfectly clear skin. Her long blonde hair accentuated her naturally pale complexion. Her real strong point, though, was her mouth: it was too large, but when she decided to open it into a smile, it was beautiful.

She'd never taken much care with her appearance; she was much more interested in practicality – and, generally, she thought she'd reached a good compromise between the two. At that moment, however, she felt deeply inadequate. Side by side, she and Monique were complete opposites in terms of class and elegance. Her friend, however, didn't seem to register these details as she walked alongside Elena, pointing out one stand then another, bombarding her with questions and listening carefully to her answers.

Elena looked around again and was relieved to see that plenty of other people were casually dressed. Comforted, she pulled her shoulders back and held her head high. After all, she told herself, posture is what really counts.

As soon as they walked into the main room, Monique suddenly stopped, closed her eyes and inhaled deeply.

'That perfume has a soul, Elena,' she whispered. 'And I want it. Can you smell that?'

Of course she could smell it. Everyone could smell it. Each person was immersed in one specific scent – the one that, more than any other, stimulated something ancestral in their memory, evoking the past in a vivid and immediate way that almost transcended the relentless passage of time.

As the two friends moved between the various stands, separated by transparent walls, Elena was surrounded by intense, penetrating fragrances. In spite of herself she was soon swept up by them, analysing them one by one, trying to guess which and how many elements they were composed of. It was a while since she'd tried; in fact, for a long time, she'd deliberately avoided anything from the world that made up her past. Now, however, the temptation to identify the aromas was overwhelming, and she decided to indulge this sudden interest. She established the components in her mind, visualizing the olfactory pyramid before analysing it then putting it to one side so she could move straight on to the next. Suddenly she found herself smiling.

When Monique stopped in front of a bouquet of roses, Elena walked over to join her, unable to take her eyes off the uniquely coloured petals. She'd found the source of her torment and her joy: centifolia roses from Grasse in France. When she was a little girl, her mother, Susanna, had travelled around the world for work, taking her daughter with her, but the French city had always been an essential stopping-point in their nomadic existence. They went back there again and again. Grasse was the very symbol of the perfume tradition.

Elena had grown up there, moving between laboratories where natural essences were distilled – tiny artisan workshops set up centuries ago, and large, ultra-modern establishments where Susanna Rossini often worked. Whatever their size, each place had a lingering mixture of smells, delicate or intense depending on what was being made at the time. In spring, the town was transformed: colours and perfumes were everywhere. Every scent had a different meaning and each one was permanently ingrained on her memory.

That was what centifolia roses symbolized to her.

She held out her hand to brush the petals. They were exactly as she remembered: silky to the touch, with a delicate, captivating perfume.

'They're amazing,' Monique said with a note of reverence in her voice.

Once again, Elena felt herself catapulted into the past.

★ ★ ★

She was a small child and the huge fields of centifolia roses surrounding Grasse stretched out in front of her. Everything was green, and then little buds appeared – ivory, pale pink, dark pink, almost cyclamen. The fragrance exuding from these flowers was so intense it enveloped her completely.

Her mother had let go of Elena's hand and walked off into the rose garden by herself. She stopped almost in the middle, her fingers amongst the petals, a distracted smile on her face. Then a man joined her, and after they'd looked at one another for a moment, he stroked her face. Susanna wrapped her arms around his neck and they sank into a passionate kiss. When she finally turned back to the child, beckoning her over to them, the man's smile had vanished, replaced by a sneer. Frightened, Elena ran away.

That was the first time she saw Maurice Vidal, the man who would become her stepfather.

'The roses have a different perfume in September,' Elena said now. 'It's more concentrated; it brings the smell of the sun and the sea with it.'

'The sun?' Monique asked. 'What does the sun smell like, Elena?'

She closed her eyes for a moment, searching for the right words.

'It's immense, hot, soft ... it's like a nest, a comforting cradle. It seeps in, but at the same time sets you completely free. The sun accompanies the perfumes. Take jasmine: its fragrance is most intense at dawn, different from the light midday scent, but after sunset, when the sun is just a memory, that's when the flower reveals its true soul. You can't mistake it, it's impossible.'

Monique frowned, watching her intently.

'I haven't heard you talk about perfume like that for a very long time.'

A jolt of panic ran through Elena and she felt suddenly vulnerable. Her imagination had got the better of her rational side. She'd let herself get carried away by memories and emotions. Like back when she was a child, when perfume ran through her and she thought of it as a friend. Playing around with perfume was one thing; letting it take over was something else. She had to keep that in mind, she had to be careful.

'Let's get out of here, Monie, come on,' she said, quickly heading towards the open glass doors. Then a wave of dizziness stopped her in her tracks. What was happening? Could it be the perfumes?

She'd always managed to keep them at bay. She had learned early on to ignore them, pushing them to the sidelines. From the age of twelve, she'd always been the one to decide when and how much they mattered. She'd loved them, feared them, and then learned to control them.

But that morning, she realized, the perfumes were getting the better of her, dragging her back, making her remember, making her look at things she'd rather not see.

'Are you all right, Elena? You look awful. You're not thinking about that idiot Matteo again, are you?' Monique took her by the arm and got her to stand still.

Struggling to compose herself, Elena looked at the high stone walls, followed their outline to focus on the steel beams. Ancient and modern. A match that might seem jarring, but which was actually charming and full of character.

'And stop staring at the walls. I won't leave you alone until you tell me what's wrong.'

Elena looked at Monique, then laughed, putting her

face in her hands. 'Has anyone ever told you you're like a bulldog?'

The other girl shrugged '*Oui.*' She tapped her finger on her bottom lip. 'It's called character, *chérie*. So, tell me what's got into you today. You're even weirder than usual.'

A sigh swept away the tension between the two women.

'It's the perfumes. I can't stand them today.'

Monique burst out laughing. 'You're joking, right?'

But Elena wasn't smiling any more, and her eyes were watery and tired.

'Listen,' Monique said, wagging her finger, 'I need your skills. I need a nose, or the nearest thing I can get. If I go back to Paris without a truly original creation, Jacques . . . Things aren't how they used to be between us, Elena. I want to surprise him, I want him to respect me.'

'I'm not a nose, Monique,' Elena objected, trying to control the wave of nausea rising from her stomach.

Her friend pursed her lips. 'No, you're much more than that. You don't just smell an essence, you see beyond it. Perfume holds no secrets for you.'

'And you think that's an advantage, do you?' Elena asked bitterly. The words left her lips before she could stop them, before she could suppress them and hide them. Nose or not, Elena didn't want her sense of smell to run her life. It had already taken her childhood, and she'd decided that that was all she was prepared to give it.

Rationality, that's what she needed. She had to think, she had to react.

There was a mixture of exasperation and patience in Monique's voice as she replied, 'Yes, it probably would be an advantage, even if you looked after sheep for a living. You'd be able to sniff out foxes. But as it happens, you're a perfumier,

32

and a damn good one. And you know enough about perfume to be able to find something unique for me, a composition that will really give my boss something to think about, set a new trend. Something to add to the Narcissus line. I'm not kidding, I really do need you. Will you help me?'

Elena looked around. A light breeze brought the scent of Florence in over her shoulder; it smelled of sun-baked tiles, dreams and traditions, whispered love and hope.

She blinked, took a deep breath and gave in.

She'd never been able to stand up to Monique. Her friend had been bossing her around ever since they were little, when they had had their first race, running through streams in the Provence countryside, and ended up tumbling in a heap.

That's how they met, in the middle of the wild mint bushes, not far from the workers collecting the flowers. They'd been friends from that moment.

Monique had taken her home, and Jasmine, her Egyptian mother, had scolded them, dried them off, and then, over a cup of ginger tea and a plate of biscuits, warned them of all the dangers lurking in the streams. At Monique's house, Elena discovered what it meant to have a real family. Her new friend had introduced her to the maternal warmth and serenity that Jasmine had in abundance. Monie made her feel like one of the family, like a sister.

'So, will you help me?'

'Seriously, I don't know what use I can be to you. You know every step in creating a perfume and you've produced some extraordinary things.'

Monique made a face. 'Come on, Elena, we both know my perfumes are simple, convenient and popular. Even the best one was hardly subtle. But you, you're like an artist who paints a picture with words. I don't know anyone with your skills or your genius.'

'Yeah, right! A genius who couldn't even cover her costs.'

'Don't give me that old chestnut about your grandmother's business,' Monique cut in. 'You closed the perfumery because you're the most stubborn person I know. As far as the business goes, if you'd followed your instincts instead of sticking to Lucia's antiquated rules, things would have gone quite differently, and you know it. We've already talked about this. I just don't understand how you could take Matteo's ravings into account. The most *he* had to teach you was how to lay a table,' she snorted.

'You never made any decisions about running the shop,' she went on, 'you just let things happen. I'm sorry, but you know I like to tell it how it is, Elena. You're a nose, that's all there is to it. And the perfumes you made for me and my mother were truly unique. They still are. And that's what people want: a special perfume.'

'You know as much as I do,' Elena insisted. 'We did the same studies, we've got the same training.' She moved over to a metal shelf where a series of different-sized vials were lined up. The glass seemed to come to life as the cold light skimmed over the sharp edges.

'Maybe, but I wasn't brought up in an apothecary's workshop. Nor am I descended from generations of perfume-makers. That makes all the difference in the world.'

Yes, that was the difference between them. Monique had had a normal childhood: parents, a brother, two sisters, school, home, university, boyfriends and, in the end, a job she liked. She'd been able to choose.

So had Elena, in a way. And she'd chosen the easy route: obedience. She'd done everything her grandmother had asked of her, or as much as she could bear. She'd studied perfumery and applied herself conscientiously. Silently, however, she'd begun to harbour resentment towards perfume. And she'd ended up cultivating that resentment until she blamed it for all her problems.

'Do you know what my grandmother's last words were?' Elena asked. She waited a moment, then, spurred on by her friend's silence, she quoted: '"*Follow the way, do not abandon the perfume*".'

'Lucia wasn't well at the end,' Monique replied.

Elena's lips curled into a gentle smile. 'Her body might have given up, but her mind was there until the end. Don't think for a minute that she did or said anything that wasn't part of her plans. It was an obsession for her – the same as it was for all the women before her, even my mother. They always put perfume before anything else.' She reached for her friend's hand and squeezed it. 'I closed the shop because I wanted a normal life, regular hours, a man to love who loved me back, and children.'

'Those things aren't mutually exclusive. You could have been a perfumier and had all that. It's up to you, *n'est-ce-pas*?'

No!

The answer exploded inside her. Perfume wasn't like that – why couldn't Monique understand? It was all or nothing. And she hated it. She hated it because she couldn't help but love it.

And so she'd decided: perfume wasn't compatible with the life she'd chosen to lead with Matteo. That was why she closed the shop. The perfume would have bewitched her in the end, like it had all the other Rossini women, jeopardizing her plans for the future. It was that fear which had pushed her to distance herself from it for ever.

'I didn't want to risk it,' she murmured aloud.

No, she didn't want to risk it. She didn't want to give in. She didn't even want to talk about it.

'I'm not sure giving up everything you are has made you happy.'

Elena went pale. 'Everything I am?' she repeated.

'Think about it, Elena: since you closed the shop and went to live with Matteo, have you ever really been happy? You gave up everything you know, everything that makes you who you are, to chase after an idea, something you thought would satisfy you. But you went from one extreme to the other. Was that the life you wanted?'

No, it wasn't, but it was still better than standing by and watching, wasn't it?

'I tried. I believed in it and I tried!' she said hotly.

Monique stared at her, then smiled. 'That's not what I asked you. But it doesn't matter. Let's stop this depressing talk and focus on what we need to do, because you're going to help me find the perfume for Narcissus, aren't you?'

'Yeah, sure.' Elena nodded mechanically. But Monique's words were still ringing in her ears. Had she really given up who she was?

3

Benzoin: composure. A dark resin with a thick and intense
  balsamic essence.
The fragrance relieves anxiety and stress.
It enables spiritual energy to grow in strength and is the ideal
  preparation for meditation.

Elena's first memory was the dazzling sun on the French
Riviera; her second was a vast expanse of lavender. Green and
blue and pink and lilac and white, stretching on and on. Then
there was the darkness of the studio, where her mother
Susanna worked, leaning over tables covered with tiny glass
and aluminium bottles.

Her mother worked in Provence for most of the year. That
was where they had a house. And that was where Susanna had
met a man, her first and only love: Maurice Vidal.

It was in the flower fields there that Elena had learned the
basics of perfumery: which herbs to pick, which to use in
distillation, which to transform into *concrètes*, which to use to

extract *absolutes*. Petals of all colours and sizes swirled around, carried by the Mistral winds, or fell like little pink waterfalls from the ledges where they were kept. The petal-pickers filled huge silos with hundreds of kilos of flowers, squashing them down before the real business of production began: with *lavage*, as it was called in perfume jargon. This process produced the *concrète*: a concentrated, intensely perfumed, waxy substance. Lastly, a final washing in alcohol transformed it into an *absolute*, separating off any impurities.

Each step was a clear image etched into Elena's childhood memory. In her solitary existence, perfume had become the only language she could use to communicate with her mother, a woman of few words, who took her daughter everywhere but rarely spoke to her. Elena enjoyed looking at the liquid perfume, she loved its colour. Some containers were as small as her hand, others so large she had to ask for Maurice's help to lift them.

Maurice was tall and strong. He owned the laboratory and the fields, and he adored Susanna Rossini. He loved her at least as much as he loathed her daughter.

Elena knew why he never looked at her. She was someone else's child. She didn't know what that meant exactly, but it was definitely something bad. It made her mum cry.

One day, she'd come home for a snack and heard her mother arguing with Maurice. It happened a lot, and that day she took no notice at first. She picked up a biscuit and was about to go back outside to play, when she thought to take another one for Monique.

'She's the image of her father, isn't she? Admit it. She doesn't look anything like you. I can't even bear the sight of her. How can you ask me to keep her with me? With us?'

Elena stood still, then. A vice clamped around her stomach.

It was the tone of the man's voice that stopped her in her tracks. Maurice was talking quietly, the way people tell secrets. But she had heard him perfectly.

She turned around. The bedroom door was open. Maurice was sitting on a chair, his head bowed, his fingers buried in his hair.

'I made a mistake,' her mother was saying, 'and there's nothing I can do about it now. And anyway, when I came back, you said the past didn't matter; you wanted us to make a new start – together. Try to understand. She's my daughter, too.'

Yes, she was her daughter. The way Susanna pronounced the word was strange. And why was her mother crying? She didn't like those words, Elena thought. They stung her throat and her eyes.

Maurice jumped up. 'Your daughter! Yes – yours and who else's? Who is her father?'

'No one – I've told you a thousand times. He doesn't even know there was a baby.'

The man shook his head. 'I can't stand it, Susanna. I know I promised you, I know, but I just can't do it.'

That was when he noticed her. 'What are *you* doing here?' he yelled.

Speechless, Elena stepped back, then ran away.

She only shed a few tears on the way back to Monique's house, because Monie hated cry-babies. Crying didn't get you anywhere. Her friend had often told her that, and it was true. The pain was still there, like a chasm in her throat. But she told her friend everything, because she listened and she understood her.

As she was talking to Monique she realized that Maurice was wrong. She'd never had a dad. Maybe she should tell him, and that would make things better.

But however hard she tried over the next few days, the man's stern glare frightened her. The words refused to come out; they got trapped in her mouth, caught on her tongue. So she came up with the idea of a drawing.

She had to use the whole page because Maurice was very tall, but she managed to fit him in. She drew the three of them together: Susanna holding her hand, and there, at their side, was Maurice, not another dad.

Before she gave him the drawing, she showed it to her mother.

'It's beautiful, darling,' Susanna told her.

Her mother really liked her drawings, even though she never had time to look at them properly. But this one was special, as Elena had insisted when she showed her mother all the details. Details were important: her teacher told her that all the time. She'd drawn Susanna's long black hair that came down to her shoulders, Maurice, and herself in the middle, holding them both by the hand. She was wearing a pink dress – she really liked that colour.

She didn't have a dad, so Maurice could be hers, if he wanted. And as for who she looked like, he was most certainly wrong. Jasmine had assured her that when she grew up, she'd look just like her mother. And Jasmine knew what she was talking about, she had loads of children.

One day, when Maurice was in a terrible mood, Elena decided to give him the drawing to cheer him up. Ignoring the sombre expression that frightened her, she mustered her courage and handed him the piece of paper. He took it without saying anything, and after giving it a quick glance, she saw his face twist with rage.

Elena instinctively shrank back, her palms sweating and her fingers gripping the fabric of her dress. Maurice turned to

Susanna, who was preparing dinner, brandishing the piece of paper.

'Do you think this will fix things between us?' he asked in a hushed voice, almost whispering. 'One big happy family? You, me, and ... *his* child? Now you're using the girl to convince me?'

Susanna turned pale. 'It's just a drawing,' she told him in a tiny voice.

'You know full well what I think,' he shouted, scrunching up the paper in his huge fist and throwing it into a corner. 'What will it take to make you understand?'

A tense silence fell over them, broken by a single sob from Elena.

As though he suddenly realized what he had done, Maurice looked at the little girl, then slowly picked the paper up from the floor, smoothing it out in his fingers.

'Here,' he said, holding it out to her.

But she shook her head. Maurice put it on the table, gave a shrug and, out of nowhere, he started to laugh.

If she tried hard, even after all these years, Elena could still remember that harsh, forced sound.

Susanna sent her to play at Monique's house. As she was leaving, Elena heard them begin to argue and then she started to run. Jasmine dried her tears, assuring her that Maurice just hadn't understood what she'd drawn. 'Grown-ups often do things like that,' she said. 'They don't understand and they get scared.' Then she took the child by the hand and walked her home.

Maurice wasn't there any more. Susanna's eyes were red and puffy. Jasmine made tea and stayed with them late into the night. The next morning, Susanna packed their bags and she and Elena left. They were away for the whole spring. But then they went back.

41

They always went back, and Maurice was always there. And that was where Elena had first encountered the smell of hatred. Cold, like the smell of a starless night after the rain has stopped but the wind continues to howl. The smell of hatred is frightening.

A few months later, Elena turned eight. In the autumn they left again, and this time she stayed in Florence with her grandmother.

'I like these,' Elena said, breaking the thread of her memory and returning to Florence and the Pitti Fragranze event.

The crystal bottles she'd been looking at sparkled under the spotlights; they were unique, all angles and character.

'No, too bold. Jacques wants something more harmonious.'

After a moment, Elena said thoughtfully: 'Harmony is a subjective concept and it's definitely not a trendsetter. If it's something new you're looking for, Monie, you have to go further. You have to be daring.'

Her friend stared at her for a moment. 'What would you choose, Elena?'

'Me?'

'Yes, you. How about we split up to find the right perfume? Then Jacques would have two choices. He loves that kind of thing. *Oui*, it's decided. We'll meet here in an hour and then I'll take you to lunch. Today there's Sunday brunch at the Four Seasons – it's quite an experience. I've got Jacques' credit card, we'll splash out, and you can do me the favour of wiping that miserable look off your face. Come on, so you lost a lover, it's no big deal. Do you have any idea how many men would go crazy for you if you let them?' asked Monique, wagging a finger. 'Loads, *chérie*. Guys would be queuing up.'

'Yeah, course they would.' Elena didn't even have the

energy to lose her temper with Monie, and why should she? Tact had never been her friend's strong point, she knew that well enough. Even as a child, Monie had spoken her mind without worrying about the consequences.

Suddenly, she needed to be alone. Monique was the person she loved most in the world, but at that moment Elena felt too vulnerable and exposed. All it would take was a look, one word, to tip the balance she was trying so hard to re-establish.

'Shall we split up, then?' Now that she was no longer afraid of immersing herself in the perfumes, that kind of respite seemed too good to be true.

Monique pulled a face. 'I'll pretend I didn't hear that hopeful tone,' she grinned. 'Go on then, go! Gather your thoughts and try to calm down. But remember – I want that perfume. I really need it. *Vite, vite!* I'll see you back here in an hour.'

Elena gave a hint of a smile, then moved away.

She'd taken just a few steps when she realized she didn't have the slightest idea what Jacques wanted. All she knew was that he owned Narcissus, the company where Monique worked, that he belonged to a well-established and illustrious family of perfume-makers, and that her friend had been in a brief and intense relationship with him. The 'best sex of her life', was how Monique had summed up Jacques Montier.

She turned back to look for Monique in the crowd. The stands were full of people intently breathing in the atmosphere saturated with smells. Elena eventually spotted her friend standing next to a huge orchid, a white *Phalaenopsis*, in front of a table lined with crystal jars. As she walked over to join her, Elena studied the liquids in the luxurious glass bottles. The different shades ranged from pale pink, through various tones of opalescent grey, to the clearest amber yellow.

'Monie, you haven't told me what Jacques actually wants,' she said, once she was standing next to her. The other woman immediately spun round, her fingers clutching a smooth, square bottle with neat corners.

'*Non, c'est vrai*. But it doesn't matter,' she replied, turning her attention back to the little crystal masterpiece. 'The perfume isn't for him. Jacques wants a new, energetic fragrance he can include in his catalogue and sell at Narcissus. He's hoping to start a trend that will satisfy high-flying Parisian women. Nothing too predictable, but something that's still feminine and harmonious.'

'Right . . . as easy as that,' Elena joked.

Monique gave her a smile. 'You're going to surprise him. Or rather, I am. I'll take all the credit, seeing as you don't know what to do with it.'

'If this is your way of getting me to consider the idea of working with perfume again, it's not going to happen,' Elena told her firmly.

Yet as she walked around the stands, running her fingers over the packaging and feeling the energy the different aromas gave off, Elena realized that the uneasiness that had always accompanied her while she worked on a new essence seemed to have vanished – along with the irksome sense of obligation and duty. There was just the shadow of a concern in the back of her mind – but she couldn't feel it any more, like an old scar.

Now, something different was stirring in her, a need that drove her to inhale deeply, to fill her lungs with one ingredient after another. The nausea had gone, too. All that remained was a sense of urgency. She was suddenly curious – she was desperate to smell, as though it were the first time she'd smelled an essence, as though this world hadn't always been a part of her life. This restlessness was almost ridiculous. Ridiculous and out of place – but there it was.

Everything she was once sure of had crumbled, along with her carefully devised plans. She decided to go with her instincts.

Just then, Elena found herself in front of a stand run by a young Indian perfumier. She stood to one side, listening to her. The woman had very clear ideas. Elena liked the description she gave of her perfumes: there was technical information, demonstrating a perfect understanding of her work, and simple language that could tap into the imagination of anyone who stopped to listen.

Amongst these exotic perfumes, she found what she was looking for. When she opened it, there was a floral explosion: patchouli, gardenia, jasmine, and then a spicy heart, with mysterious notes of cloves and coriander. Lastly, the wood: it didn't just harmonize the blend, it made it creamy. She imagined it on her own skin – the way it would dissolve, emanating elegance and refinement. She knew intuitively that this was the right perfume.

Whether Jacques would like it, she didn't know, but it was perfect for any woman who loved femininity and who didn't want to relinquish every last hint of frivolity. To Elena, it was as if this perfume was speaking to her: telling her about itself, the places it came from, the women in red and gold saris for whom it had been invented, the modern city, the metropolis that Delhi had become. Paris would love it. She decided to listen to the perfume, and she bought it.

She carried on walking around the Leopolda station with the perfume in her bag, and when she met up with Monique one hour later, Elena realized that she hadn't felt so calm in a long, long time. Of course, Matteo's betrayal still hurt, but as they were getting into the taxi that would take them to the Four Seasons, she felt something flicker inside her, a sense of expectation and excitement. Plus, she was absolutely ravenous.

Much later, when night had fallen over the city, Elena's gaze followed the lights of the plane taking her friend back to Paris. Before Monique left, they'd promised to speak to one another soon. And this time Elena had every intention of keeping her word.

4

Bergamot: hope. Lively, scintillating.
The fragrance gives energy and agility when all expectations
*   have withered under the weight of monotony.*
Lights the way and helps us see alternatives.

The palazzo on the medieval street of Borgo Pinti had belonged to Elena's family for ever. Legend had it that the beautiful building had been bought with the profits from a special perfume, an extraordinary essence secretly transported from Florence to France. A perfume that had charmed a princess. In return for this gift, the lady had given her hand and her dowry to the man who had commissioned the perfume, making him very rich indeed.

That was the story. The few people who knew what had really happened were long dead.

But the legend of the Perfect Perfume lived on.

It was known, for example, that it had been created by Beatrice Rossini, the founder of the family business. In the first half of the seventeenth century, a period which saw two Florentine queens on the French throne, this remarkable woman had left her home town to take on commissions abroad. She was an extraordinary perfumier. Florence's most famous women wanted to be among her few, select clients. Beatrice had created a unique perfume for each of them. Even powerful noblemen competed for her services. They all wanted to distinguish themselves with their own special fragrance, a perfume worthy of their grandeur.

Her fame was so great that Beatrice often had to travel to the courts of princes who requested her services. It is said that on one of these trips, she created a perfume so marvellous, so extraordinary that it would stay forever etched on the memory of anyone privileged enough to smell it. An instant success, it was as brilliant as a shining star, as balanced as the purest scented waters, as simple as a breath of air. Its notes created a surprising, even delicate harmony. It was persistent and sensual. A perfume unlike anything that had been created before.

But when she returned to Florence, richer than almost anyone there, Beatrice had no desire to talk about her experiences. She'd changed. She seemed absent, silent. She stopped going to court, gave up parties and all her friends. Deeply disillusioned by her rich suitors, she quickly married a man of humble origins, with whom she had a daughter, Laura. In the marriage contract, the man had granted her the privilege of keeping her own family name and passing it down to future generations. So she was born and forever remained Beatrice Rossini. And from then on, all the women in the family inherited her surname, like a prestigious, ancient brand.

Widowed after just two years, she never wore mourning dress. There was no need, as the only colour she'd worn since her return from France had been black. Satin, velvet, Irish lace: she allowed herself the finest materials, so long as they were in this sombre colour.

She never revealed the secret source of her fortune to anyone, and she never remarried, despite numerous offers. She spent her days composing perfumes and making soaps and creams for people who wanted something special. Special, like the perfume that occasionally, on long summer nights, with only her own breath for company, she would take out of the secret compartment in her jewellery box. She didn't open the silver vial. Ever. She just held it to her heart. That was also the only time she allowed herself the consolation of tears.

The Perfect Perfume was the source of her joy and her pain.

One December night, when her once-beautiful black hair was threaded with silver, and her breathing faltered more and more often, she knew her time had come. She asked her daughter, Laura, to bring her the chest and, after moving aside the jewellery, she showed her the perfume. She had to. Because the formula for the Perfect Perfume was the legacy awaiting her sole heir. But the exhaustion and the emotion were too much for her. She'd waited too long and she died in Laura's arms, in front of the fire, remembering the past, talking about her secret instead of telling her the whole story. Beatrice never managed to give her daughter the formula for the perfume, but she did tell her it was hidden. She would find it in her books, amongst her notes, amongst the things she'd loved best. To get to it, all she had to do was follow the ways of perfume.

But Laura never found it, nor did she manage to recreate it from the last drops of perfume in the vial. Beatrice had left too many formulas to make up, too many books to read, too much pain to deal with.

After that, the other perfume-makers in the Rossini family passionately continued the search, driven by the certainty that all her compositions had been properly written down, always. Writing recipes down became rule number one – something they learned even before they knew that perfume was a mix of floral, wood and animal extracts, diluted in alcohol or oily substances. It was a pact, a promise. Every perfume was carefully recorded and stored.

The formula was there, in the archives; of that, everyone had always been convinced – but it was like looking for a single coin in an overflowing treasure chest. How could they distinguish it from the thousands of others painstakingly stored in Beatrice's archives? Which one of these was the formula for the Perfect Perfume? There were boxes full of paper to be examined: notes, studies and thoughts that all had to be processed meticulously. And then, of course, there was her diary.

The fate of all the Rossini women was tied to their search. Each of them, in her own way, had deepened her study of perfumery. There were some who had experimented with new forms of alchemy, dared to try things that anyone else would have called madness or heresy. But they all knew that this wasn't enough to discover what was missing: the Perfect Perfume.

Elena's grandmother Lucia had dedicated her entire life to the search for the Perfect Perfume. Year after year she'd experimented with the formulas written in Beatrice's papers, with no success: none of those perfumes seemed that special to her. Based on her own knowledge and the experience she'd gathered from her ancestors, she was convinced there was a way to smell the perfume simply by reading the formula's composition. For example, she herself could predict the result of combining two or more essences. But her talents were limited and would not have been enough to identify the Perfect Perfume, as the formula surely had to be highly complex.

Instead, she focused her hopes on her daughter, Susanna; but the girl had no intention of following that path. She was fascinated by the many possibilities offered by synthetic substances, rejecting tradition and her mother's teachings.

And then Elena was born.

At a certain point in her life, when time had stiffened her fingers so much that she could no longer uncork the essence containers, Lucia decided to pass on her knowledge to the one person she was sure had the passion, depth of heart and intuition required to bring the Perfume back to life: her granddaughter. And so she left everything to her.

The palazzo walls, made of stone and bricks that had been fired in the old city's kilns, reared up strong and dark, three storeys high. On the ground floor there had always been the workshop, the laboratory and the courtyard, which was overlooked by the upstairs rooms. On the first floor were the kitchen and living room; on the second floor the bedrooms. The property hadn't changed much over the centuries; even the herbs in the corner of the garden had stayed the same.

The house had also always had a secret study, because the Rossinis had been making perfume since the days when alchemy was the natural extension of their profession. It was in the basement and no one had been down there for decades.

The building was in excellent condition, thanks to the

precious materials with which it was built: timber from ships toughened by storms and sea winds, stone straight from the rockface, bricks fired at infernal temperatures. They were silent witnesses to births and deaths, extraordinary discoveries, joy, blood, sweat and tears. The building had kept all its charm, character and a hint of mystery.

Lucia Rossini lived for perfume; everything else was superfluous. One day she'd let a man into her bed, and that was the strongest link she'd ever had with the outside world. When Giuseppe Rinaldi died, she had raised their daughter Susanna, teaching her everything she knew and, according to tradition, she gave her the Rossini name. For Lucia, like all the women before her, it was a symbol, a link to her ancestors; it was her identity and her duty.

Susanna, however, couldn't have cared less about her illustrious surname or about the Perfect Perfume. She didn't share her mother's ambitions. She was interested in perfume, but she wanted to learn state-of-the-art techniques; she'd had enough of the old-fashioned nonsense Lucia insisted on drumming into her, enough of all those dusty papers. She wasn't interested in the past: all that mattered to her was the future. So she left. She sent postcards from Alexandria, Athens, Bombay . . . and when she stopped roaming, she settled in Grasse, in France.

One day, many years later, she turned up on her mother's doorstep with a little girl.

'I can't keep her with me any more,' was all she said. The two women exchanged a long look, then Lucia threw open the door and smiled at her granddaughter for the first time.

'Come along, Elena, let's go inside. This is going to be your house now.' But the girl grabbed hold of Susanna's skirt, tugging it hard. She closed her eyes and hung her head. It was raining hard that day, at the end of November. Susanna was wearing an almond, violet and iris perfume Maurice had made for her. A wedding present.

From that moment on, Elena had always hated rain.

Starting then, Lucia Rossini had passed on all her knowledge to her shy, quiet granddaughter. Even though the girl was only eight years old, she immediately proved to be incredibly receptive. She had an extraordinary relationship with perfumes. She handled them with dexterity and knew how to measure out essences perfectly. She could really smell perfumes, and she could describe them.

For the first time, Lucia Rossini saw her hopes realized. This girl would find the Perfect Perfume, she was sure of it! And so she dedicated her body and soul to Elena's training. No silly games, no time-wasting for this one. Sending her to the convent school, getting her the best possible education would be more than enough. After all, Elena wasn't like other children. She was a hope. She was *the* hope.

In the beginning, Susanna paid regular visits to her daughter. Then the visits became occasional, and eventually they stopped altogether. Like the girl's interest in perfume.

Disconcerted, her grandmother questioned the reasons behind this sudden and absurd rejection, but the girl never answered. Later, Lucia understood. The problem was Susanna, or rather, the man she'd married: Maurice Vidal, who couldn't stand the sight of his stepdaughter, as though the poor creature could be held responsible for the choices her mother had made.

Lucia started to believe what Susanna had told her, years before, when she left Elena on her doorstep: 'It's for her own good.'

Yes, perhaps it really was better for the child to keep her distance from that man.

Men! How they were given so much power, Lucia could never understand. But Susanna had always had a weakness for this Maurice, a man she'd met when she was just a student; when what she should have done was kick him out of her life and concentrate on Elena.

Maybe it was time she had a word with that irresponsible daughter of hers. But if Susanna took Elena back, the plans Lucia had for her granddaughter, the search for the Perfect Perfume, would vanish.

The little girl was the only one who could find it. So Lucia made a choice.

'It's better this way,' she told her crying granddaughter one day, trying to console her. 'It takes time, and you need to clear your head to be able to smell the perfumes in your mind, to understand them. Creating a perfume is a very delicate process. You can't get distracted, even for a second. One drop too many and the whole thing could be ruined. Do you understand, sweetheart?'

Elena dried her face and nodded. But perfume wasn't her friend any more. It had become pain and failure.

'One day you'll understand. It's your destiny,' her grandmother told her, stroking her head.

Alone in the house, cleaning the workshop's ancient marble floor the day after Monique had left, Elena was scrubbing a very stubborn stain when one particular memory came to mind – it was as though she could still feel the intense pain deep inside her chest, a biting cold.

She was bigger by then, already twelve, and for months she'd been working on a plan, a project. Her grandmother always said that perfume was the way, that it was truth. So she tried to prepare one especially for her mother. She wanted to tell Susanna how lonely she felt, how much she missed even the sight of her. Being with her grandmother was fine, but it was hard work. All those names to learn and things to look up in books. She wanted her mum, that was all. A perfume would be better than anything else to explain what she felt in her heart. Her grandmother told her so all the time.

'The message is in the perfume.'

She put in tuberose: its flowers were white, like the dresses Susanna loved to wear. Then Elena had chosen gardenia: hot and green. Next she blended leather and wood, which could soften the bright, fruity sweetness. There was something jarring in this composition, though. It was the pain of abandonment: it was her way of asking Susanna to take her back.

She prepared it diligently, remembering everything her grandmother had taught her, and then she put it in a crystal bottle.

The Christmas holidays finally arrived and, holding her breath, she waited for the moment she could finally give her mother the present in Grasse.

'For me?' Susanna asked. 'A perfume? Did you make it yourself, darling?'

Elena loved the sound of that voice. It was light and delicate – perhaps because she didn't use it very much. That kind tone made her feel better. And since Elena had arrived, the night before, even Maurice had been kind. Maybe they would keep her with them, this time.

'Yes, Mum, I made it myself.'

Susanna opened it very carefully, smelling the contents. Smiling, she tried it on her wrist and sniffed.

'Aren't you clever, sweetheart? I like it; it's delicate, but at the same time it has character.'

She liked it! Elena's heart was bursting, she couldn't think of anything else. She went up to Susanna, one step at a time, as though she were afraid this perfect moment might vanish. But Susanna kept on smiling and talking to her.

The sunlight streaming through the window lit up the polished wood floor. Her mother was sitting on the sofa and had put the bottle of perfume in the middle of the coffee table, still singing its praises.

'An original composition. I can't work out the base notes . . . oh, but don't tell me, darling, I want to guess. Would you believe it, my little girl made a perfume just for me! Maurice, come and see – look what Elena did.'

The man came over. He was smiling, but his eyes were cold. He took the tiny bottle and once he'd smelled it, he put it back on the table.

'You shouldn't encourage her so much. There are some serious mistakes there. The top notes clash, and really, what about the structural failure? No, Susanna. You're not doing the kid any favours by deluding her like this. The perfume's no good, and you know it. Stop leading her on.'

'How can you say that?' Susanna murmured. 'She's only twelve years old!'

Maurice span round, slamming his fist on to the table. The bottle rolled along the polished surface and fell to the floor. The smell spread through the room, filling the air.

'It doesn't matter. It makes no difference how old she is. I'm just telling the truth, because you're not brave enough to do it. That perfume is all wrong – it's worthless.'

A tense silence fell over them, shattering Elena's dreams, crushing her hopes.

'There's no need to shout,' Susanna told him. Then she bent down and picked up the bottle. She closed the lid and went back to Elena.

'Spoiling a composition by using such bold notes is a mistake lots of beginners make. Make sure you have the olfactory pyramid and the fragrance families clear in your mind. To be daring you need knowledge that you don't have yet. But thank you, anyway. It was a really kind thought.'

Then she stood up, left the sitting room and shut herself in her bedroom. Maurice followed her immediately. The next day, Elena went to stay at Monique's house, and Susanna must have approved of the decision because she sent her luggage over. A long time later, Elena realized what was wrong with that perfume. Too much pain.

After that, she saw her mother less and less, and only on the most important occasions. From then on, their relationship became very formal. Fortunately, Maurice always managed to busy himself with something on the few occasions Elena went to Grasse, and Elena herself always found thousands of excuses to go to Monique's house.

She was almost seventeen when, in the laboratory where Susanna and Maurice were working, a gas leak caused a small explosion. Her mother almost made it to the door, but flames forced her back to the window. The fire spread in just a few seconds, fuelled by the highly flammable liquids in the room. By the time Maurice managed to grab the fire extinguisher, the blaze was already out of control. The laboratory was completely overcome by smoke. So Maurice took his wife in his arms and jumped out of the window. He saved her, but the accident left him with burns to his face and serious spinal injuries.

★ ★ ★

Elena sighed and dried her eyes. How was it that all she could do lately was think about the past? Her worries about the future were starting to weigh on her mind.

That morning, her thoughts were trapped in a circle, and she always ended up facing the same question: what on earth was she going to do now? She wasn't looking for a profound philosophical answer, like the meaning of life. No, her concern was more practical, immediate.

She stood up and looked around. The workshop walls were high and plain, in stark contrast to the fresco-covered ceiling. Flowers, an abundance of painted flowers, covered the entire vault, like a meadow hanging upside down. The colours of the fresco were faded: the red poppies were just a pale cherry colour; the warm, powdery tones of damascene roses were almost imperceptible; little cracks decorated the edges of the petals; the blue of the irises and the still-bright violet of the anemones were also testimony to the relentless passage of time. Her grandmother had never let the arts heritage authorities get their hands on them.

'It would change the smell. How can you not understand that?' she once yelled, exasperated by the insistence of the official who wanted to include the palazzo in plans for restoration.

It was true, the balance of perfumes that gave life to that room would be lost for ever. Modern paints would have brought the picture back to its original brilliance, a real joy to behold. But what would have become of the perfume of the place, once it was contaminated? The cedarwood table with its sturdy feet, the delicate inlaid cupboards that contained all the essences, the display cabinet lined with leather-bound books, and the Venetian wardrobe where all the utensils were kept had always been part of the place. Every single object had its own specific smell and none of it should change.

There was something else in that vast, marble-floored room. Elena looked around for it, and sure enough, there it was. It was still in the furthest corner of the room. She walked over and ran her fingers across it.

The screen's frame was flaking and the silk covering had faded a little. But it was still in good condition, if a bit dusty. The height of a door, it opened out to create a sheltered corner. It was old, very old. They said it was as old as the house and had belonged to Beatrice Rossini herself. But there were too many legends surrounding her ancestor for Elena to believe them all. She didn't care where the screen came from, she liked the feeling of warmth and privacy she had when she was behind it, and the smell that came off the silk. In the past it had been used as a partition to protect clients who didn't want to reveal their identity. And from time to time, when things got too much, or she was up to mischief, Elena had made it her hiding-place.

Elena stopped to smell it more carefully – and with a hint of surprise she realized that this was where the subtle scent of a real perfume was coming from, as though the screen had once been soaked in it. And it probably had. There were other antique objects in the house that her ancestors had subjected to experiments in an attempt to preserve fragrances for longer. Her grandmother's mahogany chest, in her bedroom, contained several pairs of vaguely scented Spanish leather gloves. Her grandmother's slippers, too, gave off an essence of Bulgarian roses. Plus several reams of paper, each with a specific scent and every one of them stamped.

But of all these bizarre objects, the old screen was still her favourite.

There were other things, too, things that actually took her

by surprise, like the comfortable sense of wellbeing. She felt as if she'd come home. And she couldn't really explain this, since she'd never previously thought of the house like that. It had never been a place where she'd felt truly at ease. Jasmine had been wonderful to her; at her house Elena had breathed in love and been happy, but she'd also understood precisely what she didn't have. That big old palazzo had always been her grandmother's home, not hers. She'd only gone back there because, after the split with Matteo, she didn't have anywhere else to hide. But she had done so very reluctantly.

Catching her off-guard, the warm feeling she'd felt on the first night crept up on her again. She knew that sooner or later she'd have to sort herself out and deal with her feelings. But this wasn't the right time.

Matteo had just brought her belongings back. Five boxes piled in the middle of the hall to remind her of a year of living together and a heap of stupid dreams which, it would seem, he had never shared. Stubbornly and blindly, she'd poured all her needs and desires into that relationship, fooling herself that she and Matteo had a connection that worked.

'You made an error of judgement, Elena. You forgot the one thing a woman should always bear in mind,' Jasmine had told her on the phone a little earlier.

'Have you been talking to Monie?' Elena asked the one person who, for all these years, had been a mother to her.

'*Oui*, it's not good to keep secrets. Don't be cross with her.'

'You know I won't,' she replied.

'Not even if I tell you I'm happy that idiot is out of your life?'

Elena smiled through the tears. '*Non, maman.*'

Jasmine's happy sigh prompted more tears. Elena sniffed them back.

'Go on,' she urged in a shaky voice.

'You can't put all your eggs in one basket, *ma petite*. Circumstances mean you have to diversify. They call it Plan B. You have to have one, Elena: a girl always needs a Plan B.'

'And what if I don't even have a Plan A?'

'Rubbish! You've got a beautiful house full of incredible objects. You've got a vocation: whether you like it or not, you're a perfumier. You know how to create perfumes, you know how to recognize them, and if you don't want to make them, you could always sell them like Monique, don't you think? And what's more, my girl, you've got us – a family that loves you.'

More tears, and this time Elena couldn't hide them.

Jasmine sighed again. 'I've never heard you cry so much, not even when you were a little girl. Are you sure you're all right? Why don't you come and stay with us in Grasse for a few days? A change of scene would do you good.'

Elena dried her face. 'You know I can't do that.'

'Why? Ever since his accident Maurice never leaves the house, so you wouldn't even see him. As for your mother . . . I don't think it'd hurt to see Susanna again. You know it would make her happy, deep down.'

'You really think so? I wouldn't be so sure. She's never been to see me.'

'True, but you know why that is. She feels responsible for Maurice; she doesn't want to leave him on his own in his condition.'

'That's ridiculous, it wasn't her fault,' Elena whispered. 'It was an accident – it could have happened to anyone.'

'But it happened to Susanna. And regardless of anything

else, Maurice was badly injured saving her. She'll never forget that.'

A thoughtful silence came over them, and then Jasmine added, 'I'm not condoning the way she treated you, let's be clear on that, but perhaps it's time you put your resentment aside. Susanna made some bad choices, and she's paid dearly for them. But she is still your mother.'

Yes, she was still her mother. But that didn't matter any more. She hadn't been part of Elena's life for years now. One day she'd simply stopped hoping Susanna could love her. But it wasn't that simple.

Even though what Jasmine was saying made sense, Elena had no intention of thinking about Maurice or her mother; right now, she couldn't face it. And it wasn't just them. Her mind was a whirlwind of thoughts, dragging her into a vortex of feelings that she didn't know how to escape. Her heart ached.

'I'll think about it,' she managed, before she hung up.

5

Lavender: relaxation. Intense and sweet; herbal with balsamic undertones.
The complex fragrance seduces and bewitches.
Refreshes and purifies the spirit; relieves exhaustion, fear and anxiety.

By day, Paris was rich and fascinating beyond belief; by night, the city showed its true character as *La Ville Lumière* – the City of Light. As Monique flew above it, gazing at the lights in the tall townhouses, the Eiffel Tower and the long, gold ribbons of illuminated streets dividing up its most stylish quarters, she knew that some of those lights, shining like diamonds, were in reality just the headlights on thousands of cars speeding through the streets. Yet from the sky they looked like jewels. Paris was a city that knew the value of appearance.

Jacques had sent her a message. He wouldn't be coming to meet her at the airport. Something had come up at the last minute, something really important. But he'd send the car.

Monique sighed. Things had started 'coming up' a lot lately; he always had something more important to do.

She carried on watching the city as it sparkled happily, resolutely staving off the wave of self-pity that was threatening to emerge from the depths of her soul. They would be landing soon, the pilot announced. The slightly distorted voice told them to keep their seat belts fastened until the doors were open, gave the final instructions for landing and ended with a curt, 'Welcome to Paris.' When the wheels touched down, a tired round of applause rippled over her. Monique unfastened her seat belt, collected her bag and stood in the queue to disembark.

'Wake up, *mon amour*. It's not like I'm going to let you sleep, anyway.'

Monique opened her eyes and jumped up, with Jacques's fingers still touching her.

'Get that hand off me, now.'

He gave a lazy smile, then got off the bed and straightened his tie. His expression was inscrutable.

'Nervous, *chérie*?'

Monique rubbed her hand over her face, trying to dispel sleep. Then she clenched it into a fist, to stop the shaking.

'What are you doing in my house?'

Jacques smiled at her again: hair perfectly slicked back, piercing dark eyes, the look of a man who knows he has the world at his feet. Standing in the middle of Monique's little loft apartment, he looked like lord and master of everything. He was confident, determined – everything would go just the way he planned it.

God, he was handsome! Monique had to force herself to keep her distance. She grabbed hold of the sheet, clutching on to it like a lifeline. The urge to beg him to continue what she'd just told him to stop was almost overwhelming.

'I wanted to put things right. I haven't treated you very well,' he replied, unbuttoning his jacket.

'That's one way of putting it,' Monique muttered.

Jacques went over to the window and opened the curtains. The sun came flooding into the room. Monique shielded her eyes, unused to the sudden brightness.

'So, how was Florence?' he asked smoothly.

'Old, beautiful, dilapidated.'

'Yes, it's a charming city. I should go with you next time,' he said, as though he really meant it. But, if there was one thing Monique had learned from their relationship, it was that Jacques said a lot of things. Words, phrases, promises, which he duly forgot. They were just another adornment for him, like the clothes he wore, his jewellery, his stylish looks. There was never any truth in what he said, even though he led her to believe the opposite. Sometimes, Monique thought he must be a magician, an emotional conjurer.

Jacques looked at her again. Lying eyes, that charmed and deceived at the same time. It was so easy to believe him, Monique thought, to delude herself that she really was important to him. He was too gallant, too handsome, too much of too many things, all at once.

She took a deep breath and got out of bed. As she walked towards the wardrobe she was careful not to catch the look in his eye that made him so irresistible. She could feel her desire for him quivering inside her. And for a moment, she was tempted to believe him. Maybe he really had missed her; maybe he did want to apologize for having behaved like the worst kind of bastard.

One glance at the coffee table brought her back to reality. The two packages she'd carried with her from Florence were open. A strip of paper – a *mouillette* – was resting next to the perfume Elena had chosen; another lay screwed-up on the floor. Her hopes faded, then disappeared altogether, leaving only a cold realization.

'Couldn't you wait until tomorrow?' she asked, trying to hide her irritation.

'Why? Would something have changed? You found what I wanted. Get dressed – I'm taking you out. I want to celebrate. The perfume you chose is just right. You're a genius.'

Monique let him approach her. It was Elena who was the genius. She was about to tell him so when he grabbed hold of her, and the words died on her lips. Jacques kissed her and ran his hands over her body.

She closed her eyes, savouring the sensation of his warm skin expertly caressing her. As their passions rose, she let out a moan. The man pressed his lips to her neck and Monique knew she had to say it.

'I'm not your genius.'

She could have lied. Elena wouldn't have minded – the perfume didn't mean anything to her. But then what? How would she live with knowing that Jacques's admiring looks, his respect . . . everything was based on a lie? She would be taking what rightfully belonged to Elena, and only to Elena.

But in that moment, none of this mattered: she wanted him, she desired him, and knew it wouldn't take much to get him back. All she had to do was lie. Despite her best intentions to be honest, Monique would have done anything to keep him.

Jacques tensed. 'Don't be silly,' he whispered against her skin, before sinking his teeth in, biting her gently.

No one could make her melt the way he could. Heaven, or indeed all the wonders of hell, were as nothing compared to what Jacques could do.

'What if it were true? What if I'd asked someone else to find the perfume for me?'

She regretted her words almost immediately. She could have kept quiet, and he would have loved her. When Jacques pulled away from her, took a step back, she could see that a doubt had found its way into her lover's mind. And then, under the layers of delusions, desire and lies, something else emerged: the bitter taste of shame.

Had she really been reduced to lying to keep Jacques? What kind of woman had she become?

She hung her head, trying to recover her pride, or what was left of it, and once again was overwhelmed by the sweet and captivating scent of ambergris. But this time she felt no shivers, she didn't see the sea or feel the sun. She quickly tied her hair in a ponytail, and without looking Jacques in the eye, she walked over to the bathroom.

'When you leave, put the keys on the table by the door. The next time I find you in my house uninvited, I'm calling the police.' She didn't wait for Jacques to reply, locking the door behind her.

It took a while, but when she came out of the bathroom Monique had calmed down. She didn't need to check to know that Jacques wasn't there any more. She could feel his absence.

She let some of the anger bubbling inside her rise to the surface and was almost happy to feel it, to let it chase Jacques and his stupid flattery out of the pathetic place in her heart that still guarded her dreams.

'Go to hell,' she swore at the card he'd left on the bed. She grabbed it and screwed it up, throwing it on to the floor. 'As if I'm going to call you.'

She was willing to bet he'd taken the perfumes as well. Both of them. Jacques was a man who liked to keep all his options open. The essence from the Indian manufacturer that Elena had chosen was what he wanted, but the other one, the one she'd found, was also a good option. She had enough experience as a perfumier to know her own worth.

The room around her was decorated in perfect minimalist style and neutral tones, striking a contrast with the elegant dresses hanging in her antique rosewood wardrobe. She picked out a bottle-green silk dress and paired it with a light purple woollen cardigan, a dash of make-up and her hair tied back. She should have her hair cut short, she thought. But she could never go through with it. She was a bit like Elena in that respect, sticking with something that had identified her for so long. She should call Elena, tell her all about Jacques, let her friend know that her formidable instinct for perfume was at the heart of it.

Whether she liked it or not, Elena was a nose. She always had been. Actually, she was much more than that, because she could even deduce emotions from smells, and she knew how to explain them. For Elena, her sense of smell was as fundamental as sight is to anyone else. The fact that she refused to admit it, that she rejected this talent, was another matter altogether.

Monique sighed. Before she went out, she glanced in the mirror, then picked up her handbag. In one of the compartments, she'd stashed a business card. It was a deep ivory colour, thick and deliciously perfumed: musk and sandalwood, she was sure. In the background, Monique could detect a bitter third note, perhaps another wood. She pondered for a while, trying to identify it. Not that it mattered. Then she stopped thinking and just breathed in the perfume, a truly captivating *mélange*.

Alain Le Notre of the perfume house La Fougérie was a smart, sophisticated man, and he'd made her a good offer. The time had come to find out exactly how worthwhile a new job might be.

6

Myrrh: security. More earthy and 'concrete' than incense.
The fragrance is strong, balanced and unambiguous.
Represents the link between spirit and reality.

Paris

The line of trees started on one side of the street and ran almost as far as the eye could see until it suddenly stopped, and began again on the other side. The trees in place Louis-Lépine followed the lines of the buildings and, a little further along, inside the flower-market, lavender, myrtle and rose-mary bushes sprouted untidily from their stands as if in protest at being confined.

With his hands deep in his pockets, Caillen McLean headed straight for the stand where he would find roses. It was a wet day, and his thick hair dripped rain on to his gaunt face. His piercing blue eyes were cold and lined with tiny wrinkles. Those eyes were daunting enough to give anyone pause when seeing him for the first time, but nothing in comparison to the deep and uneven scar running across his cheek.

Ignoring the banks of caramel-scented lilies, freshly opened tulips and freesias, he turned to look at an odd combination of dried flowers – and grimaced. Right in the middle was a bouquet of electric-blue roses.

'*Bonjour*, Cail, how are you? What can I do for you?' A middle-aged man dried both hands on a soil-covered apron. A steely glint in his eyes suggested that the hearty-looking florist might not be as calm as he seemed. Disregarding his friendly greeting, Cail pointed at the blue roses. 'Is anyone really going to buy those . . . *things*?'

The other man scratched his head. 'I've got some green and gold ones. Do you want to see them?'

'You're joking, right, Lambert?'

The seller shrugged. 'They're not that bad, actually.'

A frosty glare was Cail's only response, before shifting his gaze, as though he couldn't even stand to look at the flowers.

'Is Liliane in her usual spot?' His voice was deep, with a slight Scottish accent, and there was a hint of impatience in his tone.

'Yes, opposite side of the market,' Lambert told him, 'next to Louise's stall. The one with the hibiscuses.' Cail nodded a thank you, and after casting one final withering glance at the flowers, he stalked off. As Lambert watched the tall figure disappear into the middle of the market, he grumbled to himself, 'Roses follow fashion, just like the rest of the world. If the punters want blue roses, I get blue roses. They want green? Then green it is.' He stared at the flowers with their crumpled petals and that metallic touch that gave him the shivers. 'I don't blame him for hating them, though,' he muttered under his breath. A moment later he was flashing a dazzling smile at a woman who came looking for him with a vase of mottled purple petunias in her hand.

Cail had almost reached the back of the flower-market when he spotted the rose-sellers. He carefully examined the tired-looking blooms emerging from their spiny stems. From a distance they were no different to the fat buds of peonies. Even the colours, a whole spectrum of pink, from the brightest to the most powdery, seemed to mark them out as such. But a more careful observer wouldn't miss the delicate and slightly decadent grace of the chalice-shaped flowers, with their open petals resting languidly against one another. They were Claire Austin roses. An unmistakable, though delicate, scent of myrrh seemed to mix in with the meadowsweet, gaining strength and adding character to their docile appearance.

Cail looked at them, lifting them up in the palm of his hand and leaning forward to bury his face in the flowers. He didn't even need to smell them: their clear, characteristic perfume was all around. But there was something profoundly sensuous about the silken touch of those creamy-pink petals on the skin, and Cail intended to make the most of it. He ignored the looks he got from passers-by, as he did with anything else that didn't remotely interest him.

'Hi, Cail.' A young woman approached him. Slowly, gracefully, he straightened up.

'Have you got my parcel?' he asked, skipping the small talk. Liliane looked at him for a moment, then shook her head with a look of resignation.

'Yes, I'm fine, thanks. You're looking very well yourself,' she said curtly, before going behind the counter and coming back with a brown box. She was wearing a blue sleeveless dress with a square neckline that had provoked disapproving looks and compliments in equal measure from her customers.

Despite the chill in the air, she didn't regret her decision: she had known Cail would be coming to collect the parcel and she would have worn a bikini if it got him to notice her.

Cail, however, didn't seem to be paying any attention to her appearance. He just picked up the parcel and handed her a hundred euros in exchange. On seeing her confused expression, he pointed at the box. 'Keep the change. I'll need some more stuff for next week.'

The young woman nodded. 'Anything else I can do for you?' she asked. And she wasn't talking about flowers.

Cail was quiet for a moment, and then nodded goodbye. 'No. See you next Saturday.' Liliane could only purse her lips in frustration.

Alain Le Notre. The very name was terrifying. Monique straightened the skirt of her dress. Perched on an uncom-fortable antique armchair, she cast a quick glance around the room. Her eyes settled on a desk that might once have belonged to a French monarch and had since found its way to the *maison*'s Head of Human Resources. Marquetry, ornaments, mother-of-pearl, and rosewood. Why did men have to flaunt their power like this?

She stood up and went over to the window. Paris was dozing under a grey drizzle. Only a few brave tourists had dragged themselves out, conspicuous in colourful plastic raincoats designed to protect their state-of-the-art cameras. Monique stared at the fat raindrops clinging to the glass, a knot of anxiety in her stomach. What if Le Notre retracted his offer? What then?

Silently, Monique chided herself. She had to stop thinking about the consequences of something that hadn't even happened yet. She was just like her mother! She wondered whether Elena would accept Jasmine's invitation to visit Grasse. Not that Monique agreed with the suggestion – personally, she didn't think Elena should be wallowing in the past. Having fun, being around people, that's what she needed. But, above all, her friend needed to accept her true nature. Once Elena realized what a unique talent she had, she'd become one of the most sought-after noses in the world. Easily. Except that Elena hated being the centre of attention.

Monique was the one who needed to be in the limelight. She was so good at solving everyone else's problems, it was a shame she was completely hopeless when it came to her own.

Another sigh. She straightened her skirt again. Then she heard the door behind her.

'Monsieur Le Notre,' she said, turning around.

'It's good to see you again, *mademoiselle*.'

Alain's eyes were a cool shade of grey, but at that moment they gleamed, delighted. He must have been around forty, but his slender, athletic body showed that he took serious care of himself and his appearance. He was tall, smart and sophisticated.

'Benzoin, bergamot, vetiver, sandalwood and a mixture of cedar wood,' Monique recited. 'And tonka bean.'

She didn't know what had come over her, but she recognized the fragrance the man was wearing. It was one of her own creations. Nothing special – any perfumier could have come up with an essence like that for a man like Le Notre. He smiled, revealing a row of bright white teeth to go with his sporty and naturally tanned appearance. A boat, she'd bet. Le Notre looked like a seafaring man.

'Please, *mademoiselle*, let's take a seat.' He led her over to a small sofa and sat down beside her. It wasn't the first time Monique had met Alain. She'd already had a chance to appreciate his vibrant personality.

'I like the way you work,' Le Notre smiled, and went on: 'Your intuition is quite incredible; you can find original, solid blends at affordable prices – and that practical approach is just what I want for my new line. I want action, certainty, energy – and for it to be accessible to a wide audience. Do you think you can give me what I need?'

'Let me think about it,' Monique said calmly, her heart pounding. This man had taken her limitations, the things that made her ordinary, and turned them into strengths. She was thrilled, and so deeply moved by Alain's words that she almost forgot to breathe. It was as though she'd found someone who could appreciate her for her faults.

The man gave her a pensive stare. The perfume hung in the air, a bond between them.

'I . . . I think we can discuss it,' she said again, this time with more certainty. Then she straightened her shoulders and looked Le Notre in the eye.

'Very well, Mademoiselle Duval. What do you say we move on to the administrative side?'

Monique nodded, trying not to let her enthusiasm show. 'I'm listening, Monsieur Le Notre.'

It was almost ridiculous, waiting in the rain. He was completely drenched, his jeans and T-shirt stuck to his skin, his eyelashes dripping with raindrops. Yet Cail wouldn't have moved from the rosebush even if the sky fell in.

He looked down into the courtyard for a moment. The renovated apartments enclosing the large communal court-yard, the heart of what had once been the grand home of one of the wealthiest aristocratic families in Paris, were still cloaked in darkness.

Cail moved his umbrella to keep the rose stem dry. At the top of the spiny branch, a fat bud was about to open any moment.

He half-closed his eyes. The rain pattered relentlessly, plastering his hair to his face and soaking into his two-day-old beard. He shook himself dry, careful not to knock the rose.

He had no idea what effect getting too wet might have on a bud at that stage of maturation. In general, he'd prefer to conduct an experiment like this in a greenhouse, but this particular plant was the product of a series of events that went against any cross-breeding technique manual, and he didn't want to run the risk of undermining months of effort by moving it. It was a three-year-old rosebush, with its first mature bud.

He leaned over, desperate to protect the flower. Then he put one knee on the grass; he was so impatient he was shaking. He was excited and he couldn't wait for the dawn to come and light up the sky. It would stop raining soon, he knew it.

'Bloody weather,' he cursed. 'For God's sake give it a rest!'

John, his dog, got to his feet and plodded over to join him. Cail smiled and put out his free hand to stroke the creature's tawny coat. 'Go back in your kennel,' he ordered. 'You'll get soaked.' The dog licked his hand, and did as he was told.

Paris seemed to be waking up. The buzz of cars quickly became a roar, like a swollen stream heading for the valley. Lights were disappearing from houses, too, replaced by a sunrise growing brighter and brighter. Cail knew it wouldn't be long before the courtyard was full of people. He gritted his teeth. It was better for them if they kept their distance.

He didn't mind the quizzical looks from his neighbours, who had caught him talking to his plants on more than one occasion. But the benefit of being a solid six feet four was that none of them was brave enough to poke fun at him. At least, not within earshot. Although he was more inclined to think it was down to the off-putting effect of his scar.

'Good morning, Caillen,' a voice called up. 'I won't ask what the hell you're doing standing in the rain keeping that rosebush dry. I'm far too scared of that temper of yours.'

'Piss off, Ben!'

His friend's laugh got a smirk out of Cail. Ben waved goodbye and went about his day.

Cail knew he looked ridiculous holding a ladies' checked umbrella over the rosebush. His mother, Elizabeth, had left the umbrella on one of her visits. She would have appreciated the excuse to come back and collect it, but Cail had decided he'd post it to her at the first possible opportunity. He carried on waiting, eyes fixed on the bud.

A stream of pink eventually cleared away the black clouds, the rain slowly easing off until it was just a light patter. Piles of wet leaves at the sides of the courtyard below gave off a strong, musky plant smell.

Cail breathed in the pungent scent, concentrated by the cold air, and then turned his attention back to the rose. It was the only survivor from a group of seeds that had been very important to him, and had gone decidedly wrong. For a while they were growing normally; then they started to wilt. Cail decided to replant them in the ground, taking them out of the pot they were grown in. It was a risky move for such a young cross-breed, he knew that. But luckily his unconventional response had strengthened the remaining plant, which, thanks to all his attention, had grown quickly. Now Cail couldn't wait to see the results of the cross-breeding. It felt as if the many months he'd dedicated to this plant had been reduced to this one moment, for the rose would bloom with the first rays of sunlight.

The rain finally stopped altogether, and the sky quickly cleared, swept by a cold wind that made Cail shiver. It would be at least another hour before the flower would warm up and open its petals. Cursing this sudden drop in temperature, Cail closed the umbrella.

'I'm sorry, John, we'll have to be patient for a little bit longer.'

He looked at the dog, who had come to his side, and then back at the rose. He wouldn't move until he knew for sure whether or not it had all been for nothing.

Monique waited for Le Notre's driver to open the door for her. She could have walked, since the *maison* wasn't very far from Narcissus, but it was raining again. Alain had kindly offered a car to take her, and she had accepted: she had no intention of arriving soaking wet on what was going to be her last day at work. She settled into the comfort of the cream leather seats, breathing in the smell of leather and luxury. She could get used to this, she thought.

When they arrived at Narcissus, the driver walked her to the entrance, holding an umbrella. He waited for her to go in, then went back to the car.

'*Bonjour, Philippe. Monsieur Montier?*' she asked the manager.

The man smiled at her. '*Mademoiselle*, you're back from Italy! Did you find anything interesting?'

Philippe Renaud was something of a workaholic but he was a good man, Monique thought, if a bit of a snob. Usually, Monique liked to stay and chat with him, but just then she was nervous. Her contract with La Fougérie was signed: in a few days she would be working for a new *maison*. And Jacques would never forgive her. Monique knew that. Her move to La Fougérie signalled the end of their relationship once and for all.

'Yes, an original brief – really does the job, you'll like it. Now, where's Jacques?'

Philippe's smile lost some of its shine. He pointed at the door behind him. '*Monsieur* is busy in the laboratory. Do you want me to go and tell him?'

She should have guessed that Jacques would get straight to work on the perfume. Monique looked at Philippe and shook her head. 'No thanks, I'll do it myself.' She walked away, past Philippe and down a long corridor. When she arrived at the laboratory she didn't knock, just opened the door gently. She wasn't dressed properly and didn't want to contaminate the atmosphere.

'I want to talk to you,' she said.

Jacques greeted her coolly. 'Come in, but not too close. I don't want your scent to ruin the formula. Anyway, what is that perfume? I've never smelled it on you before.' He spoke to her without even turning round.

Monique looked at him for a moment. She was wearing a new fragrance, a perfume she'd just been given by Alain Le Notre. They were launching it on the market soon, he'd told her. It was set to be their key product for the whole of autumn and winter. To Monique, it smelled of new possibilities.

'Don't you like it?' she asked.

Jacques didn't even bother to reply; he had his eyes closed, his nose over a *mouillette*. Monique knew that Jacques only cared about his own interests, and yet she was still hurt. In the end, getting it over with quickly was the only thing to do.

'Don't worry, I've got no intention of coming in,' she said

crisply. 'I just came to clear up a couple of things.'

'If it's about the perfume, I closed the deal with Shindia today. We'll be selling their perfumes. Your second choice is good, but the other one is better. Naturally I'll give you what I owe you for finding it.'

How could he make her feel worthless in so few words? For a moment Monique thought of telling him where he could stick his money, but all that would achieve would be to close the door to Narcissus for Elena.

'In Florence, I asked a friend to help me. Like I told you, I didn't choose that perfume myself.'

A few seconds of silence and then: 'So who is this perfume wizard, this ... nose?' The conceit in his voice convinced Monique that she was doing the right thing. He was a bastard, she reminded herself. And the worst kind. She would be better off without him.

'I'm leaving Narcissus. I just came to tell you.'

Another silence, longer this time, until he finally lifted his head and looked at her.

'Isn't that a little excessive? I wouldn't have thought you'd be so touchy.'

Jacques put on his lab coat, his expression grim. In front of him stood a row of tiny aluminium bottles containing essential oils. The rest of the ingredients were in glass containers, vials and alembics of all shapes and sizes. On the steel table sat a number of droppers and paper funnels, and in the middle of it all, a measuring cylinder emitting an intense perfume. He opened his mouth to go on, and then looked at the cylinder, as if it were only then that he remembered what he was doing.

'Wait. I need to write down the last step, then we'll talk.' He leaned over the table and scribbled on a pad next to the perfume the exact number of grams of essence he had just used.

Monique watched him, then gave a sad smile. 'There's always something more important,' she said quietly. She waited a few more minutes. Jacques went over to the computer on the next table, entered a code, took his time to read something, then went back to the pad and continued to write.

'Goodbye, Jacques.'

The sound of the pencil snapping cut through the silence between them.

'I can't listen to you now. You know that full well.'

Of course. What had she been thinking? Had she really expected anything different? Something like despair rose up in Monique.

'You'll find my resignation letter on your desk,' she said after a long pause, and closed the door behind her.

As she walked away, she half-expected to hear his footsteps behind her . . . she prayed he'd hurry to catch up with her, talk to her. She stood and waited another minute in front of the exit, counting the seconds, still prepared to give him a bit more time. Then she pushed the door with both hands, walking out on to the shop floor of Narcissus, elegant, bright, brimming with customers. She greeted a few colleagues, quickly collected her things from behind one of the counters and left.

With his eyes fixed on the security camera, Jacques watched her even after she'd left the shop. When she disappeared from the video, he swore violently, running his hands through his hair, and collapsed into an armchair.

Another ruined one!

Elena wrinkled her nose, quickly pulling the bottle away. It smelled rancid. She'd cast aside around fifty essential oils that had gone bad; she'd have to throw them all away. There was no chance of saving anything.

She couldn't have reopened her grandmother's shop even if she'd wanted to. She'd gone down into the basement to check what state things were in down there since the shop had closed. She still hadn't decided to go down the perfume route – she hadn't got that far. But since she didn't have the faintest idea what to do with her life, it was as good an option as any. It was funny, she thought, smiling at the irony. Now that there was nothing stopping her from opening the perfume shop, she couldn't do it: no essences meant no perfumes. And no perfumes meant no profits. Anyway, what was she think-ing? She couldn't restart a perfume business just because perfumes suddenly didn't turn her stomach any more.

She sighed. That wasn't fair. It wasn't disgust that she'd felt when she worked in the shop, it was something else – some-thing she didn't want to think about right now.

Her mobile phone vibrated. Elena opened it, looked at the number and smiled.

'Did it go well?' she asked Monique.

'Define "well". Actually, no, forget it. Anyway, I got the job. Le Notre is a real gentleman. Tell me about you. How's the stocktaking going?'

Elena rubbed the palm of her hand on her shirt. 'All in the bin. All I've got left are a few bottles I made for a hotel that never collected them, and some really old stuff. Nothing that would be any good now.'

'Like perfumes from another era?'

Elena went up to the dark wooden cabinet, aged over time, and gave the doors a gentle tug, letting them swing on their hinges. 'Yes. My grandmother kept them in the dark, and the temperature in the cellar never changes with these walls . . .'

'You mean to say you went down there, to the secret studio?' Monique sounded incredulous and excited at the same time.

Elena said she had. 'You've got no idea what's down here. I could open a museum. There are alembics and extractors that must be hundreds of years old.'

'Did you have a look at the formulas?' Monique asked.

'Absolutely nothing has changed since the last time we looked at them together. Beatrice Rossini's Perfect Perfume is just a legend, Monique,' Elena said.

'The diary says otherwise,' her friend argued.

'We've read it from cover to cover, and there's nothing that could suggest a formula. They were just the ramblings of an obsessive woman.'

It was true: both she and Monique had read Beatrice Rossini's diary over and over again. Apart from references to a few ingredients commonly used in perfumery, and a series of symbols drawn on the pages, they'd never found anything relating to the production of one specific perfume. The symbols were interesting, of course, as were the drawings, poems and rhymes. But the main content of those pages was a heart-breaking tale of unrequited love that ended in tragedy. Beatrice had fallen for the wrong man. And she wanted him so much that she let herself be destroyed by what became an obsession. The Perfect Perfume was the essence of her delusion and betrayal. It was appearance, it was deception.

The two friends had reached a conclusion: the illustrious client had paid for the perfume in cash, rather than with his heart. That was all there was for Beatrice Rossini: tears and money. Enough gold florins to ensure that she and her family would be comfortable for generations.

'Love can have that effect,' Monique murmured.

'I don't know. I'm pretty confused by love. Apart from the urge to vomit whenever I think about Matteo and Alessia, I've just got a kind of empty feeling in my chest.' Elena paused for a moment. 'You know how much I wanted a normal family, a husband, children. A stable environment. I'm nearly thirty, Monie, I can't wait for ever. And now I'm alone, I don't have a job . . .'

'Come on, you've got a long way to go before you hit thirty. Besides, you can't just marry the first idiot who comes along,' Monique blurted out.

Elena nodded. A shiver made her decide to leave the cold, dark room. 'Matteo wasn't that bad, if you ignored a couple of things,' she said, turning off the lights and closing the door behind her. She went back upstairs, noticing that she felt tired again.

'Like the fact that you had to have lunch with his mother every Sunday. What a horrible woman!' Monique shuddered audibly. 'She's an ignorant, rude snob. And anyway, she gave me the creeps.'

'Me too. She used to give me such looks . . .'

'I'd have done a runner. I swear, I'd have made up some kind of excuse to avoid seeing her. But my God, why were you with him anyway?' Monique was as direct as always. Elena sat on the bench by the stairs. She needed to catch her breath.

'Kids. He wanted loads of them. He said they were the most important thing to him. And I wanted a baby. And then – I don't know . . . I keep asking myself how I didn't see what kind of man he was.'

'Listen, enough about him. Let's talk about you. Have you decided to go to Grasse?'

Elena closed her eyes. 'I can't. Not now. It doesn't feel right.'

'So what about coming to Paris? My job at Narcissus is up for grabs. If Jacques knew who you were, he'd take you on straight away.' Monique lay down on her bed, Le Notre's business card in her hand.

Elena frowned. 'You what? You must be joking! We're talking about Narcissus here, not just any old perfume company.'

Her friend left a thoughtful silence. 'Supposing the job's there, would you come? There's my family's old apartment in the Marais – you could stay there. Loads of Italians live in the Marais, and it's twenty minutes from my place on the Metro. So?' Her voice had become more determined, as though a vague idea that had gradually been developing had finally taken shape.

'I don't know,' Elena mused. 'A job like that, really, I mean . . . and I'd have to arrange everything, close up the house.'

Monique sprang up so she was sitting on the bed. 'Come on, Elena, think about it! A job in Paris, a new life. Of course, the apartment isn't perfect – it needs a lick of paint, some new furniture – but it'll make a nice change. Somewhere different, somewhere you can start from scratch. It shouldn't take you more than a week or two to sort things out in Florence, should it?'

Elena stood up. The silence of the house all around her only emphasized the loneliness she'd been feeling for days now. A sadness came over her, bringing a lump to her throat, but she swallowed it back down. She imagined Paris, the narrow streets of the Marais, the parks full of flowers, the wonderful museums. And a job. She could make some money, pick up the path she'd abandoned a couple of years ago, re-establish her contacts . . . Then if it all went well, she could reopen the shop here in Florence. Not straight away, no, but one day.

But she knew that these were just hopes; she couldn't truly believe in them. They were barely more than dreams.

Then something inside her stirred. It was her own will, reasserting itself. How long had it been since she'd made a decision? She realized that lately, she'd missed the satisfaction of deciding on something and accomplishing it for herself, with no motivation other than fulfilling her own expectations. She *would* go to Paris! She wanted to go, she wanted a change . . . she wanted to, end of story.

'I'll admit, it does seem like a good idea. But there's a problem. I don't know anything about new perfume technology, I'm not up to date.'

Monique went over to the table where the packaging from the Indian perfume was still sitting. 'Book the ticket,' she said. 'Email me the flight number, and leave the rest to me.'

Monique ended the call, picked up the *mouillette* that still held a slight perfume, and inhaled it slowly. Then she opened her mobile phone and dialled a number.

'I'm sending you a CV,' she told Philippe.

7

Helichrysum: understanding. Sweet as honey and bitter as a
  sleepless dawn. An intense perfume.
The fragrance of kindness; to be used sparingly, blended with
  delicate scents like rose that can take on its qualities.
Unites heart and mind, passion and reason. Evokes
  compassion.

The Marais was one of the few quarters to have retained the character of seventeenth-century Paris. Once a favourite of the aristocracy, who preferred to live next door to the royal court rather than in it, the area came through the Revolution unscathed, and survived subsequent visions for town-planning, the Seine floods that deluged southern parts of the city, a succession of kings, and Napoleon.

Elena walked through the narrow streets in search of the apartment where she was about to start her new life. In spite of the rain, dozens of tourists stubbornly continued to hunt for things, admire them and take photographs. Elena left them behind in rue des Rosiers, the ancient heart of the Jewish quarter within the Marais and entered a maze of back streets. Here, the ambience changed, and she felt as if she was somewhere else, a tiny village suspended in time.

She stopped under a *boulangerie* sign, checking the piece of paper with the address on it for the thousandth time: rue du Parc-Royal, number 12A. She carried on walking almost automatically. At one point, the wheels on her case stopped co-operating, weighed down by the rain. Muttering crossly, Elena gave the suitcase a sharp tug before realizing she'd finally arrived.

'At last,' she said, stopping in front of a stone archway marked with the number twelve, and peering through the wrought-iron bars. In the dim glow of a few beams of light, she could make out a garden, some bicycles and a couple of parked cars.

Monique had emailed the code for Elena to open the main gates – but the rain had smudged the numbers she'd jotted on a piece of paper. Annoyed, Elena screwed the note into a ball. Then, weighed down by her wet clothes and wretched mood, she leaned against the wet wall. It smelled of brick, plaster and exhaustion; the same exhaustion Elena could feel in her whole body. The journey from Florence had not been easy. The plane was late, then she couldn't find a taxi at the airport and she had had to take the bus.

At that moment, a car drew up beside her. The driver activated the automatic catch on the gate and drove slowly into the internal courtyard. Dragging her suitcase behind her, Elena limped through the gates just before they closed. The first door on the right was marked as the entrance to apartments 12A and 12B. A wave of relief swept over her.

Monique had sent her a text message saying that she'd called round that afternoon to switch on the heating and hot water, and to drop off some shopping, and that she'd left the shared entrance door ajar. Elena only had to give it a shove, Monique said, since it was inclined to stick, and she'd be in. .

Leaning both hands on the huge door, Elena followed her friend's instructions. But it didn't budge. A musty smell filtered through a tiny gap in the door: as though inside there were piles of old books, plants and moss.

With her eyes closed and her hands on the wooden door, Elena found herself suddenly transported into another world: the world of scents. Smoke rose from the charcoal fires of restaurants nearby: she could smell grilled fish and mixed vegetables – courgettes and peppers – then the icing on a chocolate cake. Semolina and freshly baked bread. In addition, the breeze brought with it the perfume of cedar trees, their leaves heavy with rain, and flowers: gardenias, Michaelmas daisies, then the seductive, delicious scent of roses. And finally, the smell of a hard day travelling without a break. Impatience, fatigue – and doubt. Then a riot of colour: red, green, purple. She opened her eyes wide. The emotions took her breath away and spiralled inside her . . . she felt them brush against her, then swirl, concentrate, and explode. It was too much. She *had* to stop them – she *had* to stop feeling.

She pushed with all her might – and the door suddenly burst open, catapulting her forward into darkness. A strong arm caught her waist, breaking her fall, and a voice said, 'What the hell . . . ? Are you all right?'

It took Elena a couple of seconds to realize what had happened. Thank God this man had caught her before she ended up on the floor. That would have been the final straw, she thought.

'Yes, thank you,' she murmured, stunned.

When he didn't respond, Elena fidgeted nervously – the man was still holding her tight.

'You can let go of me now,' she told him awkwardly.

Suddenly he let go, stepping away from her. 'I didn't mean to frighten you,' he said sharply.

Elena was struck by something in the stranger's voice, a hint of sadness. The emotions that had overwhelmed her a moment ago dissolved, and new ones took their place.

There was pain in the man's words – old and unjust suffering. Elena wondered why, and wanted to get to know him; she wanted to hear his story. This wasn't something she could explain; it was instinct.

'I can't see you – it's too dark,' she told him, taking his hand. Her fingers grasping his, she turned around to see his face. The lamplight coming through the open door outlined the strong figure of a man, but left his face in shadow. Elena couldn't make out anything more than a tall, broad silhouette. His voice was slightly harsh, but still polite, and deep.

'I'm not scared of you,' she said, and gave him a smile.

He didn't reply, just held on to her fingers. Elena knew it was irrational – absurd even, to not want to let him go. But lately she'd stopped acting rationally.

'You smell nice.' It was an impulse, this confession; the words simply tripped off her tongue.

She immediately blushed. God, it sounded as if she was trying to pick him up. Monique would have been proud of her.

'Sorry, you must think I'm crazy,' she babbled, 'but I've had a horrible day and the first good thing that's happened to me was you rescuing me. If you hadn't caught me, I'd have ended up in a heap on the floor. A perfect end to a terrible day. I was just taken by surprise because the door opened all of a sudden.'

'What of?'

Elena was confused. 'What of . . . what?'

'You said I smelled nice. What of?'

'Oh, yes,' she laughed, a light, velvety sound. 'It's an occupational hazard.'

But he didn't laugh, just kept on staring at her intensely. Elena felt his gaze on her, sensed the importance of her reply and the words that this man, whoever he was, was waiting for. So she closed her eyes, and let his perfume speak to her, telling her things only she knew how to hear.

'You smell like the rain, and the cold, but sunshine, too. Like words you've thought, long silences and reflection. You smell like earth and roses . . . You have a dog, and you're a good person, who stops to help, and who's grieving for something in his heart.'

A long silence. Then, without warning, the man snatched back his hand.

'I have to go,' he said. 'Leave the main door open, as the light in the entrance doesn't work. Take care.'

He backed away, slowly, without taking his eyes off her. Only when he reached the door did he turn around and leave.

Elena stifled a sudden urge to call him back. Then, with her eyes still on the door, she started to laugh. What on earth had got into her? She might as well have asked the guy for his phone number. She just grabbed hold of a strange man and . . . well, really it was him who grabbed hold of her. She was half-amused, half-shocked by her own behaviour. But these thoughts were soon swept away as she lifted her head, trying to breathe in that perfume again. It was a promise kept, it was the sweetness of trust; and the weight and responsibility that go with it. It was action and need. She searched for it again, breathing in the night air, trying to retrace the thread as it disappeared. But it was gone, leaving her with a sense of something close to longing.

By now, she'd got used to the strange half-light. She blinked; the hallway was large and the ceilings high. In one corner, beside a window, there was a plant, probably a weeping fig, and a flight of stairs led to the apartments on other floors. On the ground floor there was just one door marked 12A, and it seemed to match Monique's description.

Elena pushed the door, which opened easily, with a squeak. So this was the apartment. She looked for the switch, and in the first flash of light she saw a large, bare room with high walls. Someone had tried to plaster over the old bricks – unsuccessfully, to judge from the results – and had instead made do with a coat of paint. Evidently, when Monique couldn't persuade the wall it was going to be plastered, she'd ended up painting it. Somehow, she'd got her way. Elena laughed.

She walked into the middle of the room, the tiles shifting under the pressure of her feet. She frowned: they must be very old. Some of them had been taken up and piled pitifully in a corner, revealing an even older floor underneath. To her right was a window, and a door that must open straight on to the pavement, but which looked as if it had been sealed for years. Monique had told her that the apartment had been passed down through her family. None of them had ever wanted to live there, but selling it was out of the question. It had belonged to Jasmine's father, Ismael Ahdad, a first-generation immigrant, and he had spent his entire life savings on it. Jasmine had been particularly proud of the apartment. But even so, the Duvals had never been especially fond of the place. Monique had used it as somewhere to crash for a couple of months when she arrived in Paris, but had moved to another part of the city as soon as possible.

Elena went over to the staircase, which wound upwards to another floor, no doubt where she would find the bedroom and bathroom. She flicked another old switch and a bulb illuminated the landing above.

Monique told her she'd bought new bedlinen, a duvet and some towels. All Elena wanted right now was a bath and then sleep.

She set off wearily up the stairs and stopped at the top to look around. She could see three rooms: a small living room with a kitchen; a bathroom and a bedroom. Save for a few piles of books lying around, there was little furniture: a red Formica kitchen unit, a few old appliances, three chairs and a table. On the table was a plastic bag, the source of a delicious smell.

'God bless you, Monie,' Elena murmured, rummaging around inside. She bit into a piece of baguette before going back to exploring the apartment.

Once the windows were open, a light breeze brought in other smells and sounds: the voice of a beautiful, romantic city Elena was eager to see again.

She should call Monique, tell her she'd arrived. Where had she put her phone? Oh God! And her handbag? Elena looked around frantically, then hurried back downstairs. When she saw her bag by the door, she breathed a sigh of relief. Her suitcase was there, too. Suddenly she remembered that she'd actually left them outside in the courtyard. Could the stranger have brought them in for her?

She let out another sigh at the thought, grateful to the man, whoever he was. A neighbour perhaps? She liked that idea; it made her feel good. It was strange. Nothing like this had ever happened to her before. She had never had a chance encounter with a stranger.

She closed the door and went back upstairs. Submerging herself in a tub of hot water, she began to revive. For a second Matteo popped into her mind, but she was quick to push him back out. She had too much to do, too much to organize. She was busy planning her new life. There was no time to keep going over the past.

'Too busy for love, no time for hate,' she whispered, recalling a phrase she often spotted on Facebook. It wasn't strictly true. (There had been moments when she felt like gouging out Alessia's eyes and stabbing Matteo.) Still, it was a nice idea and she decided to stick to it as much as possible: she would fill her days with only good things. Thoughts raced around her mind, lingering briefly before taking off again in new directions.

Relaxed but hungry, Elena got out of the bath. Once she'd eaten the treats Monique had left her, she lay down on the bed and realized that she almost felt happy.

Cail looked at the rose he'd sheltered from the rain a few days earlier. Its petals were open now. At their edges tiny droplets sparkled, waiting to join the others and roll to the ground like tears. A delicate scent of apple tea was all the flower emitted – but it was too slight, too commonplace, barely acceptable. It was a beautiful rose, of course – and he hadn't anticipated that, when it matured, the rose would be shaped like a chalice, since it had shown no signs of this before it bloomed. The colour was baby pink with an apricot centre.

So in the end, he decided, his work hadn't been totally wasted. His German clients would include it in their catalogue, no problem. They'd pay well and he'd get to keep the royalties.

As he went back inside his apartment, he thought about the girl he'd met at the entrance earlier. From her accent, she seemed Italian. She had told him he smelled like the rain. He thought back to her words, turning them over in his mind, carefully weighing up each one, until John came over and rubbed against his legs. The animal was nice and warm; Cail bent and stroked his fur.

'How many times have I told you you're a dog, not a cat?' In response, John licked his hand and Cail smiled.'Are you hungry? Come on, let's go inside.'

The apartment Cail rented was in the part of the premises that had once been used by the stable boys from the former grand mansion. It was reached by a staircase which ended at a terrace. He'd had to pay a premium for sole use of the terrace, but it was worth it. He'd surrounded it with a wooden trellis and planted a *Banksiae lutea* rambling rose. In just two years the plant's long thornless branches had covered every inch of the fence, creating a screen for the rest of the terrace. It flowered once a year – tiny perfumed posies that lasted just a few weeks. In the sheltered area, Cail grew special roses: the mothers, the plants he would go on to use in his work. A little nylon green-house, in the middle of the terrace, contained the young hybrids he was counting on to find new varieties of roses. Around it, everything was arranged and kept in perfect order: equipment, soil, fertilizer. Next to the door to the apartment was John's kennel.

With the dog at his heels, Cail went inside, turned on the lights and headed for the kitchen. He chopped some vegetables, put them in a pan with a little olive oil, then added a clove of garlic and a couple of basil leaves.

He picked out a CD, carefully removed it from its case, and put it into the machine.

Curled up on the rug in the lounge, John dozed lazily, constantly keeping one eye on Cail. After tidying the kitchen and loading the dishwasher, Cail went out on to the terrace.

The dog followed him to the doorway, and stopped.

The air was cold, crisp. The clouds had dissipated, allowing for a handful of stars to shine through. Cail carried on looking at them for a while, and let Ludovico Einaudi's piano lift his thoughts. He then went inside and came back to the terrace carrying a long metal tube. He positioned it on a stand and adjusted it. A moment later, peering through the telescope, his own world seemed distant, black, and in some strange way, brilliant.

'Did you find it all? The shopping, the sheets? Did you sleep well?'

'Yes, don't worry. I found everything and I slept like a log. But tell me about this house. How old is it?'

Monique sighed. 'It's very old – two or three hundred years, I think. It used to belong to some nobleman who lost his head.'

'Over a woman?'

'No, on the guillotine.'

Elena shivered. 'That's not funny!'

'It wasn't meant to be. That's what happened, it's hardly my fault. And besides, the masters' quarters were in another section of the building. There's no ghost wandering around your part of the house, trust me.'

'Is that why you'd rather pay to rent somewhere else than live in your own house? Haven't you got over your fear of ghosts yet?'

Monique snorted. 'Don't be silly! Anyway, as soon as you've sorted yourself out we'll find you something more suitable.'

'No. I like it here, really. May we leave things as they are for now? Let's say I'm taking a holiday. I'm not ready to make any long-term plans. If I find a job, maybe I will stay in Paris, Monie. Otherwise I'll just go back to Florence.'

Unfortunately, Monique still had no definite news for her. Philippe hadn't told her anything about the application and she didn't want to call Jacques. She was sure that, with her contacts, she would find Elena a decent job sooner or later, but that wasn't enough. Monique had wanted to be like Elena for so long, she couldn't let a talent like her friend's go to waste. Narcissus was definitely the right place. She just had to work out how to convince Jacques.

'OK, relax,' she said now. 'I'll come and pick you up tonight. Is around seven all right for you?'

Elena stretched, still wrapped in the goosedown duvet. 'Seven sounds great.'

'Why don't you go out for a bit? The Marais has everything. Go to rue des Rosiers, buy yourself lunch and eat it outside – it tastes different, trust me.'

Elena thought for a moment, then nodded. 'Very well. Today I'll be a tourist,' she replied, looking at the fierce morning light streaming in through the curtainless windows. 'See you at seven, then. Have a good day.'

She closed her mobile and sat up. As she did so, a sudden stomach cramp made her groan. She put a hand over her mouth and sprang out of bed. She stayed kneeling by the toilet even after the retching had stopped. Her stomach was still in turmoil. The bout of nausea had passed, but she was gripped by stomach cramps so violent it was as if she hadn't eaten for days.

She slipped under a hot shower. Ten minutes later, while she was drying her hair, she decided to go out anyway. She could have breakfast in one of the bistros she'd spied the night before. And she could buy some aspirin. She picked out a comfortable pair of jeans, a white linen shirt and a red cardigan. Leaving her hair loose over her shoulders, she put on a layer of moisturizer and a dab of mascara. Then she decided to add some lipstick, too.

'In honour of Paris,' she declared, addressing the mirror.

She picked up her bag and went downstairs. As she was walking through the living room to the door, she let herself imagine what the space could really be like. And she surprised herself: these were the thoughts of someone who wanted to stay, organize and create things.

'Don't go making long-term plans. It won't do you any good,' she chided herself, closing the door behind her.

In daylight, the entranceway seemed much like any other. Maybe just a bit darker. The only window was shielded by the thick branches of a plant, and the ceiling was vaulted. Elena got to the door and, when it opened easily, she was surprised. There was no way she'd developed superhuman strength overnight: those hinges had been oiled.

'At eight in the morning?' she wondered. That was surprisingly efficient maintenance work.

She was about to go out when a thought popped into her head. She stretched out a hand and pressed the switch. The white ceiling light lit up. She stared at it for a moment, then turned it off. A smile lit up her face in turn. It was him. She couldn't be certain, but she'd bet it was.

When she got outside, it was like going back in time. An Italian-style garden occupied the central part of the large court-yard, with flowerbeds divided into coloured sections. The wet leaves of the trees dripped on to the heads of children running along the paths. She kept looking around with a mixture of happiness and astonishment. Were it not for the numbered doors around the edges, she would have sworn she was in the courtyard of a castle.

She stopped for a few minutes to watch the children,

ignoring curious looks from a group of men talking amongst themselves. It seemed she'd become the topic of conversation for the morning. And while once she would have been mortified to be the centre of attention, right now she couldn't care less. The sky had cleared, streaks of cobalt blue between neat lines of rooftops. Cold air, all the smells of a morning just beginning: freshly baked bread, coffee, croissants. Her appetite had returned.

She stopped in a café at the end of rue des Rosiers and ate hungrily. She had to laugh when, paying the bill, she discovered that Antoine, the owner, was in fact Antonio Grassi, who had been born and lived in Naples until a few months earlier. 'Come back and see us, *signora*, you won't find a better cappuccino in Paris.'

She carried on walking through the quarter's ancient streets, careful not to stray too far, losing her way and finding it again. It was comforting, walking without a purpose, without a schedule, without having to let anyone know or take anyone else into account. She felt free, completely and utterly free. She could do whatever she wanted. She could stop and look at the sky, the river, or through shop windows as long as she liked. Nobody was judging her, nobody knew who she was. It was as though, suddenly, someone had let go of the string on the balloon that was her life.

For the first time, she didn't mind being alone. Elena realized that the pressure she had felt to be with someone was no longer a need, it wasn't even a desire.

For the first time, she was happy by herself.

8

Rose: love. A difficult essence to obtain. Sweet and light.
The fragrance symbolizes feelings and emotions.
Encourages personal initiative and the arts.

'*Bonjour, ma chérie.* I read your friend's CV. If you're still thinking of putting her forward for the job, let's talk about it over
dinner. I can't pretend I'm not interested, but the fact is,
Narcissus is not a recruitment firm. You'll have to convince
me. Come prepared.'

It was the third time Monique had listened to the message
Jacques had left on her answerphone. Waves of anger rose up
inside her, spilled over, abated, then started all over again.

Jacques would send a car to pick her up tonight. She had
been summoned. How dare he treat her like that?

She picked up her bag and left. Oh, she'd convince him, all
right! There was no question he was about to see just how
convincing she could be.

★ ★ ★

'Are you ready? I'm taking you out – I want to introduce you to someone,' Monique said, walking through the front door.

'I thought it would be just the two of us,' Elena replied, giving her a hug. 'Is it me, or are you in a bad mood?'

Monique looked at her. 'I'm sorry. It's Jacques, he makes me want to kill someone. I know I'd promised you a girls' night, but this is important – it's about your future career.'

Elena held her friend's gaze. 'I'm not sure it's a good idea to force your boss – *ex*-boss, actually – to hire me. Especially now that things between you aren't exactly amicable.'

'When did you become so ... insightful?'

Elena got the feeling that wasn't exactly what Monique wanted to call her. She ignored the barb and decided to make her position clear.

'Don't get me wrong, I'm really grateful for everything you're doing for me, but I'm also quite sure I'd be able to find a job by myself.'

'I've never thought otherwise,' Monique retorted. 'The point is, you have a great talent and I don't think shutting yourself away in a kitchen and being an assistant chef is the best choice.'

'And who says that's what I'm planning to do?' Elena asked crossly.

An awkward silence fell over them.

'Why are we quarrelling?' Monique asked all of a sudden.

Elena sighed. 'I have no idea. But arguing in the hallway isn't a good idea. Come in, we can bicker more easily inside,' she said, closing the door.

Monique laughed and gave her another hug. 'I'm sorry, *chérie*, for being so grumpy. But you know me, I've got a plan.'

'You don't say,' Elena muttered. 'I'm almost afraid to ask.'

'Nonsense! Listen, Jacques went crazy for that perfume you chose. He wants you to work for him, even though he'd rather die than admit it. And you need this job – not to survive, obviously, but for your future. Think about it, Elena. Picture a shop of your own, where you'd be the one making all the decisions, from the way you arrange the furniture to customer relations. Bright and modern, just the way you've always wanted it. And you'd have a career at Narcissus behind you. Success is practically guaranteed.'

Elena listened to her friend in silence. 'I'm not stupid, Monie, and you know that it was the thought of working for Narcissus that finally pushed me into coming to Paris. But I can't let you resort to lowering yourself to deal with that man. Do you understand?'

Monique shrugged. 'I won't have to. I'll take you with me tonight, and he'll realize he'd be a fool to let you go.'

Put like that, it seemed perfectly simple, but Elena wasn't convinced. From what Monique had told her, this Jacques was a shrewd man. Elena wasn't about to be manipulated. She shook her head.

'I should have known it would be more complicated than it seemed,' she said. 'Maybe I should look elsewhere. It's not as if Narcissus is the only perfumery in Paris, is it?' She had no intention of giving up her newly discovered dream, but nor would she allow Monique to compromise herself on her account.

'No, but it's the right one. Narcissus creates, Elena, it doesn't just make do with selling second-rate stuff. You're exactly what Jacques is looking for, and in turn he's got everything you need.'

'I don't know . . .'

Monique started to pace restlessly, trying to find the words that would make Elena believe her. Suddenly, everything she'd kept bottled up inside for years came pouring out.

'Why don't you get it?' she said passionately. 'I'd give anything to be like you! But I don't have your gift! I have to settle for my mediocrity. You can't just throw away everything you know, Elena. I'll say it again: I'd do *anything* to be like you!'

Elena opened her eyes wide. 'Come on, what are you on about? Are you blind? Have you seen me lately? Have you really forgotten that a couple of weeks ago you practically scraped me up off the floor and offered me a new life in Paris?' Suddenly, she was really angry.

Monique hadn't seen so much fight in Elena for so long that she was stunned. 'That's not the point. You needed a change of scene, of everything. You'd have done the same for me.'

'Oh, I don't believe it,' Elena retorted, rolling her eyes. Then she took Monique's hand and held it between hers. 'There are things I need to do for myself, on my own. I can't let you fight all my battles. Do you understand, Monie?' she said softly.

'I'm not trying to fight your battles,' Monique sighed. 'Don't get me wrong, Elena, Narcissus is a competitive place, and whatever you get there you'll have to slave for. Even if Jacques does hire you, you'll need to do whatever it takes to keep hold of that job.'

The two friends looked at one another. Up until a month ago, Elena would never have considered a job in perfumery, and now she was discovering that this was what she truly wanted. Isn't life funny? she thought.

'If you let this opportunity slip away, you'll be making a big mistake,' Monique pressed.

It was true. They both knew it. Still, it wasn't easy to admit. Too many emotions all at once, too many things to reassess.

Monique decided to let it go, at least for the moment. They needed a break so they could both cool down a bit.

'This place is terrible. *Maman* should just get rid of it,' she said, looking around.

'I like it. I've noticed that the window and the door to the street have bars and a huge bolt – as if someone wanted to keep the whole world out.'

Monique opened her mouth to respond, then changed her mind and went up into the kitchen.

'Those perfumes you found in your grandmother's study, did you bring them with you?' she asked, sitting down and running her fingers over a bunch of tulips Elena had bought at the market. 'Incredible what a few flowers and a tablecloth can do for a place,' she murmured. The kitchen was still the same, but Elena had cleaned it from top to bottom, and put out some ornaments she'd found in the closet.

Elena sat down opposite her.

'Yes. I brought Beatrice's diary with me, too.'

Monique's eyes widened. 'Really? Fantastic! You could make a fortune. Do you realize what it would mean to bring perfumes from hundreds of years ago back to life? You'd have a line that was one of a kind, absolutely authentic. Nobody would be able to compete with that.'

'I'm not sure. People's tastes were different then. A bit like perfumes from the sixties. Who would wear those today?'

'Quite a few people,' Monique replied, still nosing around. 'Chanel No 5 is from 1921.'

'But that's different,' Elena protested. 'It was the first time aldehydes were used to enrich a perfume. It's still a classic. Nobody could ever call it obsolete.'

'And what about Shalimar or Mitsouko by Guerlain? You know better than I do how current they still are. At the end of the day, it's up to you to modernize those compositions. Do you think it would be that difficult?'

No, it wouldn't. And Monique might be the one bringing it up now, but while she was still in Florence Elena had already started thinking about possible variations of perfumes created by the Rossinis. The idea of restarting the business no longer seemed so painful. She would have to adapt the perfumes, of course, and she had no idea how, or how much she'd need to transform them. It still wasn't clear, but it was starting to look like a challenge.

'The more special and difficult it is to reproduce a perfume, the more people want it. And they'd be willing to part with some serious cash,' Monique said.

'You reckon? I don't know,' Elena mumbled, deep in thought.

'Well, I'm sure of it. And the diary is incredibly valuable, too — both historically and from a business point of view. It could solve all your problems.'

It was true. Those formulas were invaluable, they were her heritage. All of a sudden, Elena's mouth felt dry.

'When we were together, Matteo wanted me to sell the house in Florence. But I never agreed to it.' She stopped and sat down. 'I've got no intention of selling, Monie,' she said, looking her friend in the eye. 'I don't know why my life has suddenly turned upside down, or why what I wanted to do for years — get away from perfume, from the Rossinis and their obsessions — is now completely out of the question. I just know that's how it is.'

Monique paused to consider Elena's words, then she nodded.

'I think it's normal to treasure your roots, your past. Look at my mother. She hated this place with a passion, and now she can't bear to be separated from it. It can seem as if you don't care about what you've got – you can even come to loathe it. But then something changes. In the end, life's all about perspective.'

In a woman as determined as Monique, the ability to stop and listen might seem like a contradiction. But Elena had always liked that aspect of her friend's personality. Monie knew when to step back and give her friend the space she needed to express herself.

'It's even more complicated than that, I'm afraid,' Elena whispered. Then she stood up. 'I haven't even offered you anything. Shall I make you some tea?'

Monique shook her head. 'Sit down and finish talking.'

Elena reluctantly did as she was told, but maybe talking would help her restore some kind of order to the chaos her mind had become.

'I never wanted to be a perfumier, you know that,' she burst out after a little while, her bottom lip trembling. 'Looking for the Rossinis' wretched Perfect Perfume, perfume in general, it's brought me nothing but pain. But now it seems as if that revulsion, that anger I had inside me, has just completely disappeared. Can you tell? It makes no sense – it makes me feel like someone who doesn't know what they want!'

Elena's indignation was so heartfelt – and so completely unreasonable – that it brought a smile to Monique's lips.

'Come on – we've talked about this so many times in the past. It's not the perfumes you have a problem with, it's the perfumiers themselves: women who had empty lives and decided to fill the void with something they thought would make them rich and famous. *They* were wrong, not the perfume. You inherited their special gift, but not necessarily their curse.'

Elena shook her head. 'It's not that simple. Do you know, the first thing I notice about someone when I meet them is their smell? And do you think it's normal to cry over the harmony of a bouquet, or to get all worked up because you can't identify every component of a *mélange*? To give each ingredient a colour whatever it takes, to hear them talk to you through their essence? Monique, I think I am one of those crazy women.'

'Of course you are, Elena. We're all a bit mad, don't you think? But remember, there aren't many people who are as sensitive as you, who have your sense of smell. Even fewer who've had the privilege of being raised in the art of perfumery the way it used to be done: with your mind, with your heart and soul. So why don't you try and just go with it? Listen to your feelings, without caring what other people think. Who are these people, anyway?'

Indeed, who were these other people? Her grandmother, who'd loved her for the role she would one day fill. Her mother, who'd abandoned her to live with a man who couldn't stand her daughter. Matteo and his lies. She rubbed her eyes, as though she were trying to wipe away traces of tiredness, and after a moment's silence, met her friend's gaze.

'I had a dream about the shop,' she confided suddenly. 'It was right here, downstairs. And it was beautiful – small and decorated in shades of cream and pale pink, with a wood and glass counter, a table for talking to people, a little sofa and some lamps.'

Monique smiled. Never in a million years could she think this place was beautiful. Jasmine hadn't told her much about her own childhood growing up here, but she got the feeling that her mother had been very unhappy, and that was enough for her.

'So let's take the first step towards making your dream come true, *chérie*,' she said, standing up and taking Elena by the hand.

It might not have been the Ritz, but no restaurant matched the heights of the one Jacques had booked. In every sense: the Jules Verne sat right at the top of the Eiffel Tower.

Arriving at the foot of the tower, Elena looked around, keen to take in every detail. She wanted to see everything, to smell everything. She inhaled gently, in small breaths, searching through the perfumes for details that had once been a source of pain and discomfort for her. It was a strange sensation, because she knew Paris, she'd been here as a little girl with her mother – only now it seemed different.

'Good grief, Elena, I promise I'll bring you to look at the view another time, but right now we need to get a move on.'

'But how can you ignore all this?' she protested.

Monique didn't answer, she just took her hand and dragged her along behind. She wouldn't let go, for fear that Elena might even decide to take the stairs. All those steps! Out of the question. She had no intention of meeting Jacques all hot and sweaty.

It had taken Monique hours to calm herself down. She had dressed with care because she had every intention of stunning Jacques tonight. She wasn't going to give him the slightest advantage. Maybe she did have a broken heart, but that was her problem and no one else's – and he certainly didn't need to know.

When she saw Jacques, she pointed him out to Elena.

'There he is, sitting at the table in the corner.' Elena spotted a smartly dressed man staring out at the view.

'He's very attractive.'

'Some people say the same about snakes.'

'Listen,' Elena said, trying not to grin, 'it doesn't look as if he booked for three. Maybe it's best if I go.'

'Don't you dare move,' Monique threatened. 'This all started in Florence with that perfume you chose for him. So, he got what he wanted, and now you're going to get the job you deserve. It's business, Elena; nothing more, nothing less.'

Elena wasn't sure that was the best line of argument, but she was curious to see how the situation played out – though she had an inkling that before the evening was over, Jacques would be regretting a few things. She noticed Monique had her fists clenched and was trembling with rage.

'Are you still in love with him?' The question came out of Elena's mouth before she had a chance to think about it. She wasn't being nosy, she just wanted to understand. She herself no longer felt anything for Matteo, and she was quite amazed by that.

Monique didn't take her eyes off Jacques. 'Yes, but I don't want to be. It's like a curse. I wish I wasn't in love with him, I wish he'd disappear out of my life. And then, when I don't see him, I wish he was there to hold me. And you thought you were the only crazy woman in the world? Welcome to the club, chérie. Let me do the talking, OK?'

No, it wasn't OK. 'Absolutely not. If I'm staying, I need to speak for myself.' She didn't say anything else; the determined look in her eyes convinced Monique to give her the space she needed. Elena was under pressure. She was pale, and the bags under her eyes told of sleepless nights. She was trying to find herself, and she was being forced to do it in stages.

Monique sighed and nodded. 'All right, but I'll be right here with you, OK?'

'Fine, but it's me he's dealing with.' That was important to Elena; it was imperative that she should be the one to talk to Jacques Montier. She'd been watching from the sidelines for too long, letting other people make her decisions. Maybe it was realizing how foolish that sort of attitude had been, or maybe it was the loneliness she'd been feeling for the past few weeks that had given her the strength to react; in any case, she'd decided to change, and that meant negotiating her own future by herself.

At that moment, Jacques spotted them, stood up and came over.

'Good evening, Monique. I imagine your friend must be Elena Rossini.'

'Yes. I "came prepared", like you said,' Monique said tautly. 'You did mean you were going to offer her a job when you left me that message, didn't you?'

Elena stifled her laughter with a cough. Monique was as direct as a bullet from a gun. To say she was furious with this man would be an understatement.

In a fraction of a second longer than it should have taken, Jacques's severe expression stretched into a smile.

'Naturally. Pleased to meet you, *mademoiselle*. The perfume Monique brought back from Florence is very interesting. My compliments on your selection. We've decided to market it here.' He took her hand and held it in his for a moment.

'Great,' Elena replied, slightly taken aback. She hadn't expected such gallantry. This Jacques really knew what he was doing when it came to women.

As he escorted them back to the table where a waiter had

hurriedly set a third place, Elena started to understand why Monique was so caught up in their relationship. Jacques Montier radiated an impressive energy and self-confidence. A woman could feel protected by someone like that. Or oppressed.

She instinctively pulled back, trying not to touch him, even when he very politely pulled out the chair to help her take her seat. Then she noticed it: the smell of his anger. It was bitter and well-hidden under the delicate aroma of oakwood, the base of the scent he was wearing. And there was something else – suspicion, maybe a hint of curiosity. It smelled like resin, sharp and balsamic. Elena wondered whether Monique could smell it, too, that strong, almost irritating odour. She followed his gaze and saw that it was fixed on her friend. The two of them still had a lot to talk about, she thought.

'The perfume you chose is exactly what I was looking for, Mademoiselle Rossini,' Jacques continued, after he'd signalled for the menus to be brought over. 'Do you have specific training, or was it just happy intuition?' He had his eyes fixed on her now, and was studying her coldly.

Elena forced herself to match his penetrating gaze. She had no intention of letting herself be intimidated. Her heart was pounding and the tension between Jacques and Monique seemed to crackle in the air.

She cleared her throat and began to explain. 'Intuition, no. That's not it.'

But before she could explain any further, Jacques started talking again. 'The mixture is well-calibrated: a pleasant balance with no distracting flashes, yet the composition has some sparkling notes.' This time his tone was hard, his words chosen with care. 'You need quite a specific understanding to choose a *mélange* like that. Let's cut to the chase, *mademoiselle*. What skills do you have?'

The question hung between them for a moment. That wasn't what Jacques really wanted to know. In her head, Elena translated what he was actually asking: 'Why on earth should I hire you in my company?' He hadn't said it openly, he wouldn't do that. But his tone of voice and the haughty look on his face spoke volumes. His style, she saw, was to alternate between politeness and a series of quite unkind remarks. And Elena suspected she wasn't the adversary Jacques really wanted to beat.

Behind him, the Paris night seemed to explode with colours, and Elena watched them while she decided what to say. She was sorely tempted to stand up, tell him where to go, and leave. But she couldn't do that. Giving up simply wasn't an option. Monie had been as good as her word and was sitting there in silence, intently studying the china on the embroidered tablecloth.

She didn't need her help, Elena thought. She didn't need anyone's help. She turned her attention back to Jacques and nailed him with a glare.

'I know every extraction technique, from the oldest to the most modern. I can make perfumes, creams and soaps, for people or for environments. And I didn't just learn all this from books, but working with it. Separating, purifying, re-combining, fixing. Those skills aren't common in modern perfumery, but I can carry out every single step because it's what I've been doing since I was old enough to hold an alembic. That also means I have a perfect understanding of distillation and *enfleurage* techniques.'

A glint in Jacques's eye betrayed his interest. So this woman was saying she'd mastered the ancient art. Nothing special about that, really. They were things anyone with an under-standing of perfumery could have listed. But if what she was saying was true, her skills could turn out to be useful.

'Right. What can you tell me about *Peau d'Espagne*?'

Elena licked her lips and replied, 'A complex perfume, dating back to the sixteenth century. Neroli, rose, sandalwood, lavender, verbena, bergamot, cloves and cinnamon. Sometimes they used to add civet or musk. A fascinating mixture of smells, no basic brief, no specific personality, so many expensive fragrances all combined together.'

Maybe it was the pride he sensed in these words that made up Jacques's mind, or maybe it was Monique's stiletto heel pressing into his ankle that elicited the burst of laughter which suddenly broke the tension between them.

'Bravo! Just the answer I was looking for.' He was lying, and he was doing it for Monique. He'd made her sit next to him. The long tablecloth gave him a certain freedom to move. She sat motionless beside him while he touched her leg and ran his hand along the hem of her dress. And a bit further. Then Monique picked up a full glass, a warning look in her eye. So he stopped – there would be another opportunity to get her back.

All he had to do was hire her friend. And who knows, perhaps that would actually be a good move. This Rossini woman seemed as if she had an in-depth knowledge of perfumery. Besides, he'd put her in sales to begin with. She was nice enough, nothing special, but she'd look pretty good in the right dress. Yes, he decided. He'd hire her, but not as a perfumier. He wasn't stupid enough to put that much trust in a stranger, whatever credentials she might have. The decision cheered him up. He was starting to enjoy this game he was playing with Monique. He was going to win, he was sure. No matter what she might think, in the end he was the one calling the shots.

They finished their dinner in a more relaxed atmosphere. Jacques really turned on the charm. Yet the conversation never broached anything serious, just touched on a little of this and a little of that, like a light breeze, sometimes warm, but unreliable.

Later, several hours after her taxi-ride home, Elena was still tossing and turning in bed. She didn't like the way they had left things. Of course, now she had a job at Narcissus ... but she was also convinced that she hadn't got it on her own merit. And that made her angry, because even though a job at Narcissus was exactly what she wanted, this wasn't the way she'd imagined getting it.

She plumped up the pillow, tried lying on her stomach, but the worry wouldn't leave her alone. Monique had stuck to their deal to let Elena handle the situation herself, but that didn't change anything. That job was still a gift. If Montier hadn't had his eye on Monique, and if she hadn't been Monique's friend, she doubted he would have given her a chance. What's more, at the end of dinner he'd made it very clear which job he had in mind for her. He wasn't interested in her experience as a perfumier. At least, not for the moment. First he was going to give her a trial as a simple sales assistant. It brought a lump to Elena's throat to have to accept such humiliation. For a moment she'd even thought about saying no. But then she caught Monique's eye: she knew how much trouble she'd taken to arrange this meeting. So she swallowed her pride and accepted. She didn't want to disappoint Monique. Besides, the important thing was to become part of Narcissus, wasn't it? There would be time to make this man rue his air of superiority. She just needed to be patient for a little bit longer.

She fidgeted, then she sat up. For God's sake, she'd spent her entire life being patient. Patience was her middle name. And she was absolutely sick of it.

The uncomfortable feeling in the middle of her chest turned to rage. How dare he? Who did this guy think he was? Her family had been producing perfume for centuries, and she was willing to bet she knew more than all the Narcissus employees put together, including Jacques himself.

Her grandmother would just have given him a look; she wouldn't have needed to say a word. She could almost see Lucia putting the arrogant bastard in his place. That made her feel better; but she still couldn't sleep. For a minute she thought about putting on the essence lamp; a few drops of lavender in the water might help her relax and drop off. But she knew she was too wound up.

She got out of bed and put on some clothes, deciding to go for a walk. The night was mild – warm enough for her to go out without a jacket. Once she was in the courtyard, however, she stopped, suddenly frozen by fear. Not because of the dark – she wasn't afraid of that – but of what she might find in the night-time city on the other side of the gate. All she wanted to do was relax, sit down somewhere and look at the stars. She knew it wasn't sensible to go out alone at this time of night, so perhaps she could go up to the roof and find somewhere secluded enough to get some peace and quiet.

She turned back. Once she was inside the entrance to the building, she headed for the stairs. At first, she couldn't work out how many floors there were above her apartment. She'd climbed just three flights when, pushing a door, she found herself out in the open. In front of her, under a starlit sky, there stood some sort of pergola. An intense perfume hung in the air.

Roses. Someone was growing roses up here.

How was that possible? For a moment, she thought she must be mistaken. Come on, they were in the Marais in October, more than thirty feet above ground. Who could possibly have a garden on the rooftop? But despite what logic told her, her nose wasn't wrong. They were roses all right: tea roses, Damascus roses, Gallic roses, and mint, basil ... other aromatic herbs. A whole garden. She could smell those perfumes, clear and distinct, as they were carried away and brought back together, drifting on the night-time breeze. Curious, she tiptoed forward, partly because of the dark and partly because she felt as if she was intruding. That harmony of fragrances was calling to her. Wet, rich earth. Fruit. To taste and to touch. So many flowers, but predominantly roses. Whoever looked after this garden had created an extraordinary *mélange*, something with top, middle and base notes. A full, strong, intoxicating perfume. A man, she would have said. A practical, decisive man, someone who did things carefully and above all with precision. And then she remembered him.

'Who's there?'

His voice stopped her in her tracks. She turned to leave – her heart pounding. Then something grabbed hold of her sleeve, pulling her back. A dog! Fear coursed through her. When she felt the animal's teeth on her hand, she let out a scream.

9

Frangipani: unparalleled charm. Extracted from the plumeria
  flower and intensely floral.
The fragrance of blossoming femininity opening itself up to
  life.
Bold and voluptuous.

'What's going on? John, stay!' Cail ordered.

What on earth was a woman doing on his terrace at this time of night?

'Don't panic, John won't do anything to you.'

'How can you be so sure?' With her back against the wall and her hands stretched out defensively in front of her, Elena was trembling with fear. 'I'm scared of dogs,' she managed to say.

'That much is apparent. But like I said, John won't attack you. If you hadn't come sneaking into my house like that, he would never have gone for you.'

The harshness of these words didn't make Elena back down. 'I didn't know that anyone lived here. I . . . I just wanted a bit of peace,' she said. 'And anyway, you should have put something outside, a bell, a nameplate, something like that.'

A fraying cloud suddenly dissolved and let the moonlight through. Now she could see the man, not clearly, but enough to make out his strong features, his penetrating stare. He looked silver; in a world full of greys the white jumper he was wearing really stood out. Long hair fell down over his shoulders and there was something across his face, a scar.

Then she recognized him.

'It's you! You helped me yesterday.'

The perfume woman. Cail recognized her, too.

'Nobody comes up here. There's never been any need for a lock.'

'There's a first time for everything, you know. And anyway, the fact that you never have visitors isn't a good enough reason.'

'No, true. Some people are just nosier than others.' Cail leaned his head to one side, still looking at her. Elena scowled. She wasn't being nosy; she'd gone up there for a specific reason.

'Why are you scared of dogs?'

She thought about telling him – at least then he would understand there were real reasons to explain her terror. Then she changed her mind. She didn't actually know him at all; she didn't have to justify anything to him. 'I was bitten, obviously,' she retorted.

The man shrugged. 'You say that as if it was my fault.'

Elena peeled herself from the wall. He was a few steps away. He was so tall, yet he didn't frighten her. The shiver running through her now was due to something else – to the memory of that time when she was a girl and Maurice's German Shepherd Milly had bitten her. And the night air had turned cold.

As Elena moved, Cail stepped back away from her, his arms crossed over his chest in a defensive, almost hostile pose. Perplexed, Elena wondered if she had offended him in some way.

'No, of course it's not your fault,' she said. 'But you don't live on top of a mountain here, do you? There are other residents, and someone else would have come up here, sooner or later.'

'No. You're the only one.'

Elena was speechless. 'What?'

Cail pointed at the door. 'You and I are the only ones who live on this staircase.'

'Ah,' she replied. Things were starting to make sense. 'I see. Even so, you should still get a new lock.'

He carried on looking at her calmly, the same way he'd spoken to her, enunciating his words, no rush. Elena took a breath. The man's perfume was different that night, a bit warmer, a bit more complex. She realized she'd woken him up. He must think she was crazy.

'Why *did* you come up here?' The question took her by surprise. What was she supposed to tell him? The truth.

'I just wanted to look at the sky.'

She didn't know why she'd come out with it. Why should this man care about her inner turmoil, her need to lose herself in contemplating the night? She stood there, unsure what to do with herself until Cail spoke again.

'Give me your hand,' he said.

'Why?'

Cail pointed at her arm. 'I want to check John didn't hurt you.'

No, not even a scratch. Elena felt a little ashamed. The dog had just given her a warning, not used his teeth with any force. Maybe he'd just licked her hand – but even if she'd overreacted, it made no difference. Dogs scared her to death.

Elena fidgeted nervously. 'You're not going to punish your dog, are you? I can assure you he didn't hurt me at all and, besides, it's not his fault.'

'That's very strange, coming from someone who hates dogs.'

'I don't hate dogs,' she insisted. 'I'm just careful to stay well away from their teeth, that's all. Anyway, look, I'm totally fine. But, is there no light on this terrace?'

Cail tensed. 'To see the stars, you need darkness.'

'I don't understand . . . the stars?' For a moment she thought she'd misheard him.

'Yes. You said you wanted to look at the sky, and I've got a telescope.'

Unbelievable. This man smelled like roses – and he looked at the stars.

'Come on, over here. It's nothing special, but it's enough to get a clear view of Alpha Centauri, Sirius and Altair. To be honest, you could see them with the naked eye, but you get a different effect through the telescope.'

Elena didn't know much about stars; it was enough for her to look out into the night and stare at the blackness punctuated by so many sparkling lights. It made her feel peaceful . . . and then it was easy to let go and contemplate infinity. But she'd always admired people who could identify the constellations. She was happy she could even name Ursa Major and Minor.

'Look inside, like this.'

He showed her what to do. When he stepped aside to make room for her, she bowed her head and put her eye to the lens. It was like slipping into a world of black velvet, where enormous objects glowed with a unique, profound light she'd never seen before, making her feel small and humble. Awe stirred up inside her, as the bright wake of the Milky Way shone so close; in reality the distance was infinite.

She looked up. The stranger was right there, beside her. If she'd stretched out her arm, she could have touched him. He was looking at her, too, lost in the same silence. Yet there was no awkwardness between them; rarely had she felt so in tune with somebody. It was like knowing, sharing. She bent down to the telescope again, and in that half-light discovered how deceptive the huge, mysterious stars could be.

'I don't even know your name,' she said after a while, lifting her head.

'Does it matter? I don't know your name either.'

It was true – and it was strange, to say the least. Suddenly she started to laugh, a delicate, feminine sound, then she held out her hand to him. 'Elena Rossini.'

'Caillen McLean. Cail, if you like,' he replied, shaking her hand. 'You're Italian.' It wasn't a question. Caillen McLean had a very direct, almost brusque way about him.

'Yes. I just moved here. And you?'

'Me, what?'

'Have you lived in Paris for long?'

He shook his head. 'Five years in December.' A shadow had appeared in his voice: it was little more than an inflection, but it was there. Elena stared at him, but the night was too dark to work out what that look was hiding. Then she realized he was probably just tired. Not everyone suffered from insomnia like her.

'I'm sorry,' she said. 'Sometimes I lose track of time. I should get going.'

Cail didn't object. He just looked at her, expressionless. 'I'll walk you back.'

She felt a twinge of disappointment. For some reason she'd expected him to ask her to stay a while. That was ridiculous, she told herself. Then she instinctively stretched her hands out in front of her, worried that she'd bump into something in all that darkness. Once again, they'd met in the dark. 'Thank you, you're very kind.'

Before she went on to the landing, Elena stopped. 'John, I mean, your dog . . . I didn't see him again. Do you think he was frightened?'

Cail laughed quietly. 'No, he's just a bit offended. Don't worry. Maybe next time you can make friends.'

Make friends with a dog? Never in a million years. But Elena didn't tell him that. She liked that 'next time'. Then, all of a sudden her natural reserve got the better of her and she said stiffly, 'I . . . I don't think so. Thank you, and I'm sorry for keeping you up. I can't get to sleep at night and I tend to forget it's not the same for everyone.'

'No problem, Elena,' Cail said quietly.

'Remember that lock,' she said in the doorway.

'OK.'

'Good night, then. And thanks again . . . Cail.'

He remained where he was, looking in her direction even after she'd closed the door behind her. Then he went back into the apartment, yawning. 'Come on, John, let's get some sleep.'

A few days after their dinner at Jules Verne, Jacques asked Monique to bring Elena to Narcissus.

'How about we walk there?' Monique suggested to her friend.

'Is it very far?' Lately, Elena tired easily, and she was none too enthusiastic about the prospect of a long walk.

121

'Half an hour, but Place Vendôme – where the perfumery is – is almost straight down rue de Rivoli. We won't have time to get bored.'

'OK. Fine by me.'

A couple of hours later Monique was waiting for her at the entrance to the apartment. Both women were feeling a bit stressed, but they soon relaxed. Rue de Rivoli was quite a sight, bustling, lined with all kinds of shops, and as she walked along with Monie, chatting and giggling, Elena felt calmer. The worry of having such an important appointment disappeared. And then, there it was: the perfumery she'd heard so much about. Beneath the majestic colonnade of thick stone arches surrounding the famous square, a massive wooden door was wedged between two large windows; above it, a simple, old-fashioned nameplate: *Narcissus*.

Gold. If she'd had to define Narcissus by a colour, Elena would have chosen gold. She walked around the inside of the shop, looking up at the high walls covered with mirrors in elaborate frames, wood panelling, pink marble worktops and glass shelves. There were bottles of all shapes and sizes waiting to be filled, and others already brimming with the most classic and simple scents. Even the floors were made of pink marble, reflecting the light. Everything seemed to sparkle; there was luxury in abundance. Hopes, dreams, delusions and seduction – this place had everything.

Yet the perfume Elena could smell in the air wasn't right; it was too rich . . . almost suffocating. It seemed as if the shop had no consideration for the needs of people who came in looking for something for themselves. The space was completely occupied by intense fragrances. There was no suggestion, only imposition. Wonderful, luxurious . . . but always decided for you.

Elena felt a kind of oppression weighing down on her. It was like Jacques. That shop *was* Jacques: it reflected the way he lived, the way he managed everything.

She understood why Monique had decided to sever that link. She was quite sure her friend was still in love with Jacques, but letting him control her life . . . no, not Monique. The man was vain and selfish, and only wanted to possess her. Jacques was dominant in every sense of the word.

Elena took a deep breath and the moment that all-pervading perfume 'invaded' her she regretted it. It wasn't that it was nauseating – no, that wasn't the problem. It was more like seeing a jumble of mismatched colours: it was over-whelming. Had it been up to her, she would have done everything she could to make the room as neutral as possible. She would let just a few light base notes filter through; some-thing simple and discreet that would go with any composition, from the most intense to the most delicate, and never over-whelm. She would have *suggested* essences, never *imposed* them on her customers.

She turned to Monique to say so, when she saw that her friend was now accompanied by an extremely well-dressed man with a gaunt face and shifty eyes. He had a thin, black moustache above a smile he'd mustered for the occasion; his hair was the same colour. He was wearing a sickly-sweet perfume, almost saccharine, that concealed something more pungent: ammonia. Elena frowned at the confusion. There were other aspects of Philippe that didn't add up. He didn't seem at all happy to meet her, for example. Something bothered her about the look he gave her, his circumspect expression. He was judging her.

It was obvious he felt hostile towards her, and Elena wanted to know why. Before that moment, she'd never set eyes on him. All of a sudden, the man reached out his hand and waited for her to extend hers. His outstretched hand was soft, the palm wet. She struggled to return the greeting. She couldn't wait to wipe her hand on her skirt.

'*Bonjour.*'

Up close, he seemed a bit more cordial. Even his look was less sharp. Then he smiled at her, but Elena couldn't shake off the twinge of anxiety. It was a good job she'd decided to put a bit of effort into her appearance, she thought. Taking Monique's advice, she'd worn a simple black dress with black high heels, and had tied her hair back and put on a touch of make-up. The transformation had been immediate and satisfying. That was part of the new life, too, wasn't it?

Like her new neighbour, Cail McLean. She had felt good around him, comfortable, despite the awkwardness of the situation. She hadn't told Monique anything yet. She should, she thought. Cail was . . . remarkable. Brusque, yes, but with a fundamental kindness that was part of him, part of the man he was. But this was no time to think about all that. She had a bad habit of losing herself in daydreams.

'Elena, let me introduce Philippe, the backbone of Narcissus.'

Philippe, meanwhile, had put his head on one side and half-closed his eyes as if he was delightedly savouring Monique's words. 'When women start giving one compliments like that, it's time to be worried,' he said, turning to Elena. '*Mademoiselle* is giving me too much credit. I'm not the backbone, just the manager.'

Elena noticed that sickly-sweet smell again, but now it had turned dusty, with the stench of false modesty.

'Jacques Montier is the real backbone of Narcissus, like his father before him, and his grandfather before that. You know this is one of the few companies in this business that can boast centuries of tradition? And the shop has always been here, in Place Vendôme.' His tone had suddenly turned serious and was full of respect and consideration.

Philippe went on to explain the history of Narcissus, listing the important clients the perfumery had served. The two women stayed quiet, each carefully avoiding the other's eye.

'Monsieur Montier permitted me to smell the perfume you chose. My congratulations, *mademoiselle*. Working together will be . . . interesting. You have a certain aptitude – one might even say a sensitivity – for perfume, which is rare these days.'

He made a feature of long pauses throughout his entire speech, which seemed interminable to Elena and put her on edge. Then he gave her that shifty look again.

'I assume you're aware, young lady, that we don't just *sell* perfumes. Here at Narcissus we *create* them,' he said suddenly, as though the notion had popped into his mind right that second. 'Naturally, that's handled by the composers, the noses. You will need to listen to the customer, collate their requirements and explain them to the perfumier. It might seem difficult at first, but you'll get used to it.'

The two friends exchanged a surprised look. Jacques clearly hadn't told Philippe about Elena's skills. A surge of heat bubbled up inside Elena, reaching her face. The owner of Narcissus had been clear about the job she would be doing here – he'd said that, at least to begin with, she would only be selling perfumes. But why had he kept her real talents hidden from Philippe? Somewhere deep in her soul, that kernel of pride for what she was, for her heritage, stirred angrily. She felt deeply humiliated, as though someone had suddenly taunted her. Philippe's words were like a shower of stones on what she now realized had become her dreams.

'I'll do my best,' she replied, looking away.

Philippe didn't appear to notice Elena's reaction: he was too busy talking. 'It takes years of experience, dedication and in-depth study to create a perfume,' he waffled on. Another pause, this time accompanied by a snort of derision. 'Many people think they can invent perfumes because they have an instinct — but it's not as simple as that. Nowadays, perfumiers are popping up all over the place. It's irritating and, frankly, it's embarrassing.' His voice was monotone, flat.

'I can imagine,' Elena murmured.

The man went on for a bit, explaining things that Elena knew perfectly well, and exponentially increasing the irritation she was trying to keep at bay. Politeness was proving a real struggle. Philippe might well be a perfumier, but he'd never be able to identify an emotion even if it smacked him in the face, she decided, holding his gaze.

'Here we have oils, waters, essences. I won't go into detail, since these are technical processes that you wouldn't understand right now, but don't worry: with the right dose of patience and application, you'll learn.'

She wouldn't understand them? She swallowed it down, but her indignation was strong and pressing on her lips.

Again, Philippe hadn't noticed anything untoward and gave her a good-natured smile, looking thoroughly pleased with himself. Elena felt her irritation die down. It was still the right job, wasn't it? She just needed to be patient for a little while longer. Philippe would soon be eating his words.

'There are few rules for employees here at Narcissus, but the ones we have must be followed to the letter.'

The man's voice had suddenly hardened. Even his expression had changed. Now he looked like an owl, with his round eyes and hooked nose. He wasn't being so kind any more.

'I'm sure you'll have no problem sticking to them. I can tell you're an intelligent woman.'

Oh really? How? What a condescending little man. Elena forced herself to calm down; it wouldn't help anyone if she started shouting. Even though she was dying to. She unclenched her fist and stretched out her fingers, then she took a deep breath. It wasn't Philippe's fault, she told herself. It certainly wasn't *his* fault she'd left her old life and was trying to start a new one from scratch. She couldn't skip the stages, she knew that. So she searched inside herself for the drop of patience she had left and forced herself to listen to the house rules.

Monique had wandered off. Elena watched her walking around the shop, lost in thought, staring at things. When she saw her take her tablet out of her bag, she could guess her friend was already trying to find her another job.

'Is it all right with you if I start straight away?' she asked outright.

Philippe blinked. 'I don't know. That's not the usual procedure.'

But Elena wasn't giving up. She didn't want Monique to have to keep worrying about her. The little bit of independence that had started to grow inside her wanted both space and autonomy. In fact, it demanded them.

'I won't bother you, I'll stay out of the way and just watch. That way it'll be easier to understand how to handle sales and what kind of relationship to build up with the customers, don't you think?'

The man shrugged. 'Yes, actually that might be a good idea. But I would point out that your contract doesn't start until next week, and only then will you receive your agreed salary which, I must say,' he paused, looking her in the eye, 'is very

127

generous. No one in the whole of Paris would have offered those terms to a sales assistant.'

Elena gulped, but she held his gaze. 'Right, a sales assistant.' She stretched her lips into a forced smile. *You can do this*, she told herself. Empathy certainly wasn't one of Philippe's strong points, but she could ignore that. She made sure she kept a polite expression on her face.

'Perfect,' he said. 'Now I'll go and say hello to Monique, if you'll excuse me.'

Elena knew that if she didn't start looking at things from the right angle, her adventure would be over before it had begun. She'd have to go back to Florence. And there was nothing for her there. She didn't have enough money to re-open the family business, and she didn't want to see Matteo again, or their mutual friends who had carefully avoided calling to see how she was.

She wanted to stay in Paris. She wanted to walk through the Marais, go back up the Eiffel Tower, she wanted to look at the stars with Cail again, smell the roses he was growing on the terrace. That was what she wanted, and that was all that mattered; she'd enjoyed the taste of the few decisions she'd made by herself and she wasn't about to give that up.

Now she just had to face Monique. Her friend might have been the one who'd convinced her that Narcissus was the right place for her, but Elena was willing to bet that, after the way Philippe had behaved and thanks to Jacques's arrogance, Monique had changed her mind.

'*Chérie*, you mustn't worry. I'll call a friend. You don't have to put up with all this.' Just as Elena had thought, Monique had already come up with a Plan B. 'I'll soon find you another job.'

That promise, so full of diligence and concern, was the last straw for Elena. The anger she'd bottled up came to the surface, like an unbearable fever. She wasn't a child, she could look after herself. Why couldn't Monie get that into her head once and for all? She was about to tell her as much in no uncertain terms, but suddenly she realized how upset her friend was. She was pale and had tears in her eyes. Elena's anger dissolved. Sooner or later, she'd deal with Jacques, she promised herself. No way did he deserve a generous woman like Monique. Elena wondered whether he was the reason her friend had so little belief in herself and her own abilities.

'No, why? This will be fine,' she replied, acting calm and serene and ignoring the genuinely astounded expression that came over the other woman's face.

'You're joking, right? Jacques won't let you in the laboratories, didn't you hear Philippe? As long as you're working here, you'll only be able to sell perfumes over the counter like a common or garden sales assistant.'

Elena shrugged. 'Have you got something against sales assistants?' she asked with a beaming smile, determined to play things down. Intent on having the last word, she walked Monique to the door. 'Don't you have an appointment with Le Notre?'

Monique nodded, still looking uncertain. 'If you need—'

'No. Please go – everything will be all right.' And this time Elena's voice was uncompromising. She left her friend in the doorway and went straight back into the perfumery, determined to do whatever it took to meet the requirements set by Jacques, Philippe, and anyone else if she had to. Her anger was now a knot squeezing her throat. She forced herself to breathe slowly and, when she was calm enough, she went back to join Philippe. It was time to focus on the internal organization of the shop, to carefully observe the way perfumes were arranged, and the approach to customers.

At the end of the day, as she was walking home, clutching her jacket around her, she had quite a clear idea of what was seen to be important, and what wasn't. Yet Elena was bewildered. Working alongside her grandmother in the shop for years was her basis for comparison: and none of what she knew fitted in with the way Narcissus operated. They cajoled their customers, undermined their certainty, drew them in with what was effectively an olfactory trap.

But who was she to say they weren't on the right track? That shop was successful, whereas she had closed down her grandmother's business because she didn't even have enough customers to cover her costs. When Lucia got ill, Elena's world had collapsed around her. Her grandmother had known how serious her illness was from the beginning, and had insisted on staying at home. She wouldn't hear of hospitals, except for absolutely essential treatment. Elena had no choice but to go along with it.

After a few months, Lucia was consumed by her illness. She kept talking about the past, about Beatrice and the Perfect Perfume. She recounted the history of her family so many times: everything her ancestors, the Rossinis, had achieved. She told her granddaughter again and again how important it was to follow the 'ways of perfume'. Elena knew these stories by heart but she listened to Lucia attentively, and was always by her side, which left her with scant time for running the business. Closing the perfumery after Lucia's death was the only thing she could do. She no longer had the strength or the will to carry on with it.

Out of nowhere, the notes of 'La Vie En Rose' suddenly broke her chain of thought. She realized she'd already reached the Marais and there, right on the crossroads with rue des Rosiers, was the old man selling antique prints of the city on his stall. Every evening, Edith Piaf sang the well-known words of the beautiful, classic love-song. The old man insisted on playing the song on a loop, come rain or shine. A gesture tinged with regret, disappointment, longing and lost love, or at least that was Monique's take on it when they had walked past one evening.

Previously, Elena had always sung along under her breath without ever really thinking about it. She liked the singer's deep, almost scratchy voice, the flavour it gave of days gone by. This time, however, she looked straight at the old man and saw only the shrewd expression in his watery eyes, and his crafty smile. Yes, he might be playing the song because it reminded him of a love, a woman, a past life – but more likely it was a ruse to attract tourists, to encourage them to open their wallets and take home a little piece of Paris and a tear-jerking story. When faced with this picturesque stall while holding hands with the current love of their life, even the most cynical of individuals would allow themselves to be bewitched by the most famous song in the world, to be told that life would be infinitely better when seen through rose-tinted glasses. Even Elena had sometimes found herself standing in front of the stall, under some kind of spell.

But this time she stalked past, and as she turned off at the first crossroads, heading towards rue du Parc-Royal, she felt both sad and cynical. She didn't like that kind of exploitation of people's feelings. And then a thought of Matteo surfaced, bringing the usual tangle of emotions with it.

The memories didn't hurt as much as they had at first, but she still didn't want to think about him. Sadness, that was all it brought her. And a foolish desire: she'd like to see *la vie en rose*, too. She started to think about what she had, and not about what she had lost. She had a job, and a prestigious one at that. Somewhere to live – somewhere she really liked. And a chance. She had a chance.

All in all, things weren't so bad, were they? As she entered the courtyard of number twelve, she could still make out the enchanting voice of Edith Piaf, singing about nights of love that would never end, and a happiness so intense one could die.

10

Jasmine: sensuality. Flower of the night, it only gives off its perfume at sunrise and sunset.
The fragrance is heady and warm. It evokes a magical world, blurs boundaries, bestows well-being and happiness.
The real pleasure is hidden in its small white petals: picking it is just the beginning.

The motorbike raced through the night. The road was dark, and heavy rain had made the tarmac slippery. Then the deafening horn of the truck tore through the silence.

Bathed in sweat, Cail stirred in his sleep. His fingers gripped the sheets. He couldn't remember much about the accident, but the sensation knotting his stomach was all too familiar. Other sensations came to mind, and into his soul. He swam through them, trying to breathe, desperately trying to find something that would allow him to rest at least long enough to regain his strength.

'A perfume of earth and roses.' Those words made their

way through the nebulous layers of sleep, through the darkness and the torment. He clung on to them, keeping them with him, searching his memory for the face of the woman who'd spoken them.

He sat bolt upright, panting, his breath trapped between clenched teeth, his throat burning. When the furniture came into focus, he realized he was in his bedroom, in the Marais. Relief flooded over him. It was just a dream . . . just a dream. Slowly, his confusion subsided. He rubbed his face and got out of bed.

John came straight to his side. Cail ran his hand through the animal's fur, then rested it on his head.

'If I hadn't let her drive, it would never have happened,' he said aloud. But that was a lie and he knew it. If he had been driving instead of Juliette, his girlfriend, the accident would have happened anyway. The lorry would still have hit them. But Juliette might well have survived – that was the thought that tormented him. With his fingertip he traced the scar that disfigured the right side of his face.

He went out on to the terrace, without a shirt, and felt the cold morning air on his skin. When he reached the door that led to the stairs, he opened it and checked the lock. He would have to call in at the ironmongers to pick up one that worked. He'd promised his new neighbour he would, he thought, frowning. That way, he wouldn't find her on his property unannounced again. Not that he minded; he was quite honest with himself in admitting it – but that didn't mean that finding strangers in the house should become a habit. After all, he was fine as he was – on his own.

The nausea wouldn't lessen its grip. Elena gently inhaled the morning breeze, bit cautiously into the end of a croissant and waited another few minutes. Insomnia, nausea, fatigue: she felt like a wreck. Finally the feelings passed and she was able to get up from the table where she'd had breakfast. She waved her thanks to Antonio and his wife, crossed the road and checked the time. While she was walking to work, she decided to take a detour. It did her good to explore Paris. She would have liked to ask Cail to give her an itinerary. In reality, she could just as well have asked Monique, and her friend would surely have kept her company. Yet she liked the idea of wandering around with Cail. She carried on strolling, looking at the buildings – this part of Paris was so pretty. She left Saint-Honoré behind her and shortly found herself admiring the enormous column in the centre of Place Vendôme, before carrying on under the arches. When she went into the shop, she looked around for Philippe.

Could nobody apart from herself really tell how intense and overpowering that fragrance was? She wrinkled her nose, hoping she'd soon get used to such a strong smell. She'd have to learn to ignore it.

'There you are, at last,' Philippe said, looking up from a table where he'd arranged a series of silver bottles.

'You told me nine o'clock,' she replied, looking at the glass clock on the shelf.

The man glared at her. 'We get here an hour before the shop opens. Bear that in mind.'

He'd kept that part to himself.

'I didn't know,' she said.

'Make sure you find out, then. I expect the most from the staff here. If you want to stay with us, you'll need to get used to that, *mademoiselle*.'

Elena was about to respond, then thought better of it. She gritted her teeth to hold back her response. A woman came over to them and Philippe cleared his throat.

'This is Claudine,' he said, introducing a blonde, poker-faced woman of around thirty-five.

'*Bonjour, madame*,' Elena greeted her.

The woman just nodded. The half-smile she was feigning didn't move. It reminded Elena of the Mona Lisa. She wasn't expecting hugs and kisses, but she had hoped for some signs of life, rather than this strange, almost catatonic trance; there was absolutely nothing in that smile. There wasn't even anything in her perfume – Elena could barely smell it. And it wasn't because it was light, or delicate; it simply disappeared into the smell of Narcissus. She tried to concentrate. A whiff of benzoin reached her, intense and soft; then came incense, followed by a series of woods and musks. Then smoky notes, that gave an original balance to the fragrance, enhancing its character. It was clear, sparkling, but distant. Like a perfume that had been applied the previous day. Or before a shower.

Prada: the woman was wearing 'Benjoin' by Prada, and she'd covered it with something that mingled with Narcissus's ambient perfume; something she'd bet was from their own range. It was like one painting hidden beneath another. It struck Elena as a strange decision. Everyone had the right to wear what they wanted. Why go to such lengths to hide it? Perhaps Narcissus didn't appreciate its staff using perfume from other houses?

'You'll be working with Claudine today,' Philippe went on. 'You should follow her instructions – make sure you do,' he finished, and then, after exchanging a complicit nod with Claudine, he went over to the other side of the shop, lingering by a set of shelves.

At last the statue came to life and turned to Elena. The

136

woman had blue eyes mottled with green, and they were icy cold.

'You do speak French properly, don't you?'

'Yes,' Elena replied quietly.

'Good. I hate having to repeat things. Follow me and pay attention. And don't touch anything.'

Off to a good start, Elena thought, wondering whether, at certain levels of seniority, good manners and warmth were optional. 'Of course,' she said.

The Mona Lisa didn't turn out to be too bad in the end. Systematically, without pausing even for a second, she explained the display of all the perfumes, the premises, the tasks Elena would have to do, the official rules – and just as importantly, the unofficial rules – and then she took her into the laboratory.

'You only go in here when you're invited,' she told her, staying outside the door.

'Of course.'

Claudine looked at the inscrutable expression on Elena's face and raised a curious eyebrow. 'Have you ever worked in a laboratory?' she asked.

Elena nodded. 'Yes.'

The woman stared at her for a moment. 'Florentine school, right?'

'Amongst other things,' Elena replied.

'Do tell.'

This sudden interest made her uneasy. Now what? Elena sensed that it was probably best to keep a low profile with Claudine, but her sense of pride in herself and her family came to the fore at the most unlikely moments. She might as well tell it like it was. Of course, she'd be careful not to let this woman know that she'd created her first perfumes under the supervision of her grandmother at the age of just twelve. She was better off keeping that to herself.

'I started studying in Grasse: cultivation, extraction, all the stages up to the final perfume. I finished my studies and perfected my technique in Florence.'

If she was impressed by Elena's words, Claudine didn't let it show. She just nodded her head and gave a hint of a smile.

'You'll have a chance to show me what you can do. Some customers prefer personalized compositions; in general we just change a few ingredients in the formulas that have already been tested. You'll see it being done.'

Elena's heart skipped a beat. Composing perfumes at Narcissus was only a matter of time.

'Follow me. Today we'll be working with customers. Pay attention and don't interrupt, whatever I say. Understand?'

Claudine kept talking and, for a while, Elena pretended to listen; but her mind was too busy getting excited about the prospect that she would soon be able to concentrate on things she already knew inside out. Eventually the woman showed her to her place and went to get ready to welcome the first customers.

Many people came in that morning. All the perfumery's employees were busy. After she'd committed a fair number of Jacques's perfume creations to memory, Elena went over to the sales counters, but kept her distance. Claudine had started to serve a gentleman of a certain age who wanted a special perfume. He was clearly annoyed, his gnarled fingers gripping the handle of his luxurious walking stick.

'No, I don't like that one. It smells old – it smells like moth-balls, for God's sake!' he exclaimed indignantly.

Claudine was still wearing her indestructible smile. 'May I

suggest a more discreet *mélange*, if you'd prefer? How about adding some sandalwood?'

The man pursed his lips. 'How should I know, if you don't let me smell it?'

He was standing at the counter, eyes blazing and disappointment written across his face. A dozen used *mouillettes* lay on the table. Claudine's smile was starting to show the first signs of collapse.

'They assured me you'd find what I wanted. Well, that was clearly an exaggeration. Why should I waste my time with you?'

He'd raised his voice and some of the other customers were turning to look. Claudine tried again. 'Tell me exactly what you want.'

'Haven't you been listening to me? I need a new perfume! I don't want the same old fragrance.'

'Every single one of these perfumes,' Claudine replied, pointing to the various bottles lined up on the counter, 'matches your description. Do you want to try them again?'

The old man half-closed his eyes. 'Are you suggesting I don't know what I want?'

The woman's delicate nostrils flared, she was losing ground rapidly. 'One moment, please,' she said.

Elena had been watching this scene from the sidelines. The man's outfit was original, but smart. He was nervous, and every so often he'd slide a finger under his neckerchief, trying to alleviate the tension. He was looking around at the perfumes, and that look revealed his need for something new: a second youth, something that could disguise old age, give him faith. Men made that kind of choice, trying to rejuvenate themselves, hoping for some small miracle − like a new love. Elena didn't know where this idea had come from, but if that's what it was, if what this elderly gentleman wanted was a change, she knew exactly what he needed.

'Try this one, I'm sure you'll like it,' Claudine said, handing him another *mouillette*.

The man smelled it and shot her a suspicious look. 'Do I look like a boy to you? Do you really think I'm going to go around smelling like *that*?' he replied, indignant.

Claudine's voice turned frosty. 'If you'd be kind enough to wait another minute, I'll see what I can find for you.'

When Claudine walked past Elena, she still had that smile plastered on her face like some kind of stamp. That's professionalism, Elena thought. But it appeared that Claudine really had lost her patience, since instead of continuing to help him, she went to serve another customer who'd come in for some rosewater.

The gentleman visibly deflated; the anger had passed but the disappointment remained, deep and stinging, and clearly nothing to do with the perfume. It was vulnerability – it was an attempt to stop the relentless passage of time and seize another chance.

'May I ask which perfume you used in the past?' Elena asked him, walking over. Claudine had told her not to interrupt, but she hadn't said anything about talking to customers. Technically, she wasn't disobeying any orders.

She softened her tone and, seeing the man was lost in thought, repeated the question. His head shot up, as though he'd only just noticed she was there. She held out her hand, saying, 'My name is Elena Rossini.' Her grandmother had always introduced herself to her customers.

'Jean-Baptiste Lagose,' he replied. But instead of shaking her hand, he took it in his own and leaned forward to kiss it, like an old-time gentleman.

Leather, labdanum and bergamot, Elena noted when he got closer, almost brushing against her. The smell was strong yet sophisticated, with a deep, musky base scent. She could almost see him, Jean-Baptiste, watching the merry-go-round of life that had thrown him off. She could sense the shock and, hidden beneath layers of heartache, the burning desire to get back on it.

'Are you a saleswoman?' he asked.

Elena nodded. 'Today's my first day.'

The old man looked around and when he caught Claudine's eye, he turned back to Elena. 'Is that your boss over there?' He didn't even bother to hide the fact that he was pointing at her.

'In a sense.'

'You poor thing,' he said, shaking his head. He cast another glance towards Claudine. 'Some people have a real knack for being unpleasant.'

She'd thought the same herself. But that was not the sort of thing you would tell a customer, so Elena steered the conversation back on to more appropriate ground.

'You're wearing a chypre. It's very nice, but if I understood correctly, you're looking for something new?'

Suddenly, Jean-Baptiste lost all his belligerence. 'Yes, that's right. I wanted a perfume with character. Something clear, but original. But that . . . erm . . . *she* didn't understand. She wasn't listening to me.'

Elena was thinking of another chypre. Yes, it was a classic perfume with a base of oak moss, but she could put a spring in its step with lemon and vetiver to make it fuller and fresher. This man would wear it well. He seemed to have very particular and unconventional taste, judging from his outfit of blue jacket, pale blue striped trousers and red neckerchief. He was sporting a large gold ring on his right hand. There was nothing shy about him, just a real determination. He was a man with a plan. The perfume he wanted was part of a scheme to conquer a lady; it was so important to him that he was convinced he should handle the matter of a perfume personally.

'Why don't you smell these fragrances again? We can vary them to your taste,' Elena suggested, needing to buy some time. She had to speak to Claudine. She was sure that some-where in the shop there would be a new-generation chypre. After all, Montier was a professional; he wouldn't be without the latest version of the most universally loved classic perfumes.

Jean-Baptiste immediately went back to sulking. For a moment Elena was genuinely afraid he'd refuse. She looked at Claudine, and then back at him. Maybe because of the worry on the new sales assistant's face, or simply because he wanted to spite the witch who'd treated him with such arrogance, Jean-Baptiste stretched out his hand and started to sniff a *mouillette*.

'I'll be right back,' Elena told him with a relieved smile.

'Take your time, my dear,' he said.

When Elena found Claudine, she explained what she had in mind.

'Have you got something that would have neroli, pink grapefruit, or even lemon as top notes; jasmine, gardenia, magnolia or another floral *mélange* as the middle, amber, sandalwood and musk? Vetiver, for example, would be perfect.'

Claudine thought for a moment. 'Yes, it's a chypre. We've got one that might be what you need. I think there's some leather in it, too.'

Elena couldn't have wished for better. Leather was a potent, ancestral, masculine perfume.

'That would be perfect.'

Claudine didn't return Elena's smile, but got straight to work. They didn't use chypres very often; they were too strong, too rich – they were perfumes with a lot of personality, not easy to wear, and almost always thought of as women's fragrances. But in certain compositions, with the right ingredients, they could be intensely masculine. Why not? Elena's intuition might be spot-on. Claudine checked the storeroom, found what she was looking for, and went back to the man.

Elena followed, a few steps behind her. Jean-Baptiste was still offended. When Claudine offered him the *mouillette*, he pretended to be looking the other way.

Claudine bit her lip. '*Mademoiselle*, could you show the perfume to this gentleman? I need you to take over from me, as Philippe requires my assistance.'

When she had left them alone, Jean-Baptiste turned around once more.

'Is it for a special occasion?' Elena asked him.

The man took the strip of paper with his fingertips and lifted it to his nose.

'Yes, very special,' he admitted.

'Sniff it gently and think about what you want, what you would like to happen. See whether it feels right or if it's missing something.'

He did as she said. In silence, almost reverently. Then, after a while, he started to talk.

'Things ended badly, and all over nothing. We were young, proud. Now . . . things are different. I never married, she's a widow.' He kept gently wafting the chypre-soaked paper back and forth. Elena stayed quiet, entranced by the story.

'She wasn't the only woman I ever loved, it's not like that. But she was the one I suffered for the most. And she's always been in my thoughts; it's surprising how long she's stayed there.'

He paused and shook the strip of paper. 'She's annoyingly stubborn,' he said, frowning again. 'But when she smiles, her eyes light up and she looks straight into your soul. She's beautiful, she really is, in spite of all the years that have gone by. She's beautiful to me.' He smelled the perfume again. 'It reminds me of a garden, not just flowers, but plants. I feel as if I can hear running water, lemon . . . or maybe it's orange. We once went to a citrus grove together. It was a lovely day, we laughed so much; we were very happy in those days. Then we came back to the city.'

He'd gone back to his memories . . . and it was all thanks to the perfume. Elena was almost moved to tears.

'Have you ever been in love, *mademoiselle*?'

'No, I . . . I don't think so,' she said honestly, after a long pause. He gave her a strange look.

'Don't worry, you're pretty and you're kind. You'll find the right man soon enough. It's sad to be alone, my dear. Pride may look hot on the surface, but it makes a cold companion. Try to follow your heart.'

Suddenly Elena felt the need to tell someone about a man she'd only met twice, in the dark. She didn't even know what he looked like, really. But his smell, she knew that well enough. She felt a flutter in the pit of her stomach, but then chased away those thoughts and focused on Jean-Baptiste.

'Well, I was engaged once,' she told him, 'but he . . . he'd rather . . . it didn't work out,' she concluded. Jean-Baptiste reached out a hand and placed it on top of hers.

144

'He's an idiot, that's for sure. Don't worry, *ma petite*. Life may present us with things, God may provide, but we have the final say on everything.'

'True,' Elena murmured, although she didn't really believe it.

'I like this perfume very much,' the man went on. 'It reminds me of the past, but it has something new. It's exactly what I wanted. Hope. Life has no meaning without hope, as you know, *mademoiselle*.'

Yes, she knew. That was what had brought her to Paris, almost without even thinking about it. She'd done it even though she knew it wouldn't be easy. So why did she have a lump in her throat? And tears stinging her eyes? She chased them away and forced a smile.

'So I'm learning,' she said.

Jean-Baptiste beamed. 'You're a clever girl. Now, give me a package of this perfume – but not too big, mind. That way I'll have an excuse to come back soon.'

He winked and Elena saw that he must have been a real heartbreaker in his youth. Who knows what stories she might have, this mysterious woman who'd prompted him to seek out a special perfume, something to remind her of the good old days and convince her to try again, to give their relation-ship a second chance.

That wasn't the only sale Elena made that day. Under the watchful eye of Claudine, she served several customers and took two big orders.

On her way home, tired but very pleased with the way things had gone, she tried to remember what she knew about composition – but she was too tense to concentrate. The customers' emotions had invaded her, and she could hear them speaking to her. She'd tried to fight it and push them back, more out of habit than anything else. But they'd managed

145

to get through her defences, and there they were, like birds perched on a branch, never taking their eyes off her, not even for a second. She listened to their requests, but more than anything she wanted to give them what they wished for. Because she knew how to do it: that was the one thing she could do better than anything else. And that scared her. She was terrified of her own abilities, terrified that the Rossinis' obsession would manifest itself in her, the way it had in her mother and grandmother.

Her ancestors had given up everything for perfume. Would she be able to resist it? Could she make her peace with perfume without becoming enslaved to it?

She didn't know. Or rather, she wasn't sure, because right then, she was enjoying herself. Being at Narcissus, helping customers find the right smell for their lives and their dreams had made her happy. No, it was more than that: it had given meaning to her day.

When she entered the courtyard, she walked up to the door without even looking around, so lost was she in her thoughts. She rummaged through her bag for her key, and slid it into the lock.

'Hello, Elena.'

Cail. She looked up and there he was, a few metres away, casually leaning against the wall. The light from the streetlamp outside sharpened the angular features of his face. He had deep, dark-blue eyes, she saw, and brown hair with reddish hues. She felt her heart skip – and it was as though her mind cleared just by looking at him.

'Finally we see each other in the light,' she said with a pleasant smile.

Cail suddenly switched moods. In one swift movement, he peeled himself away from the wall and took a step back. His hands were buried in the pockets of his leather jacket and his expression was forbidding. Elena's smile died. What on earth had got into him? She hadn't meant to offend him.

She turned the key, but it wouldn't move. She tried again; still no luck. 'Damn it,' she cursed before giving the door a kick.

'Let me do it,' Cail said, moving forward almost reluctantly. Elena glared at him.

'Sure you want to get that close?'

He frowned, then glanced around. 'It's just that it sometimes bothers people if I get too close.'

'You're joking, right?'

But he didn't look as if he was joking.

Elena shook her head. 'OK – look, we barely know each other, you don't have to explain yourself to me.'

She could tell he'd got closer, because she heard him catch his breath. For a moment she thought about moving out of the way, or even being rude, but she was too tired to start arguing with him. She took a deep breath and the burst of anger that had seized her completely disappeared. Then she smelled his perfume again, altered this time by his discomfort, and something like a hint of disappointment. She sighed, then stepped aside.

'Fine, you try,' she said.

Cail stretched out one hand and gave a tug on the handle with the other. At that point the key turned. The click echoed loudly around them.

'There we go,' he said, opening the door.

Elena walked into the main entrance hall. 'Come in, I'll make you a coffee.'

Cail didn't answer; he just stood there in silence, his hands back in his pockets. Elena immediately regretted the invitation.

It was a stupid idea: you could see from a mile away that he wasn't remotely interested.

'OK, forget it,' she mumbled. 'See you later. Thanks for the door.'

'I'd prefer tea,' Cail's deep voice resonated, undoing Elena's worries. He flicked on the light switch. 'Do you *have* any tea?' he asked, looking straight at her again. 'If you don't, it doesn't matter. I've got some upstairs.'

Apparently they were going to have a cup of tea together; apparently he wasn't completely hostile. She needed to relax, Elena thought. Being on the defensive like this was doing her no good. She smiled faintly, telling him, 'No, it's OK. I think I've got some tea bags somewhere.'

He seemed about to say something, but then just walked over to the door of her apartment.

'Could I have the keys?' she asked, stretching out the palm of her hand towards him.

'Shall I do it?' Cail offered, waiting for her permission.

Elena found herself nodding.

'Yes, OK. Go ahead.'

It only took him a moment to open the apartment door and then he stepped aside to let her through. Elena went inside, a little troubled. She didn't understand what it was, but she knew something had happened between them. Acutely aware of his presence and his perfume, she walked quickly past him and over to the staircase.

'I've never been in this apartment,' Cail said, taking a long look around. 'It's really interesting – the original structure is completely unchanged.' He stretched out his arm, pointing to the series of arches supported by the thick stone walls. 'You see how high it is? They used to keep carriages in here. And the servants' quarters were upstairs.'

He kept talking, describing the architecture of the ancient building. Slowly he began to bring it to life, and at one point it was as though the walls around them had lost their layer of mould and the plaster had regained its strength.

'It's a shame to leave the ground floor like this,' he concluded. Elena was still watching him from the bottom step.

'If it were mine,' she said, 'I'd refurbish it and turn it into a shop – you know, a perfumery.'

'Is that what you are?' Cail asked. 'A perfumier?'

Suddenly everything made sense. 'A perfume that smells of earth and roses . . .' Perfume had an important place in this woman's life. There was something else, Cail mused. For a moment he'd thought she was the same as everyone else. His scar wasn't that terrible, but people are instinctively repulsed by anything that isn't perfect. He'd got used to it over time, and besides, not everyone was his cup of tea either. When he'd felt Elena looking at him, he'd noticed her surprise and he'd recoiled, like he always did; people hated being too close to him. In general, he just needed to give them a bit more space, keep his distance, to make them less nervous. But she had amazed him again, by getting angry. Then she'd gone back to being friendly, even invited him in for coffee.

'That's right, yes, I'm a perfumier. For what it's worth,' she replied, and turned to go up the stairs.

'That's up to you.'

Elena looked at him over her shoulder. 'How do you mean?'

'What it's worth, I mean.'

She laughed wistfully. 'You're right. In the end, it's all up to me.'

Cail couldn't take his eyes off Elena's slender figure as she made her way upstairs; he liked the long blonde hair swinging across her shoulders, and her frank, direct look; but what struck him straight away was her smile. When she smiled, she was beautiful.

Suddenly, Elena staggered. She'd reached the landing, one hand on the wall. Cail rushed up to her, taking the stairs two at a time. 'What's wrong?' he asked brusquely, grabbing her by the shoulders.

Elena took slow, gentle breaths, and the dizziness started to pass. 'Nothing — I'm just a bit light-headed. I'm probably coming down with the flu or something,' she said. But her vision was still blurry, she couldn't breathe properly and she was starting to get really worried. She'd been feeling unwell for a few weeks now — and on a regular basis, too.

'Can you manage?' Cail asked, still holding her up. He spotted the kitchen and led her there. 'You're pale, sit down. Where do you keep things?' He started to look through the cupboards. 'A cup of tea will do wonders for you,' he added.

'Really?' she asked, still a little fuzzy, leaning back in her chair.

Cail saw the kettle, filled it with water and put it straight on to the stove. He found the tea bags and put one in each cup.

'At least, that's what my mother says. So it must be true.' He stood still and looked at her. Then he went over and put the palm of his hand on her forehead. 'Have you eaten?'

'Yes.'

He kept looking at her, as though he was analysing her answer. Then he nodded. 'It's probably just low blood pressure. The tea will do you good.' He left her and went back to the cooker, lowering the flame.

'Were you waiting for me before?' she asked, partly because

she didn't like thinking about mothers, and partly because she was curious to know.

'Yes,' Cail said. 'I wanted to tell you I put a new lock on the terrace.'

Elena stared at him, and the cold teeth of disappointment bit away any happiness she'd felt watching this man busying himself in her kitchen.

'But there's no doorbell, so I thought I'd give you my mobile number and ask you for yours. Next time you fancy looking at the stars, call me first. I . . .' He paused. 'I'm not used to having guests.' His voice was so quiet that Elena had to strain to hear him. 'Anyway, you still need to tell me why you're afraid of dogs,' he added.

As he spoke, he took a card out of his jeans pocket and placed it on the table. 'There you go,' he said, and went to pour boiling water into the cups.

Elena didn't know what to say. He'd waited for her to give her his mobile number. No, better than that: to exchange numbers. All of a sudden she felt light-hearted, like a naive teenager.

'So, what happened to you? When did you get bitten?'

Cail's question brought her back to reality.

'I was little.'

He sat down in front of her, looking into her eyes. 'OK, we know you were a child. Then what?'

Elena started to smooth the fabric of the tablecloth with her fingers. She found it hard to dredge up the memory, and didn't do it willingly. It was one of those things that she preferred to forget had ever happened. Then she sighed, and the shadow of a smile emerged.

'I was nine and I was very inquisitive. Our dog Milly – a German shepherd – had just had puppies. I didn't know dogs were fiercely protective of their babies.' She paused.

Maurice had told her not to go near them, but Elena disobeyed him. She waited until he was back in the laboratory and sneaked over to the basket. Milly and she were friends – surely she would let Elena hold one of her puppies? They were so cute, so chubby and soft; Elena couldn't wait to stroke them. But when she picked one up, the mother snarled at her. Shocked, Elena instinctively held the puppy to her chest. It was then that Milly threw herself on top of her, biting her arm and then her leg.

She couldn't remember much of what happened next. There was a lot of screaming. Maurice was furious. Even her mother had shouted, blaming Maurice for something; then he had walked away without calling the animal off.

The ambulance siren, the pungent smell of disinfectant, and the fear of that long night spent in hospital, alone, were etched on her young mind. They weren't serious injuries – the dog hadn't sunk her teeth in – but Elena hadn't forgotten.

Cail put a cup of tea in front of her. Her eyes were still darker than usual; a muscle twitched on one side of her jaw. 'Here, sip this slowly, it's very hot.'

He sensed that Elena was angry, but he had no idea why. She blew on the sweet tea, breathing in its perfume, savouring the sensation of the steam caressing her face.

'That man,' Cail said, after a few seconds. 'Who was he?'

Elena creased her forehead. 'Maurice?'

Cail nodded. 'Milly's owner.'

Elena put the cup to her lips and took a sip.

'When I was eight, he married my mother. Now they both live in Grasse. He owns a laboratory that produces essential oils – roses, mostly, but tuberose and jasmine, too.' Her voice had become monotone: she almost seemed to be talking about someone else, someone who didn't have the slightest connection to her own life.

Cail could tell there was more to this confession. He controlled the rage that had caught him by surprise as he listened to Elena's story. What kind of man would leave a little girl at the mercy of a dog who only wanted to protect her puppies? In such a situation even the most tame creature could become dangerous. It was a miracle Elena had come out of it with just a few stitches. Anger was coursing through him now – and it was ridiculous. He barely knew her: she meant nothing to him. But Cail had long since stopped analysing the rationality of his own reactions. A long time ago he'd learned to accept them, and then to keep them under control. So he decided to do something for the woman sitting in front of him, trying not to brood over such a painful memory. He wanted to help her. He owed it to her, because even though she didn't know it, she'd be the one to help him through his recurring nightmare about the crash.

'It's Saturday tomorrow, and I need to go out. Seeing as you've just arrived in Paris, I could give you a tour of the city centre, if you'd like that.'

With her hands wrapped around the still-warm tea cup, Elena shook herself out of her memories.

'That would be wonderful!' she exclaimed. 'Although technically speaking, it's not really my first time in Paris.' She smiled and shrugged. 'Mind you, the previous times I was probably too little to appreciate it, because everything seems so new to me now.' The truth was, she only had vague memories of the city, and the prospect of rediscovering it with Cail filled her with joy. She thought he would make a very special guide. She stood up and smiled at him. 'Yes, yes. I can't wait.'

Perhaps it was Elena's enthusiasm, or perhaps it was the smile that lit up her face, making her truly beautiful, but something made Cail's heart beat faster. He was thrown by the strength of his own reaction. For a moment, just a moment, he regretted having made the offer.

'All right, I'll pick you up in the afternoon.'

He didn't hang around but simply said goodbye then, leaving his cup of tea on the table, untouched.

For a long time, Elena stayed sitting at the table, wondering about herself and about this man, until she realized she was actually very tired. She picked at a plate of grilled vegetables, had a shower and decided to take a look through Beatrice's diary. But however hard she tried to concentrate on her ancestor's neat handwriting, the words escaped her. When her mobile rang, she already knew who it would be.

'Hi, Monique.'

'Hello, *chérie*, I couldn't wait to hear from you. So, tell me, any news?'

Elena bit her lip, thinking. She was tempted to tell her friend what was happening, that she kept feeling dizzy and unwell. But maybe it would be better to just ask her for her doctor's number. 'Actually, yes,' she said with a sigh.

Monique picked up on that sigh, trying to interpret it. Then she decided she didn't have the patience to decipher her friend that evening.

'If you can't deal with the situation at work, we'll find you something else. I mean, you were right, Narcissus isn't the only perfumery in the city.' There, she'd said it. She was sure it *was* the right place for Elena, but Jacques could be a real idiot. She didn't want Elena being bullied by her former lover.

'It's not about Narcissus, which is actually much better than I anticipated.'

'So what is it?' Monique asked, sounding worried.

Elena opened her mouth to answer, then closed it. Monique already had too much on her plate: her relationship with that impossible man, her new job . . . why give her something else to worry about? Elena decided she would handle this one by herself. If the dizziness came back, she'd go to the doctor. Besides, it couldn't be anything serious, it was bound to pass. Cail was probably right about the low blood pressure. Right now, in fact, she felt completely fine.

'I'm going out tomorrow,' she said instead. 'I've got a date, can you believe it?'

Over in her apartment, Monique sat up straight in bed. 'Yes, I can believe it,' she said. 'Look, it was you who had so little confidence in yourself that you felt you had to make do with that chef guy.' Secretly, she was trying to hide her astonishment. So, things *were* going much better than she'd hoped. Soon Matteo would be a distant memory.

'Tact really isn't one of your strong points, is it?' Elena said. But she was too happy to take offence at her friend's bluntness, so she let it go.

'I say what I think – what's wrong with that? Anyway, stop changing the subject and tell me who's the lucky man?'

Elena made herself comfortable between the cushions and looked at the ceiling.

'Did you know there was a man who lives on the top floor of the building here?'

'Now that I think about it, I do. Isn't he some kind of researcher?' Monique racked her brain, trying to piece together everything she could remember about the neighbour. 'Scottish guy, yes. He grows roses . . . yes – yes, that's it, I think he breeds them,' she said, as her mind turned over all the details and scraps of conversations she'd had with her neighbours when she lived in the Marais. 'I've seen his roses in magazines a couple of times. He's won prizes, you know.'

'No way.' Elena's eyes widened. 'That's why he's got so many plants on the terrace. To be honest, it's not as if I've seen them,' she continued, 'but the scent is unmistakable. You can smell it on him, too.'

'Shame he's a bit odd. Now I remember his face . . . he must have been very attractive once.'

Once? Elena bridled. 'Come on, have you looked at him properly? He's not just handsome, he's so much more. There's something about him that draws you in. And the perfume he wears? I've got no idea who created it, but it's extraordinary.'

Monique seriously doubted that Cail McLean put on perfume before he left the house, but she didn't say anything. Elena sounded as if she was infatuated, and there was nothing better than a new romance for getting over a lost love. She smiled happily. From what she could remember, Cail was quite forbidding. He walked quickly, with long, confident strides. He looked out for himself and didn't seem to care about anyone else. A bit too strange for her liking; but if Elena had smelled perfume, maybe he had changed. You never know.

'Is he taking you somewhere nice?'

'It's a surprise. To quote: "city centre". That's it, he didn't elaborate. He doesn't seem like one to mince his words. Let's just say he's very concise. Did you know he's got a telescope? He knows the names of the stars.'

'No way. Don't tell me you looked at them together?'

'We may have done – I'm saying nothing.'

Elena was laughing now. Monique hadn't heard her sound

that happy for a long time. She might have her doubts, but she knew Cail had lived in the Marais for years and that people respected him. Besides, he couldn't be that bad, if he'd set his sights on her friend. So Monique skipped the usual advice and just asked Elena to stay in touch with a text now and then.

'Of course, don't worry. I'll send you a message when we get back tomorrow, OK?' Elena ended the conversation and put her mobile down on the bed. A rose-breeder – it was such a fascinating job. That explained the smell of earth and roses.

Tomorrow, she decided. Tomorrow, she would ask him to tell her about himself and his work. She'd soon satisfy her curiosity.

Later that night, before he fell asleep, Cail analysed every moment he'd spent with Elena but couldn't find any specific explanation for the interest he was developing in this woman. He liked her – it was as simple as that. And that was something he really couldn't understand.

11

Iris: trust. Precious and essential, like water, air, earth and fire.
The fragrance is bright and intense.
Relieves tension and renews faith in the soul.

It was the third time Monique had been over the formula. She dipped the *mouillette* into the graduated cylinder and sniffed, then waited for the top notes – almond and grapefruit, both volatile – to disappear. She inhaled again, looking for what made up the heart of the perfume: white musk and tonka bean. She waited again, because there was something missing from this compound that should bring to mind the skin of a strong, determined man, the kind women dream about: sandalwood and vetiver.

Nothing – she could smell nothing apart from the sharp tang of vetiver. It wasn't good enough. She wanted a scent that symbolized the purest essence of masculinity – an intense fragrance that promised what no words could ever explain. What she really wanted, in fact, was the smell of Jacques.

'Why can't you just leave me alone!' she burst out, slamming the palm of her hand down on the table.

The graduated cylinder holding the mixture swayed. Monique put out her hand to grab it, but it slipped through her fingers, tipping out its contents. A straw-coloured halo spread across the worktop, spilling on to droppers, paper funnels, and all the equipment Monique had set out in front of her, including her notebook.

Speechless, she stared at the disaster, and then she swore. She almost ripped her lab coat in her hurry to take it off. She needed air, and space. She opened the door and walked down the corridor. Outside the laboratory that Le Notre had assigned to her, she met the cleaner. 'Get rid of that mess – all of it. *Now*,' she ordered brusquely.

She reached the stairs and ran down to the terrace. Despite the bright sun, her breath turned to cold mist almost straight away. But that wasn't what was clouding Monique's eyes. It was tears of frustration.

She wiped her face and then took a deep breath of icy air. 'I'll start again from the beginning,' she vowed. 'It doesn't matter if it takes me all day, I *will* make this perfume.'

Claudine had been watching Elena Rossini all morning. She liked the way this young woman did things. She was competent, polite but firm – and she wouldn't be fobbed off by customers, suggesting alternatives instead. Yes, she was a valuable addition. And Claudine had every intention of making the most of her. After all, a practical woman like herself knew that life as a manager had its advantages. She'd offered her support to Elena Rossini because she could tell she was going to be very useful.

Just then, a sophisticated-looking woman stopped right in

front of Claudine's counter. 'I want a light perfume,' she said. 'Something suitable for a very young girl.'

She hadn't waited to find out whether Claudine was free: she expected to be served immediately. The woman was smartly dressed and looked around condescendingly, her fingers poised on the arm of a pair of half-moon Gucci spectacles.

Claudine knew this kind of customer all too well. After seven years of serving Narcissus's clients, she'd developed a kind of sixth sense. She'd bet this one was going to be both difficult and stingy. One of those women who are rolling in money, and who want everything to be instant and unique, while expecting it to come cheap – less than they tip their waitresses.

'I'll call the sales assistant,' Claudine replied with her usual serene expression.

She didn't give the customer a chance to respond, savouring every second of the astonished look the woman gave her, as she blithely walked away. As soon as she caught Elena's eye, she beckoned her over and discreetly pointed out the woman. '*Madame* needs a young, delicate perfume. Try to find something for her.' With that she turned and marched off, leaving Elena to it. If and when the customer pulled out her wallet, only then would Claudine need to make a reappearance, just in time to register the sale in her own name and take all the credit.

Elena had a special afternoon ahead of her. All morning, thoughts of her date with Cail popped into her mind at the most inappropriate moments. She couldn't wait to go for a walk with him, and felt happy and slightly nervous.

She was very pleased with the way things were going at Narcissus. Even though at first it had sounded less than promising, she'd settled in pretty well. Every day, she understood the dynamics of sales a little better, and that morning she'd had some really enjoyable moments.

A super-chic woman, who looked like an aristocrat, had bought a perfume for her daughter. She wanted to give her a special present, she said. Things were tense between them. Just like that, her little girl had vanished and been replaced by a gloomy, depressed stranger who was always picking fights. Eloise Chabot wanted something that would make her daughter realize how much she meant to her.

Her own mother, Susanna, had given her a perfume once. Elena had almost forgotten. The memory cropped up out of nowhere, taking her by surprise. It was a birthday present. She'd never opened the perfume; it must still be in Florence, somewhere in the enormous chest in which her grandmother had kept everything.

Elena recommended a simple composition for the woman: almond, honey, peony, chocolate and tonka bean; and as a base note, the warmth and velvety softness of amber. It had a flavour of childhood, but also a hint of malice and seduction.

'It's not a girl's perfume, but it's not an adult's either. It doesn't have the certainty of someone who's arrived. There's still a way to go.'

Eloise thanked her with a big smile. When they said good-bye, the woman almost gave her a hug.

It was never like this before, Elena thought as she hurried home. She'd never felt the deep sense of satisfaction that came from knowing that her work was important, that she'd done something significant for someone.

Her mind went back to the perfume her mother had made for her. When she first received it, she felt ridiculously happy for a moment, almost crazy. It was always like that when she got something from Susanna. She held the parcel in her hands . . .

then her happiness gradually faded. It felt as if she was holding a broken glass container, full of cracks, and all the contents were seeping out. She made herself put the present away without opening it. She didn't need that kind of gift from her mother. A perfume, for heaven's sake. She could have all the perfume she wanted. Her grandmother was always creating new ones. And besides, if she really wanted a perfume, she'd make one herself.

What she actually wanted from her mother was quite different, the young Elena thought, as what remained of her momentary happiness turned to anger and bitterness. What she wanted was a hug, hours of conversation, attention, laughter, even tellings-off, the kind that end with tears and promises. She wanted to tell her about the time Massimo Ferri from 3B had asked her out and how disappointing it was when he kissed her. And the way he smelled . . . so wrong.

Oh God! Where had she unearthed that memory from? The blast of a car horn brought her back to reality. A smile crept on to her face. How silly! Massimo Ferri . . . She'd had such a crush on that boy whose name she could remember, but not his face – a crush that disappeared just as quickly as it came.

As ever, she banished anything to do with her mother, and all the pain that went with it, to a suitably deep, dark part of her soul. But she was still curious about the perfume: what Susanna had ended up choosing for her, whether it was vanilla or gardenia, neroli or lavender.

When she reached the crossroads with rue des Rosiers she glanced over at the print-seller. He was huddled up in his big old jacket and had put on a red woolly hat which left his eyes uncovered and made him look younger. She stopped for a moment to watch him, stamping his feet that had frozen stiff in the cold. When she got home she'd put boots on, she decided.

She wanted to be warm on the walk and to see everything Cail had to show her.

In the meantime, the old man had turned on the record player. There it was: *La Vie En Rose*.

She smiled and headed home.

When Cail arrived, she'd been ready for a while. She was wearing a midnight-blue skirt, a white shirt and a wide-necked sweater. She'd bought it just after she arrived in Paris, in one of those little vintage shops that had cropped up all over the city. It was soft, thick and powder pink; she would never have dreamed of wearing that colour when she lived in Florence, and now she loved it. Besides, according to the assistant, it looked divine on her.

'Di-vine,' she repeated to herself as she walked down the stairs, trying to recall the exact inflection the woman had used.

'Hi,' she said, opening the door.

Cail stared at her without saying anything. Elena felt him look her up and down. She held her breath, her heart was racing.

'You should wear a jacket,' was all he said.

'Oh.' Elena scowled. Short, sharp and to the point. God, it wasn't as if she was expecting a kiss or anything. *Liar,* she scolded herself, fighting the sting of disappointment.

'Right, here it is,' she said, turning around. On the wall was one of those old-fashioned coat-racks, and on it hung a long wool jacket.

Cail took it out of her hand, felt the material, and shook his head. 'That won't do. You need something thicker.'

'I'll be right back.' A few minutes later she came down wearing a leather jacket and a scarf around her neck.

Cail looked at her and nodded his approval. But he didn't

return her smile; he appeared to be deep in thought. Now what was wrong? He almost seemed angry.

'Look, if you've changed your mind, if you don't feel like going any more, that's no problem.'

He ignored what she was saying. Instead, he asked: 'Are you all right?'

No, of course she wasn't all right. She was confused and couldn't understand what had got into him. She frowned. 'Yes. Are you?'

'Seriously, Elena. We're taking the motorbike and it'll be cold.'

Motorbike? She'd never been on one – she'd always been a bit scared of the noise. Then all her doubts disappeared. Cail had a motorbike and he wanted to take her on it!

'I didn't know you had a bike. But won't I need a helmet? I don't have one,' she said with a hint of disappointment in her voice.

Cail raised an eyebrow. 'There's a spare helmet,' he said. Then he stretched out his hand and, with the tip of his forefinger, he lifted a lock of hair that was hanging in her face and tucked it behind her ear.

'Do your jacket up.'

He stepped back and cast that moody look over her again, from top to toe. Elena felt her heart flutter.

'Let's go, it's getting late,' he said, putting an end to their strangely charged moment. Two minutes later, Elena was looking at a giant chrome racer, metallic black, with red flames painted on the petrol tank. Hermione, Cail told her it was called.

Elena didn't bat an eyelid. Who was she to tell him it was ridiculous to give a motorbike a woman's name? So she bit her lip until the urge to giggle had passed, focusing on the best way to get herself on to the thing.

'Here, I'll show you,' Cail told her.

'It's easy for you, but my legs are nowhere near as long as yours,' she protested, looking apprehensively at the seat of the Harley. Cail shook his head. Once he'd fastened the strap on her helmet, he slid an arm around her waist. A moment later she was on the back of the bike. The engine rumbled, low at first, then louder. When they set off, Elena was clinging so tightly to Cail she was afraid he might object. In the end, she decided nothing would have convinced her to loosen her grip.

City of Light.

If three little words could describe Paris, it would undoubtedly be those. The city shone and sparkled with life. It was only five in the afternoon, but a veil of cloud had dimmed the sunlight and the whole of Paris had lit up in response to the invitation. And, as Elena thought about it then, it was that glow that had lingered in her mind since childhood – that and the perfume. The city smelled of cars, people, food and tobacco. There was another perfume that came off the Seine, too, hot and stifling. Only now it was different, for there was also the smell of this man she was holding on to so tightly: strong, warm and intriguing, a mixture of herbs and leather, and sweetness.

It was comforting to have his firm back to cling to. She also felt slightly concerned, as if she was about to do something stupid. After all, he was a stranger, a charming man who had decided to show her a wonderful and very romantic city. If only she could hear the strains of 'La Vie En Rose', she thought to herself, the moment would have been even more magical.

They reached Île de la Cité and drove towards a car park.

'Here we are,' Cail said, helping Elena, who had already started struggling with her helmet strap.

165

'Urgh, I can't wait to get this thing off,' she grumbled. She was hot and, despite the fact that she could see her breath condense in front of her, she could feel her face burning up. But most of all she was happy. She'd felt joy and dread in equal measure and she'd loved every minute of the adrenaline rush. She couldn't wait to do it again.

There were people milling around everywhere, and after a while Cail took her hand. 'Stay close,' he said, gesturing towards the crowd.

'If you insist,' Elena replied, rolling her eyes.

Puzzled, Cail squinted at her; when she laughed happily, he realized she was joking and found that he wanted to laugh along with her. He felt good – she made him feel good. They stood there, in the middle of a crowd, staring at one another, searching for some unspoken understanding.

'Come on, let's go,' he said brusquely, once again snapping them out of that strange intensity they'd fallen into.

'Where?'

'You'll like it.'

No, he wasn't the chattiest character, but Elena was starting to get used to his style. Besides, she felt safe with him, holding his warm hand in hers.

'Come on, give me a bit more. You can't expect me to follow you if you don't even tell me where we're going.'

Cail seemed to think about it, then he turned to her. 'Chocolate,' he whispered, getting close to her lips for a moment. Elena started to giggle. Chocolate was, by far, her biggest weakness.

'If this is a dream,' she grinned, 'don't wake me up.'

Cail tutted, but when he went to take Elena's pulse, brushing his thumb over the network of veins on her wrist, her heartbeat was racing. It was a tender and intimate gesture. Elena could

166

have taken her hand away at any point – Cail was only holding on gently – yet she felt bound to him, and it troubled her.

They carried on walking, hand in hand, in silence. When the crowd got busier, Cail pulled her closer, putting his arm around her, and after an initial moment of surprise, she let herself sink into his embrace.

There were lots of tourists in front of Notre Dame. A long queue had formed from one end of the square to the other.

'We'll never make it up there,' Elena murmured, staring mournfully at the tops of the bell-towers. She would have loved to see Paris from above again, and she would have loved to see it with Cail. The view from the bell-towers was magnificent, it was unique. She could still remember it, after all these years. Then a thought struck her from somewhere: if they saw it together, they would have something to share.

'We'll find a way, trust me,' Cail assured her.

Elena looked at him, and she could tell that he meant it.

The bakery wasn't far from the cathedral, no more than 100 metres. It was all pink – Elena could hardly believe her eyes. She stopped a few metres away and breathed in the perfume coming from this beautiful shop. Forest fruits, honey, chocolate, peach. And the unmistakable smell of melting sugar, seconds before it browns and turns to crunchy caramel.

A sudden wave of lethargy made her realize she was starving. Then the tingle in her stomach became a vice-like grip and she froze, scared that she was going to feel ill again.

'It's not Ladurée,' Cail told her suddenly, as though he felt the need to apologize.

Elena shrugged. 'If it tastes even half as good as it smells, it will be heaven.' The strange pang of sickness had vanished again, leaving just ravenous hunger.

Inside, everything was a shade of cream, from the seats to the shelves stacked with jars in every size, shape and colour.

Elena could tell immediately that the smell of freshly baked cookies wasn't coming from the kitchens, but was the sophisticated composition of a perfumier. She smiled to herself as Cail helped her take off her jacket. Olfactory psychology. Lots of shops had their own perfumes made nowadays to associate them with a happy feeling, and to leave an unforgettable impression on their customers. This place was a sheer delight for the senses: the wonderful view, the smell, the taste, the feeling of well-being.

A girl dressed in white served them straight away, bringing a selection of pastries, fruit *macarons*, a hot chocolate topped with cream for Elena, and a black tea for Cail. Wasting no time, Elena dived in. The desserts were delicious. As she sank her teeth into the thin, fruity crust, the soft pastry melted in her mouth.

'It's so good,' she said, snatching up another straight away.

Cail watched her in silence, an amused glint in his eye.

'Have you had . . . Hermione . . . for long?' Elena asked between mouthfuls.

'Five years. I had another bike before.'

He tensed up. Elena watched him fiddling with one of the napkins the waitress had put on the table. She could tell that this wasn't his favourite topic of conversation, so she dropped it, and instead bit into a *macaron* such a bright shade of lilac it seemed unreal. An explosion of blackcurrant cream made her close her eyes. It was a pleasure she could hardly describe; the perfume was intense and the cream filled her mouth like warm honey.

'Oh my God, this is one of the best things I have ever eaten,' she whispered.

Cail looked at her again, and his expression softened. It wasn't really a smile, she wouldn't say that much, but it was close enough to let her see how handsome he might be.

'Have you been working with perfume for a long time?'

'All my life,' she told him after a moment. Then it was her turn to look away.

Cail pushed the plate of pastries towards her; he was enjoying watching her eat. He liked watching her full stop. He waited patiently for her to take another. Elena chose one, took a bite, and then started to talk.

'Lots of women in my family were perfumiers. The most talented ones created famous perfumes, and the others helped with the family business, too.' She paused and looked outside. 'You know, we actually made our fortune in France. One of my ancestors created a very special perfume. It was so intense, so perfect, that it seduced a princess. The man who commissioned it married the princess, gained her kingdom and paid the perfumier an unbelievable sum. The perfumier, my ancestor, then left the country and went back to her home in Florence.'

'I get the feeling there's a bit more to it, something you're not telling me.'

Elena held his gaze. 'She never forgot him – the knight, I mean. She always loved him, even after she married someone else. She used to write about him in her diary. It's a sad story.'

Cail put his cup down on the table and leaned back in his chair.

'Maybe they weren't destined to be together,' he said.

'You can change your destiny,' Elena replied. 'You just have to really want to. That's the only way you can alter the course of events.'

'Not always. Sometimes things happen that you can't change.' He was distant again now. Suddenly the look in his eyes was as hard as the line of his lips. He seemed sad, and Elena sensed that a deep pain lay beneath Cail's words. And then she understood.

'You're talking about death.'

'No,' he replied sharply. 'Only good things today.' That wasn't much of a response, Elena thought. It raised more questions than it answered, but the message was loud and clear: he had no intention of talking about death and destiny, even if she wanted to.

'Tell me about you,' she said, changing the subject. 'What do you do apart from live in the Marais and look at the stars?'

'My work is a bit like yours, really,' Cail told her. 'I breed flowers, specializing in scented roses. I try to keep the look of the old roses – the ones with real character, bold colours and unique perfumes. Complex perfumes, ones that have different levels of smell – that's what I'm aiming for. The perfume might start with simple fruits, but then it might bring in citrus or myrrh, scents that can say something intense, something unique. I don't want the new creations – which barely have a fragrance – to overshadow the old roses just because they're outwardly beautiful.'

'So you protect them?'

Cail raised an eyebrow. 'I'm not doing it for the good of the world, Elena. I make a lot of money.'

'That may be so, but you still do it. If you hadn't decided to create an alternative, the old roses might have been doomed to oblivion.'

They carried on talking. Cail gave her a few, brief answers, and spoke about his latest creation: very disappointing, if he was honest, but it might make a good mother rose.

'It's a bit like it is with people. A mother with blue eyes and a father with green eyes could have a child whose eyes are also light, but a different colour altogether.'

Elena listened, enthralled. More than once she lost the thread of the conversation, but she kept her eyes firmly on Cail. When they left the pink bakery it was already dark, but under a thousand coloured lights the Île was as bright as day.

'It's too late to go anywhere else. Notre Dame is right there – come on.' Cail pointed towards the looming cathedral with its arches reaching up to the sky, the pinnacles topped with stone gargoyles that seemed to be ogling passers-by.

Elena looked up. 'I didn't know you could get in from this side,' she said as they reached the enormous doors.

'This entrance is on rue du Cloître. There are four hundred spiral steps,' Cail said, by way of warning. 'The lower part of the cathedral is very pretty, though, if you'd rather not climb all the way.'

'I know. But I wouldn't be able to see the bells from there.'

'No, you wouldn't, that's true.'

'They all have beautiful names,' Elena added.

Cail nodded. 'Angélique-Françoise, Antoinette-Charlotte, Hyacinthe-Jeanne, and Denise-David are the most recent. The largest is Emmanuel: almost thirteen tons.'

'Amazing,' Elena murmured. 'The sky seems so close from up there,' she said, recalling the last time she'd climbed those towers. Then she turned to Cail. 'Let's go up. If you want to,' she said, patting him on the back.

He took her hand, squeezing it for a second, then nodded and let go. 'All right.'

Luckily, the queue of tourists had thinned out. They started to make their way up, slowly, their fingers numbed by the autumn air. The steps kept appearing, endlessly, one after another. There was an ancient smell trapped within the walls, the smell of damp, of centuries of footsteps, old incense and beeswax. How many people had climbed these stairs before her? Elena's imagination drifted off with the perfume and everything it evoked. Women, men, everyone with their own past, their own story.

Suddenly she stopped, unable to breathe. She bent her head and raised it again. Panic made her blood run cold. No matter how hard she tried to catch her breath, the feeling of suffocation was overwhelming.

Cail was behind her. When he realized something was wrong, he took her by the waist and turned her round to face him. He quickly saw that she was about to faint.

'We're going down now, don't worry,' he said gently.

He didn't wait for her response, but picked her up as if he were lifting a child. Jostling through the tourists on their way up, tight-lipped, ignoring their complaints, he made his way down, one step at a time, holding her to his chest. It was only when they were finally outside and he set her down that he realized Elena wasn't responding. He unwound her scarf and carefully brushed back her hair. She was pale, but breathing normally.

'Elena, can you hear me?'

Her eyelashes fluttered, then she blinked, and looked at him as though nothing made sense.

'What happened?'

'You fainted. I'm taking you to hospital.' The emergency department of the Hôtel-Dieu was just a few metres away. Taking her in his arms again, he crossed the road.

12

Vanilla: protection. The warm, sweet perfume of childhood.
The fragrance gives comfort, boosts mood and relieves tension.
Goes well with leather. A few drops combine to direct affairs
of the heart.

Monique sniffed the *mouillette* again, closed the graduated cylinder tightly, and shook the *mélange* so the alcohol would start to dilute the molecules that made up the essences. Then she put it back in its container to keep it in the dark. She checked one last time that the formula she'd entered in the program matched her notes, threw out the used paper filters, stretched – then left the laboratory.

It would be another twenty days before she would have a clear idea of the nuances of the perfume she had just created. 'A month to mature', as Lucia Rossini always used to say. Even though Monique had not strictly followed the procedure Elena's grandmother had taught her, the structure of the scent was still clear, and the end result was in sight. Yes, she'd had a productive day. After the twenty days had passed she would add water, filter the compound again, and only then would she determine whether it would become an *eau de parfum*. But that decision had to be made with Le Notre.

She went down the stairs and straight into the underground car park, saying goodbye to a few colleagues on the way. Once she was in the car she switched on her mobile phone.

'There you are,' she said, hearing it vibrate. But it wasn't a message from Elena. She skimmed the dinner invitation from Jacques and deleted it.

'Idiot,' she muttered, ignoring the temptation to call him and tell him exactly what she thought of him. She waited a few more moments, staring at the screen as other messages appeared one after another. It was strange that she hadn't heard anything from Elena, but then her friend was probably too busy enjoying herself, she decided, smiling as she started the car. She couldn't wait to take a long, hot shower. Afterwards, she was planning to watch television and call her mum; she hadn't spoken to her for a few days. She needed some TLC, and Jasmine always knew how to cheer her up.

Sitting on a hard chair in the hospital waiting room, Cail's gaze was fixed on a random spot on the floor. They'd taken Elena away an hour ago, and he'd done nothing but check his watch every five minutes since. He hated hospitals. They reminded him how helpless people were, how fragile life was.

He ran his hands over his face and then through his hair, brushing it back. It was nothing serious, he told himself for the thousandth time. Otherwise he would have known by now. And besides, if she was really ill, Elena wouldn't have refused to sit in a wheelchair – she'd only agreed to be seen by a doctor if they let her walk to the examination room by herself. He felt a pang in his chest, and the same fear that had struck through him when she fainted.

As she walked to the examination room, Elena had waved at him, like a child, her eyes fixed on his, her face white with fear. He would have given anything to go with her. Once more he felt that irrational need to hold her to his chest, to feel her warmth, smell her perfume.

What was taking so long?

He got up and started to pace nervously. Reaching the window, he stopped, faced with the wonders of the city and its thousands of lights. With his palms pressed against the thick glass, staring out into the dark night, he felt as if he was being sucked into the past, into a previous life.

He wasn't there when they took Juliette away. After all these years, his memories were blurred and what he knew, he'd learned from the police reports. He could vaguely remember the deafening truck horn, the screech of tyres on asphalt a few seconds before he was thrown from the seat of the motorbike. It was a miracle he'd escaped with just a scar and a few broken bones. But he was sure of one thing: that night, a part of him died with Juliette. He hadn't been the same since.

He swallowed, and closed his eyes. A moment later he re-emerged from that dark place in his soul where he buried everything, and where he very rarely went. Reflected in the window he saw the nurse who had accompanied Elena; he turned to her and asked: 'Is there any news?'

The woman stopped, then she seemed to understand. 'Ah, yes,' she smiled. 'Are you Mrs Rossini's husband?'

Cail stood there, speechless, and somehow managed a mechanical nod.

The nurse patted him gently on the arm. 'Don't worry, it's nothing serious. Your wife just needs to rest and take her vitamins. Dizzy spells are normal in her condition. With a bit of luck the nausea should pass after the third month. Pamper her a little bit – women love that, you know?'

He didn't reply. He had no idea what to say. She smiled at him again, almost amused by the sudden pallor and look of astonishment on the man's face. Cail thanked her, then he found a seat and sank into it.

'She's pregnant. Elena's pregnant.' He sat staring at his hands, as a mass of contradictory emotions swirled inside him.

When the nurse came back into the waiting room around half an hour later, he stopped her.

'Could I see . . . erm . . . my wife?'

'I think that would be a good idea. She's in quite a state,' she told him with a searching look.

This time, she didn't seem so friendly, and she set off down the corridor without even bothering to wait for him. After a short walk she pointed him to a door and said frostily, 'There. You can go in. You'll need to wait for the last test results before you can leave, fill out the forms and get her discharge slip. It'll take at least another hour,' she warned. 'Like I told your wife, if you decide to intervene, you only have a couple of weeks. After that it would be too late.' She turned and disappeared round a corner.

Intervene?

Cail knocked and opened the door. Elena was sitting on the edge of a bed with her head in her hands. She looked lost, with her hair in her face and her shoulders hunched. Occasionally she would shudder. She hadn't even noticed him.

He walked over to her and knelt down, so that his eyes

176

were at the same level as hers. Then, very gently, he lifted up her chin.

'Hi. Are you feeling better?'

Elena shook her head, her eyes glistening with tears. 'I'm pregnant,' she told him in a tiny voice.

She was approximately two months' pregnant and alone. How could she not have realized? Elena asked herself. OK, so she'd never had a regular cycle, but not to put two and two together? So much had happened, so much all at once. Now she had a baby on the way and no idea what to do. A deep fear, fear such as she'd never known, gripped her. She couldn't think, she couldn't speak. She'd always thought that one day she would do this with a partner, a husband. But Matteo ... The very thought of him made a wave of revulsion wash over her. No, she didn't want to think about him right now. She didn't want to think full stop. How could it be possible? she kept asking herself. Why now?

Cail swept a strand of hair off her forehead and then another, stroking her skin gently. He wasn't doing it for her, but for himself. He needed to touch her. Just touch her. There would be consequences, and many, he knew that for sure. But he decided he'd cross those bridges when he came to them. One at a time. There was no point in thinking about it now, not when Elena's fingers were clutching his sweater tightly.

'It's a good thing, a baby is always a blessing.' Where the hell did that come from? What did he know about babies?

But it didn't matter what he thought. Right then, she needed all the support she could get. The single tear that had tracked a damp furrow down her cheek, and the way her fingers still clung to him, told him that. Cail had no idea of the right thing to say – he wasn't good with words or big speeches. So he let his instincts guide him, and somehow he found the strength to give her the smile he'd still never shown her. He dried her face with his thumb without saying a word, waiting for her to calm down enough to say something. Anything.

'I always wanted a baby.' Elena's voice was less than a whisper.

Cail held his breath.

'What about you? Or maybe you already have them?' she asked him.

He shook his head. 'No, I don't have any children. I've never thought about it, to be honest. I suppose one day, sooner or later, I will. But it's not on my list of ten things to do before Christmas.' He forced himself to keep his tone light. 'Anyway, look at me, I wouldn't even know how to hold one. Newborn babies are tiny.' Just the idea of holding a child in his arms brought him out in a sweat. Not to mention the fact that his scar would probably scare it to death.

'Why only ten things?' Elena joked weakly.

'I'm a realistic kind of guy.'

Cail stroked her hand. 'So, this is a good thing, then? I mean . . . the baby. You said you wanted one,' he asked, concerned by the despondent look on her face, her eyes swollen from crying.

But Elena couldn't speak. She felt as if she was falling apart.

Instinctively, Cail opened his arms and she sank into his embrace. He held her like he'd wanted to all afternoon, hugging her close. Elena buried her face in Cail's neck, clinging on to him with all her might, to his warmth, his perfume. So good, so perfect.

He stroked her hair, let her pour her heart out and listened as Elena told him how much she'd wanted a child, but with

Matteo it hadn't happened right away; how life seemed to be playing a joke on her; how her world was turning upside down. She was thinking out loud, saying things that made no sense, except they did make a worrying kind of sense. Cail continued to hold her, and in that moment nothing else mattered to him. Nothing. Just her – just Elena.

'I don't even know what to call it,' she said a little later, taking deep breaths, searching for the composure she'd been struggling to find.

He felt his heart leap. Relief and a flash of joy: Elena was going to have the baby.

'I don't think that's a big problem.'

She chewed her lip, then agreed. 'Right, that's not a problem.' But actually, it was. What was she going to call this baby? And what if it was a girl? Her thoughts instinctively turned to her own mother, and the despair she felt became deep and biting. Again that sense of loneliness and dread.

'Don't think about that. You've got plenty of time.' Cail's voice cut through her train of thought, brushing everything else aside. He was here, now. And he was the most real thing she had. She didn't know what she would have done if it weren't for him.

A huge wave of gratitude joined the feelings she already had towards this man. And there was something else: a sense of pleasure stirring inside her like the delicate beating of a pair of tiny, very fine wings. She moved closer to him, then traced his profile with her fingertips, lingering softly over his scar.

'Have you ever wanted something so much, so badly, that you couldn't think about anything else? That made everything else seem pointless?' she whispered.

Cail nodded, looking into her eyes. 'Yes,' he said.

He could see it again, the desire she felt when they were together. He'd noticed it straight away: in that extraordinary speech she'd given him in the dark at their very first meeting. He'd recognized it immediately, because it sprang from the same illogical attraction he felt towards her. And it was still there, between them, even now that everything had changed.

'Want to tell me about it?' Elena sounded calmer now. She was sitting up, and looking at him inquisitively.

The question surprised him. Despite being deeply upset by the news of the pregnancy, she could still find the strength to think about him. In the order of Elena's garbled, frightened thoughts, he was still important. He shook his head. 'Another time. But tell me yours. Now that it's about to happen.'

'I thought it was the thing that I wanted most, but when I realized what the doctor was telling me, that the pregnancy test was positive, I was terrified. The thing you see as the finish line ... when you actually reach it, you find out it's much more complicated than you thought and you're actually only at the start of a very long journey.'

'One thing at a time. You don't have to think about everything at once – it'll be too hard if you do that. But if you take one thing at a time, it makes it, if not easy, at least do-able.'

Logical, straightforward, and above all practical. Again Elena wondered what else lay behind this man's wisdom. He always knew what to say and he was direct. It was like he didn't have time to waste on anything unnecessary. Everything he'd said to her was true. She decided to listen to his advice, and after a while she felt better. Of course, fear was still bubbling inside her, along with worry and thousands of questions she didn't know how to answer, but there was also a subtle, hidden joy that every now and again made her smile and rest a tender hand on the place where her baby was growing. She wanted to cry one minute and laugh the next. Thinking about it now, she realized she'd felt like this for a while. In fact, her pregnancy explained everything – it all made sense. Even changing her mind about perfume: it was back in her life – or had it simply never left? It was she who was different now.

'Do you want to let someone know?'

Cail struggled to get the question out. There was another man in Elena's life. Or there had been. And however well things were going between them, a baby changes everything. It forces you to alter your perspective. It is nature's way of settling things. He'd be sorry to let her go, even if she didn't mean anything to him yet; he would just stand aside. In reality, all he had to do was get on with his own life; nothing could be simpler.

Yet the thought troubled him. Because, whether he liked it or not, what he had just told himself was a complete lie. He waited for her to answer, studying every nuance of her expression.

'No, I don't need to tell anyone. Anyway, I don't want to. I don't want to talk about it.'

Relief, then anger again at the burst of happiness he'd felt. It was a thoughtless reaction; even if there was no man, no boyfriend, there was still the baby.

'Whatever you want.'

There was no point in trying to resolve it now.

'What do you say we fill out these forms and get out of here?'

Elena nodded. She was so very tired. Utterly drained. She was happy, but she was also terrified. Her head felt as if it was stuffed with cotton wool. The only thing giving her any stability was Cail; she was still clinging to him. She forced herself to let go and sighed.

He stood up to leave. 'Come on, let's go.'

They walked to reception hand in hand, their minds heavy with thoughts but their hearts a little lighter.

Philippe Renaud went over the sales list again. Since she joined Narcissus the Rossini girl hadn't made any big sales; with the exception of a couple of perfumes, she'd only sold the cheap stuff. What's more, he'd had reason to admonish her on a couple of occasions. She had appeared distracted, and at times looked as if she was on the verge of passing out. And when he asked her what was wrong she had the cheek to suggest that the ambient perfume ought to be subtler. To him, Philippe Renaud, who had personally measured out the fragrance that was the very symbol of Narcissus! He was almost snarling with rage. Then there was her sickening niceness: but those false manners didn't fool him. They were fake, like everything else about her. He'd noticed how keen she was to waste time with the customers, and wondered if she was engaging in more than a friendly chat. She knew the job well enough, so why wasn't she making any sales? The woman was definitely hiding something. And he was going to take it upon himself to find out what.

He'd give her another few days, Philippe decided, and then he'd tell *monsieur* she was up to something. It was his job, after all. Not that he was expected to supervise the sales assistants – that was Claudine's responsibility. But he did like to keep everything under control, make sure he had an overview of the whole business.

He took off his glasses and placed them on the table, careful not to touch the lenses. The little office he occupied wasn't fitting for someone in his position, and he had to share it with Claudine. High walls, painted a ridiculous mint green, and absurd white furniture; he hated it. Like he hated incompetent freeloaders. He hadn't liked that foreign girl from the start: too much pride behind that sweet façade. She was a liar, and he knew it. He could tell straight away that she was hiding something: when he showed her the laboratory she seemed on edge. Not that she could get at the perfume formulas, of course. Their surveillance system would have stopped her even getting close. No, that didn't bother him. It was the fact that the woman wasn't who she said she was.

He'd discussed it with Claudine a couple of times. But she took no notice, playing everything down. At the end of the day, Philippe thought, his colleague was just like every other woman: weak and emotional. She'd even suggested he should give Elena more time, even though she really was very slow – which Claudine had noticed herself. However, despite the fact that Elena often seemed distracted, Claudine said, she did know how to deal with customers. What Philippe couldn't understand was what Elena Rossini could possibly have said or done to gain the sympathy and support of Claudine, who had never shown the slightest solidarity towards any of the other sales assistants the company had seen come and go. Indeed, before they left, the girls would often complain about Claudine's unorthodox style and inappropriate conduct.

The fact remained that Rossini wasn't any old sales assistant. He sighed and stroked his moustache between his thumb and forefinger. To be honest, what was bothering him most was the fact that hiring Elena had put paid to his own infatuation with Monique. As he thought about it, his irritation turned to a burning resentment.

Since that woman came into the shop, they'd neither seen

nor heard from Monique Duval, despite her promises to the contrary. It was driving him crazy. How dare she make fun of him?

Still, he would personally see to it that things were put right. Taking on Elena Rossini had been *monsieur*'s choice . . . but certain decisions could be reversed. He just needed to find a convincing argument.

Elena finished packaging up the scented water she'd just sold. As usual, Claudine was taking care of the payment and smiling. It was good to see her like that, and Elena was happy with the way things had worked out between them. After their none-too-cordial start, now they were getting along much better. Claudine had started to trust her. Plus they could talk about perfume, compositions, *mélanges*. Elena thought she was very bright, and she enjoyed talking to her. Apart from Monique – and Cail, of course – there weren't many people who would be amazed by how much the perfume of a rose can vary depending on the species or where it's grown. Or how a perfume can be so complex that it can be interpreted many different ways.

Claudine had asked her to go into the lab to create a new fragrance, saying that she would sort out any problems with Montier. She was keen to see her at work; and Elena was thrilled to bits.

'There you go, Madame Binoche, I hope we'll see you again soon,' she said, turning her attention to her customer, handing her the golden Narcissus bag.

'I'll be back soon, *mademoiselle*. My sister-in-law Geneviève needs a special perfume, something personalized. She's an artist, you know, a writer. I've told her about you and she's very intrigued.' The woman moved a couple of steps closer and lowered her voice. 'Not everyone can transform one's desires into a perfume. But you, Elena my dear, you can work magic.'

She liked that definition, it made her smile. If only Madame Binoche knew . . .

'When I was little, my grandmother drove herself mad trying to teach me to listen to perfumes. I used to run away and hide behind a dusty old screen,' she confided.

The woman's eyes widened. 'Really? This is your family tradition?'

Elena nodded. 'Yes. More or less.'

'Oh . . . how wonderful!' Madame Binoche was enthralled. 'I would love to stay and hear more, but I'm going to be late for my meeting. Have I told you about my club, *mademoiselle*? No? Well, every Tuesday we meet to talk about the latest books we've read, over a nice cup of tea and some pastries. What could be better in life?'

One or two things sprang to mind for Elena, and they all involved Cail. Every time she thought about him, she felt her heart beat faster. Since they had found out she was pregnant, something between them had changed, and not because she wanted it to. Cail had become a friend. To be precise, the best friend she could wish for. But just a friend.

'I've always been fascinated by perfumes,' said Adeline Binoche. '"Because perfume is the brother of our breath". I think that's a remarkable thought, don't you?'

Adeline quoted the Yves Saint-Laurent aphorism with such earnest enthusiasm that Elena secretly wanted to laugh – but Adeline was a genuinely nice woman. She had a silver bob that swayed whenever she moved and, as she didn't stand still for a second, it seemed to flutter constantly. Her huge grey eyes made her look quite dreamy. She was one of Elena's favourite customers.

185

'I'm delighted with this perfume,' she told Elena, 'but tell me, speaking of your grandmother, what was her name?'

'Lucia – Lucia Rossini.'

'Ah, what a beautiful name. Very Italian,' Adeline replied. 'From Florence, right?'

Elena nodded. 'Yes. If you know Santa Maria Novella: there. My family's house is in that part of the city.'

'Who knows how many stories those walls could tell,' Adeline whispered, looking at her. 'Mysteries, family secrets maybe.'

Elena laughed. 'Are you really interested in all that?'

'Yes, very! Italy is full of wonderful legends. And Florence, well ... One of the most famous French queens was from Florence.'

'Yes, Catherine de' Medici. She was the one who introduced rose cultivation to Grasse. She loved the smell, and then her relative Marie followed in her footsteps, both as Queen of France and as a lover of art and perfume.'

Adeline drew closer. 'I have an old book about that, you know. And a lady-in-waiting's diary. They're very interesting. It was said that Catherine had her perfumier sent from Florence. His name was René, and he didn't just do perfume. It seems he also made poisons . . . There's nothing better than a diary to show you what life was really like in those days.'

It was true. Entire chapters of Beatrice's diary were dedicated to events from the time. Elena's ancestor had a great gift for observation and a sharp sense of irony. The castle where she stayed, for example – whose name she never wrote down and which none of her descendants had ever found – had towers and gargoyles guarding its walls; in the village below there were fields of lavender and tuberose, and the villagers spun silk. Beatrice described whole days spent picking the flowers she used for her perfume. It was absolutely fascinating. Such a pity that bitterness and regret had come along and tainted her life.

'Now I really do have to go,' Adeline said. 'See you soon. And thank you.'

Elena said goodbye with a smile. As she got back to work, her thoughts returned to the diary. Maybe she'd take another look at it this evening. She'd just started to set out a display of a new fragrance that would be launched to the public in a few days' time, when Philippe Renaud called over to her.

'If you've finished, I'd like a word with you.'

Elena left the bottles she was arranging and waved to him. The man took a little while to respond, as though he had to make a real effort. No, being pleasant was not one of his virtues, she decided, ignoring her manager's scowl.

'I just need to finish arranging these,' she told him, gesturing towards a box of silver bottles. 'Then I could use a box for a chypre *pour homme*. I've got a customer coming to pick up a bottle in a bit.'

Philippe half-closed his eyes, irritated by her response. 'A customer? I didn't realize you had any – at least not ones that come into this shop to buy perfume. I assume you must be referring to another kind of service.'

Elena stared at him. Her face started burning up. For a moment, she was speechless, astounded by the harsh insult. When she realized the full extent of what Philippe had just said, she put both her hands on the gleaming shelf and leaned towards him.

'I don't know what you've got into your head, and I don't want to know, but don't you *dare* speak to me like that ever again!' She hissed every word, her eyes flashing with rage, her throat aching from the effort of holding back what she really wanted to scream in his face.

Philippe blushed. He slipped a finger into the knot of his tie, loosening it, and looked around. What if someone had seen? He hadn't anticipated that kind of reaction. Elena was so rude! How dare *she* address *him*, Philippe Renaud, in that tone? With relief, he saw that business in the shop was carrying on as normal. Customers were waiting at the counters, sales assistants were proffering various options, and the high-resolution screen on one wall of the shop was playing the quiet background music that accompanied adverts for perfumes made by the house.

'Don't take that tone with me,' he retorted.

Elena shot him a withering look. 'Actually, I think you might be right. I was too polite.' She moved away from him, her fists still clenched, so tense she was almost at breaking-point. As she went, she walked past a customer she didn't recognize straight away.

'*Ma chère*, are you all right?'

'Monsieur Lagose! No, I don't feel at all well.'

'Is there anything I can do for you?'

Elena burst out: 'What gives a man the right to insult a woman like that, to imply she's a whore?' When she realized what she'd just said, it was too late to take back her words.

She blinked back the tears and the absurd desire to run to Cail and tell him everything. Maybe she was unusually emotional because of the pregnancy, but she found herself in a complete state in the middle of the shop.

'Frustration, *ma chère*,' said Lagose, offering her a hand-kerchief. 'When a man has no real argument,' he continued, looking daggers at Philippe, 'he trots out the same old story. It's convenient, it's devious. Don't pay too much attention.

188

Laugh about it, sweetheart. And remember, if someone has gone to such lengths to be unpleasant, it's because you're the one with the power. Now, let's calm down. I need to collect a bottle of perfume and, if you've got time, I'd like a little chat with you. Perfume I can get anywhere, but not the pleasure of an intelligent conversation with a beautiful woman.'

If looks could kill, Philippe Renaud wouldn't have stood a chance. Jean-Baptiste Lagose shot him another scorching glare, before focusing all his attention on Elena. She took a deep breath and gave back the handkerchief she'd balled up in her fist. She hadn't used it, she hadn't needed to. No tears, just indignation and fierce anger. 'I'm sorry, I'm quite emotional at the moment,' she told Monsieur Lagose.

'There's nothing to apologize for, *ma chère*. Sensitivity is one of the most interesting things about a kind soul. Feeling better now?'

Elena nodded. 'I'll be right back with your perfume.'

'Go ahead, I'll be here.' Jean-Baptiste waited until Elena was far enough away, then he went over to Philippe.

'Can I help you, *monsieur*?' the manager asked him, trying to regain some ground.

Jean-Baptiste flared his nostrils, squeezing the handle of his walking-stick as if he'd like to throttle the man.

'No, Mademoiselle Rossini is seeing to everything I need. She's a lovely, sensitive woman. I wouldn't like to see her in that state again.'

Philippe hid behind an indignant look. 'She's just a sales assistant, that's all. You shouldn't give her so much importance.'

'Don't make the mistake of thinking for one second that you may tell me what I can and cannot do. You have neither the intelligence nor the authority.' Jean-Baptiste's tone was calm, but there was a clear threat in those words. 'You think you're worth more than this woman because you have a better job, but you're wrong. Only a person with no class would put someone else down.'

Lagose then turned his back, leaving the store manager of Narcissus feeling very small. As soon as he spotted Elena, Jean-Baptiste walked over to her, wearing a big smile.

'Did I tell you about the perfume?' he began, conscious of the young woman's still-fragile state. He'd decided he was going to distract her. Sometimes it was the only thing to do. 'It was a real success, my dear. And it's all down to you. The perfume you recommended for my ... girlfriend, it did the trick,' he sighed, and a spark appeared in his eyes, mischievous yet manly.

Elena tried to concentrate on what Monsieur Lagose was saying, but it wasn't easy. There had to be a reason why Philippe was so angry with her. She should demand an explanation; he sure as hell wasn't going to offer one. As soon as Jean-Baptiste had made his purchase, she'd go and find Philippe to ask what had got into him.

She'd never been so confrontational before; she'd always avoided conflict, always stepped back. But in that moment, she was burning with rage. It was one thing having to put up with someone, however unpleasant they might be, but it was something else entirely to let oneself be so vilely insulted.

'You're still upset, my dear,' Jean-Baptiste said. 'Why don't you go home? You can do that, you know. Actually, look, I've got the car outside and it's no problem for me to drive you home.'

Elena looked at him. Why not? She'd been insulted: right now, she had no desire to stay. 'Thank you, *monsieur*. I'll take you up on that offer.'

She called Claudine, who arrived after a couple of minutes. The woman could immediately see that Elena was upset.

'Try not to take too much notice. Philippe is acting strangely at the moment, but I'm sure there must be a misunderstanding at the bottom of all this. I'll look into it, if you like.'

'I don't care if he's having a nervous breakdown, Claudine, I want an apology. If he wants to fire me, it'd be better if he just came out with it, without sinking so low!' Elena exclaimed. 'It's not the fact that he as good as called me a prostitute, it's that he wanted to insult me, and he thought he could get away with it. I don't understand it – I thought things were going well.'

'They're going very well, Elena. You just need to be less dramatic. You can't make a tragedy out of every little thing. You Italians are so theatrical! Now, I'll speak to him, and tomorrow everything will be back to normal, you'll see. Go home, you're very pale. You've not been looking well the last few days,' Claudine said, walking her to the door.

Maybe it's because I'm pregnant? Elena thought, putting on her jacket and pulling up the collar. That appeased some of her anger, filling her with sadness instead. She really needed this job. Babies don't come cheap, and even though Monique had cast herself as godmother and offered all her support, especially financially, Elena wanted to be independent. She already had problems with Cail, who was still doing her shopping and refusing to take any money for it.

Even though it was not yet November, the cold weather had already arrived. Outside, it was snowing heavily – ledges and rooftops had started to disappear under a layer of pure white. Breath condensed immediately, rising in gentle puffs of steam. Rather disconcerted by this unexpected event, people in the street were hurrying to reach their destinations. As Elena got into the car, Claudine went to look for Philippe. What in God's name was he playing at? She had plans for Elena Rossini: that girl had a real talent and Claudine had no intention of letting her go.

'Have you seen Monsieur Renaud?' she asked one of the sales assistants.

The girl nodded. 'I think he's in the office, *madame*.'

Claudine thanked her, then gestured towards a woman who was just coming in. 'See to her,' she ordered peremptorily, before disappearing into the back.

She didn't knock like she usually did, even though it was just as much her office as his. She was too worked up. She wanted to know what Philippe could possibly have against Elena. No way was she going to stand by and let the advantages she stood to gain from that woman slip through her fingers.

She found Philippe engrossed in his records, a kind of sales database he insisted on keeping by hand, even though they had a whole sophisticated computer program he could use.

'What on earth has got into you?' she demanded, standing right behind him.

Philippe looked up. 'I don't know what you're referring to,' he replied, 'and I don't much care for your tone.'

'I'll tell you in two words: Elena Rossini.'

Philippe tensed. 'Ah, you're talking about *her*. Well, I've decided to fire her. She doesn't bill anything, we're carrying her – plus, she's arrogant and rude.'

Claudine stared at him. 'Rubbish.'

Philippe's eyes narrowed. 'Why are you defending her? What's in it for you?'

'I don't know what you're alluding to. But I'm warning you: leave her alone.'

192

Indignant, Philippe placed his glasses on the end of his nose. 'We have a clear duty to maintain the high quality standards of this shop,' he protested.

'Monique Duval — she was the one who recommended Elena, right? Is *monsieur* aware of your . . . let's call it "admiration" of his lover?'

Philippe turned white. 'Nonsense,' he said, brushing her comments aside and going back to scribbling on the papers on the desk. 'Besides, Montier's engaged to be married now. You've heard that, too.'

Claudine smiled. 'Yes, but you know that means nothing.' She paused and pointed at the paper. 'Try turning the pen round. That end doesn't write.'

Claudine left the office with her thoughts whirling. If Philippe really wanted Elena out of Narcissus, that idiot would find a way to fire her. Especially now Monique was out of the picture. Of course, she couldn't tell him that Elena had made some major sales for which she herself had taken the credit. She had to find a way to protect her investment: the girl had to carry on working at Narcissus. Of course, the situation was only temporary. As soon as Elena passed her probation period she'd be able to make sales by herself, including putting them through the till. But until then, Claudine had every intention of making the most of the situation. She smiled to herself. Soon, she would put the girl to the test. She wanted to see whether her talents extended to perfume creation. Montier would pay very well for a new fragrance . . .

13

Hay: calmness. Ancient, ancestral, akin to fire, sea and earth.
The fragrance is etched deep in the ancient spirit we
   all possess.
Evokes tranquillity.

Elena looked at herself in the mirror, then turned to check her profile, one hand on her flat stomach. She was three months' pregnant, but you couldn't tell yet.

For a moment, as she was on her way home with Monsieur Lagose, she'd wondered whether Philippe had noticed something, and taken offence because she hadn't told them she was pregnant yet. Could she have inadvertently got herself into trouble at work? How was she to know – maybe French maternity laws call for immediate notification? But the more she thought about it, the less likely it seemed. Not to mention the fact that Philippe had still treated her disgracefully – even more so if he had guessed her condition.

No, she decided, it couldn't be the pregnancy that had

sparked Philippe's resentment. Besides, no one knew about it except Cail and Monique. She hadn't even told Matteo yet.

That thought put her in a bad mood. She sighed, took her phone out of her pocket and went to sit down. It was time to tell him. She didn't want to, and she wouldn't have done, if Cail hadn't told her in no uncertain terms that this wasn't something that only affected her. They'd actually argued about it. She disagreed, and wasn't afraid to say so. But he could be very stubborn. Just like that dog of his, who hadn't learned to stay away and followed Elena around, watching her with his big, brown eyes. It was getting increasingly difficult to keep her distance. That dog had the same protective instinct as his master. She shook her head.

Cail wouldn't let her go on the motorbike any more. Actually, now she thought about it, she hadn't even seen Hermione parked in the garage for a while.

She counted to ten, then gathered up her courage and dialled Matteo's number. One, two, three rings. No answer, Elena thought, relieved. She was about to put the phone down, when she heard the man's voice.

'Hello?'

She waited a couple of seconds, hoping he would hang up, then decided she would respond. 'Hello, Matteo. How are you?'

'Ah, Elena . . . I'm fine, thank you. How are you? We haven't spoken in a while – I've been meaning to call you.'

'I'm sure you have,' Elena said.

He cleared his throat. 'I know you're still angry with me, but try to understand. It wasn't something Alessia or I planned. It just . . . happened. It was love at first sight for her – you can understand that.'

Elena scowled at the phone. 'I see you still have a very high opinion of yourself.'

He was like Maurice, Elena suddenly thought. The idea struck her as a truth so evident, so disconcerting, that it almost took her breath away. How could she not have realized it before?

Matteo sighed. 'I know it's hard, and I know you invested a lot in our relationship, but that's just how it goes. I'm not coming back to you.'

What – did he really think that she was going to suggest something as ridiculous as getting back together? After what he'd done? Anger started to bubble up inside her.

'No, I didn't call to ask you to start over, believe me. Actually, I can assure you that that hasn't even crossed my mind.'

Silence, and then his voice changed. 'Really?'

'Yes, really. Don't worry.'

She wanted to laugh. Matteo had summed himself up with that one word: his tone was actually surprised. Really? *Yes, really.* As if there could be any doubt, after his treachery! What kind of man was he? And even worse: what kind of woman had she been to live with someone like that?

Her mind ran through Monique and Jasmine's many veiled comments. But her grandmother had been more direct than anyone.

'Elena, the man's an idiot. We've already got one in the family – and believe me, my girl, we don't need another!' Elena felt a sudden rush of love towards Lucia. She wasn't angry with Matteo any more – just slightly contemptuous, perhaps. The rest had vanished, cancelled out by something infinitely stronger, something she felt for another man, something she still hadn't been able to analyse but that was there, in a corner of her heart, waiting.

'Oh, good. You don't know how pleased I am to hear you

say that. Especially now. You see, I'm going to be a dad. Alessia's having a baby. You've got no idea how happy I am, Elena.'

Oh God, what now?

'Ah. Well, that's great news.'

Matteo gave a deep sigh. 'I know it must be a tough blow for you. We tried, and you could never get pregnant. But hey, you know, some women are just made to be mothers, and others . . .' he paused. 'Well, I mean, you're good at . . . other things.'

Elena didn't know whether to take offence or burst out laughing. The arrogance of the man! So she was good at other things, was she? Like what? He'd never bothered to find out about her interests, he'd just dismissed everything with a shrug of his shoulders.

'Listen, Matteo, it's actually a very similar thing I wanted to talk to you about,' she said, after a moment's silence.

'You mean . . . you're not trying to tell me you're pregnant as well?'

'I'm not trying to tell you anything,' she said, exasperated, closing her eyes and rubbing her forehead. She was getting a terrible headache.

'Thank God, because I wouldn't buy that.'

'Why not?' she asked, perplexed.

'Look, I'm sorry, but you disappear and then you turn up again right after we announce I'm going to be a dad. Isn't that a bit strange? Anyway, we've already had the banns read. We're having a church wedding.' Then suddenly he mellowed. 'You need to move on, Elena. Try going out with someone, make new friends . . . just – live. Life's too short.'

Life is short? What the hell had happened to this man? For a second she was tempted to tell him about Cail, really make

197

it hit home that she wasn't harbouring any romantic ideas about him and he was completely off-track. But she decided not to: first of all, she really didn't care what Matteo thought, and secondly she would never have used what she had with Cail, whatever that might be, just to make a point. She didn't feel the need. It was then that she realized Matteo meant nothing to her any more.

She stood up, drew back the curtains and opened the window. Maybe Cail was at home. It had stopped snowing a while ago, and a quick look at the night sky was exactly what she needed.

'But let's say for a minute that I am pregnant, too . . .'

A long silence, then laughter. 'Oh, that's a good one!' he replied. 'I get that you're still in love with me, but don't think you can take advantage of the fact that we were together to lay claim to . . . hello? Hello? Are you still there?'

But Elena had ended the call. There was only so much she could take.

She turned off the phone, letting it fall on to the bed. She knew Matteo – he would never call back, but she didn't want to risk it. As far as she was concerned, the matter was closed. And later, when she was in the right frame of mind, she would delete his number from her address book, too. Not now. Now she didn't have time. Her heart was racing and she felt sick.

'I'm not coming back to you,' she mocked. Maurice, Matteo. She let out a low, throaty laugh. The wrong men, men who needed to dominate others and abuse their power. Egotists. And while there was nothing she could do about Maurice, she was the one who had gone looking for Matteo, the one who had wanted him.

The knot in the pit of her stomach tightened. She wished she'd never called him. Even though, deep down, she knew it was the right thing to do, she couldn't ignore the anger and disgust she felt after talking to him. A strong sense of how wrong this man was made her shiver. The anger intensified, wiping out any trace of what was left of Matteo, her memories of him, what he had once meant to her.

Enough! She was done with men like that. Never again! *Never again*, she told herself fiercely. She'd started over, and wasn't about to make the same mistake twice. She alone would make the decisions about her life, and her child's life.

Perhaps things with Cail would move on, or perhaps not. That, she didn't know. But no man was ever going to take over her life again.

Elena changed out of her skirt and into a pair of soft cigarette pants and a red jumper. Her hair was still damp from her shower. She tied it up in a ponytail and added a touch of make-up. Then she felt like putting on perfume, but not the one she normally used. Tonight she wanted a special one; she wanted her own. She went back into the bedroom and opened the heavy wooden box where she kept her things. There it was, still where she'd put it: the perfume she'd made a few years ago, when she created one each for Jasmine and Monique. She wondered whether it would have lasted this long. It might have done. It had always been kept in the dark, in the thick, impermeable cedarwood box, away from heat.

She carefully removed the simple opaque glass bottle from the metal cylinder where it had been stored. Her grandmother didn't believe in the seductions of modern packaging. For her, substance was all that mattered. Elena hadn't cared about the container either: she'd decided to make the perfume because she wanted something special for her friends and for herself. Things had changed so much in such a short time, she thought.

Very gently, she turned the cap. The perfume was intact, as fresh as if it had just been made. At first, she felt a sudden discomfort, but it soon passed. It wasn't the first time a scent had irked her like that; since she started working at Narcissus, she'd walked into the shop a number of times and felt irritated by its perfume. Now she knew why – it was quite normal for pregnant women to be extra sensitive to smells.

Now she could smell the top notes. She closed her eyes and found herself in a field of lilies. Then came sparkling bergamot and neroli. The smell faded, and rose again, like the beating of wings. Jasmine this time, then gardenia and hints of magnolia. The aroma was intense and full of life. Then came musk, and last of all, amber. But just a hint, like a flake of snow that melts as soon as you look at it.

It was as though she could feel Lucia's presence beside her. Her grandmother had watched her make that perfume and then congratulated her on the result. That wasn't something that happened often. Yet, that perfume no longer smelled like her own.

She was the one who had made it, yes, and she had personally selected, tested and determined each one of those essences, but she was no longer the woman who'd created it. It was too soft, too sweet. It didn't have enough character, that was the problem. There was no verve in that range of gentle, soothing fragrances. This was a perfume that suited the old Elena. Now she needed something new. She wanted a perfume that reflected her needs, her taste. The thought of creating a new one made her happy, and it swept away the last vestiges of her unpleasant conversation with Matteo.

She looked in the mirror again, and picked up her keys. As she made her way up the stairs, she thought about the father of her child. No, she decided: Matteo might be the biological father, but the child didn't belong to him any more. He'd rejected it, and that was the final word on the subject. She would remove every trace of him from her life, and the baby would be hers and hers alone.

It was funny how history was repeating itself. She hadn't known her own father either. Susanna had never told her who he was, and in the end Elena had stopped asking. Maybe he was a perfumier, too. It was possible; her mother had a lot of colleagues. Maurice wasn't the only one Susanna had lived with, but he was the one she'd married. If she really tried, rummaging deep in her earliest memories, Elena could remember at least another two. She'd forgotten their names; they were mere shadows from her past. She had been too little to take it all in, then.

It was possible that her mother had never told her anything because she was ashamed of being foolish enough to get pregnant by a man she didn't love. Much how Elena was feeling right now.

How on earth had she managed to spend so long with someone who thought only of himself? That phone call was so absurd that she had to laugh. Sometimes you have to laugh or you'll cry. That was one of her grandmother's favourite sayings, and until now Elena hadn't realized just how perceptive Lucia Rossini had been to see that Matteo was a real idiot.

As for herself, she was adamant that the telephone call absolved her of any obligation. She'd done her duty and that was it. The pact she'd made with Cail was to tell Matteo about the pregnancy, not convince him to take any responsibility for it.

She put on her jacket and closed the door to the apartment, slamming it a little bit louder than she needed to. She was about to go up to Cail's when, standing on the first step, she changed her mind and went out into the courtyard, deciding that she needed to be by herself.

It was very cold that night and everything was dark. A few beams of light were reflected in the dusting of snow on the ground. Nothing silences a place quite like snow. Life itself seemed suspended: sounds, smells, even time. Everything was black and grey, soft and delicate.

With her arms wrapped around her chest, Elena thought again how much her life had changed, and in such a short space of time; how much she herself had changed. Her thoughts slid deeper inward, guided by a place in her soul that called to them.

She was about to become a mother. Maybe then she would be able to understand Susanna, to finally understand why she had abandoned her own daughter. But then her old resentment came to the fore, chasing that notion away. There was nothing *to* understand, she thought bitterly. *She* would never give up her baby. She hugged her belly instinctively, as if to protect the tiny being inside. The truth was: her mother had made a choice that did not include her.

Elena started walking, the snow crunching under her black leather boots – high heels, a present from Monique to celebrate the happy news. Cail had given her a rose plant – one of his first creations, he told her. Its name was Baby, and Elena looked after it as best she could, afraid that her inexperience would have fatal consequences for this beautiful plant. At first, sceptical about keeping it in the house, she'd put it by the window, so that it could get as much light as possible. Outside, it would have lain dormant as it was already late autumn, but Elena hoped that, by keeping it sheltered, it might still flower for a little longer. She'd read in several places that roses continue to grow, even in the winter months – of course, probably not at that latitude, but she still wanted to try.

Her by no means green fingers had picked up every book they could find on rose cultivation. She didn't want to run the risk of killing Cail's creation, which he had entrusted to her in what she considered a moment of extreme recklessness; nor did she want to pester him with a thousand questions. Baby had a complex perfume: it was fruity, plant-like, but there were chypre notes in the *mélange*. In the afternoon, the heat helped the flowers to exude their fragrance, and the petals smelled different. Perfume was at the heart of these roses; the brightly coloured petals, from the amber edges to the bright pink bases, seemed to diffuse the essence everywhere. From time to time Elena would talk to the plant. She'd read that establishing a dialogue was important for a plant's well-being. In general, she made sure she was alone before she started one of her monologues, but increasingly she'd stopped caring and, if she had something to say to the plant, she just came out with it. As much as she hated to admit it, her old fear of being alone had resurfaced and it kept her awake at night.

She carried on walking until she reached the hedge, her eyes fixed on its frozen branches pointing up towards the sky. The previous morning, she'd seen one of the roses planted nearby crystallized in a thin casing of ice. It was red and beautiful. It seemed to her that the frost, so unusual for the time of year, might have saved the rose from its fate of decay – but instead it had ripped out the flower's heart, freezing its perfume. All that remained was a set of scarlet petals, which in the first rays of autumn sunlight would scatter on to the stone floor, helpless, devoid of their essence.

She was staring at the rose when she noticed him. She didn't hear him arrive as much as feel his presence.

'You'll get cold,' Cail said. A moment later he wrapped his jacket around her. The warmth enveloped her like a cocoon. Elena tilted her head and closed her eyes. Then she straightened up.

'What about you?' she asked.

He shrugged. 'I'm not cold.' He was never cold. Elena smiled and pulled the jacket tighter.

'I called Matteo,' she announced, out of the blue. She wanted Cail to understand, to know what it had taken.

'When is he coming?'

Elena turned to face him. 'Never,' she said. 'His new girl-friend is expecting a baby – they're getting married soon.'

'What the hell? Is he crazy?'

Elena looked away. She didn't want to see the pity in Cail's eyes. She wouldn't be able to endure it. Despite everything she'd said, everything she'd done, and the control she thought she had regained, her emotions were gathering in strength and threatening to overwhelm her. She wouldn't be able to keep it together much longer.

'It's funny, don't you think? I mean, all that time trying to have a baby and nothing ever happened. And then . . .' Her voice cracked. She swallowed and took a deep breath. 'This child is mine, Cail. Just mine. I'm not asking for anyone's help. I will raise it, do you understand?'

She felt him come closer, ready to console her. She waited for him to touch her, but Cail didn't even brush against her. Elena looked down at her toes. He'd surprised her again. He was always surprising her.

'There are special nights, when it's almost completely dark, when if you're lucky, you can see stars that are usually invisible. Shall we go and find out whether this is one of those nights?'

She closed her eyes, taking in the sound of Cail's slightly anxious voice. He was on the way back from his evening run. He was the only man she knew who went running at night, in the dark. 'Yes, I'd really like that,' she whispered.

Now he was right behind her. Cail wrapped his arms around her, and they stayed like that for a moment, the desire flowing between them, each a prisoner to their own fears, the words they hadn't had the courage to say . . . but still unable to let go and give up what little they had.

When Cail kissed her hair, Elena closed her eyes, abandoning herself completely. Her half-closed lips let out a muffled groan, almost a prayer. He turned her to face him and Elena stood on the tips of her toes, lacing her arms around his neck. Cail leaned down towards her, slowly, giving her all the time she needed. He could have held back. He could have.

First Elena felt his warm breath and then a gentle touch on her face. He continued to stroke her skin delicately, but when Elena grabbed his sweater, pulling him towards her, he embraced her, lifting her up. Elena buried her fingers in his hair and Cail kissed her the way he'd wanted to, the way he'd been imagining for days.

They went up to Cail's apartment and, while he took a shower, she decided to wait for him in the greenhouse. She hardly knew anything about him, about his work, about how he lived his life. She realized then that she was at the centre of their story. Cail always kept himself on the sidelines.

'One-year-old seedlings,' he said shortly afterwards, when he joined her.

Elena was leaning over a pot sprouting tiny pale green leaves with jagged edges. They were adorable, so small and pretty.

'They're beautiful,' she whispered.

'Every one of those is a hope. If they survive, they could become a special rose – perfect, even.'

Elena raised her eyebrows. 'The Perfect Rose . . . that's quite a title.'

Cail slipped his hands into his jeans pockets. 'Imagine a red rose: extraordinary, bright colours, strong petals, resistant to disease, with an intense perfume of fruit and spices.' He looked at her. 'That's every rose-breeder's dream.'

'But you've created so many roses like that,' Elena replied.

Cail shook his head. 'Not really. Lots of them are barely passable – and there are no red ones. But I've got a couple of two-year-old plants. I might get lucky.'

'Is this where you work?' she asked, curious, casting a look around.

'Yes.' He leaned over a pot and tore out a few blades of grass. 'The real laboratory is near Avignon, down in Provence. Here I have the plants I'm working on for the competition.'

'For roses?'

He nodded. 'It's more than a competition, really. It's a show open to people in the trade: breeders, sellers. There are some keen gardeners, too. During the gala evening, the last night of the fair, there's a prize for the rose that best meets the criteria for quality, beauty and perfume. The international competition for new roses, the Concours de Bagatelle, is held at the beginning of June.'

Her baby would be born around that time, Elena thought. 'Will you enter?'

Cail looked at her. 'Yes, it's a very important event.'

She started to wonder. 'How come you decided to live in Paris if your business is in Provence?'

'Because Paris is where most of our clients live, or have

their offices. And I like the city. Come on, let's go inside, it's freezing,' he said, walking over to take her hand. It was true, it was really cold; but Elena had the feeling that Cail didn't like talking about himself – and that filled her with questions.

Jacques knocked at Monique's door and waited. He could have got in anyway. Despite what he'd let her believe, he still had a copy of the keys, and he used them regularly. He did it when she wasn't at home. He never touched anything, he just looked at her belongings, breathed in the perfume she left on the sheets, like a love-struck fool.

One minute, two, three, five. Jacques smiled, then murmured, 'I know you're in there, *mon amour*. Open the door, I'm not going anywhere.'

A sharp click, then the lock turned three times and Monique appeared.

'Close it,' she snapped, heading back into the lounge.

How did she manage to look so beautiful in a baggy old jumper and a pair of knee-high socks? Legs, Jacques decided. It was all down to those legs that went on for ever.

'Isn't it a bit late for house calls?' she asked coldly.

Jacques ignored her hostility. 'How are you? I haven't heard from you for a while.'

Monique just gave him an icy glare, picked up her book and opened it where she'd left off.

'You don't answer my calls, or my messages. Are you too busy, or maybe it's something else?' he said, getting closer. 'Is Le Notre taking up all your time? Tell me, *chérie*, can he satisfy you like I used to?'

He watched her tense up, take the blow and let it wash over her. With his heart in his mouth he waited for a smile; watched the anger disappear under her fierce self-control, the very thing that was keeping her away from him. Yes, this woman was a fighter. And he wanted every bit of her, every breath, every thought.

'Go to hell, Jacques,' Monique replied. She smiled at him and he felt a pang of lust. The game had begun, and this time he had no intention of losing. He joined her on the sofa, where she was curled up. He took off his jacket, then his tie. He unbuttoned his shirt and removed the solid gold cufflinks, letting them fall on to the rug, without ever taking his eyes off her.

Monique was mesmerised; she wanted him desperately – but that didn't mean she was going to give in. She stood up, because she'd never resist Jacques if he got any closer. And he had exactly what he wanted written all over his face.

He grabbed her arm, stopping her from moving away.

'I've had enough of your games. I've done what you wanted, I even hired your friend, now I want what I'm owed.'

'You're the one who should be paying me, Jacques. Elena is an incredible perfumier. Tell me, are you still keeping her out of the laboratory? Are you really so scared of having your mediocrity exposed by a woman?'

She said it to hurt him, yet when she saw the flash of pain in his eyes, she wanted to take back every word. But it was too late. Jacques stretched his lips into a kind of fierce smile. He pulled her to him, pressing her against his chest, then he ran his fingers through her hair, coiling it in his hand, his lips a breath away from hers.

'She's not that good, according to what Philippe tells me. She hasn't even made a decent sale. I think *you* should give *me* compensation.'

'That's not true,' Monique protested. 'Elena told me everything was going well.'

But Jacques pressed his lips to hers, preventing her from saying any more.

'I don't give a damn about that woman. I want you, do you understand?'

'Get lost, Jacques. Go back to your wife-to-be. How long till the wedding now?'

He ignored the provocation. He wasn't going to waste the time they had, talking about another woman. 'It's a business arrangement. You're different,' he replied.

'Yes, I'm the one you want to screw.'

'Precisely.'

She slapped him across the face, but Jacques blocked her other hand, twisting it behind her back.

'Let go of me,' she snarled.

'Only if you calm down.'

Monique struggled and he released one of her arms, holding her tightly by the other.

'Why are you resisting me?' he whispered.

Monique said bitterly, 'Let go of me, Jacques. Let go and get out of here. Go back to that girl and stay there. It's her turn. You've made your choice, now go away.'

'No, you'll never be free of me. We're the same, Monique. We were made for each other,' he breathed.

She closed her eyes, feeling that familiar sense of shame and pity. But then he started to caress her again. His lips were soft on her skin, and warm. And she'd needed him more than anything in these long, lonely days. When Jacques picked her up and carried her towards the bed, Monique buried her face in his chest.

14

Angelica: self-knowledge. Angels' grass, a captivatingly sweet,
*   honeyed perfume.*
The fragrance awakens the hidden essence of everything.
Promotes self-awareness. A remedy for all ills.

'You're wearing a different perfume,' Cail noted. 'Is it new?'

Elena reached over to take another pastry from the tray in the middle of the coffee table.

'No, I made it a couple of years ago. But I need to adjust it – it's not right for me any more.' She made herself comfortable on the sofa next to Cail, pulled the warm coverlet across, and went back to reading Beatrice's diary. Despite being almost four hundred years old, the little book was in surprisingly good condition. After reading it, every Rossini had always kept it wrapped in a cinnamon-scented silk cloth. For a while now, Elena had been wanting to go over a few passages in the diary, and tonight was perfect: it was freezing cold outside, and they were staying in.

'Have you changed that much?' asked Cail, setting down the botany journal he had in his hand.

'You're the most perceptive man I know. Yes, I've changed a lot.'

'What were you like before?'

She gave it some thought and then smiled. 'Stupid.'

The word came out so spontaneously, so sincerely that Cail couldn't help but laugh. That throaty sound, so instinctive and unexpected, soared above the silence in the room. Elena looked at him, enthralled. Cail very rarely smiled, but when he did it seemed as though he'd never had a care in the world.

Elena felt the urge to run her fingers through his hair, to caress the scar that ran down his cheek, to kiss it, to hold him close and smell his perfume.

Then she remembered the baby, and her plans for the future. And the spell was broken. However much she liked Cail, she didn't want to complicate what was already a delicate situation; she'd decided that on the night of their first kiss.

'I'm serious,' she said. She closed the book, stood up and put it on the table.

The Marais apartment had changed drastically since her arrival in Paris. Cail had decided that a place with such history and character should be restored to its original glory. Monique had pointed out that even in its finest days the ground-floor room had never been more than a basic shelter for horses and carriages. But he wouldn't listen, and so, once he had permission from the Duval family and moral support from Elena – seeing as he wouldn't let her lift so much as a paint-brush – he refurbished and redecorated the whole place, from the juniper ceiling beams to the door and leaded-glass window facing the street.

It was incredible to see those wonderful exposed brick walls and think that just a couple of weeks earlier they were buried under several layers of mouldy plaster. Cail had also taken up the tiles, revealing the original grey stone floor. He'd treated it with special oils until it shone like pewter. The first time she saw it after the restoration, Elena was lost for words.

They'd bought the sofas at the Porte de Vanves market, one of the city's oldest and most authentic antiques markets (or flea markets, as Monique put it). Cail had bought two prints and a Tiffany lamp, Monique a weeping fig which, according to her, was in desperate need of someone to talk to.

'Why stupid?' Cail asked. He'd stood up, too, now and was watching her closely.

'Because that's how I acted: stupidly.' Elena smiled, then her expression turned serious. 'I don't know how to explain it to you. Look . . . it's something I only realized a while ago. Now I take each day as it comes; everything I do is new – it's as if I'm doing it for the first time. It must be because of the baby . . .' she said, pensive. 'Maybe Jasmine's right when she says a mother takes on her children's personalities and their tastes. Do you know, when she was pregnant with Monique she couldn't stand strawberries? She only started eating them again after she was born. And Monie never liked them, even as a child. Yep, I bet it's the little one interfering with my choices.' She thought about it then she looked over at Cail. 'Stop laughing.'

'I'm not laughing at you.'

'But you are laughing,' she said, standing with her hands on her hips.

'Because I like what I see.'

Elena stopped. 'There! You see? You say things like that to me and I . . . I ask myself why I ever wasted my time with

Matteo when I could have spent it with you. And I don't even know why I was like that for so long. I hate it and I can't stop thinking about it.'

Cail walked over to her and took her hand. 'Come and sit back down. We can talk about it, if you want to.'

Elena let herself be convinced, because she knew that talking to Cail always did her good. He listened properly and he helped her overcome her obstacles. Once they were sitting together on the sofa, under the coverlet, they looked at one another. Then he started to kiss her; his lips brushing hers, gentle but determined, and increasingly so, as though every time they shared a kiss the bond between them got stronger. But despite that, he never went any further.

Elena, though, drew him to her chest. When he kissed her neck she melted into his caresses; they were more confident now, more possessive.

Suddenly, Cail pulled away from her. Every time it was harder to stop. He wanted her more than he'd ever wanted anyone. He knew that she wanted him, too, Cail could feel it in every bit of his body. But once they had been together, when their relationship changed, what would happen then? The baby would arrive, and a whole stack of problems along with it. Sure, Elena said she would never go back to her ex, but what if she changed her mind after the birth? That thought drove Cail crazy. He didn't want to let go of her, but he couldn't cross the boundary they'd set.

Damn it, he cursed in his head. Cail held her again, tenderly this time, resting his forehead on hers, his heart pounding beneath the palm of her hand. Elena looked and saw that his expression had hardened, as though he regretted losing control. He probably did. Instinctively, she wriggled free. Cail immediately let her go and she took the chance to stand up.

She kept forgetting she was a pregnant woman; pregnant by somebody else, she reminded herself with a hint of bitterness. And she knew from experience how unsettling that could be for a man. Oh, she knew! An image of Maurice flashed through her mind, but she dispelled it. Cail was nothing like Maurice. There was no chance he would behave like her stepfather. He was there, wasn't he? With her. He could have left whenever he wanted; there was nothing between them, no promises, no obligations. Yet there he was. He was always there. Besides, he acted completely differently. Cail had never forced or persuaded her to do anything she didn't want to do. He talked to her openly . . . when he did actually talk.

She sighed. Then she realized that however sure she was about Cail, there was always a doubt – a subtle, intangible doubt. After all, Elena didn't know how charming Maurice had been with her mother. She'd only seen the worst side of their relationship. Even if Cail was interested in her, what if he didn't want the baby?

She brushed her hair back with her fingers, feeling a sudden urgent need to talk to her mother. As strange as it sounded, Susanna was the only person who would understand. They were both in love with a man who wasn't the father of their child. But was it love that she felt for Cail? Elena had no idea. After Matteo, she was being very careful when it came to putting her feelings on the line. And then there was the baby to think about.

'Come back over here,' Cail said, patting the sofa beside him.

She was tempted to refuse, or much worse, maybe even ask him to leave. But that wasn't what she really wanted.

'Let's talk for a bit, OK?' he suggested again. 'Or do you

want me to leave?' Cail's question broke the tense silence that had settled over them like a heavy cloak.

'No.'

'So, come over here, let's sit down and talk.'

'I don't think so. I don't want to talk about . . .'

'About us?' Cail asked.

Elena nodded, her eyes glued to the floor. She wasn't ready to define this thing between them – not yet, and not right then, not when she was so close to bursting into tears.

'OK. We don't have to. Let's not argue.' Cail's voice was more relaxed now, more amenable. He took a lilac *macaron* from the tray, Elena's favourite, and held it out to her.

'Peace-offering?'

She fought back the tears and an involuntary smile. 'You're terrible,' she told him. But she took it and bit into it, savouring the delicious blackcurrant cream. 'I'm not doing this for you,' she continued, wagging a finger at him. 'We're making up because of the cakes. Seeing as you brought them, I wouldn't want you to take them away again.'

He didn't reply, but as he tucked a lock of hair behind her ear, his touch was warm, gentle.

'One question each?' she suggested.

Cail thought for a moment. 'All right, but I go first.' He paused. 'You once told me you had two wishes: one was the baby . . . what's the other?'

Elena licked her lips. 'Is there an alternative question?'

'No, but you don't have to answer if you don't want to.' His voice was low and serious.

With a deep sigh, Elena tried to explain herself better. 'It's not that simple. And it's not that I don't want to answer, but it involves you. I can't reveal my plan. I have to play my cards right, don't you think? Come on, ask me another question,' she said, waving her hand at him again.

Cail seemed surprised. He held her to him again and kissed her, his hands in her hair. Then he pulled away, as though he'd been overcome by an irrepressible urge and then regretted it. He cleared his throat and a moment later he picked up the conversation. 'OK, another question. Let's see . . . Do you miss Italy? Do you want to go back?'

Still thrown by the kiss, Elena shook her head, as though it would order her thoughts.

'I like Paris,' she said. 'I think it's one of the most beautiful cities in the world – I feel I can say that, even if I haven't visited them all. You know, when I was little, my mother moved around all the time, before she settled in Grasse. I saw Bombay, Cairo, Tokyo, New York . . . She went anywhere they needed her skills as a perfumier. And I went with her. I've visited more playgrounds and zoos than you can imagine. When I went out with the nannies, I took it all in. There were places I liked, where I felt at home, and others that frightened me, even though they were beautiful. A place is like a perfume, like a dress, you have to try it on to understand whether it suits you.' She paused. 'Paris, the Marais, the Île de la Cité, they're all places I like.'

'So you won't go back to Florence?'

'For a visit, every now and again, yes. To see the house. You know, that's another thing I can't understand. Before, I hated the place; now there are moments, especially at night, when I wish I was there. Maybe it's because of what it represents, because of its past. Everything my grandmother taught me is there, everything that was created and left by the women in my family. You should see the laboratory: there are glazed porcelain jars taller than me. They're amazing.

216

Every room has antique furniture, and an old oil lamp.'

'Like that one?' Cail asked, pointing to a glass vase with a candle burning under a little plate that was giving off a light, aromatic perfume.

'Yes. My grandmother always used the same oils: orange for happiness, sage to combat confusion and doubt, mint to stimulate the imagination, lavender for purification. The perfumes are all over the furniture now – it all smells as if it has herbs, flowers and fruit stuck to it. When I came from Florence, I slipped that one into my suitcase, along with a few essences.'

'I really like this perfume.'

'Jasmine and two drops of helichrysum,' she explained.

'It's very stimulating,' Cail went on, half-smiling.

Elena blushed. When she had measured out the jasmine, she'd had an intimate atmosphere in mind. Taking a deep breath, she tried to pick up where she'd left off. 'On the ground floor, there's the old perfume store. There's a fresco on the ceiling. When you look up, it's as if you're looking at a meadow full of flowers and angels, and in one corner, a little out of the way, there's a man and a woman. They're holding hands and walking towards an arch of roses. It's really striking. There's also a huge screen in the corner of the room: if you open it up, it turns into a little house – the perfect hiding-place.'

'Is that where you used to go when you were up to something?'

She nodded. 'I was a terrible disappointment to my grand-mother. I used to make her really angry. Some days we got on and everything seemed to be going well. And she was happy. But there were times when I hated her. So then I mixed up perfumes, ruined compositions, refused to study, refused to speak to her.'

'You really were a terrible child.' Cail laughed, but soon his happiness turned into bitter reflection. He understood the young Elena's anger, how overwhelmingly powerless you feel at that age. Cail himself often used to get angry, especially when his father, Angus McLean, would disappear. His mother, Elizabeth, stayed on her own with him and his little sister to look after the business. Somewhere deep inside, he could still hear his mother's stifled sobs. He'd even tried to ruin his own father's work: one of their best roses was actually the result of his attempt to sabotage a seed.

'Your roots are in that house, Elena,' he said now. 'It's normal for you to feel attached to it.'

She shrugged. 'It would be normal, if I hadn't hated every minute I spent there.'

Cail looked into the distance. 'Hate is a very complicated emotion. We hate the things we intensely desire but can't have. We hate what we don't understand, things that seem too different. Hate and love are too close; their edges get blurred – they don't have clear boundaries.'

Elena stared at him. 'I'd never thought about it like that.'

'Why did you hate that house?'

'My mother left me there. She told me it was for my own good, that I'd be better off with my grandmother. They were excuses – she just wanted to get rid of me. The truth was, Maurice hated me and she wanted to start a new life without another man's kid under her feet.'

'Your grandmother . . . she never hurt you?' His voice was low and serious, his eyes solemn.

Elena shook her head. 'My grandmother loved me very much, albeit in her own way. You know she used to come into my room at night? She'd wait for me to fall asleep, then come in and sit by my bed. After a few minutes, she'd get up, give me a kiss, and go back downstairs. That's the only affection she ever showed me. During the day, though, she talked to me as if I was an adult. She had no time for mistakes, but she respected me.'

The feeling came back with the memories, little incidents that popped into her mind like lost objects she thought had disappeared without a trace. She'd forgotten how much her grandmother's respect had mattered to her.

'Whenever I said something – especially if it was something to do with perfume – she'd stop, put down whatever she was doing and listen to me. She wanted me to go beyond the concept of perfume, beyond the fragrance itself. She wanted me to look for the perfume in my mind, to find it in my heart. She said perfume was the way, the path to a deeper understanding, an understanding of the soul. She insisted that words, images, sounds and even taste could be misleading, but never smell: "it transcends everything else".'

She paused; in her mind she could still hear Lucia Rossini's exact words. They were as vivid now as they were then, deeply engraved on her memory.

'*The smell, the perfume, enters you, because you invite it in with your breath, then it follows its own path. You can't decide whether you're going to like it or not, because it travels in another dimension. It's not a matter of logic or reason. It will take you over, demanding the absolute truth. You'll love it, or it will disgust you. But nothing in your life will be as genuine as that first emotion. Because that response comes from your soul.*'

Cail stroked her hand. 'What else?'

Elena turned to him. 'In the shop she followed rituals that were generations old. She wouldn't even hear of changing our techniques or instruments. For her, there was only what

219

she'd learned; nothing else. She was obsessed. Like my mother, like Beatrice. Like all those women.'

'Your mother . . . is that why she left? Your grandmother wouldn't let her run the business?'

Elena sighed. She didn't like talking about the past. Yet, as she told all this to Cail, the bitter taste of her lonely childhood began to fade. She welcomed that sensation with a hint of surprise. She could bear it now. It was as though by drawing it out, showing it to someone, it had lost its intensity.

Elena focused. She wanted to be clear, to get it right.

'No. My mother wasn't interested in that kind of perfumery; she didn't believe in it. She wanted to travel, see the world. My mother loved anything modern. According to her, the future of perfumery was chemistry, synthesis. She said Beatrice's perfume would be good for nothing nowadays. Too antiquated, too different. My grandmother, on the other hand, thought the exact opposite. For her, Beatrice's Perfect Perfume was special: it was the concentration of ideas, sensations and emotions from previous generations, the things that reside in our family memory and are passed down together with genetic heritage. A sort of olfactory code. Beatrice's perfume would always be relevant, she believed, because it was the human soul. It was love, hope, generosity, value, trust – all the good the human race knew and had produced.'

'Utopia?'

Elena shook her head again. 'It's not impossible, you know. It's true that perfume is subjective, but a fire smells of heat, comfort, danger, action, and it's the same for everyone. Just like rain means hope and the future. For some people, it can also represent anguish, but it's always synonymous with abundance. Then there's the smell of the sea, wheat, wood . . . I could go on for hours. Smells, whether good or bad, are processed by the brain instinctively, before the conscious mind is aware. And smells trigger a reaction that comes from the most ancient part of our soul.'

'And what do *you* think?'

Elena shrugged. 'I just know it was perfume that took them away from me. Both of them.'

Cail hugged her, hoping he could banish the grief her whispered words revealed. He wanted to ask her about Susanna – he had a feeling she was the key to the worst of Elena's pain. But he sensed she was too upset to talk about that right now. So he searched deep inside himself for the right words, and he found them in what they shared, that mixture of love and hate that he'd felt towards his father when he was a boy, and had grown out of in later life.

'Maybe it's even more complicated than that,' he said gently. 'From what you've told me, from what you've become and from what you're doing, perfume could be the thing that brings you together.'

The thing that brings you together. Instinctively, Elena flinched at those words. Then, while Cail told her about how cross-breeding roses was the only thing he had in common with his father, she considered what he had said from all angles, the way you approach a potentially dangerous stretch of water, one you have to cross at any cost to reach the other side. Eventually, she realized it was true. However determined she was to believe otherwise, perfume *was* probably the one thing she had in common with her mother and grandmother.

At that moment, she thought of something Monique had once said – that it was Susanna and Lucia's obsession, the influence perfume had over their lives, that led Elena to reject perfume. That was why she'd pushed it out of her own life. But perfume was a part of her. Slowly, patiently, and in spite

221

of her efforts, it had found its way back to her and drawn her in.

'What if *I* neglect my baby, too?' she said in anguish. 'What if *I* abandon it for this foolish obsession? What if *I* don't have time?'

There, he'd finally got her to say it, Cail thought. At last Elena had revealed what was really tormenting her.

'You could deal with it head on, without going round the houses.' Like you do with everything else, Cail thought.

Elena scowled. 'What do you mean?'

'Open your own shop, make your own perfumes, look for the lost formula. But make sure you're in control. It's all right there in front of you. Choose. Make it your own choice.'

Elena heaved another sigh. 'One day, maybe. Now, I need to think about the baby.'

'What's stopping you doing both?' Cail wanted to know.

Well, what was stopping her? 'I don't know. I'm not sure.'

'Have faith in yourself.'

'It's not just that. It costs a lot to open a shop. And you need a sponsor, someone to introduce you to the right people, to get you into distribution channels, and that's not even the biggest obstacle.'

Secretly amused, Cail asked, 'And what would that be?'

Elena looked him in the eye. 'Do you know how it works? How you go about making a perfume?'

Cail shook his head. 'Only when it comes to roses, but I don't think that counts.'

Elena snuggled into his arms and rested her chin on his chest. 'It starts with an idea. It could be an event, a dream, a walk . . . you see, a perfume is like a story, it's a way of communicating – although it's more subtle, more immediate. Once you've established the brief – that's what it's called

– you can choose the essences. I feel them all: they turn into colours, emotions, they overwhelm me, possess me. I can't stop thinking about the perfume until it's finished.'

Silence.

'It's amazing,' Cail said quietly, 'the things you say, who you are, the passion you put into your work – that's not an obstacle, that's a real gift. You're a very special woman.'

He spoke from the heart, and every word expressed his admiration, respect and consideration. This was the moment Elena really began to fall in love with him.

Paris glittered like magic in November. By now, Elena was used to the tall houses with their sloping roofs and skylights that caught the sun's rays, reflecting them on to passers-by. She knew the parks and local markets. She walked around with Cail, exploring ice rinks, museums with paintings, furniture and jewellery – and one very special place that housed all the perfumes in the world.

The Osmothèque museum, located in the heart of Versailles, was an archive of more than 1800 fragrances, some of them otherwise extinct, others that hailed the end of an olfactory era and the start of a new one. Cail had smelled Hungarian Queen, from 1815, used by Napoleon Bonaparte, and he liked it. Elena had introduced him to Coty's Chypre, then they discovered the sensual Mitsouko, created in 1919 by Jacques Guerlain, and the more recent Shalimar. Based on an iris and vanilla blend called Guerlinade, this perfume evoked the famous Shalimar Gardens, an Indian prince's homage to the memory of his beloved. It was incredible to think a perfume like that could be the result of an accident: a small vial of vanilla was accidentally poured into a bottle of Jicky and the result formed the base for Shalimar.

The museum was also home to Chanel N° 5, created in 1921. On their tour, they chanced upon Joy by Jean Patou, created by Henri Alméras. It was, in its day, one of the most expensive perfumes in absolute form: it needed in excess of ten thousand jasmine flowers and three hundred roses to make just thirty millilitres of fragrance. Launched after the war, it became a symbol of luxury and revenge.

Alongside these famous perfumes, there were also some ancient fragrances: the 'Regal Perfume' created in first-century Rome, Queen of Hungary's Water from the fourth century, and scents made from recipes handed down by Pliny the Elder. In 1927 Madame Lanvin, from the perfume house of the same name, gave her daughter, Marguerite, a delicate floral perfume with classic top notes: neroli, peach, a heart of rose, jasmine, lily-of-the-valley, ylang-ylang, and finally sandalwood, vanilla, tuberose and vetiver. The perfume was a gift for the girl's thirteenth birthday, an elaborate composition prepared by two of the great names of that time: André Fraysse and Paul Vacher. The girl named it Arpège. On the apple-shaped bottle was the house logo: the image of a woman dancing with a little girl.

What surprised Elena more, though was that the list of perfumiers' names included Giulia Rossini, one of her relatives. Her ancestor had been an expert perfumier, one of the best – and of her prolific repertoire, the Osmothèque had kept Enchanted Garden, a perfume Elena knew well, and which Lucia had often cited as a point of reference. It was a delicate fragrance, but at the same time very confident. There was orange flower, angelica and tuberose; then rosewood, cedar, myrtle, and finally amber. Knowing that it had been created by a Rossini, seeing it there alongside the most important fragrances in the history of perfume, filled Elena with happiness and pride. The affinity that she felt when she recognized it had given her a warm glow. She was one of them, a Rossini. Enchanted Garden, as it was first released: it was marvellous. Smelling it, imagining the feelings, the emotions that led her ancestor to create that fragrance was a real highlight of her day.

15

Thyme: clarity. Energizing, invigorating.
The fragrance dispels confusion and opens the mind to logic.
Deciphers the uncertainty of dreams. Restores mental stability.

Since she had started taking her vitamins, Elena had been feeling better; even the sickness had passed. Her pregnancy had turned into something that filled her with wonder and fear in equal measure. She would start talking to the baby, then stop and listen, almost as though she expected a response. It was still too early to feel it move – the doctor had told her that wouldn't happen until the fifth month – but Elena didn't care, she knew her child could hear her. Talking to the baby had become vital to her. Susanna had never talked to her much, and that always saddened her. She was going to be different, Elena vowed: she would tell her child everything.

She started out with short phrases, then moved on to whole conversations and real secrets. At last, Elena had someone to confide in.

'Who were you talking to?' Cail asked one morning, as he came into the apartment.

'The baby, of course.'

He stared at her and then, without saying a word, went over to give her a hug. He liked touching her, holding her close to him, keeping her safe. It was something he couldn't understand, this attachment: but he had a bad feeling about it. *Look at the past*, he reminded himself bitterly: it was best to bear that in mind.

The pain was still there. If he thought about it, if he looked for it, he could find it – and with it, memories of the young love that had come to a tragic end. He shouldn't be throwing himself into a complicated relationship, and with Elena things would certainly be complicated. He'd even thought about leaving. But he couldn't; it was a matter of honour. And Elena needed someone to take her out, someone to make her laugh.

He asked her to go and get ready, trying to restore a bit of normality, create some distance. He took her to the flower-market to pick up the rosehips that were waiting for him, the ones that would produce the seeds for his new plants.

Elena loved the market, the flowers, the perfumes, and the respect everyone had for Cail. All apart from the woman who served them, who was apparently called Liliane. She was constantly smiling and flirting. Elena hadn't warmed to her at all.

Everything in Elena's life seemed to be going well now. Even at Narcissus things had improved. Philippe had never properly apologized for his appalling behaviour, but he'd kept his distance and let Claudine deal with her. Fortunately, shortly after that nasty little episode, Philippe had to go away for a while. Montier wanted to open a branch in London and he needed Philippe to handle the logistics and find suitable premises.

★ ★ ★

It was almost closing time when Adeline Binoche came into the shop, followed by a woman in her fifties with very short red hair and an intense expression. She reminded Elena of summer: bright and golden. A hint of bergamot, freshly dried hay lying in the sun, and wildflowers.

'Do you remember my sister-in-law?' Adeline asked with her usual friendly smile. 'I told you about her the last time I came in.'

'Of course, *madame*. Geneviève, isn't it?' Thank goodness the woman had an unusual name, Elena thought with a hint of relief. She had no memory for people's names, perhaps because she could remember their perfume perfectly.

Adeline Binoche, for example, smelled of vanilla, with middle notes of rose and oak moss. Composed, sharp and lively. The fragrance suited her, Elena thought. Clean and clear, no compromises. Just as direct as that look of hers.

'Geneviève Binoche,' the woman said, holding out her hand. 'I've heard a lot about you. May I call you Elena?'

'Yes, of course.'

'Great,' said Geneviève. She was sophisticated, elegant, and she had a very frank, straightforward manner. 'I hope you'll be able to help me. I need a perfume – the perfume of Notre-Dame.'

Elena felt a quiver of a laugh in the back of her throat, but she forced herself to contain it. If Claudine managed to stay serious when faced with similarly absurd requests, it must be possible.

'In the metaphorical sense, you mean?'

Geneviève shook her head. 'No, literary. I need to smell something that will inspire me, give me a sign. I'm writing a book about Victor Hugo's *Notre-Dame de Paris – The Hunchback of Notre-Dame* – and I want it to be different to

228

anything that has come before. Hugo wrote a wonderful work that brought together the sacred and the profane . . . Good and bad, beauty and ugliness. I want a perfume that does all of that. That is as big and solid as Notre-Dame, that has the cathedral's purity, together with Esmeralda's innocence and sensual vitality. I need something that can evoke Phoebus's cruelty, Frollo's madness and, most of all, Quasimodo's unique, all-consuming love.'

Everything went silent for a moment. It was the concept of life itself, Elena thought. Life in the most profound sense of the word.

'I'm wondering what could come out of a combination of perfume and literature,' Geneviève continued. 'The story stirs the imagination, and that means also stirring your sense of sight, sound and touch. Music, melody, that's all very well, but what if we could turn these concepts into a smell? In reality, Notre-Dame has its own perfume: incense, candles, antiquity, that nice musty smell of centuries gone by, the glaze that millions of breaths have put on the statues. The perfume would bring together all the senses to create a three-dimensional impression.'

Something similar had been tried before. Perfumes had been inspired by paintings. Laura Tonatto, the famous Italian perfumier, had come up with the idea when she saw Artemisia Gentileschi's *Aurora*, and then decided to create the fragrance evoked by Caravaggio's *Lute Player*. It was a great way to draw the viewer into the masterpiece. Make them smell it as well as see it. Elena had liked Tonatto's idea so much that a visit to the Hermitage Museum in St Petersburg, where one version of the Caravaggio is kept, had gone straight to the top of her to-do list. After all, it's quite natural to imagine the perfume of a painting, and inevitable when you see it. But the perfume of *Notre-Dame de Paris* . . . now, that was such a complicated concept, so profound that it was everything and nothing all at once.

'Tell me what you're thinking of, exactly.'

And Geneviève did. In immense detail, she described how the perfume she had in mind should show the path through different stages of life, feelings and emotions. How it should represent the complexity of the human soul.

'You realize this would take me a long time to develop.'

Geneviève nodded. 'Of course. To be honest, I'm not even expecting it to be a finished perfume. It could just be a selection of essences for me to smell and draw inspiration from. But if you could create a whole perfume, that would be amazing. Of course, money isn't a problem.'

'So, let's see. Give me a few days to think about it. How about we meet again next Monday?'

'That sounds like a great idea. Thank you. Here are my details.' She handed Elena a blue business card. 'Speak to you soon, I hope. This means a lot to me,' she smiled. As Geneviève and Adeline walked towards the exit, deep in animated conversation, Elena overheard Adeline say: 'What did I tell you? If there's any way to find that perfume, Elena will do it.'

If only it were that simple, she thought.

That night, if she wasn't too tired, she'd take another look at the diary. Lately she'd done nothing else. Maybe somewhere in those ancient pages she'd find a clue, a sign to follow. If she was honest, she'd never cared that much about Beatrice's famous perfume. She'd always heard about it, of course, but to her it was just a legend. She'd never really thought about it; and it was probably about time she did.

She recommended a violet-scented cream to a customer, then went to find Claudine. She'd never seen the woman laugh, and maybe Madame Binoche's request would be the thing that cracked her blank expression. She was keen to find out.

The perfume of Notre-Dame, no less . . .

As she walked down the corridor, she started to think about the idea seriously. The middle and base notes would need to come from the novel. Incense, of course, wood, and wax. The more volatile notes, though – the top notes that hit you straight away, they could correspond to what Geneviève thought of as purity, carnal instinct. White flowers, perhaps. Because yes, this perfume began with an objective vision, but obviously, the woman's feelings had to come into it, too. In the end it was a subjective concept. And that meant they would have to work together.

'I've just been commissioned to make a perfume,' she told Claudine when she went into her office, knocking politely first.

'Tell me everything.'

Elena recounted Geneviève Binoche's proposal and Claudine's smile did make a brief appearance, but was gone just as quickly, and replaced by a look of greed.

'And you're telling me she'll pay whatever price we ask?'

Elena shrugged. 'That's what she said.'

'Can you do it?'

Elena had been waiting for that question. Somewhere inside, she could feel her enthusiasm stirring. Yes, she could do it, but much more importantly, she wanted to do it.

'I can give it a go,' she said. Better to err on the side of caution, she thought, although the truth was she wanted to get straight to work; she was both fascinated and tempted by the idea.

Sitting at her desk, Claudine raised her hand and gestured

towards the seat in front of her. 'Sit down. We need to have a serious think about this. We could do it as a simple personalization.'

Elena shook her head. 'No. If I'm going to do it, I need to work from the text. I can't use a ready-made *mélange* and correct it. I need to find the right essences; only then will I be able to come up with a formula to prepare. Then I'll change all the possible variants, according to the customer's requests.'

Claudine stared at her. 'How long will it take you?'

Elena felt a flicker of happiness. Claudine was going to give her the go-ahead to make the perfume. She couldn't wait to tell Cail. A major perfume, the perfume of Notre-Dame, no less!

'At least two months, probably three.'

As Claudine counted the days on a desk diary, Elena cleared her throat.

'Yes?' The woman's voice turned cold; Claudine's rapid mood swings always made Elena feel uneasy. She should have been used to them by now, and yet they always took her by surprise.

'What if Monsieur Montier wants to take care of this perfume himself?' Elena asked.

Claudine pursed her lips. 'He's too busy at the moment. But I'll let him know. For now, just get on with the project yourself. As soon as you're ready we'll start preparing the *mélanges*.'

Elena stood up. 'Very well.'

She'd got as far as the door when Claudine called her back.

'I expect the utmost discretion from you. If this project comes off, there's a lot to be gained – both financially and in terms of reputation. The perfume of *Notre-Dame de Paris*: you realize what that could mean for us? And for you, too. Philippe will really have to eat his words, my dear.'

Elena looked away. 'Of course,' she said.

Deep in thought, she closed the door behind her and went back to work. In spite of Claudine's assurances, she couldn't shake off the feeling that something wasn't quite right; and her unease was in no small part due to the expression on her colleague's face. There was something shifty about that look . . . Whatever it was, it gave her the shivers.

Cail had to knock twice before Elena decided to open the door.

'Hi, are you all right?' he asked, studying her face.

'Why do you keep knocking when you've got keys?' Elena said irritably.

'Those are for emergencies.'

'Just another way of keeping your distance,' Elena muttered. She was in a bad mood, and trying to decipher passages from Beatrice's diary hadn't made her feel any better.

They had never discussed the need to keep their relationship within precise boundaries, but they were both trying to stick to some sort of unspoken agreement they believed was best for everyone. Every once in a while, though, Elena forgot. And he found it difficult to keep his distance when he wanted her so much. Every time he touched her he had to force himself to stop and take a step back.

He went over to her and kissed her on the lips. 'Not feeling great?'

She made a face, then said more gently, 'You smell good. I could sprinkle you with oil and distil your perfume like Grenouille, the character in Süskind's novel. I'd make a fortune, and I wouldn't have to torment myself with this diary ever again. Nostradamus made himself perfectly clear by comparison,' she joked bitterly.

He kissed her again, running his fingers through her hair and letting it fall down over her shoulders.

'Like strands of silk,' he told her, moving away a little.

Elena half-closed her eyes. 'In a book I had when I was little, the main character was a tall, dark count. He had a scar running down his face, too. And instead of spoiling his appearance, it made him devilishly handsome. I loved him. I was absolutely smitten.' She stopped and looked into his eyes. 'You've got him to thank for your success with me, you know.'

Cail smiled. 'So, come on, tell me what's wrong.'

Elena went over to the sofa, handed him the diary, and sank back into the cushions.

'OK, look – tell me if you understand any of this,' she said. 'Because I give up.'

Very carefully, Cail picked up the tiny book, opened it and frowned. 'I've only got schoolboy Italian. This bit looks difficult.'

'Not really, it's just a poem.' She held out her hand. 'Give me the diary, I'll translate it for you.' And she started to read.

> *'Rose, heaven-sent laughter of Love . . .*
> *above other flowers Lady sublime*
> *purple of gardens, splendour of meadows*
> *eye of April, jewel of spring . . .*
> *when pretty bee flies to find food,*
> *or gentle breeze blows, thou shouldst*
> *have them sip nectar from thy ruby cups*
> *a dewy, and crystal-clear drop.'*

She stopped reading. 'Apart from the quotation from *Ode To a Rose* from Giambattista Marino's *Adonis*, there's not much here you can use to make a perfume,' she commented.

'Why are you so intent on this one passage?'

'It's the only thing that could constitute a recipe. The rest, before and after, are just her observations of places and courtly life. There's another poem, also by Marino. That one's about precious stones. Then the final part of the diary is all about *him* – the man who commissioned the perfume. Beatrice stayed in his castle while she was making it, a whole spring and summer. In the autumn she went back to Italy, and a few months later she got married. It was only just before she died that she told her daughter everything and gave her the diary. But she never revealed where she'd put the formula, or the identity of the woman the perfume was made for, or the man who commissioned it. She doesn't even give the name of the castle, the family, or the village. It's a complete mystery. My grandmother spent years poring over the archives looking for the formula. She was adamant that Beatrice must have kept it somewhere. But my mother has always thought that Beatrice would have destroyed it.' Elena passed the diary to Cail.

He carried on looking through the tiny book, a thoughtful expression on his face.

'I can't help you with the text – the Italian is too archaic for me, but there are some words in Occitan, and I understand those.' He paused. 'May I make a copy?'

Elena nodded. 'Yes, why?'

'There are a couple of things I'd like to check. Have you seen the drawings?' he asked, standing up and walking over to the small desk in the corner where Elena had her computer.

'Yes. They're not alchemy symbols, I'd know those. They look like a mixture of some kind of code and just doodles, like Monie says. I thought one of the symbols was a lion's head, although to tell you the truth, it could be a wolf. It's quite stylized. But I don't think Beatrice just started scribbling because she didn't have anything better to do. I mean, it's not as if they had biros, and paper itself was a precious commodity. But I digress.' She turned her attention back to Cail. 'What are you doing? Leave the scanner, you can take the original,' she told him.

Cail hesitated. That diary had been in Elena's family for nearly four centuries; it was an extraordinary document, maybe their greatest family treasure. And she was offering it to him. He turned it over and ran the palm of his hand gently across the cover.

'After the baby's born, I'll remember this moment, and I'll make it worth your while.'

Cail's voice was low and hoarse. Elena felt every word. Her heart started to race.

'Once this baby's born, I'll make sure you do.'

Claudine saw to it that Elena focused all her energies on the Notre-Dame perfume. With Philippe out of the way and Jacques almost always in London, she'd managed to arrange things so that Elena could use the laboratory whenever she needed to do so.

Geneviève had already been back twice. The first time, she'd brought Elena an illustrated copy of Victor Hugo's *Notre-Dame de Paris*. The next time, a CD from the famous musical. Not that she needed it, seeing as Cail had managed to get hold of two tickets for the show from his friend Ben. The musical had fortunately just come back to Paris, and Elena had been desperate to see it. The three of them – herself, Cail and Geneviève – had visited the cathedral together the following Sunday. But no towers. That was another thing that would have to wait until after the baby was born. The hospital had made that very clear: no exertion. And Cail had followed the doctor's instructions to the letter. Motorbike included. When Elena saw a dark blue Citroën in Hermione's place, she was so upset that she refused to get in. Cail had to swear that he hadn't got rid of the bike; the Harley was actually safe and well. He couldn't keep it in Paris, because he didn't have two parking spaces, so he'd been forced to take it home, to Provence, where it would stay for the time being.

He was quite firm about that. There was no way he was bringing it back to Paris. *You can't put a baby seat on a Harley.* His explanation left Elena lost for words.

'So, how's it coming along?' Claudine had washed her hands before coming into the laboratory and, careful not to touch the aluminium flasks containing the essences, she went over to take a better look at the contents of the cylinder Elena had in front of her.

'I've got the top notes,' she told her, her eyes fixed on the dropper. 'And maybe the middle. But I still can't get the base.' She was pale and tense. The essences were mixed, but the combination wasn't balanced. Something was missing – she felt it instinctively. She'd concentrated hard on what colour she should be seeing, but her efforts had brought her nothing but exhaustion. Fortunately, Cail was coming to the shop to collect her later. By now she was getting tired very easily.

She rubbed her belly – she'd started to do it often now. Every day, the bump was more visible. Soon she'd have to tell Montier she was pregnant. And that was worrying her; she didn't know how he'd take it, and whether the news would have repercussions for Monique. She knew the two of them were still seeing each other, and that Monie was unhappy.

Their relationship was toxic, not least because they had to keep it a secret. If the newspapers were to be believed, Montier would soon be married.

'Let me see,' said Claudine, dipping a *mouillette* into the compound. She leaned towards it, closed her eyes and took one deep breath, then another.

She couldn't believe it. The perfume, which according to Elena was still unfinished, was one of the best compositions she'd ever smelled. It recalled the complex structure of a *chypre*, but this was something new. Harmonious, captivating – fresh, even. It was perfect. The best way she could describe it was 'just right'. She breathed in again, filling her lungs: hesperidium, definitely. But she couldn't say whether it was lemon, neroli or bergamot . . . no, it was something more delicate. She was still thinking about it when the fragrance changed, turning into a garden full of flowers at sunset. Roses made way for jasmine; it, too, disappeared, to be replaced by an earthy, musky smell. Finally, at the end of this journey of the senses, Claudine felt herself enveloped in sensual sandalwood and myrrh.

'Tell me the composition again,' she said after a few seconds.

Elena nodded. She could have read out the formula, but she preferred to go through the *mélange* in her head, dividing, sectioning and recomposing the essences one by one.

'Pink grapefruit, lavender and lime as top notes. For the middle: rose, jasmine, peach, artemisia, angelica. Finished off with myrrh, oak moss, leather and amber.'

Claudine shook her head. 'I can smell something else. Have you added a *fougère*?'

Elena nodded. 'Yes, vanilla and lavender.'

'You didn't mention that.'

Elena frowned. Claudine seemed to be interrogating her. Why was she making such a fuss when the formula was written on the pad in front of them?

'I told you, I'm still working on it. The perfume isn't ready, it's still missing the idea of the cathedral, its grandeur – and that's one of the key aspects. I need to try the blends again and replace some of the elements,' Elena said.

'*No!* It's more than perfect as it is!'

'What's wrong with you? It's certainly not perfect. You can tell that from a mile away,' Elena argued. She was starting to get really annoyed. She couldn't understand why Claudine was behaving like this.

Suddenly, the door opened and Philippe Renaud strode into the laboratory, followed by Jacques Montier.

'What is going on?' Jacques's tone shifted from surprise to outrage in the space of a second.

'Hello, I didn't know you were back already,' Elena said.

'Obviously not.' Philippe's response troubled her. The man folded his arms across his chest, an accusatory look on his face.

Elena looked at Claudine, who stood there in silence, stiff as a post. The tension in the room was palpable. A shiver of apprehension ran down her spine, intensifying the panic her colleague's behaviour had already provoked. She decided to take charge: it was best to explain everything. Perhaps Claudine hadn't told Montier they'd be researching *mélanges* that day.

'I think the perfume is missing a note,' she told him, leaning over to pick up the pad where she'd written down all of that day's steps.

'Do not touch that notebook!' Philippe yelled, reaching out.

But Claudine got there first and snatched it out of his hands. Elena instinctively recoiled, frightened.

'Have you all gone completely mad?' she demanded.

Claudine didn't respond, she just held on tight to Elena's notepad. Philippe was still glaring at Elena with contempt.

'What do you think you're doing in the laboratory? You're not authorized. How did you get in?' Montier snarled.

'Of course I'm authorized – you're the one who signed my pass.' Elena couldn't understand what was going on. She grabbed her card and showed it to him.

Jacques's face turned red with anger. 'That's fake.'

'Did you hear that, *monsieur* – what she just said to you? It's shameless! She clearly has no qualms about lying,' Philippe hissed. By this point he was purple in the face. 'Wanted to steal the formulas, did you? Well, they're – not – here.' He enunciated every word, as though he were talking to an idiot. 'There's nothing you can do here. Apart from ruin the equipment, obviously.'

'What on earth have I done to make you treat me like this?'

Philippe stiffened. 'You haven't been honest from the start.'

'What do you mean?' Stress was creating a knot in her stomach. 'This is ridiculous.' Elena tried to gather her thoughts and explain everything. He probably didn't want her working on the perfume. But it was Claudine who'd given her permission – they must know that!

'The Notre-Dame perfume is an ambitious project, I know, but—'

'What the hell are you talking about?' Just two steps brought Montier face to face with Claudine, who so far had not opened her mouth. 'I want to know what you're doing. What's all this about a Notre-Dame perfume?' he barked.

'Nothing – it's silly really. Elena, Mademoiselle Rossini,

made a big sale today, so I thought I'd give her an incentive and show her how a perfume is put together. One of the customers asked for a fragrance that evokes the magnificence of Notre-Dame. She's a famous writer called Madame Binoche. We were testing out blends and Elena showed me a few ideas.'

Philippe ground his teeth. 'She is not authorized to be in the laboratory,' he insisted.

'Like you said before, there's nothing in here she could take,' Claudine replied, still not looking at him.

'Silence, both of you.' Jacques held out his hand. 'The note-book, please.'

Claudine gave it to him. Jacques stared at it for a moment, and started to flick through. There were pages and pages of formulae, scribbles and notes. He knew Claudine's hand-writing, and this wasn't it. Yet he'd never signed a pass for Rossini. He didn't even bother to ask what Claudine was trying to do that secretly involved Elena. Because he already knew. He'd deal with both of them later. All he really cared about at that point was the perfume, not who had made it. He cast a quick glance over the *mélanges*. They showed real vision, pure intuition. She'd used an obsolete technique, building it around individual notes and starting from the top until she found the base. No one these days would have made a gamble like that. But the perfume was good, it was more than good. He re-read some of the more complex passages, then gently picked up the cylinder and brought it to his nose.

Luck, pure luck, he kept telling himself. But the perfume was bursting with heady notes. How on earth had she managed to achieve such a balance without using any of the latest tech-niques? Jacques took this as a personal insult. In a flash, his annoyance turned into open hostility.

Elena Rossini might very well think she was a perfumier, but he wasn't about to let himself be swindled just because she'd somehow managed to hit on a good *mélange*. That thought made him feel better. Yes, he'd make sure this woman stayed well away from his laboratory.

'There's been a misunderstanding, *mademoiselle*. You were not hired by this company to make perfumes, remember? We talked about this. I have expert staff to handle that. Your job is sales. You should apply your efforts there and leave the composition to someone qualified. As you can see, you're obviously not suited to such a delicate task. Perfumery is not an improvised art form.'

Elena was stunned. She'd simply stood and listened to what Claudine had said because she had no come-back. She'd trusted this woman, and she'd been deceived. Suddenly, it all made sense: Claudine wanted the perfume formula for herself. That's why she was so keen to let her make it, keeping their bosses in the dark. And Elena had fallen for it. She hadn't checked whether Philippe or Montier knew about her project, she'd never even thought to do so because she'd been so wrapped up in creating the perfume of Notre-Dame. In the end, it was her own fault.

But she wasn't going to stay and work there: she knew she couldn't stand another moment in that place.

'You know what, Montier, you're quite right. There has been a very serious misunderstanding,' she said, taking off her white coat. 'I'll get my things and leave you to make, sell and wear your own perfumes.' She finished her speech as she reached the door. Then she stopped and turned around.

'Give me back my notebook.'

A sneer spread across the man's face. 'You mean this?' he said, holding up the pad.

'Precisely.' Elena gritted her teeth, she was at the end of her tether. She focused on Jacques, because if she'd looked at Philippe or Claudine, she would have started screaming.

'This doesn't belong to you. Everything that is formulated, tested or simply experimented with inside Narcissus is mine. Didn't you read your contract?'

'What are you talking about?'

Jacques smiled. 'Come to think of it, that clause probably escaped you. After all, it applies to perfumiers and you, *mademoiselle*, as I have already told you, were a sales assistant.'

It wasn't the first time Elena had encountered such pettiness but this intention to hurt, to wilfully humiliate someone, was completely new to her. Jacques's malice was cold, slimy. It turned her stomach, but there was no way she was going to break down in front of those people. She had to be tough. She could think of only one thing: finding the exit, getting out of that place and forgetting all about them. She poured every ounce of her contempt into the look she gave Montier. Then she left: she didn't even want to breathe the same air as them.

'Keep my notes,' she muttered.

They wouldn't do him any good. They were just observations, the odd paragraph. Elena had made a note of the *mélanges* but she'd changed them at the last minute. She was about to write down the new quantities when Claudine came in. Of course, Elena knew that a good perfumier would be able to work it all out – but they'd have to use gas chromatography. That test was the only way they had of finding out for sure which essences she'd used in the composition, and in what quantities. It was scant consolation, but enough to give Elena the strength to push the open button. Once she was out in the corridor, she walked to the cloakroom at the end, put on her coat, took her bag out of her locker, and slipped out of the back door.

The air was like a wall of ice against her skin. She stood for a few seconds, trying to adjust to it. She felt ill. A pain had started in her chest and ran all the way up to her throat. She wasn't crying, that wasn't it. Maybe that would have been better. Instead, this anger, this knot was caught inside her, like a warning. She'd been tricked and cheated because of her foolish trust in other people. She'd just lost her job, her future, her dreams, at the hands of someone she'd all too lightly assumed to be a loyal colleague. This was the second time she'd put her trust in the wrong person.

She slid her hands into her pockets for warmth and started walking. People rushed around her but she paid no attention. She couldn't hear anything; she was wrapped in a numbness that protected her like a cocoon. She just needed to walk: soon she'd be in the Marais, and home. She'd have to move out, she realized. But she didn't want to think about that. Suddenly, she heard a voice behind her.

'Elena, what's wrong? Why didn't you wait for me? I told you I'd come and pick you up.'

She kept on walking, putting one foot in front of the other. He wouldn't stop calling her, but she didn't want to answer. What could she possibly say to him? 'I didn't wait for you because I couldn't bear to stay in that place a minute longer?'

Cail followed her for a few metres. When she still wouldn't speak, he took her arm and led her into a café.

'A cup of tea will do you wonders,' he said, helping her take off her coat. He ordered tea for them both, and asked for a slice of sachertorte.

'Can you sit down on your own, or do you need a hand?'

Cail kept his tone light, but he was worried sick. Elena was frighteningly pale and shaking. But her eyes sparked with fury.

'I walked out,' she said, out of nowhere, still standing up.

Cail wanted to storm off immediately to Narcissus and demand an explanation from Elena's boss. But for now, it was more important for her to sit down, drink her tea and start breathing normally.

'OK. You'll find a better job. Obviously that one wasn't really right for you.'

'He stole my notes. He said he owns everything that's produced there.'

Cail gestured towards the seat. 'Why don't you start again from the beginning?' he said gently, forcing himself to stay relaxed. Elena blew her nose. When the waiter came over with their order, she finally decided to sit down.

'Drink it while it's hot.' Cail gave her a generous portion of cake, put sugar in her tea and added lemon. When she picked up a piece of cake he breathed a sigh of relief.

It was a while before Elena started talking. He filled the difficult wait by telling her how his day had been, lingering over John's exploits and what he was going to make for dinner later.

'Do you remember my mentioning a Madame Binoche?' Elena said finally.

Cail nodded. 'Sure, the woman from Notre-Dame.'

'I was working on her perfume today . . .' Elena recounted the whole horrible episode. When she'd finished, she swallowed down another sip of tea and blinked back the tears stinging her eyes, which she refused to shed.

'Jacques took the book where I kept my notes.'

Cail clenched his fist beneath the table.

'I don't know how Monie can be with him. He's awful,' Elena whispered, then she put her hand over her mouth. 'I don't feel very well.'

'Do you want to go home?'

Elena shook her head.

Cail reached for her hand and held it tightly in his. It was soft and cold.

'I wanted to tell him that he was a despicable human being,' Elena went on.

Cail thought about having a word with this Montier himself. Only he'd say something quite different.

'Are you still hungry? No? Do you fancy a walk then? We could go down to the river?'

Why not? It wasn't as if she had to go to work the next day. Elena put on her coat and followed Cail outside. The night was like a sheet of icy black glass.

16

Black pepper: perseverance. Warm and stimulating, the 'King
of Spices'.
The fragrance awakens the senses, promotes inner strength.
Teaches us that when it seems there is nowhere to go, we've
just lost our way.

'Might I ask why you're not using your keys? And don't even think about pretending you forgot them.' Leaving Cail and Monique standing in the doorway of the apartment, Elena hauled herself back upstairs to the living area. The two exchanged a look, then followed her. Upstairs, Cail put the kettle on the stove and opened a box full of colourful *macarons*. He'd been all the way to the Champs-Élysées to buy them from Ladurée. He put them on the table and a subtle perfume of meringue and fruity cream emerged from the box, drifting through the kitchen.

'Elena, we have a proposal for you,' Monique said.

'Is that so,' Elena mumbled, taking her favourite seat in

247

front of the window. She threw a blanket around herself and started fiddling with the tassels. She was in a foul mood. She hadn't left the house for a week, and her skin was so pale it looked almost transparent.

Cail stole glances at Elena out of the corner of his eye as he made the tea. He hoped Monique's plan was going to work, otherwise he'd have to come up with something else.

'Cail and I have put our heads together,' Monique went on. 'We think the time has come to open a perfumery. Or rather, for you to open one – we'll give you financial backing.'

There, she'd said it. Monique took the cup that Cail handed to her and focused on the amber-coloured liquid. She really needed something warm. The air in the apartment was frosty. Didn't Elena have the heating on?

She waited a few minutes, then asked: 'So, what do you say?'

'I'm tired. I'm going to bed,' Elena replied. She stood up, her head bowed. She'd almost made it to the bedroom when Cail blocked her way.

'If you don't like the idea, if you don't feel like it, you at least have to tell us why.'

Elena had had enough. For days she'd been trying to work out what to do, but there was nothing she could do, nothing she could say. However she looked at it, her plans were in ruins, along with the ifs and buts of what remained of her self-esteem. Claudine might have been the one who had double-crossed her, taken advantage of her, but Elena herself had let her do it. She hadn't even bothered to check with Montier to see whether he knew about the perfume Madame Binoche had ordered; she hadn't even spoken to him about her new role in the laboratory. She'd just taken her colleague's word for it. For everything.

What made it worse, what hurt the most, was knowing that deep down she'd been fooling herself. She should have questioned Claudine's strange behaviour – but no, she'd ignored it, dismissing it out of hand. Because she *wanted* to make that perfume. She couldn't forgive herself: she'd put her trust in the wrong people and she felt a fool. And the mistake would cost her dearly, because how could she get another job with a baby on the way? And this put her in another quandary: money. She didn't have much left, nowhere near enough to see her through the rest of the pregnancy. She would have to leave Paris. Go back to Florence, where she had a house. It was the only option she had left, but it meant giving up her plans. And Cail. Because she wasn't going to take her friends' money. She had nothing to offer them in return, nothing she could put down as her stake. This wasn't a company, it was a gift.

She lifted her head and retorted, 'I don't have to explain anything to you,' but before she could finish the sentence, she burst into tears. 'I'm not a charity case. I can find another job. I can . . .'

Cail let her carry on for a moment before folding his arms across his chest and saying, 'Have you quite finished?'

Monique decided to give them a few minutes alone. She went downstairs, hoping Cail could make her friend see sense, or at least drag her from the depths of self-pity she'd been wallowing in.

Once Cail was reasonably sure Elena wouldn't have another meltdown, he took her hand and pulled her into the bathroom.

'Take a shower, calm yourself down and come back downstairs. We've got a serious business proposal to make – it's not charity and it's not a gift. And there's another thing: I wanted to ask you to come to Provence with me. I need to go there for a couple of days. A change of scene would do you and the baby good.'

'I'm not coming with you.'

'Why not? I'll take you to meet my mother. She's a lovely woman, you'll like her, you'll see.'

'I said no.'

'Not even if I told you I think I've found where Beatrice wrote her diary?'

Despite herself, Elena's eyes widened. 'That's not true,' she whispered.

Cail shrugged. 'Have I ever lied to you?'

Silently, she shook her head, then gave a long sigh. 'I'm going to take a shower. Can you leave, please?'

He closed the bathroom door and went downstairs, a hint of a smile on his face.

'She'll be down in a bit,' he told Monique.

The woman lifted her head from the magazine she was flicking through and said, 'Thank you for being there for her.'

Cail frowned. 'You don't need to thank me. I'm not just doing it to be neighbourly, if that's what you're thinking.'

'I know exactly why you're doing it, and I didn't mean that.' Monique was tired and she'd just had a nasty argument with Jacques. The last in a long line. The last ever, she hoped. As long as she could resist him.

'That guy . . . that Montier, he's not a nice man,' Cail stated, and he shot her a warning glance.

'Jacques told me everything,' Monique replied. 'He said you went looking for him at his office.'

It was true. Cail had gone to Narcissus to have a word with him. The next day, Elena had her notepad back, along with a written apology and an invitation to return to work.

250

'He told me he fired Claudine,' Monique continued.

'He stole Elena's perfume.'

'Technically he only tried to,' she said. 'And anyway, as soon as the perfume is finished Jacques will put it on the market, and then he'll pay Elena what he pays all the perfumiers who work for him. And believe me, it's a handsome figure. He was very sorry about what happened.' She looked over at the staircase. 'He's not a bad person underneath,' she concluded.

'It'll be best for him if he stays away from Elena,' Cail replied coldly. 'He seems like the kind of man who brings nothing but trouble.'

Elena came down just in time to hear the last few words. And she felt ashamed. She'd been horrible to Cail, and instead of leaving and slamming the door behind him, he was still there, waiting for her. He'd even brought her the best *macarons* in Paris.

'I . . . I wanted to say I'm sorry. I haven't been in the best of moods lately,' she said quietly.

She was pale, but she'd had a shower and changed her clothes. She looked very young in a black, ribbed dress with her hair loose over shoulders. Cail looked at her, as Monique went over and wrapped her arms around her.

'One of these days it'll be your turn to look after me,' Monique said, patting Elena's slightly rounded stomach, just visible under the tight dress. 'Don't think for a minute that you're going to get off lightly.'

'Can you wait a few years, though? Let me get myself together first?' Elena smiled, hugging her just as tightly.

'No worries. How does a decade sound?'

Elena laughed and shook her head. 'Too long.'

'Let's sit down. We need to talk.' Cail took a bundle of papers out of his pocket and handed them to Elena. They

251

were creased, but the handwriting was neat and everything was set out in an orderly fashion. He hadn't used a computer, he'd written it all out by hand.

'Remember Ben, my friend who lives round here?'

Elena nodded.

'His girlfriend, Colette, works for a big accountancy firm. She can handle the shop licence and, at least in the early stages, I think it'd make sense if she handled the accounts as well. That way, you can focus on the business.'

'You're talking as if this is a done deal.'

Monique sighed. 'Don't make it so difficult, *chérie*. I'm exhausted. We all know that opening a perfumery is what you want. You've got what it takes, you've got the skills, and you know how to deal with customers.'

Elena stood up and started to pace up and down. But Monique kept up the momentum; she got to her feet and followed her.

'Would you just hear me out?' Monique asked, exasperated.

'I can't contribute to the costs now, so it's not a company,' Elena replied stubbornly.

'If you'd just stop for a minute, if you'd actually listen, you'd know that Montier's going to pay you for the perfume.'

'You didn't tell me that,' Elena said, standing still.

Monique rolled her eyes. 'Yes, I did. You just didn't listen to me!'

'Why don't you two sit down?' Cail ushered them towards the sofas. 'I can't keep up if you're constantly walking around me.'

The two of them went over to him. Elena sat beside him, Monique on the sofa opposite. They looked at one another for a few seconds, then Elena straightened out the papers Cail had given her.

'How much will he pay for the perfume?' she asked tentatively.

'Enough to settle the bills and keep you going for at least a year,' Monique replied. 'Including a full stock of essences.'

That last bit wasn't true, but she'd take care of the stock herself, by speaking to Le Notre's suppliers. Le Notre was very pleased with the perfumes Monique had created and would be happy for her to use his contacts. She hadn't even told Cail; she was keeping this one to herself. Truth was, she felt responsible for what had happened. She should have kicked Jacques out of her life for the way he'd treated Elena. Instead she'd listened to his excuses – and worse still, she'd accepted them.

'Let's say we do go into business,' Elena said, as she looked around the room. 'To be honest, there is enough space here.' The room was in pristine condition thanks to all the work Cail had done, and it looked straight out on to the street. 'We could have the laboratory upstairs and anyway, in the beginning I could use ready-made essences. But how would we find customers?'

'Advertising,' Cail replied. 'Yours won't be just any old perfumery. You can read people's feelings, you can give them what they want. As soon as word gets around, you'll have more clients than you know what to do with.'

'Exactly,' confirmed Monique.

Elena couldn't deny that talking to people who wanted to have their own perfume made was the thing she liked most: this creative side of perfumery made her feel important. Like an interpreter, she was the point of contact between the perfume and the customer.

'What about furniture?' she whispered.

'That's easy, I'll get it all at the market at Porte de Vanves,'

Cail said. 'I enjoy restoring it. Plus it'll give the place some character. I'll just need to put in some spotlights to brighten up the room.'

'Yes. That's an excellent idea,' Monique nodded.

Elena thought of the huge glazed porcelain pots crammed into her grandmother's storeroom. They would have been perfect. Maybe even a few books on the display shelves. Slowly, the strange, bitter apathy that had come over her in the last few days dissipated, making way for hope.

'OK, so saving on the fittings will help, but it won't be enough.' She gave it some thought and then looked at them both. 'I could use the Rossini formulas to start with. They're very simple, natural perfumes. The essences aren't too expensive, and I could use them at least until I have the chance to create some myself.'

'Or you could use synthetic products,' Monique said.

'Yes, I could do that, it's just . . .' She paused. 'If I want it to work, if I want to stand out from everyone else, every perfume has to connect with the consciousness of the individual wearing it. And without natural essences I won't be able to create a special perfume, just a good one. Plus, I can't compete with the big brands unless I'm truly authentic. Of course, chemical products are much cheaper, and they have infinite potential, but they're completely lacking in mystery.'

'Mystery? What do you mean?' Cail asked, intrigued.

'In alchemy, every natural essence is composed of sap, or juice – that's the physical part – and mystery, the part that contains the essence's potential, virtues and benefits. It's an energy field. Only living organisms can release it. That means that perfumes made with natural essences are different to synthetic ones. They're alive. And I will use every technique I know,' Elena continued. 'Every secret I learned from my grandmother, who really believed in this philosophy. Perfume is life, it mixes with the body's energy and strengthens it. I'll bring out the whole repertoire, I'll look through the family journals. I could adjust the perfumes according to the customer's needs, recombine them on spec. That way, everyone gets their own personalized perfume without having to wait.'

Cail agreed with her entirely. After a few minutes Monique nodded too, but reminded her: 'You realize that at the most you'll have four, maybe five hundred fragrances rather than three or four thousand.'

'I've thought of that,' Elena replied.

'Right, if that's your choice, OK. I agree.' Monique grinned. 'Your grandmother would be jumping for joy. It's been so long since I heard that word. "Mystery": the alchemic part of a plant, its vitality.'

They talked for a long time, making notes, agreeing on some things, arguing about others. But by the time Monique decided to head home, they'd laid the foundations of the company. Jasmine would receive a rent for their use of the property, even though she didn't know it yet. Cail would handle the fittings, maintenance, advertising and any admin. Elena would make the perfumes and manage the shop. Ideally, it would open in time for Christmas, but as it was already the beginning of December, they'd have to wait for their commercial licences before deciding on an opening date.

'Are you sure you don't want to stay for dinner?' Elena asked at the door.

'No, I told you,' Monique said. 'I've got to be somewhere else.' She smiled – she was thrilled at the outcome of their meeting. 'I absolutely love this idea, *chérie*. Just think: a shop of our own, a dream come true!'

As Monique left, Elena realized she was feeling just as excited as her friend. She went back inside, shivering. Cail was upstairs. The smell of tomato sauce drifted towards her, reminding her that she hadn't had anything to eat since that morning.

She took the stairs gingerly. There was a lot she wanted to say, and a lot more she wanted to do. Their relationship was one long series of postponements. It was as though the baby were an obstacle between them. Suddenly she stopped. The memory of her stepfather turned her stomach. Even if Cail ... but she couldn't finish the sentence. Because she knew there wasn't the slightest chance that he would act the same way. Cail had been happy about the baby from the start. No, Cail wasn't Maurice. He was . . . but she couldn't find a comparison. There was nothing in her past that came close to their relationship. She only knew that she felt wonderful when she was with him. She didn't even have to say anything and he knew what was on her mind. When he was away, all she did was think about him. Being around him was the only time she felt truly alive.

'*Merde*,' she cursed under her breath. She would have loved to have a chat about *l'amour* with dear old Monsieur Lagose. Unfortunately, she'd probably never see him again.

'I'm draining the pasta in two minutes,' Cail said, hearing her come into the kitchen. Elena looked at him, leaning over the stove, a strand of spaghetti between his lips, and felt a pang inside her heart. It was like pain, but it felt good: it gave her a warm glow, but at the same time it scared her to death.

'I'll lay the table,' she said, forcing her hands to move.

He nodded, distracted. He put the pasta into a bowl, added

a couple of ladles of sauce and a generous handful of Parmesan. He had been to buy it specially from a shop selling Italian products; he told Elena he'd been doing this for a while. He was crazy about tomato sauce. He'd been taught to make it by an American woman who used extra virgin olive oil, a little bit of onion, a clove of garlic, and ripe tomatoes, blanched and crushed with a fork, all cooked together in a silver pan. At first Elena couldn't believe it, then Cail showed her the photographs on his phone. 'Those pans must have cost a fortune,' she'd remarked, her eyes widening at the thought.

She sliced the bread and finished laying the table, deep in thought.

'Do you really think you've found the castle that belonged to Beatrice's lover?'

Cail filled her plate with spaghetti. 'Eat first, then I'll tell you all about it.'

Elena was too hungry to argue. And the spaghetti smelled wonderful.

'So, how did you find it?' she asked not long after she'd started eating.

Cail shrugged. 'There are a few clues in the diary about locations, if you look carefully. Things that only mean something to you if you've already seen them. But remember, this is just a theory.'

Elena shook her head. 'True, but finding the formula for the Perfect Perfume doesn't matter any more. I expect Madame Binoche will buy the Notre-Dame perfume from Narcissus.' She should telephone her, she thought. But she didn't know what to tell her about the unpleasant situation with Montier. She'd just have to tell her the truth: that from now on, another perfumier would be handling the project.

'That doesn't mean anything, though, don't you think? If we solve the mystery, you could still use Beatrice's formula as the basis for a particular line,' Cail replied.

The more Elena thought about it, the less she believed in it. 'We have to concentrate on the business now. But you said something before, about recognizing the place, the château?'

'I said there's a good chance,' he pointed out. 'It's not far from my parents' place. So, will you come with me?'

Elena thought about it. 'A weekend … yes, I think I can spare that.'

'That's my girl,' Cail smiled.

17

*Cinnamon: seduction. A full-bodied, sensual and intensely
    feminine perfume.*
The fragrance is exotic and spicy.
*Passionate and warm like the sun in the faraway lands where
    it is grown.*

Montier kept his word. The money eased Elena's worries
about the future and she gradually gained in confidence. She
was a little sad not to be working on the perfume for Geneviève
Binoche, and she still thought about it occasionally, but she
didn't have time to dwell on it. The business was almost up
and running and she was rushed off her feet in the last days
before opening.

'Is here OK?' Cail looked at her, waiting for a decision.
Elena chewed her lip, thinking.

'A bit more to the right. There, that's it.' But then she
changed her mind. 'No . . . no, that's not right. Let's try it over
there.' Ben shot Cail an exasperated look, as both men went

back to lifting the heavy bench to the opposite side of the room.

'Couldn't you do her an artist's impression on the computer?' Ben whispered, stifling a curse.

'Shut up and keep moving,' Cail panted.

'We've had this in practically every possible position,' his friend hissed.

'We still need to carry the armchairs and the coffee table inside and put them in place. Save your breath, you'll need it,' Cail replied with effort.

Elena joined them. 'I can't hear you if you whisper,' she said, eyeing them suspiciously.

'That's the idea,' Ben replied with a smirk.

'You volunteered for this,' Elena snapped. 'You said arranging the furniture would be "a piece of cake". I remember it quite clearly. Would you like me to quote the exact words you used?'

Cail rolled his eyes. Then he placed a hand on his friend's shoulder and steered him outside.

'She's pregnant, Ben. You don't stand a chance against her. She'll tear you to shreds and you'll be the one apologizing.'

Silence. 'Is that how she treats you?' Ben asked.

Cail fixed him with a beady eye. 'No. I'm a different story.'

'I don't understand why she's getting angry with me anyway – it's not like I'm the one who got her into this situation. It should be you she's sharpening her claws on.'

Cail was about to explain to his friend that the baby wasn't his. But the words stuck in his throat.

'Apparently she still likes me,' he mumbled, picking up the heavy armchair.

'When are you getting married?'

Cail stifled a grunt. He gave the chair a tug and lugged it

inside. Ben, who had no intention of dropping the issue, followed him inside with a wide grin on his face.

'Don't you think you've skipped a few stages?' he kept on. 'First you get married, *then* you start with the kids. Didn't your mother tell you? No wonder Elena's so grumpy . . .'

'That's not grumpy. You haven't seen her get grumpy,' Cail said, panting. 'And if you've quite finished, there's another shelf to sort out.'

'Another one!' Ben exclaimed. 'What the hell are you supposed to put on all these shelves?'

'Soaps, essences, water, everything you need to make perfume.' Cail pointed at the door. 'The distiller's going upstairs, in Elena's laboratory. And be careful, it's very fragile.'

Ben decided he'd keep his mouth shut from then on. Every time he opened it to start complaining, Cail found something else for him to pick up, dust or move.

'I can hear a mobile,' Elena said out of the blue. Not far from her, next to the perfume shelf, was Cail's leather jacket.

'It's mine,' he told her.

Since Elena was closest, she found the phone and handed it to him. 'McLean,' he said, without checking who was calling, as he smudged some dust from the end of Elena's nose with his thumb.

'What?' he repeated, sounding concerned. 'What happened? Calm down, Mum, and start from the beginning.' He reached for Elena's hand, grasping it tightly.

'Where is he now?' He listened for a few seconds, then ran his fingers through his hair. 'I'll get on the first flight.' He closed his phone and grabbed the jacket Elena was holding. 'My dad had a car accident. I have to leave straight away.'

Ben stared at him in silence. 'Can I do anything?' he asked.

Cail nodded. 'Finish helping Elena, please.'

She walked him to the door. 'I'm really sorry, Cail.'

'I'll call you later. Ben will bring the rest of the furniture inside. Phone Monique, tell her I don't know when I'll be back and say that you need some help,' he replied hurriedly.

'I can manage quite well by myself,' she said, following him into the hallway.

Cail whipped around. 'For God's sake, just for once could you do as I ask!' He didn't wait for a response, but left her there as he bounded up to his apartment, taking the stairs two at a time. Elena stood in the doorway. It was the first time Cail had spoken to her like that. She understood that he was upset, but she was hurt by the look he'd given her, by the harsh way he'd acted.

They'd almost finished arranging the furniture when Cail strode past her door. Elena saw him heading for the front entrance. He didn't even wave. She turned around, forcing herself to focus on the bottles she was unpacking.

'Elena, can you come here for a moment?'

She looked up and saw Cail in front of her. He was tense, the angry scar looking as if it was about to burst out from his anxious face.

'I thought you'd already left.'

'I came back. Is it OK if we talk for a minute? Come on, let's go outside.'

In the hallway they stared at one another in silence.

'Haven't you thought this might not be about you?' he asked. 'Maybe I'm the one who needs to know you're safe. Maybe I can't leave knowing you're going to be on your own.'

Elena crossed her arms. 'I'm not an invalid.'

'You're pregnant, Elena. I know you're not an invalid, but

you are pregnant, you could faint. Remember? You nearly fell down the stairs once.'

'But I didn't,' she protested. 'You can't worry your head about something that didn't even happen. You can't live like that,' she told him crossly.

He stared at her for a moment, then half-closed his eyes. 'OK, fine. Have it your way. I won't go.' He grabbed the back-pack he'd put down by the door and went back up the stairs to his apartment. Elena watched him go and bit back a couple of choice words. The man was as stubborn as a mule.

'Fine! I'll phone Monique,' she shouted after him.

He turned around and came back down.

'Promise?'

'OK, OK, I promise,' she said unwillingly. 'Now hurry up or you'll miss the plane.'

Cail leaned over and brushed his lips against her cheek. 'Thank you,' he whispered.

He'd reached the door when she called out, 'What about John?'

'Ben will look after him. Now go back inside and wrap up warm.'

Elena lost what little patience she had left. 'Don't order me about like that, Cail. I don't like it.'

He tensed up immediately. 'Just do what I say. We'll talk about it when I get back.'

'Maybe. Maybe not.' Elena watched him go with her heart in her mouth and a distinct urge to break something.

Once the mood subsided, she was just left with a sharp sense of loss and guilt.

Cail was away for a week. Their phone calls were brief, and once Elena knew that his father was out of danger, she

263

delegated the job of answering to Monique. She was dying to hear his voice, to see him – and that made her angry. She forced herself to work, to focus on what she needed to do, but quickly discovered that the head was one thing, and the heart quite another.

When Cail got back, the shop was almost ready to open. The retail licence had arrived swiftly, thanks to Colette's expertise and contacts, and Monique had done the rest using Le Notre's suppliers. They still had to get what they needed for the laboratory, but that wasn't a priority.

'Hello,' he said.

'Hello.' Elena was nervous, and her hands were shaking. She kept her eyes fixed on the bottles she was arranging.

'You've done a great job,' he said, looking around.

'Yep,' she replied.

Cail came over and held out a rose. 'Peace?'

'I don't like orders.'

'Neither do I.'

'That's funny, because you make a pretty convincing general, believe me.'

Cail just kept on waving the beautiful flower under her nose. It had warm gold petals that turned carmine pink at the edges. 'It's called Peace,' he said. Elena, fascinated by the mild and fruity perfume emitted by its silky petals, reached out and accepted the rose.

'But its other name is Joy,' he went on.

'How so?'

Cail stroked her face with his thumb. Elena was pale and the circles under her eyes were deep.

'Because every country gives it their own name. In Italy it's Joy, in America it was Peace, in Germany Gloria Dei. For Meilland, its creator, it was just Madame Meilland, and it

264

changed the fate of his family. Although they were almost ruined by the Second World War, with this rose they were able to recover and make their fortune.' He stopped, and looked at her tenderly. 'So . . . Peace?'

She nodded slowly, and he pulled her to his chest, pressing his lips against her temple.

Someone had hit Cail's father's car from behind. He'd escaped with a broken arm and a few cracked ribs, but that was all Cail would say about the trip. He didn't want to talk about it, and Elena decided not to push him. Her questions could wait. Besides, preparations for the opening were taking up all her time and energy.

For the next few days, they worked from morning until late in the evening. Elena occasionally noticed Cail looking at her intently. His gloomy, almost furtive glances unnerved her.

'We'll have to postpone the trip to Beatrice's castle,' he told her one night. They were sitting at the bottom of the stairs, exhausted. Cail had just finished installing the fire extinguishers in the laboratory. For the time being Elena was restricted to using ready-made essences, but as soon as the authorization came through she would be able to start extracting them herself.

She nodded, thoughtful. She was quiet for a while, then rested a hand on his, asking, 'What kind of woman do you think Beatrice was? I mean, you've been reading her diary for a while . . . have you managed to get a sense?'

Cail stared at a patch of ceiling and said, 'She was a dreamer. She had her moment of glory, but it wasn't enough for her. Nothing was ever enough for her. She was one of those people who are never satisfied, who have to try everything, who always push themselves that little bit further.' His voice was flat, distant. This conversation was too intense, too personal.

'It sounds as if you're talking about someone you knew.'

Cail shrugged. 'What about you? What do you think of her?'

'That she followed her heart. And I don't think that's a bad thing.'

'No, but she paid the price.'

'Everything has a price, Cail. It's up to you to decide whether you're prepared to pay it and take the risk, or whether it's better to stand back and watch someone braver.'

'We're talking about Beatrice, right?'

'Right.' She took back her hand. A heavy silence fell over them.

'I'm sorry we have to postpone the trip.' After a long pause, Elena started talking again. More than anything she did it to fill the gulf that had suddenly opened between them. She would have liked to go deeper into what Cail was saying, but he was lost in his own thoughts, wearing a sombre expression.

'Beatrice, her life, her ill-fated romance – it's a fascinating mystery,' she went on. 'You know, I was thinking about the perfume she created. Everyone in my family has always talked about it as though it were the greatest perfume in the world, a genuine elixir, able to change a person's mood. The Philosopher's Stone of perfumes. I wonder what the basic ingredients were?'

Cail yawned. 'I don't think they would be much different to the ones you use now. But maybe there weren't as many then. Lots of substances have been discovered recently, right?'

'Yes, but that doesn't mean there were fewer ingredients, because in Beatrice's time other essences were available that you don't find today, like civet, musks, roots and some kinds of sandalwood, not to mention ambergris.'

He gave this some thought. 'What do you say we pick up

our research again in the spring? The shop will be up and running by then.'

'Yes, I think we'll have to wait until then.' It was upsetting, because Cail seemed to have turned back into the man she had met when she first arrived in Paris. Distant, uncommunicative.

'Are you still interested in finding the hidden formula from the diary?' she asked.

'I don't know whether it's that, or whether I just want to see if my theory is right. But I know I want to see it through.'

He stroked her hair, and she closed her eyes, resting her head on his shoulder.

'I like what you decided to call the shop.'

Elena sat up and smiled at him. 'Really? *Absolue*, the purest part of an essence. Yes, I really like it, too.'

'Tomorrow morning I'm going to pick up the flyers. We'll hand them out everywhere.'

Elena sighed. 'You know, I was afraid they wouldn't be able to get them done in time, with it nearly being Christmas. Lots of places close at this time of year.'

'But we will be opening,' Cail replied, with a smile that shot straight to her heart.

Christmas, it was almost Christmas.

'When are you leaving?' she asked in a small voice.

Cail gave her a quizzical look. 'To go where?'

'Aren't you going home for the holidays?' She tried to keep the question casual, but the thought of spending those days alone made her deeply unhappy.

'I *am* home. And anyway, this is our first Christmas together. We should celebrate, don't you think? For the New Year, maybe we can go out, do something special?'

267

Elena looked at him, her mouth dropping open in amazement.

'I'll do the cooking, though. At the very most I'll let you make the cake, OK?' Cail told her, stroking her face.

'Fine. Perfect.' She was so happy she almost couldn't get the answer out. They chatted for a while longer, then he gave her a gentle kiss and said good night.

Lying in bed, Elena stared at the ceiling for hours, trying to keep all her questions, thoughts and fears at bay. Since she arrived in Paris, she'd learned to live in the present and for the first time she felt she was getting things right. In the past she'd done everything she could to keep herself away from perfume. But it had found a way to make her listen, regardless.

She thought about Cail, too. Sometimes he was an enigma. But whatever happened, he was always there. Elena still wasn't ready to define how she felt about him. Perhaps it was best to handle one problem at a time: it didn't make sense to do things any other way. Elena just knew she loved every magical moment she spent with him.

Eventually she closed her eyes and let exhaustion draw her over the hazy border between waking and sleeping.

It had been raining all day. Elena was walking around the shop, looking at everything, moving bottles, rearranging a display, often caressing her bump. She was starting to feel the weight of the baby. Now and again she'd cast a nervous glance at the window. Monique was pacing from one side of the room to the other, while Cail was chatting to Ben. That night, Colette, Ben's girlfriend, was there too. Everything was ready: champagne, glasses, canapés. There should be a lot of guests and a few journalists. This was the big event. This was Absolue's opening night.

'At least it's stopped.' Monique had gone over to the window, lifted the curtain, and was scrutinizing the sky. She let out a deep sigh and went back over to Elena. 'It is what you wanted, isn't it?'

'For it to stop raining?'

'No, I mean Absolue.'

When Elena looked puzzled, Monique went on: 'I wouldn't want to have forced your hand. You don't seem very happy.'

Elena looked pretty in a black silk maternity dress, her hair plaited. But her eyes showed she was nervous. 'Sometimes I'm so happy I think I could burst. It's almost scary,' she confided to Monique. 'And sometimes I'm paralysed by fear. The doctor told me that mood swings are normal during pregnancy, but I don't know whether it's that, or just realizing that I've been given another chance. This has to work at all costs, because there is no alternative. Before, life used to just wash over me. Absolue is the line between what I was before and what I'm going to become. And it's a warning: it reminds me of the things I should never, ever do again.'

Monique understood only too well. 'Going with the flow sometimes seems like the only thing you can do. Then one day you wake up and you realize everything's been decided – but not by you. Convenience comes at a very high price. It's like staying with a man who doesn't respect you, someone you'll never be able to build a life with.' She paused and looked very sad. 'If he can show you heaven, you think it doesn't matter, that you don't need to build anything together to be happy. Then the next morning, you look in the mirror and you find a new wrinkle. You start asking yourself questions, you sit by the phone, holding your breath, waiting for a call that never comes.' Her voice had dropped to a whisper. 'Bit by bit, he takes all the space you give him, while you yourself disappear. Of course, you still have your work, your family – and I suppose that's enough for some people. I admire you, you know – you're different.'

'Really?' Elena asked. 'You're going to have to explain that one to me.'

'I've always admired the way you can find incredible combinations – fragrances that capture you with their magic. I wanted that for myself.' Monique held up a hand. 'Don't interrupt me, please. I think I even hated you for it, sometimes. Not in the true sense of the word, don't get me wrong,' she added quickly. 'You've overcome the limitations that were put on you, like the break-up. You've even kept the baby. You're living. You're dealing with it all.'

'I didn't make that choice, you know that. I had plans, then things went in a different direction. The point is, there was nothing I could do but find a new path ... which actually turned out to be the old one.' Elena rolled her eyes. 'Wow, I'm even confusing myself.' She tucked a strand of hair behind her ear and smiled. 'But I like the spin you put on the truth, Monie, you've always been good at making me feel better.'

Monique had that look of deep sadness in her eyes again. Elena feigned a happiness she didn't feel; her friend's words had dismayed her.

'Thank you for the flowers,' she said, changing the subject by referring to the bouquets of dried roses Monique had managed to have sent from Grasse. She'd put them in the middle of one of the tables, and apart from perfuming the entire room, they were extremely pretty to look at. The tiny buds that still had their original colours gave off a seductive fragrance.

'Are you ready? Is it opening time?' Monique asked.

'Yes, I'm ready.'

A deep breath and Monique opened the door that led directly on to the street. Cail had turned on the spotlight to illuminate the sign. Everything was ready. For a long while, absolutely nothing happened; there was total silence, all eyes focused on the door.

'How about a toast? You can't have an opening without a toast,' Ben said, breaking the tension. He pulled a bottle of champagne from a small portable fridge, popped the cork, and filled the glasses.

'Mmm, that's good,' Monique said, drinking to Absolue's success.

'So it should be!' Ben launched into a detailed explanation of the origins of the wine produced by his friend in northern France. But Elena soon lost the thread of the conversation. She was incredibly anxious – but she'd never felt so alive.

And then the first guests started to arrive. One, two, five. All of a sudden, the shop was full. Monique was standing by the entrance. Cail was behind the counter. Elena went over to the other table. There were lots of industry faces, invited by Monique. All people who worked with perfume: models, technicians, PR consultants. Then Cail's colleagues arrived, and Ben's and Colette's.

Elena's heart was racing. She had a chat with a journalist, set up some interviews; answered some dull questions, and some bizarre ones. And then she made her first sale.

'Hello. Do you really make customized perfumes?' asked a man in his mid-thirties. He had a kind face, thin, with bulging eyes.

Customized? It was a strange way of putting it, but it was right, Elena thought. 'We prefer to call them perfumes of the soul.'

'Really – why's that? I mean, does the soul have a perfume?'

271

But before Elena could respond he'd turned round. 'And these?' he asked, pointing at a pyramid of coloured packages.

'They're scented waters, obtained by distilling herbs and flowers. Did you have something in mind, or do you want to have a look around?'

'No idea. I'm no good at buying presents. But this time . . . You see, my wife and I have been going through a rough patch. I'm working two jobs and by the time I get home I'm dead tired. She does nothing but complain. She says I'm neglecting her.' A dejected look darkened his smile. 'It's true, you know. I am neglecting her. So when I saw the advert for your perfumery I thought that maybe I could get her some-thing special. So, you would put her name on it, is that right?'

He was a customer; her first customer. Elena decided she was going to give him what he wanted, whatever it took. She smiled warmly, trying to put him at ease, because he almost seemed more nervous than she did. He'd done nothing but shuffle from one foot to the other, looking around, running his finger along the table-top. His anxiety was apparent from the way his gaze darted from side to side, and it was contagious.

'Yes, that's one of the things we do. Tell me a bit about your wife. What's her favourite flower? What perfume does she usually use?'

'I don't know . . . is that important?'

Elena took a deep breath; she knew she could do it. She would just start from the beginning and take this fellow through the process step by step. 'Why do you want your wife to have a special perfume, Monsieur . . . ?' she asked, putting out her hand.

'Leroy, Marc Leroy.'

'I'm Elena Rossini, pleased to meet you.' She shook his hand and he seemed to relax. 'You were telling me about your wife. If I understand, you want a special perfume . . .'

'Yes. So she knows I think about her. It's something only she would wear, she and no one else.'

Elena nodded. 'It would be unique – just like her, right?'

'Yes, yes. Unique.'

'Let's go back to flowers. Do you remember any she particularly likes?' Difficult question. A vacant look came over the man's face again, then suddenly it lit up.

'Roses. She really likes white roses.'

Thank God, thought Elena. She had plenty of different kinds of rosewaters, from centifolia to Bulgarian roses.

'Does your wife have a favourite colour?'

'Green,' Marc answered, buoyed by having remembered. Elena had something prepared, with citrus and fresh notes of mint, that could work even though it was a simple scented water. 'Come this way, and I'll show you something I think might be just right for her. It's not a perfume. That takes time, at least a month, and if I'm right, you want something you can take home today.'

'Yes, straight away,' he said enthusiastically.

'I thought so. Here, tell me whether you like the smell of this.' Elena prepared a *mouillette* and held it out to the man. He inhaled slowly, then closed his eyes and did so again.

'I like it. It's delicate, but it smells really good. I'll take it,' he said.

Elena prepared the wrapping, and under the ribbon she slid a card trimmed with the Absolue colours and logo.

'Could you write "Marie Leroy"?'

She did as the customer asked and, once it was wrapped, she sprinkled it with a few drops of vanilla.

'And what do we do about the perfume?' Marc asked.

'Have a little talk with your wife, ask her anything that comes into your head, because it takes a lot of answers to make a personalized perfume. You have to like it, too, but the person who's going to wear it has to feel that it belongs to them,' Elena explained. 'Don't limit it to objects, get her to tell you about her dreams, her ambitions, her most secret desires, and then come back.'

'Secret desires.' He repeated this solemnly. Of everything Elena had said, it seemed only these two words had made an impact. Apparently he knew nothing of his wife's most secret desires. But Elena would bet he was about to fill in some gaps . . .

Perfume was the way; following it meant finding your own path. Always.

Who said that people disappear when they die? It doesn't work like that; there are moments when their presence is so sharp, so powerful. Elena found herself in the middle of one of those moments. Her grandmother's words were no longer just a distant echo. She'd never truly understood what they meant until then.

As she watched her first customer leaving the shop weighed down with thoughts and the little bag in his hands, Elena caught Cail's eye. Her heart gave a flutter in her chest, as it did whenever he looked at her like that. She wanted him desperately, she wanted to run over and embrace him – but he turned away and a moment later she got back to work, serving another customer.

18

*Geranium: intensity. Resembles the perfume of a rose without
its subtlety.*
The fragrance symbolizes beauty, posture and humility.
The ultimate feminine flower.

It was a success. The next day the customers came back, even
if it was only to have another look around the shop. Elena
welcomed, explained and remembered. That was perhaps
what she did most, remember: words, moments, whole scenes
from her life. It was as though they'd always been there, waiting until she decided to admit them, to lift the veil of the
past.

She started to make perfumes. First in her head, recalling
the smell of the individual essences and putting them together,
one at a time, imagining what they would be like combined.
In those moments she worked feverishly, letting herself be
carried along by the feelings these fragrances evoked. Each
smell was like a word, but with no language barriers. Perfume

has always been the most subtle, immediate and effective means of communication.

Elena composed the perfume in her mind, starting with the top notes, then adding the middle, and finally the base notes. Before she started the physical creation, the perfume was already made inside her. But the really important thing was knowing she was happy at last. Every time she used the first essence, breathed in its fragrance, she felt a surge of joy, a deep sense of well-being flowing through her. In those moments, she experienced a sense of completeness, as if she had finally rediscovered a part of herself that had been lost.

She prepared all kinds of fragrances. Perfumes that recalled everything from passionate nights to fresh mountain walks, or the hot, flower-filled gardens of Southern Italy. Rock rose, lemon, mint, and then rose, sandalwood, iris, violet, musk, moving from fruity to more intense, almost hypnotic notes.

She let her hand be guided by her emotions, or the story she wanted to tell. And that made her think about Notre-Dame and Madame Binoche's perfume. She was sorry she'd had to give up that project. Words could never express how she felt when she walked into the cathedral – or rather, they could only ever express part of the feeling, whereas perfume could go straight to the consciousness, to its very source.

Unlike words, smells have no ambiguity. Smell is our over-riding sense; it lurks in the dark recesses of our primordial soul and responds to a series of olfactory archetypes with which we are born: it is pure emotion.

Elena mulled it over, and in the end decided she would make the phone call she'd had in mind for a while. Late one evening, she called. Geneviève answered quickly.

'Madame Binoche?'

'Yes.'

'Hello, this is Elena Rossini.'

'Finally! I was starting to give up hope of ever hearing from you again. How are you? They told me you'd left Narcissus.'

'Yes, that's right. Look, I wanted to talk to you about the Notre-Dame perfume.' Elena broke off, racking her brain for the right words. 'I had prepared a version along the lines of your original idea, and I was planning to show it to you before I finished it, since there were a few things I wasn't sure about. But the situation is . . . well, rather complicated now. I'm not sure how they decided to proceed at Narcissus, but perhaps you could ask them to let you smell some suggestions.' She paused again. It was a difficult conversation. She'd made a commitment and she hadn't seen it through. The fact that it wasn't her fault was just a technicality.

'I don't think I will. Actually, to tell you the truth, I've already made it clear to Monsieur Montier that I'm not interested in the perfume he offered me. I don't even want to smell it,' Madame Binoche said forcefully. 'You know, my dear, you just get a feeling about these sorts of things. At least, I do. I need to see the face of the person I'm dealing with. I need to be able to trust them. I'm a very instinctive person. This work, the book about *Notre-Dame*, is enormously important to me. I'd like to be able to crown it with the perfume. It would make the perfect launch. The thing is, I wanted *you* to be the one to do it.' She gave a sigh. 'Never mind, this is probably the way it was meant to be. How are you, anyway? Are you all right?'

'Yes, under the circumstances,' Elena replied. 'I've opened an artisan perfumery called Absolue, and so far there seems to be quite a lot of interest – well, certainly a lot of curiosity.'

'Could I come and see you?' Geneviève asked. 'I'd like to have a bit of a chat. I'm not sure I understand what the difference is between branded perfumes and the ones you make. Aren't they made the same way?'

'Not quite. First, in brand industry, compositions are generally synthetic, whereas in artisan production they're almost always based on essential oils. So really, even the basics are quite different. Then the customer, the person who's going to wear it, isn't just some average, standardized figure, but a very specific individual with particular requirements. This all needs a great deal of consideration, because the perfume is being created for them – and it represents everything they dream of and identify with. A bit like the conversation we had about Notre-Dame.'

'Extraordinary,' Geneviève remarked.

'It is. Please do come and see me,' Elena said. 'We can talk in more depth. I'll show you my notes – maybe they'll be of some help to you, even if I'm right in thinking the first draft of the book is already done. The perfumery is in the Marais, rue du Parc-Royal.'

'Oh, great! The Marais is a wonderful area. I'll talk to Adeline, and we'll both come. I'm really glad you rang me. I knew I wasn't wrong about you.'

'I'll look forward to it,' Elena said, as a comforting warmth rose up through her chest. 'Give my regards to your sister-in-law. See you soon.'

Christmas Eve was a frenzy. Cail had to stay in the shop and help Elena. Even Ben was drafted in. Monique had had to leave again and would be away in Russia for the whole holiday period. Elena was hoping this trip with Le Notre's staff would help her friend work out how she felt about Jacques. Monique was growing ever more difficult and demoralized. The shop had become the only safe place to meet and talk to her.

In the end, they had to order in artisanal perfumes made by other perfumiers. The ones Elena had made wouldn't be ready for a few months. Absolue wasn't going to get by on talcs, creams and soaps, so they'd decided to sell products made elsewhere but still of the highest quality. The bouquets were simple, all designed around seasons and moods. And the customers loved them. The important thing was that every fragrance was made using natural substances. The trendy perfume world full of glitz, glamour and synthetic products was extraordinary in many ways, but it wasn't for Elena Rossini. She was sure of that now.

'Are you ready?'

Elena had just closed the perfumery and was sitting on one of the sofas. 'Yes. More than ready.'

Cail helped her put on her heavy coat. 'It's getting too small for you,' he noted.

'I need to buy something else. Nothing fits me any more,' Elena acknowledged, stroking the swell of her belly.

Going outside was like walking into a block of ice.

'This cold is ridiculous,' she shivered.

Cail put an arm around her and pulled her towards him. 'It'll pass, you'll see.'

'How do you do it? I mean, look at you! You're wearing a jacket – open, by the way – and what's under there? A jumper? What kind of wool is it made of to keep you that warm?' She was indignant.

'I'm Scottish, that's why I never feel the cold.' Cail grinned, picking up the pace. 'Look, we're almost there,' he said, pointing at the bridge that led to the Île.

Light and gold, everywhere she looked, filling the night,

reflected in the Seine, standing out against the sky. Even the bridge was just one long band of gold. Elena and Cail walked in silence, holding hands, immersed in the kind of atmosphere and festive smells that lift the soul and make you cast aside bad thoughts, because they simply don't belong in the middle of such beauty.

It was easy to relax on her way to Notre-Dame. To enjoy a spectacle that was a real treat for the soul. It wasn't about religion. Elena hadn't been to church for years, nor had Cail. But that moment, that place, was the most beautiful thing human genius could produce; and sharing this notion of good was something they both firmly believed in.

When they reached the doors of the cathedral, the six o'clock mass had already started. They found a corner to sit in and stayed there until after the service had ended, listening to the treble choir who took up their singing again after a short break. The melody rose up and filled every corner of the church, mingling with incense, melted wax, smoke, myrrh and the perfume of centuries gone by.

Elena closed her eyes. Cail had taken off his gloves and was holding her tight. His skin was warm and comforting. At that moment she realized she was feeling something that, even if it wasn't true happiness, was very, very close.

'Hey, it's snowing!' Turning her face to the sky, Elena felt the flakes melting into frozen droplets on her skin.

Cail looked at her, then dried her cheeks with the end of his scarf. 'It's just a dusting,' he said.

'But it's Christmas Eve, it's special.'

They began walking home, but the snow was falling heavily now and Cail decided to hail a taxi. When they reached the Marais, it was like entering a fairytale: chimneys, turrets, and gables all white, buildings taken straight from one of those Christmas cards where everything looks magical.

Once they were at home, Cail left Elena downstairs in her apartment. 'Wait a minute before you come up to my place, OK? I need to do something. And no cheating, or else.'

'You know, I find your lack of trust deeply hurtful,' Elena said haughtily. Cail chuckled and ran upstairs.

When Elena was quite sure he wasn't going to come back, she darted into the shop. The present she'd bought him was in the drawer where she kept Beatrice's diary. She took out the parcel and held it in her hands for a moment, tutting at the slightly crooked bow. Before she closed the drawer again, she ran her fingers over the little book.

'No sad thoughts today. Today we're celebrating,' she told it quietly, pushing it to the back.

As she walked up to his flat with the present in her hands, Elena wondered for the thousandth time whether Cail would like it. She was hopeless with presents, and even worse at wrapping them. But this one had struck her immediately. She'd found it at the Christmas market on the Champs-Élysées, where she'd gone by herself and had a fantastic time finding gifts for her friends.

'I'm coming in,' she called.

The door was open and the terrace was completely dark, except for a tiny light to guide the way. Elena went in, treading carefully, a sense of anticipation dancing inside her. When she reached the glass doors to the lounge, they were half-closed. She walked in, and as she did so, in one corner of the room, a tree lit up. Cail walked over to her and took her hand so he could bring it to his lips. Then he placed a gift into her palm.

'Happy Christmas.'

Elena fought back tears. 'Thank you,' she whispered, and held out his present.

'It's not quite midnight yet – let's leave them under the tree,' Cail said, taking the parcel.

Elena was about to protest, then she noticed that there were lots of other gifts. Maybe Cail was expecting visitors? That thought made her panic. She'd never met any of his family before, and she wasn't very good with mothers-in-law and all that stuff. An image of Matteo's mother came to mind and she shuddered.

'Are you expecting someone?' The question came out before she had time to think about it. 'Sorry,' she said hurriedly. 'I didn't mean to intrude.'

Cail laughed. 'Elena, we got past the point of intruding quite a while ago. And I told you this a few days ago: I've got everything I need and everything I want right here.'

If that wasn't a heartfelt statement, nothing was. But a trace of Elena's old caution still held her back. Lately Cail seemed to be getting more distant, more absent. And she'd made a promise to herself and the baby she was carrying that she wouldn't let the wrong man into her life, wrong for her or for her son or daughter. She didn't want to find out the sex of the baby, she wanted it to be a surprise.

They ate by candlelight, relaxed and chatting in a way they hadn't done for a long time. Cail had prepared a dinner of pumpkin risotto, cheese soufflé, omelette, filo quiches and vegetables. The wine was sweet and fragrant and the cake for dessert was light and fluffy. And she hadn't had to lift a finger.

Everything was simple, delicious and wonderful. And Elena felt that she mattered – she *did* matter – to herself and to Cail. She savoured every moment, breathing in the aromas of the food, the dessert, the room . . . and him. Ah, that man's perfume was perfect; it made her feel complete and content.

After dinner, Elena helped Cail tidy up and they went to sit together on the sofa, wrapped up in a Scottish tartan blanket.

'You'll have to make do with the blanket for now,' he told her. 'Maybe one day I'll show you the real *feileadh breacan*, which is a proper Scottish kilt, and not that skirt thing some people insist on wearing. But that's not going to happen today.'

Elena pouted. 'And there was I, thinking that was my Christmas surprise.'

'Wrong!' he exclaimed. 'And anyway, it's midnight now, and these,' he said, pointing at the stack of presents, 'are waiting for you.'

Elena stared at him, astonished. 'All of them?'

He nodded. 'All of them. But open the little one last, OK?' There was a hint of uncertainty in his voice. Elena felt the urge to hug him tightly, to kiss him.

John came over and looked at her hopefully. Elena still hadn't got over her old fear. Yes, she would smile at the dog and talk to him sometimes, but she still found it very difficult to stroke him.

She looked at the parcels and went over to the decorated tree, almost nervously. She sat down on the rug beside the presents and carried on gazing at them.

'For the first few years when I lived with my grandmother I'd go back to my mother's place for the Christmas holidays. Maurice wasn't religious and he didn't even like the tree and decorations. He said it was all rubbish. Once, they'd had a fight and he kicked over the nativity scene my mother had set up for me. She collected up all the little statues in silence, without complaining, and put it back together.' For a moment she could picture the scene vividly, right before her eyes. She pushed it away, and with it the bitterness and pain. 'I never went back there for Christmas again. A couple of times I got invited to Monique's house.' She paused. 'There are moments when loneliness can sink into your bones,' she said quietly. 'It doesn't matter how many people you have around you. It doesn't matter . . .'

Cail was kneeling beside her now. 'One of these days you ought to introduce me to your stepfather,' he said, handing her the first present. He didn't touch her, he didn't console her: there was no need. Elena could feel him there with her, part of her. He was there, no question, a promise kept.

'You wouldn't like him. And anyway, it's been so long since I saw him . . . You first,' she said suddenly, breaking the tension and pointing to his present.

Cail picked it up gently and started to unwrap it, with a care that made Elena nervous.

'This slow-motion thing can wait until you decide to do me a striptease, or when you put on your kilt, or that unpronounceable thing you told me about before. Now hurry up and open the present, or I'll do it for you.'

'You worry about your own presents, this one's mine and I'll open it however I like!' Cail retorted, pulling such a strange face that she had to laugh.

A moment later, an antique pocket-watch, in solid silver, appeared in his large hands. He opened it carefully, noticing that the wheel to wind it was actually a tiny stylized rose. Cail was lost for words. It was beautiful and encapsulated the perfection and fragility of the flower he loved above all others. She understood him. This was her way of letting him know. There was respect in Elena's gesture, and consideration. Cail had never really minded the mocking smiles people gave him when they found out he worked with flowers and roses. But he was deeply touched by such a delicate gesture.

Elena held her breath. Then she reached for his hand. When she realized it was trembling, she let go. 'Don't you like it? I – I'm sorry. I thought for you it would mean . . .'

Cail didn't let her finish. Clasping the watch in his hand, he grabbed Elena and gently pulled her on to his lap. 'Thank you. It's the most wonderful gift anyone's ever given me,' he murmured.

Elena would never forget the look he gave her then. She hoped she'd be seeing it many, many more times but, since she was a practical woman and Cail's lips were right there, a whisper away from hers, she thought she'd show him the kind of gratitude he would enjoy.

She kissed him with all her heart, putting all the passion she felt for him into the caresses she gave him, forgetting any doubts and silences. Cail let himself be swept up in it, reciprocating slowly, until things between them became red-hot. Then he stopped, with Elena's face cupped in his large hands. He brushed her lips, swollen by his kisses. His expression was sombre, his eyes darkened by desire and what he didn't have the courage to finish.

'Thank you,' he said, before he helped her up.

'Thank *you*. You don't know how much this evening has meant to me.'

Cail took her hand and brought it to his lips, kissing her palm. 'It's not over yet – there are some other things to see to,' he told her, pointing at the many parcels lying unopened.

Later, before she gave herself over to sleep, Elena ran her fingers over the antique gold pendant Cail had given her. It was an eighteenth-century French perfume-holder. She didn't dare think how much it must have cost. The other presents were in the wardrobe. A red cashmere coat, a pair of boots, two thin but extremely warm sweaters in shades of blue, a scarf and gloves that seemed to have been made just for her. Two dresses and a pair of trousers. He'd been busy, even though Elena could see Monique's touch in it all. And to think her friend hadn't breathed a single word; Cail must have sworn her to secrecy.

Nobody had ever done anything like this for her. And there was another surprise still to come, Cail had told her, before he gave her a long good-night kiss in the doorway. Elena's thoughts immediately went in one particular direction. Being around Cail and putting limits on a relationship that was getting more passionate by the day was really starting to get to her. She wanted him and she could tell he felt the same about her. She was a grown woman, she knew the signs, and as if that weren't enough, his perfume was speaking for him, growing stronger and more intense each time they were together.

She touched her lips . . . What would it be like, making love to Cail? She found herself fantasizing about him, but her thoughts soon drifted in another direction. Why didn't she dare go any further? And why didn't he?

Then the answer came with a little shudder, almost a caress from her baby. She was pregnant, and that was the end of it. The answers would have to wait until after the baby was born. Elena relived Cail's kisses. Those kisses . . . She shivered and wondered whether there would be a price to pay for all this happiness.

Red, blue and a dash of gold. Absolue had welcomed the holidays with its three partners' favourite colours. The shop was flooded with sunlight, too, which was a bit of a worry for

Elena. But it was so long since she'd seen the sun that she decided to let it in and move the perfume packets to protect them from the heat.

'Sun-kissed! I should have known you'd do just fine,' announced Jean–Baptiste Lagose as he walked into the shop.

Elena went over to greet him. '*Monsieur*, what a nice surprise! How are you?'

'All the better for seeing you, my dear.' He kissed her hand and took a look around. 'Cosy, welcoming, very nice. And seeing as this is where you live, I assume it's yours.'

Elena smiled. 'Partly, but come in, sit down. Can I offer you a hot drink?'

'No. I can't stay too long. I must admit I didn't know what to expect. I went back to Narcissus, but you weren't there. And I couldn't find that witch . . . er, woman, your boss, either.'

Elena didn't say anything. She'd rather not talk about Claudine.

'You did the right thing by quitting, my dear,' Lagose went on. 'At first I had some problems tracking you down, since there's no Elena Rossini in the phone book. But then I decided to come round in person, since I remembered where you lived. Lovely area. The Marais has always been one part of Paris that's a pleasure to live in.'

She agreed; the Marais was a world of its own. 'How's your lady friend?'

'She's never been mine. And if I ever had any doubts in that regard, she set me straight.' Lagose was tense. 'She's as stubborn as a . . .' He mumbled the end of his sentence. 'She says she's too old to get married. Can you believe that?' He wrinkled his forehead, genuinely baffled.

'Do you really need to? I mean, perhaps she needs a

different kind of relationship now.' Elena would never have believed she could come out with something like that – she, the girl who had sacrificed everything for security. But her relationship with Cail had really changed her view of life. Now she lived every moment as though it were unique, not determined by something that might happen sooner or later. Living like this had forced her to take life as it came, putting herself and her baby first.

'What are you going to do?'

He shrugged. 'I don't know. Nothing, I suppose. It didn't work before, why should it work now?'

'But this lady feels the same about you, doesn't she?'

'I thought so. But people like to delude themselves, you know. It's one of many people's favourite pastimes. And right now, I'm not so sure she feels the same.'

'Did you argue?' She hoped she wasn't being indiscreet, but she was genuinely curious.

'Got it in one,' he said, and checked the time on his watch. 'I'm very glad I came round this morning, but it's getting late and I have to go.' Lagose said he would come back soon – he wanted another perfume. A *chypre* like the other one, he explained, but one even better suited to his personality. Like his clothes, he wanted to be unique, the only man who smelled a certain way. Another customized perfume.

Elena felt sorry for him. He seemed resigned, and that was a dangerous state to be in. A resigned person doesn't fight, they let things go. Thoughtful, she went back to arranging the perfumes.

After Monsieur Lagose, Elena saw another of her old customers: Eloise Chabot. She remembered her well. Rather, what she could recall precisely was the perfume she'd adjusted for her daughter.

'I really hoped it was you when I read the flyer,' the woman said. 'It's such a coincidence. You see, I live on rue des Rosiers.'

'*Madame*, how nice to see you! Just round the corner . . . this is a real coincidence.'

Eloise gave her a hug. A cloud of strong, sweet perfume enveloped her, tickling her nose. There was something strange in the *mélange* the woman was wearing. A discordant note – something that didn't suit her style. Her appearance was always immaculate: from her hairdo to her charcoal-grey dress. Chanel, probably. So why was she wearing such a strange perfume, if she could afford to buy herself something better?

'Absolue, what a lovely name. Is this your shop?'

'Yes – well, partly. Let's just say it's also mine.'

Eloise looked around, taking in every detail. She was fascinated.

'Perfume has always been important to me. I can't do without it. It's the first thing anyone notices about a person, and the last. Do you know that my daughter Aurore wants to become a perfumier? It's partly because of you, my dear. She really liked the perfume you recommended for her. When I told her you'd corrected it to suit our needs, it was as if I had opened the door to a whole new world. Since then she's done nothing but mix together my perfumes. She's even moved on to her father's. There's no point buying any more because she just keeps on playing with them. It's becoming really quite . . . embarrassing.'

Elena had to stop herself from smiling. 'You mean that perfume you're wearing has had an unfortunate encounter?'

'It used to be a wonderful Chanel Coco Noir. Now, I just don't know. She doesn't do it maliciously, it's just that at some point the balance goes completely. It makes me think of an elegant, beautifully painted fingernail that suddenly starts scraping down a blackboard.'

Elena laughed. 'How old is Aurore?'

'Eighteen.' Eloise let out a long sigh more eloquent than any words. 'Until she was thirteen, everything was fine. But I'm telling you, the last few years have been really difficult. And now she's happy. Just like that, from one day to the next. I just don't understand it.' She paused and put her hands up. 'Nothing changed, apart from the fact that she's playing with perfumes. Don't get me wrong, there are still times when it's difficult to talk to her, but at least now we see her smile. In general, that happiness coincides with us wearing her creations. As soon as my husband gets to work he has to have a good wash. Aurore doesn't seem to be able to tell the difference between masculine and feminine notes. Last time, she mixed her father's aftershave with violet water.'

'Have you thought about sending her on a basic perfume-making course?' Elena wanted to know.

Eloise raised one of her perfect eyebrows. 'She's not a very ... sociable girl, you know.' She didn't say any more, but Elena could tell she was concerned.

'She could come to me. Maybe one afternoon a week.'

'Really? You'd give her lessons? Here – in the shop?'

'Actually, I have a laboratory upstairs. I've got a half-day free, and they wouldn't really be lessons. I'd call it more of a chat; a few meetings that would give Aurore a basic under-standing of natural perfumery. If she's still passionate about perfume, she could make a career out of it.'

'Her father wants her to be an engineer like him. You know, she'll finish school this year.'

'Parents nurture these kind of hopes for their children.'

Eloise looked at Elena and smiled. 'I'm afraid you're right. Did it happen to you, too?'

'More or less. In the end, I found out that creating perfumes was what I really wanted to do. But if I'd come to that conclusion by myself, I'd have saved myself an awful lot of grief.'

'I suppose that's how it goes,' the woman replied, thoughtful. 'Now, tell me, do you have any candles?'

'Yes, of course.' Elena showed her a few options. The candles were very stylish, in simple, sophisticated packaging. They were square or round, in colours as bold as the perfumes they gave off. The fragrances were floral, full-bodied, or spicy, and always enchanting.

'I really like this one.'

'The base is jasmine: sensual, heady. In aromatherapy it helps people break down barriers, to be open to life and feelings. Have another sniff: doesn't it make you think of a hot summer's night?'

'Yes, you're absolutely right.'

It was true. A hot summer's night, on Cail's terrace, under a sky full of stars . . .

19

*Scotch broom: courage. As rich as the colour of its flowers, it is
   fresh and heady, with exciting floral notes.
The fragrance announces the spring, the transition from old
   to new.
Helps us not to lose heart.*

'Are you Elena Rossini?' A direct question, no hello, no pause
for thought. The new arrival didn't even stop to look around.
Elena pulled her head out of Beatrice's diary and looked over
towards the door, where a blue-haired girl with a long dress
and a child's features underneath heavy make-up was staring
brazenly back at her.

A few moments earlier Elena had been in another era, in
another world – Beatrice's world. Her heart was still racing,
her throat was tight, and a thread of desperation ran through
her thoughts. But they weren't her thoughts, she'd just
borrowed them: they belonged to Beatrice.

She stood up, set down the diary and went over to the

girl. 'Yes, that's me. You must be Aurore. Come in, please.'

She couldn't be mistaken. Eloise had warned her that her daughter would be coming round that afternoon, and that she was quite a character. Very thin, dyed hair, lip-piercing, a wool jacket over a white lace dress, and a pair of shiny boots. She'd been playing with perfumes again: this time she'd used lavender – unusual and attractive. There was lily and carnation, too. Then the fragrance changed suddenly, becoming dusty, almost sickly. Then out jumped the sandalwood. There was something else that was uniquely hers: a slight aroma of orange flower that lingered on her skin, no doubt as the result of her latest experiment. Elena would have put money on it.

Calling her a character was certainly an understatement. If the girl was trying to stand out, she'd succeeded, there was no question of that.

'My mum told me you're going to teach me how to make perfume.' The girl stood stock-still in the doorway, her face tense and her eyes suspicious.

'Right. To start with,' Elena replied, 'I'll explain the basics of natural perfumery, then you'll be able to decide what to do next. Whether you want to study more, or drop it altogether. Perfumery is not a simple path; it requires both discipline and sacrifice.'

Aurore narrowed her eyes. 'I know perfectly well what that means. You're judging me on my appearance.'

'Your appearance is the only thing you've shown me so far.'

'I knew it,' Aurore grumbled.

Elena knew she needed to make things clear. Apparently the girl used her appearance as a mask to hide behind, that could serve as cause or effect, as required. Elena had done something similar herself in her time, even if it was the other way round. Elena didn't like being the centre of attention. Invisible was the word. If no one can see you, no one can blame you.

'I haven't judged you. I would have said the same thing even if you'd turned up dressed in pink and wearing angel wings,' she explained. 'The perfumes I create are composed of natural essences extracted using procedures that require meticulous attention, with timings and calculations that have to be respected. Even the slightest drop will change the perfume. You have to count, calibrate, keep everything in your head. You have to know that certain substances will mask more subtle ones, that others will enhance them. You have to study hard. Perfumery can be dull – deathly dull, even. Like anything it has a technical side and a creative one. You can't have one without the other, so you decide, Aurore. This is my half-day break; I've got no intention of wasting it.'

Elena said what she had to say, then went back to her seat. Ignoring Aurore took great determination. But the girl didn't need kindness and Elena wasn't about to offer her any. She could give her something else: she could make her want to achieve something.

The truth was, she hoped Aurore would accept her conditions. This girl had really got to her. There was a deep vulnerability behind all the apparent aggression. And she'd bet that, for Aurore, perfume was a way of communicating – her language.

'And if I study? Let's say I follow all these rules, will you teach me?'

The desire was all there, in that fearful request, with none of the arrogance she'd been hiding behind before. Of course, the word 'rules' came out of her mouth like a curse, but it could have been worse, Elena thought, relieved.

'I will. At least, I will if you listen to me.'

Aurore came further into the shop. Soft, timid steps, almost tiptoeing. Everything about this girl was a contradiction. The look in her eye, her appearance, her clothes. But most of all, her perfume.

Just then, Monique came in. She'd got back from her trip the night before. Elena suspected she'd come straight from Jacques's place, but she hadn't asked any questions and Monique had remained tight-lipped. They'd only talked about their Christmas presents. Elena was dying to know what Cail had promised Monique in order to get her to help him, and then to keep her mouth shut. 'Nothing,' she said. 'It was just that he really wanted it to be a surprise for you. That man really knows how to win over a woman.' And the pain she saw glistening in Monique's eyes made Elena regret her curiosity.

'Good afternoon,' Monique said, turning her attention to Aurore.

That day, Monique was wearing an elegant, classic mini-dress in emerald green chiffon. She'd straightened her jet-black hair so that it fell to her waist like a cascade of silk. Aurore was gaping at her. Monique often had that effect on people, Elena thought with a smile.

'Sorry I'm late, darling. Everything all right?' Monique went on.

'Yes, I've left you a couple of notes. There are some deliveries to sort out. This is Aurore, she's keen on perfume.'

Monique knew exactly who the girl was, and she was very happy about the idea of perfume lessons.

'Hello, Aurore. Nice to meet you. Elena tells me you want to learn the art of composition. I can't wait to smell some of your creations. I think it's going to be . . . interesting,' she said, looking the girl's eccentric outfit up and down.

Elena smiled. 'She can smell one of them right now, can't she, Aurore?' The girl nodded. Finally, her face lost its sullen expression and relaxed. Monique blinked. Oh God! That eye-watering reek was coming from this strange girl?

'Erm, I'm sure a few lessons will sort out the problems with balancing fragrances,' she replied, taking a couple of steps back. 'You'll start with those – right?' she addressed Elena meaningfully.

'Come on, Aurore,' Elena said, smiling. 'The laboratory is upstairs.'

In reality, they were going to have their first lesson in the kitchen. It was much cosier and she didn't want to put her new pupil off. She placed the kettle on the stove. 'Would you like a tea?'

'Yes, please.' Aurore was perched on the edge of a chair, stiff as a board, her back straight and a serious look on her face. She was desperately tense.

'See these herbs?' Elena said, pointing to a bundle of myrtle branches she'd just received from a farmer in Sardinia, who also supplied her with rock rose and wild rosemary. 'If you distil them, you get a liquid that is part water and part oil. Most essences are obtained this way. You need thousands of leaves for just a few millilitres of product.'

'And that's how you make your perfumes? With herbs?'

Pleased that the girl was sounding more relaxed, Elena shook her head. 'No, that's just the start: that process gives you a perfumed liquid composed of water and oil. The water you get from the distillation is called hydrolat, and the oil is the essence, or essential oil. To make perfume, you use the oil.' She paused – creating the essences was an important concept, and she wanted Aurore to really grasp it. 'However, there are other fragranced substances. They're obtained by other extraction methods, but they have the same name: essence, substance or fragrant matter. So, to summarize, essences are a fundamental element of perfume. They're obtained from flowers, leaves, musk, wood, roots, fruit, bark, vegetable or animal resins, or by chemical synthesis. In short, they can be natural or synthetic. Essences – or fragrant substances, or matter – are mixed together and then diluted in an inert medium that supports them. It could be alcohol or another oil. The result of this process is the perfume itself.'

Aurore stared at her wide-eyed for a moment, then she bit her lip and looked away. 'I use perfumes that are already made,' she said quietly.

'Yes, so I noticed,' Elena replied. 'But what you need to bear in mind is that what you're doing cancels out the message the perfumier wanted to give, and it doesn't create a new one. Your perfume won't say anything; it will simply be a mixture of all these smells that don't know where to go.'

'It almost seems as if perfume is telling you something.'

'Exactly. Perfume is the most immediate language that exists, and the most widely understood.'

'I'd never thought of it like that.'

Elena poured the tea.

'But how do you decide which essences to put in a perfume?'

'A perfumier understands smells, remembers them and knows which substances can mask or enhance the essences. They select on the basis of that knowledge, and their own intuition.' She fetched the chocolate biscuits Jasmine had sent her, put them out on a plate and offered them to the girl. Aurore, however, seemed immersed in deep reflection.

It was always like that, Elena thought. People thought perfume was simple, and they were usually quite baffled when they learned that there was a whole world behind it. Perfume isn't just something beautiful one puts on as an accessory: it has far-reaching implications.

'You see, Aurore, perfume is something we recognize ourselves in, something we feel contains our dreams, aspirations, memories, or just a real sense of well-being, or even – and why not? – an instinctive dislike. It's something that comes from a much deeper balance of objectivity and subjectivity. Which means you might absolutely love one thing, and other smells might make you feel alarmed, anxious or disgusted.'

'That's amazing. I mean, it's such a complex subject.' Aurore sipped her tea without taking her eyes off the red tablecloth. Then she turned her attention back to Elena. 'But where do I start when I make one? I don't understand.'

Elena bit into a biscuit. 'Let's try to start with the basics, OK? We'll get there one step at a time.'

Aurore nodded.

'Perfumes can be divided into seven fragrance families: hesperidia or citrus; floral; *fougère*, meaning fern; *chypre*, meaning Cyprus; *boisé*, meaning woody; amber or oriental; and *cuirs*, meaning leather. When you're creating a perfume, you need to bear the seven families in mind.'

'But how do you know which elements you can mix and which you can't?' Aurore wanted to know.

'You could start with ones that belong to the same family – that's why it's essential you know the classifications. It's a bit like mixing colours. When you put two together you get a range of shades, don't you? You create a new colour. If you use pastels, you'll get a pale shade, and the same way with bold colours: you'll get strong hues. The same thing happens with perfumes, but instead of seeing, you smell.'

'Wow!' Aurore said.

'You also need to bear in mind another very important thing. Perfume is always a path, an idea. People who make perfume get called "noses", because they can tell the difference between the essences – that's three thousand different smells – and blend them to make a perfume come alive. Every single one is created according to an established framework: straight away you'll smell the top notes, then the middle, and lastly the base notes. This system, called the olfactory pyramid, is a perfume's identity card. That means, if you wanted to know what was in, for example . . .' She stopped to think. For a moment she considered giving Aurore a reference to an artistic perfume, but she doubted the girl would know it. They were niche products, after all. So she fell back on something universal. A famous perfume. The important thing at this point was that the girl understood the concept she was explaining to her. 'Let's say For Her by Narciso Rodriguez: straight away, you smell orange flower and osmanthus, then vanilla, and lastly woody scents, and musk which acts to stabilize and fix the other fragrances. These are the basic ideas. We'll go over them each time, we'll have a general discussion, then look at a specific theme. If there's anything you don't understand, stop me.'

But Aurore seemed hypnotized; she was hanging on Elena's every word. The hour flew by. When they said goodbye, the girl was smiling. 'And then we're going to make a perfume? But I'm not a nose,' she said, her voice tinged with disappointment.

'We don't know that yet, and besides, anyone can make a perfume. The results obviously vary according to the extent of your knowledge, skills, technique and intuition. But that doesn't mean someone can't come up with some extraordinary, crazy, or successful composition just by mixing together the essences that fascinate them.' That was about as likely as winning the lottery, but Elena didn't say so. There was no point bursting the girl's bubble. She would give Aurore a basis to work from, and the rest was up to her. There was always the chance that the girl could have a natural 'nose' and the mental predisposition for perfumery. The fact that she loved perfumes enough to play around with them was already a good sign. 'We'll make a perfume. Or rather, you'll make it.' She gave Aurore an encouraging smile, which the girl timidly returned.

'I can't wait to tell my mother. Thank you, I really enjoyed it. When can I come back?'

'I'd say next week. What do you think?'

Aurore nodded. 'Same time as today?'

'Perfect,' Elena replied, walking her to the door. The shop was quiet, Monique was busy with a customer. Everything seemed to be under control. Elena had a night off ahead of her, and she already knew how she was going to spend it. She went over to the table, opened the drawer and took out Beatrice's diary; then she went back upstairs.

'Was it something I said?' Elena asked.

Cail rubbed his wrist across his forehead and looked at her. She'd been standing in the corner for a while, watching him work, although these were the first words she'd spoken.

'Sorry – I don't get it. What do you mean?' he asked, plunging his hands back into the grass. The pots were full of weeds and Cail had decided that this sunny Sunday was the best time to make a start on his backlog of work.

Elena wrapped his old work jacket around her. She had her hair loose over her shoulders, and seemed dejected. Even John had sensed what mood she was in. Since their first encounter, John maintained a safe distance of precisely two metres between them. He looked at her, maybe even followed her, but he never set foot inside that space. They were actually very similar, Cail thought.

'So, is it something to do with the baby?' she tried.

They were in the greenhouse. They'd just finished tidying up the kitchen. Elena had chattered all the way through lunch; Cail didn't feel much like talking. Then they just stopped. Silence was sometimes the only possible means of communication.

'What's that about the baby?' he asked, confused.

Elena lost patience. These days, it didn't take much; she didn't like beating around the bush. 'Look, I'm not going to say sorry for something I don't even know I've done, so if I've offended you in some way, then have the decency to tell me, or how am I supposed to apologize?'

He burst out laughing. It was always like this with her. 'Why do you think I'm cross with you?'

Her face was red and her eyes were sparkling with rage. She threw caution to the wind and told him: 'Because you don't talk to me like you used to, and you don't laugh any more. You just sit there all day stewing over whatever it is that's wrong, wallowing in it, as if you've nothing better to do. If you can do something about it, then for God's sake, do it! And if you can't, then what are you dwelling on it for?'

Cail stared at her. Elena was now about half a metre away from him.

'You really want to know what's bothering me?'

She had known something was wrong. An icy ball of fear started to form in the pit of her stomach.

'That's the idea. I'm listening,' she replied, forcing the words out one by one.

Cail took off first one glove and then the other. He held her gaze as he stood up and took a step forward.

'Time,' he said.

Silence, then Elena took a deep breath. There were days when it wasn't enough to dream of hugging him, holding him, being with him. Then there were other moments, like this. Not only did he throw her off-course, he made her chase after him.

'Would you care to explain how time comes into it?'

He didn't move. Just kept on staring at her intensely. 'Time marks out our lives. Time changes everything.'

That was true. But Elena had no intention of engaging in philosophical speculation.

'I'm waiting, Elena. *That's* what it's all about.'

She looked at John, who hadn't moved a millimetre since the last time she checked, then turned her attention back to Cail. She was pretty calm, she noted approvingly. She could have a conversation without shouting; she could do it.

He gave her a smile she hadn't seen for a long time. 'I promised you a surprise. Today's the day. Let's go.'

He was giving her an easy way out. And for a moment Elena thought about taking it. 'I do like your surprises,' she said, 'much more than your enigmatic comments. But this isn't the end of it.'

He shook his head. 'That's what I was hoping for.'

'Hoping?' He wasn't the type to put his faith in simple hopes. Now she felt she'd never understood anything about their relationship. She had decided she couldn't wait any longer to find out why he was being so reserved with her. And besides, she didn't want a way out; the time for that was long gone.

'Instead of going round in circles, why don't we just sort this thing out?' she said reasonably.

'What if there isn't anything *to* sort out?' Cail replied.

Elena held her ground. She wanted answers and she wanted them now.

'Is there a particular reason why you think you don't have any time?'

'I never said the problem was the time I don't have.'

Elena bit back the swear word that sprang to her lips. She took a deep breath to recover her composure, and took a step forward. Now she was a few inches away from him, she had to lift her head so she could look him in the eye.

'You know, Cail, it is scientifically proven that pregnant women have very little patience. They use it all to stop themselves thinking about how much pregnancy changes their appearance. After all, you spend your whole life keeping fit and then in the space of a few months, all your hard work goes up in smoke. It's the kind of thing that would dent anyone's self-esteem, don't you think? So you see, there's not much patience left for anything else. Which is why I'm asking you to be clearer. I'm on the verge of a meltdown, I'm warning you. There'll be screaming; maybe even crying. And you'll be sorry you didn't listen to me.'

'That's a rather cruel threat.' Cail put an arm around her shoulders, and kissed her hair. 'I like your spirit, you can always joke about things. Come on, let's go back inside, shall we? I'll make some tea and we can sit on the sofa and talk.'

Joke? She was furious, torturing herself over what might lie beneath Cail's overly reserved behaviour. 'I'll have some tea, but I'm being serious. I want to know all about your time, about what it means to you.' Now she felt she'd finally breached his defences, she wasn't going to back down.

Cail's kitchen was bright and very tidy, with John's blanket next to the door. The sun filtered through the curtainless window, illuminating the jars of shoots and emerald leaves arranged on the windowsills. The smell drifting through the apartment was in part due to the essences given off by the aromatic seedlings. On the table was a bunch of yellow tulips he'd bought at the flower-market a couple of nights ago. It was a habit by now. Two bunches of tulips, one for him, one for Elena. And always the same colour. They both adored them. At the other end of the room, Cail had created a living area with sofas, tables and a television that spent most of its time switched off.

Elena, sitting on the sofa, watched him busying himself at the stove. They were still in silence. But now it wasn't tense, it was more like searching for the right words. Cail placed the tray on the coffee table in the lounge and sat down next to her. He put an arm around her shoulders and started to play with her hair.

'Do you remember the accident my father had?' he said, after a couple of minutes.

'Oh God, is it that? Is he ill?' she asked, sitting upright.

Cail shook his head. 'He's fine. It's not about him. Not directly, anyway.' He sighed, and closed his eyes for a moment. 'You see, five years ago, I had an accident, too, on the motor-bike. What happened to my father brought back some old memories.' He thought the time had come to tell her the whole story, to talk about Juliette and how she died. But he couldn't do it. There would be a better time, he decided. What they were going through at the moment was just about the two of them. And he realized he didn't want to talk about his past. It had gone, just like Juliette – but he had survived. He paused, took a slow breath in and out. There were plenty of reasons behind his decision not to tell Elena, not least his reluctance to reveal the constant sense of guilt that kept him

304

awake at night and made him behave in a way that meant he could always control the consequences of his actions. 'I don't remember much about it. But a deep sense of helplessness has stuck with me. Some things can't be avoided, only endured.' He took her hand, bringing it to his scar. 'This is a reminder of that day.'

There were others, Elena would bet. As deep as that scar, only better hidden. 'Were you very badly injured?'

He nodded. 'Six months of rehabilitation.'

Elena had had no idea. Cail had the agile movements of an athlete; he didn't seem like someone who'd been the victim of such a traumatic accident. Cail was sure of himself, he moved confidently, he went straight on his way with no compromises. Of course, he was also a practical man: it was as though he were more focused on substance than anything else. For example, he made very few concessions when it came to his outward appearance. Paris was full of men who made an emblem of their clothes. In that regard Cail stood out for his sobriety. Not that it was a problem: Elena couldn't help but notice that the simple sports gear he wore suited him perfectly.

'Yet you still go on the bike, you still use it. You're the one making the decisions, not your fears. So it's not about that.'

That was true. He was no longer afraid for himself. Cail thought about telling her how important she'd become to him, and how much this frightened him. But what he was really afraid of was the emptiness he felt when they weren't together, when he didn't see her, or when he couldn't talk to her. It didn't take much to make him happy: he just had to look at Elena. His life had changed now that she was in it. And that itself was difficult, because she was pregnant by another man. A baby should bring them together but it couldn't, because no matter how much he wanted things to be different, that child would always link her to someone else. And that was something he couldn't change. All he could do was wait.

He'd never been good at sharing. Even at work, he preferred to be alone, avoiding teamwork. He'd made an exception for Absolue. But that was another story. He wanted Elena to be happy and her happiness was what had driven him to invest in the business. In the past, he'd tried to change his ways, and the mistake had cost him dearly: the result had been that awful accident in which Juliette lost her life. If only she hadn't convinced him to let her drive, things might have been different. Never again would he be persuaded to do something he wasn't sure about. He knew what it meant to have to put the pieces of your life back together and carry on, knowing that you'd done something horribly wrong, made a mistake with disastrous consequences.

With Elena, he was only going to do what he thought was right. Even if it cost him every ounce of his determination to stay true to his intentions. He would wait. He would wait because there was nothing else he could do.

'I could have prevented it. Ultimately, that's the point.'

Elena took a few moments to think about it, then she said, 'I've never thought you were one of those men who want to control everything. That's more Jacques Montier's style.'

Montier? What the hell had *he* got to do with it? 'What do you mean?' Cail didn't like that comparison at all. More to the point, he didn't understand it.

'He makes all the decisions, he doesn't worry about the consequences, and he expects things to go his way. It's madness. Things can only go the way they go.'

306

'I didn't know you had a fatalistic side.'

'It's not fatalistic, it's practical. Cail, I didn't think you were arrogant enough to claim to have control over everything that happens.'

There was a long silence, then Cail looked her straight in the eye. 'I'm a man, Elena. Of course I want to control things. Don't think for a second that I don't have desires; that I don't feel the need to take this relationship to where it should be. Or that I don't want to keep you safe. Because you'd be wrong.' His voice was deep and penetrating, like the look in his eyes. His fingers found the hairline at the base of her neck; he stroked it and moved down to find her skin, his caresses becoming more intimate.

Elena swallowed. There, she had her answer. And while she sensed there was still more to Cail's words, at least now she understood that their situation was difficult for him, too. Perhaps difficult wasn't even the right word. His frankness filled her with admiration and fear in equal measure.

'I'm waiting, too, Cail,' she whispered.

Just for a moment, she thought she felt lighter. They'd gone a funny way about it, but in the end they'd told each other how they felt. Yet knowing that didn't solve anything. The fact remained that they were on the edge of something that was much more than a simple friendship and less than a relationship, and it was driving her crazy. Sometimes she wished that the baby had already been born so she could work out whether they had any chance of being together. Sometimes she just wanted to let herself go, without a second thought.

He smiled at her. 'So, you see? Time is our problem. We'll have a better idea of how we feel after the baby's born. We need to be patient – but that's not always easy.'

She leaned against his shoulder, breathing in his perfume.

She liked the way she felt in his arms. Cail pressed his lips to her temple, and she sighed with pleasure.

Finally, the thoughts that were whirling around in her head started to take shape. She'd always thought his seemingly self-assured attitude came from a deep self-awareness. She found it strange now, to think that he actually had his own problems just like everyone else. She felt as if she hadn't given him enough respect or consideration, and she was ashamed of that. As he kissed her, he was so close she could feel the warmth of his breath on her skin, and smell his perfume, warm and spicy, the smell of soap and aftershave.

She brushed his face with the tip of her thumb, softly tracing the scar down his cheek. 'What would you do . . .' Her voice broke, but she had no intention of stopping. 'What would you do if things were different?'

Cail leaned his forehead against hers. There was no sweetness in his gestures now. Just desire. Elena felt the effects of that look, the strong sensuality of his movements. Cail moved back just a little, took her face in his hand and kissed her on the lips. Gently at first, then with more certainty. Leaning towards her, the thousand doubts about their relationship continued to haunt him.

Then Elena ran her hands over his arms, across his chest. When Cail realized she was looking for his heartbeat, he was deeply moved. She pulled him close, erasing any space that was left between them. Such honest desire cast aside his worries. He held her tightly, pressing his lips against her hair.

He was happy. Just happy.

20

Ambergris: beauty. The oldest of perfumes, sweet and
   seductive, adored by women.
The fragrance is transported by the sea and deposited on
   beaches like a precious gift, after which it still retains its
   profound, mysterious charm.
Evokes the awakening of femininity, elegance . . . and the
   heat of a summer's night.

Elena and Cail put on their coats and went outside. The sun
set early at this time of year, but there was something he
absolutely had to show her.

'Wow, now this is a surprise,' Elena whispered, looking at
the giant greenhouses in the Jardin des Plantes. They walked
alongside them until they came to one that was smaller, but
just as pretty. Elena went inside with a sense of reverence, and
was captivated. Even as she stood in front of the thick vegeta-
tion, she couldn't believe her eyes – but the smell, there was
no way that could deceive her: intense humidity, fern, moss

and flowers. She should have known Cail would leave her speechless.

She didn't know where to look; every corner of the place took her breath away. She moved forward, unable to tear her attention from bunches of colourful *Phalaenopsis* orchids, but there was too much to see to be able to dwell for long on one flower, however wonderful it might be. Nearby, a tuft of fuchsia-pink miltonias sprouted from the trunk of a tree, next to the ferns; they looked as if they had violets inside. Elena felt the urge to touch them, to smell their perfume. Some plants had huge, bright green leaves, others seemed to be made up of long ribbons. She'd never seen anything like it.

She started to walk down the path. Immersed in the humid, perfumed air, she took off her coat, and felt light and happy. She'd gone from a frozen winter to the heat of the jungle in a matter of seconds. When they had first arrived, she would never have guessed that these giant steel and glass domes concealed a little corner of the rainforest.

She couldn't get her head round such an extraordinary contrast. Under Cail's amused gaze, she walked up to the glass walls and peered outside at the layers of ice surrounding the structure. The frost had encrusted everything; the silver patina reflected the lights of the greenhouse and everything seemed to be immersed in a pearly grey. But when she turned back again, as if by magic she was catapulted into another world, one overwhelmed by colours: every possible shade of green, the pink of the orchids, yellow, fuchsia, even blue. A little stream ran across stones where dozens of even stranger-coloured butterflies had settled; some of them with transparent wings. Then suddenly they took flight, forming a teeming cloud, only to return to the stones and sand a moment later.

Elena was entranced. But when a butterfly with enormous

310

yellow wings landed on her shoulder, she grabbed Cail's arm and closed her eyes.

'Don't tell me you're scared of a little moth?' he teased.

'It's bigger than a parrot – have you seen it?' Elena hissed, her eyes still closed.

'But it hasn't got a beak. It won't hurt you, relax. Look, it's gorgeous.'

Elena opened one eye. A moment later the creature took off. Its wings were a pure, brilliant yellow, with two bold orange spots and two long tails of gold. She had never seen a butterfly so big.

'Comet Moth,' Cail told her, as she watched it go.

'Moth?'

'Yes. Not all moths are nocturnal; there are some diurnal ones, too. This one is crepuscular, so it comes out in the early morning and evening.'

'I thought it was a butterfly.'

Cail shook his head. 'Look at the antennae: a butterfly's are long and thin, moths' are bigger and different shapes. Some of them look like tiny combs. Butterflies close their wings like a book, and moths fold them differently.' He pointed at the insects sitting on the sand at the edge of the brook.

Elena was dying to know much more. It was always like this: every time she found out something new, she had to know everything she could on the subject. She'd always thought that butterflies were beautiful creatures, but she'd never stopped to properly consider them. She was about to ask Cail another question when a butterfly landed on her head. 'Thank God this one's smaller,' she whispered, in case her voice disturbed the insect. She didn't want the marvellous creature to fly away. She stretched out her arm and waited for it, unmoving: when her perseverance was rewarded, she

311

focused on the feeling of the butterfly's legs on her arm, the bright colours of its wings and the smell of the place. She breathed it in a few times, fixing it in her memory. Because she wanted to remember this for ever.

'I had no idea you knew so much about butterflies,' she said to Cail.

'Actually, I just know the name of the Comet Moth and a few others. In the spring I was a consultant for the Rose Garden here. Lucien Musso, the manager, told me about this project, and he showed me the different phases of introducing the insects into the garden. Putting butterflies in the Exotic Species House is just an experiment for now. The idea is to recreate a corner of tropical rainforest, and to include all the species you might find there. Butterflies are disappearing, Elena. Even though there are lots of breeders striving to reintroduce them to their natural habitats, they keep dying before they've completed their life cycle. They often fail to lay eggs.'

'Let me guess – pesticides?'

'It's a lethal cocktail, molecules designed to destroy insects. They make no distinction between a fly, a bee, or a butterfly.'

It took Cail a long time to convince Elena to leave the greenhouse. But in the end she let him drag her out into the open. There was a dreamy look on her face and a wonderful new perfume in her heart.

'I'll bring you back in the spring!' he promised, and now they were walking through the tree-lined avenues of the Île de la Cité, hand in hand. The spire of Notre-Dame stood out against the black sky, all lit up, and the Gothic statues seemed to be watching over the city from on high. The couple carried on walking, chatting as their breath condensed into clouds, talking about their hopes, their dreams, everything they wanted to do.

'Exactly what is your field?' Elena was asking. 'You said you were a consultant for the Rose Garden at the Jardin des Plantes.'

'I still am. I've got a degree in agriculture, and my specialism is diseases in roses. But cultivation, as you know, is my job – it's what my family has done for generations, it's how we make a living.'

Elena nodded. 'So, you're a real authority on the subject.'

A broad smile and a kiss on the lips. Cail wrapped an arm around her shoulders and carried on walking. 'Roses have always been here . . . let's say I make sure they stay where they're supposed to be.'

That was it, in a nutshell. He made sure everything went as it should. No fuss, no arguments. Cail just did what he did in silence. That attitude was typical of him, Elena thought. He had his place in the world, and he was determined to leave his mark.

And what about her? That thought brought her joy and despair at the same time. There were times in the past when she had only existed: indeed, for a while she had merely survived. But she'd managed to distinguish, with some degree of certainty, the things she didn't want, and from there she'd established what she did want. Then she'd pursued her goals without caring about anything else. Including herself. She'd been stubborn. And now? What were her plans, really?

'Everything's changed now,' she whispered, thinking aloud.

Cail's grin warmed her heart. 'A baby changes the way you see things.'

Yes, she was well aware of that. 'I've got an ultrasound next week.'

'Would you like some company?'

He really did want to go with her – it was written in that direct look of his. He was asking her permission to enter her life a bit more. It was always like that with Cail, Elena thought. He gave her space, he didn't pressure her; it was easy to be herself with him. Yet something still wasn't right between them. Something was bothering him, something he hadn't told her yet.

'Yes, I'd really like that,' she answered.

There were still so many questions. She'd have to deal with some of them, she knew she couldn't put the issue off any longer. One by one her thoughts and problems had lined up, waiting patiently for her to come along and address them, resolve them and finally put them aside. First of all: the questions about Cail.

FROM BEATRICE'S DIARY

Today I gave the perfume to him. Gazing sweetly at the vial, he warmed it with the palms of his hands. I long for the heat of those hands, and I would have them hold me, as they held me in the depths of the night, when the icy wind blew through the stone walls and he embraced me.

We have reached the end, and I fear there is nothing left for me. There is a great, breathless anguish in my soul, but my work here is done.

Now I am cold. He still stares longingly at the perfume, but he does not notice me, my tearful eyes. He is blind to everything else, lost in anticipation of the joys of victory. If what I have delivered is what was agreed, he will lavish gold on me, and strings of pearls. That was his promise.

Now there is nothing to do but wait and see . . .

'Are you still reading the diary?' Monique's voice tore her from a past she was slipping into more and more often now. Beatrice had an eloquence very different from her own time. Her words never sounded forced or artificial; they had an immediacy – her feelings were laid out plain on the page. Almost shouted. Every word was passion and pain.

Elena looked up at her friend and swallowed. 'It's heart-breaking. She knew he was going to leave her.'

'Yep. She was a brave woman. She faced up to everything, went back to Florence and made a new life for herself.'

'Without the man she loved.'

Monique shrugged. 'You know, sometimes I wonder about that. How do we know that afterwards, with her husband, Beatrice was never happy? She even had a daughter. Love has many faces, not like lust. Lust devours you and leaves you constantly on the edge.'

Elena would bet that Monique was speaking from experience. She didn't want to ask her about Jacques, it wasn't something they discussed openly and they couldn't exactly joke about it. For a while now, Monique hadn't been asking how things were going with Cail either. Somehow, the two friends had both become reluctant to speak openly. They tried, and sometimes it even worked, like now – but they didn't feel comfortable with each other the way they once had.

'Are you seeing Aurore today?' Monique asked.

Elena nodded. 'I was thinking about showing her the difference between natural essences and something synthetic. She's really talented, you know. I think she could go far if she keeps studying.'

'In Grasse?' Monique asked.

'She could do, or even at the Institut Supérieur International du Parfum, in Versailles. Her parents can afford it. The only potential problem is the board that would have to assess her attitude and give her a reference to get into the school.'

Monique pursed her lips. 'Or she could learn from you.'

Elena frowned. 'Come on, Monie, what do you mean? You know full well that the basics are one thing, the stuff we learned, but there's a whole other world of aesthetic and food perfumes. At the ISIPCA, she'd stand much more chance of joining a qualified staff, getting a top job.'

'There's still the fact that to get into that school you need to have a certain look. Appearance is their watchword. And I don't disagree with that, because perfumery is a world that teaches you to make aesthetics your life philosophy. But Aurore . . . I don't know. She'd have to change, and I don't think that's fair,' Monique replied thoughtfully.

'It's still a bit early to be making conjectures like that. Maybe she'll just keep it as a passion, who knows.'

But Monique disagreed. 'I've noticed the way she sniffs anything within reach; she's like Grenouille in a skirt.'

'Careful she doesn't hear you,' Elena scolded gently. 'She can't stand the character of Grenouille. On the other hand, she adores Proust and his madeleines.'

'I'll bet she does.'

Monique stayed for the whole of Aurore's lesson, then she had to leave. Elena was just about to close the shop when a woman arrived.

'Good evening, *madame*. A friend of mine bought one of your perfumes. He told me you make customized fragrances, is that true?'

'Yes, of course. Come in and sit down,' Elena said, gesturing towards the sofa.

The woman was in her sixties, very elegant, wearing her hair up, a midnight-blue dress and a string of pearls that stood out brightly against the fabric of her dress. Elena smelled creamy vanilla, refined and understated like her appearance, and then a hint of iris, musk, bitter almond, eccentric and full of character. The perfume spoke volumes about her, about her feisty nature. It had the scent of the countryside and the rain, drops of which were still dotted all over her clothes. The woman set down her umbrella and calmly took off her coat, looking around.

'Did you have something particular in mind?' Elena asked, resting a notepad on her knees.

'Yes. I'd like a simple, suitable perfume,' she replied, making herself comfortable beside Elena.

'For what?'

The woman frowned. 'How do you mean?'

'You said you'd like a suitable perfume – but suitable for what?'

'Well, for me, of course.'

'And what are you like? What makes you tick?'

The woman was baffled. Elena smiled to herself. It was always like this. Customers rarely had clear ideas when it came to sounding out their desires; what they believed to be certainties were actually just vague ideas.

'Tell me, Madame . . . ?'

'Dufour, Babette Dufour.'

Elena started to work her way through the usual questions, from what the customer loved to what she hated. As their rapport developed, the woman began to confide in Elena about her feelings, and what she thought she wanted. Elena encoded everything, imagining the kind of fragrance that might suit her needs. Every ingredient she selected to

317

compose Babette's perfume came together in her mind, giving her an idea of which path to follow. She would take a number of things into account, not least the synergistic effect the natural ingredients would have on her customer. This *tête-à-tête* was essential: it was the heart of the creative process. And this was what set Elena apart from all the other perfumiers, what made her an artistic perfumier: her extraordinary ability to feel the ins and outs of what people wanted for themselves, and to transform that into a harmony of fragrances, a real melody.

'I'll start working on it, and then I'll give you a call to come in and smell the different variations. We'll start with quite a classic, light composition: a base of delicate citrus, a floral middle, quite a lively background.'

Babette nodded. 'I like that: "lively".'

Elena would bet she did. A pinch of transgression made life much more interesting.

In January the snow was replaced by ice. The Parisian air smelled of woodsmoke, mixed with car fumes and heating systems, and smoke from the homeless camps set up under the bridges on the Seine; it was dense and sticky, lingering in the air and clinging to you. Elena couldn't stand it, longing for the wind to come and disperse the layer of smog that was weighing down on the city. She recalled the Mistral winds that blew through Grasse, turning the sky blue and crystal clear.

Of course, the fact that Cail had been away for work didn't improve her spirits. But it was also partly due to feeling nervous about the ultrasound she was to have that day.

'Hello.'

Elena dropped the bunch of flowers she was holding and

ran towards Cail, who was waiting for her at the door. He held out his arms and swept her up in a hug.

'What took you so long?' Elena gasped.

Instead of an answer, Cail gave her a gentle, devoted kiss. Elena decided that, with such a valid and convincing argument, no words were necessary.

'I got here as soon as I could,' he said, with one last kiss before he let her go. 'So, the ultrasound is this afternoon?'

'Yes. We need to be at the clinic at five. But if you're too tired . . .'

'Get ready for four, it's best to be early. Will Monique mind the shop?'

'Yes.'

'Good. I'll see you later.'

Elena watched him disappear up the stairs.

'Damn you, Cail McLean,' she sighed, going back inside.

The first time Elena had heard her baby's heartbeat, she was so excited she didn't sleep a wink all night. That time, Cail had waited for her outside the clinic; when she came out to find him there, he told her he just happened to be passing. She didn't believe him. So this time, she'd told him the date and time well in advance.

'There, that's a little hand,' said the doctor. 'Do you see? Everything looks fine.'

Dr Rochelle looked at the couple clinging to one another in an almost fervent silence, their eyes glued to the ultrasound screen. The man was a striking figure: tall and masculine with a hard, frank stare. At least until he looked at the girl.

'This is your first baby, I'm guessing?'

'Yes!'

They answered in unison. Then Cail tensed and moved a

319

few inches away. Or at least, he tried to, before Elena grabbed his hand again and held on to it.

That evening, as Dr Rochelle was checking through the paperwork for all the patients she'd seen, she noticed that something was missing from Elena Rossini's file. There was a blank space in the box for the baby's father's name.

How strange, she thought. So she wrote it in: *Caillen McLean.* Fortunately, she remembered the man's name. In fact, he had left quite an impression.

A couple of weeks later, Cail went away again. In the days she spent alone, Elena dedicated all her time to Absolue. She crushed, distilled, filtered and composed. What she didn't make herself, she bought from other herbalist perfumiers, who bought her creations in exchange. They belonged to a chain of producers who had made the collection and processing of herbs and essences their philosophy. And so they prepared talcs, hydrolats and candles using the same methods employed by their predecessors, who in turn were inspired by the most exquisite artisan traditions from centuries and centuries ago.

Elena was managing almost everything now. Monique was away more often. If it wasn't because of Jacques, it was Le Notre. But if Cail left, Monique arrived. They were synchronized; Elena would bet the two of them had made a pact she didn't know about. She wasn't entirely happy that Cail had asked Monique to keep her company, although there were moments when she felt flattered by all this extra attention. She'd been alone for a long time, and having someone dedicate himself to her with such unshakable commitment made a very pleasant change.

★ ★ ★

320

With the pregnancy progressing, Elena was getting tired quickly. Fortunately, Aurore had started coming into the shop more often.

'Thank you for coming.'

'You know it's my pleasure.' And it really was. Aurore no longer resembled the girl who had introduced herself to Elena at Christmas, all skin and bone and attitude. As the lessons went on, she was gaining confidence and composure. She no longer mixed ready-made perfumes; Elena had shown her how to put a few essences together, nothing difficult, just a couple of combinations, and Aurore had demonstrated that she could handle everything she was being taught. The girl was clearly longing to make a whole perfume. And she was studying non-stop to make sure she was up to it. If Elena recommended reading a few pages of a book, Aurore devoured it from cover to cover and then went looking for another one. Perfumes were no longer a mystery to her. She knew the techniques, since Elena had explained them to her step by step. Soon, very soon, she'd be making her first perfume.

Aurore had changed her look, too. Elena was almost certain that was down to Monique and her fabulous wardrobe. Monie was the epitome of style and elegance. The ripped jeans and black jumpers the girl used to wear in defiance had been replaced by happier colours and shapes that accentuated her figure. One day, she turned up at the shop with a mane of amber-coloured hair so lustrous it left Elena and Monique momentarily speechless.

'I know people who would kill for that hair colour,' Monie breathed, 'and all the time she kept it hidden under that ghastly blue Smurf thing.'

Unlike Monique, Elena had made no comment. But now,

as an adult herself, she finally understood what her grandmother must have thought of all the mischief she used to get
up to.

FROM BEATRICE'S DIARY

The scent has triumphed. My darkest fears have come true.

Soon they will be married.

*Never have I created a more precious substance. There is
nothing to match it in the entire Kingdom of France or beyond.
At times it gives the sense of walking beneath an arch of roses,
with a sweet and favourable sun: and then at night, when the
fleeting moonlight bathes the leaves in silver.*

*He is happy, laughing, eager for what will soon be his –
those great riches. He steals the joy from my heart, the light
from the stars . . . and yet he knows nothing of it.*

*Can one die from love? How much pain can a single heart
endure? I ask myself, as I smile and wish that tears would
soothe my pain. His fortune is my disgrace. I brought this
torment upon myself. I was deceived by his love.*

He will abandon me.

*I have no honour and I care not. If he wanted me, I would
rejoice at his feet, but such reflection is futile now. Futile and
hard.*

What he needed is already his.

I must leave before he drives me away.

Elena closed the diary, that same pain in the back of her throat.
How many times had she read those lines? She knew the text
by heart now. But the pain these words evoked was always
deep, perhaps because she knew that they were not just the

fruit of an author's imagination, but came from a life that had been all too tragically real. It was part of her past: Beatrice Rossini and her magnificent perfume.

Elena let it drift away, the sorrow and the deep sense of regret that clung to her after she'd read the diary. The Perfect Perfume was utterly sublime: nothing could compare to the celestial fragrance which the knight had had stored in a golden vial as a gift for his princess.

What in heaven's name was in that formula? Elena thought desperately. What *could* Beatrice have put in there in seventeenth-century France?

'Still got your nose in that diary?'

Elena closed the little book and stood up. 'I can't find the ingredients, Cail, and it's driving me mad. I mean, when my ancestors were looking for them, they didn't have the internet; information didn't travel at the speed of light. They didn't have half the knowledge I've got at my fingertips. I'm so frustrated that I can't work out where Beatrice hid the formula.'

Cail thought about letting her in on his suspicions. He'd come up with a theory: if Beatrice had described the castle, but never given its name or the title of the gentleman, or the princess, there was a high chance there was something in that place – the village or its castle – that was linked to the formula for the perfume, something that could reveal the mystery. He was convinced of it. Before he talked to Elena about it, however, he wanted to look into it himself.

'Madame Binoche got in touch with me again,' Elena went on. 'She told me she's almost finished writing the book. She still likes the idea of the perfume of Notre-Dame. She didn't go back to Narcissus . . . She wants me to be the one to make the perfume.'

'Yes, you told me. But that will have to wait, as I need to go away again, but this time I'll have a free weekend in the middle of my trip. How about you come with me? We can finally go and see Beatrice's castle.'

21

Cedar: reflection. Extracted from the wood, this is one of the
   oldest known essences.
The fragrance strengthens and guards the spirit.
Helps maintain clarity, balance, and a sense of proportion.
   Encourages profound observation.

Perfumes and colours. That was Provence. Elena remembered
it well, and feelings swirled around inside her, never knowing
where to settle – a bit like those butterflies she'd seen in the
greenhouse with Cail. They flew around and around, and it
was impossible to know where they were going to rest.

'We're almost there,' Cail said. 'Are you feeling OK?'

'Yep. Just fine.' But that wasn't true. Suddenly, going on this
trip didn't seem like such a good idea any more.

'If you keep pulling the seat belt like that, you're going to
rip it out.'

'We've got insurance,' she replied, distracted, her eyes glued
to the windscreen of the SUV Cail had hired at the airport.

On both sides of the road, lavender bushes marked out a silver path with no end in sight. The bushes clambered through hills, down valleys and then rose skywards again before disappearing – only to reappear moments later. When they flowered in June, the pearly grey of the leaves would be offset by the deep blue of the heads. And then there would be the wonderful perfume . . . Nothing could compare to the scent of lavender in flower. By day it was accompanied by the buzzing of bees, by night the chirping of crickets.

That April morning, the sky was clear, almost dazzling.

'Twenty minutes and we'll be there,' Cail told her.

Elena tensed. 'Can't we stay in a hotel?'

He changed gear and slowed down. 'Yes, of course. We can do whatever you want. Why?'

'I wouldn't want to cause problems for you.'

'You're not. So relax, OK?'

Elena ran her fingers through her hair, pulled it back and tried to tie it in a knot. As soon as she let go, it fell back over her shoulders in thick golden waves.

'You do that all the time lately,' Cail remarked.

'What? What do I do all the time, sorry?'

'Play with your hair, try to tie it up then let it go.'

Elena tugged at the seat belt again, letting it out a little. She felt suffocated.

'I'm nervous, that's all.'

'OK, now do you want to tell me what's going on in that head of yours?' Cail asked.

Elena took a deep breath. 'In general it doesn't bother me, OK?'

'What – that people like you? I beg to differ. You want everyone to like you. It's crucial for you.'

'But . . . that's terrible,' she stuttered, staring at him with

326

bright, wide eyes and a mixture of bewilderment and indignation.

Cail shook his head. 'No. Terrible would be thinking that someone cared about you just because you act the way they want you to. Terrible is being so insecure you don't know what you're really worth: letting yourself be manipulated by someone whose only concept of a relationship is crushing other people. *That* would be terrible, Elena.' He spoke calmly, without changing his tone, in the same voice he'd just used to point out something so insignificant she could no longer remember what it was. '"Terrible" is the perverse way some people subjugate children and adults,' Cail went on. 'People who threaten not to love you any more if you ever do something they don't like. Look at you, Elena, you're beautiful inside and out. Don't be ruled by your vulnerability.'

A long silence, then she let go of the seat belt and turned back to the window. 'I don't like being psychoanalysed.'

Cail smiled. 'Because I'm good at it, and that winds you up. Besides, I always tell you the truth. I don't care what you say or do. You know those things wouldn't make me change my mind about you. That's why you like me.'

Elena shot him a burning glare. But when she saw the look on Cail's face she had to bite her lip to try not to burst out laughing. 'It's not you I like, it's the perfume you wear,' she said haughtily. 'I'm sorry to disappoint you, but that's how it is.'

'I never wear perfume,' Cail said. 'I wouldn't be able to smell the roses if I did.'

'But . . . that's impossible,' Elena said.

'I swear, no perfume. Ever.'

Elena was baffled. She could smell Cail's perfume – even in that very moment. It was intense, spicy and enthralling. And it

327

was the first thing she had noticed about him, even before she saw his face.

Elena stretched out a hand to turn on the radio. But after a couple of minutes she turned it off again.

'Relax,' Cail said. 'It's all going to be fine. My parents will adore you. They couldn't not, even if they wanted to. You sneak into people's hearts by the back door, unassumingly, which makes it practically impossible to kick you out. As for Beatrice, I don't know if we'll find the answers at the château. I guess we'll find out when we get there.'

Silence. Cail looked fleetingly over at Elena, who was curled so far into her seat it seemed as if she wanted to disappear into it.

'Hey, what's wrong? Do you want me to stop the car?' he asked gently.

'Couldn't you just say you like me?'

Cail smiled. 'That would be an understatement, don't you think? And I can't really explain anything right now. Time, remember? We talked about this.'

Elena smiled. 'Yeah, yeah . . . time . . . the baby, blah blah blah.'

They drove peacefully for a few miles. Once they'd passed Avignon, they left the main road for a smaller road, heading into the countryside. The meadows soon made way for hills. Elena noticed that right at the highest points there were clusters of houses and little villages. Covering the slopes, like a colourful blanket, were fields of flowers, vineyards and olive groves.

'There. That's home – La Damascena,' Cail said, pointing to an iron gate set in a stone wall. 'There are ten hectares including Mediterranean scrubland, hundred-year-old olive trees and the greenhouses where we keep the roses. There's also a stream running through it. Angus, my father, diverted it into an artificial lake, so during the wet season the water is contained and the fields don't flood any more. Up on the highest part there's the main house. Then an outbuilding where my sister Sophie lives, and a bit further down, there is my house.'

His voice held that subtle pride that comes from years spent improving, organizing and caring for your own land. In the end it becomes part of you. Elena felt the same about the Rossini house in Florence. The house she'd never considered home and had now made her own again, just as Cail had done with La Damascena.

'And where are we staying?' There was a hint of apprehension in her question.

'Together, obviously. My house isn't very big, but it has two bedrooms and we should be quite comfortable. We'll have more freedom. Once my mother gets her hands on you, it'll be difficult to tear you away from her.'

'I . . . have you told her about the baby?'

Cail didn't reply.

Elena moistened her lips and said in a small voice, 'I don't want to cause any problems.'

'You won't, don't worry. Look, we're here,' he said, still ignoring the question that was burning in her mind.

Even if she had wanted to say something else, there wasn't the opportunity, for the road they'd taken after Cail had activated the automatic gates opened into a gravel-covered courtyard. Ahead of them were the walls of a picturesque old mill; part of its structure was still visible, the wheel plunging into the stream . . . the waters singing many a story about the property. The house was about 100 metres away, to the right. It was certainly the most recent building in the complex:

three storeys high and built entirely in white stone. In the midday sun, its neat blue shutters seemed to smile. On the wooden porch stood a group of terracotta pots very similar to the ones Elena knew from Florence. And then roses, a profusion of roses like she'd never seen before. They were climbing along the walls, spilling from vases, carpeting the flowerbeds. Red, yellow, pink, in every possible shade and form, tapered, globe- or chalice-shaped. Some buds were simple and elegant, others round like marbles.

Cail parked in front of the house, jumped out, and opened the door for Elena.

'Finally! I was starting to think you'd changed your mind.' An attractive, mature woman with a confident walk and a friendly smile came towards them.

Elena tensed. 'Don't leave me,' she said in a panic. Cail reached for her hand and interlaced his fingers with hers.

'Never,' he whispered, with a gentle squeeze.

'We stopped to admire the view,' he said. 'Mum, this is Elena.'

'Of course it's her, who else would it be?' Elizabeth replied, unravelling herself from her son's embrace. 'Welcome, my dear. Now, if my son would be so kind as to let go of your hand, I'd like to greet you properly.'

'Thank you,' Elena said quietly.

Elizabeth smelled of roses, but her perfume was delicate, discreet, like the scent coming from the rosebuds. First came gardenia, then vanilla. It was sweet, like the look she was giving Elena.

She hadn't expected such a warm welcome. And when Angus McLean arrived, a few moments later, she needed no introduction. Looking at him gave Elena a fairly good idea of what Cail would look like in another thirty years.

Giving her a big bear hug, he kissed her on each cheek. 'Good gracious, my boy. You've always been one for surprises, but this is two for the price of one!' he said, gesturing towards Elena. 'I think you've outdone yourself this time.'

Elena, Cail and Elizabeth tried to ignore his allusions, but he continued to congratulate his son, patting him heartily on the back and grinning. Like Cail, Angus smelled of roses. Both men were well-built and strong, so confident in themselves that they weren't afraid of sporting a supposedly feminine fragrance. There was nothing vulnerable or affected about them. In Angus, however, there was something else: black pepper, cedar and other woods. It was unusual, this perfume, and strong. How a couple as talkative and exuberant as these two had produced a reserved man like Cail was beyond her.

Elena was pampered by them all. While Angus took her to see the garden and showed her the greenhouses, Cail got Hermione out of the garage and took the bike for a spin. Elena saw him disappear with a deep roar that resembled the panic in her stomach. But before there was time for it to develop into anything more substantial, she heard him come back – and when he took off his helmet and gave her a wink, she burst out laughing.

Then Sophie arrived. Cail's sister was a real beauty, without seeming to put any effort into her appearance. Simple, like the scent of golden citrus that spoke of long hours in the sun, she also smelled of roses. Gentle, subtle, combining with jasmine to become complex and intense.

She asked Elena all about perfume. She was very well-informed about the plants the essences were extracted from, especially when it came to protecting endangered species. Cail had told Elena that the environment was an issue close to his sister's heart. She was a primary school teacher and spent her free time cultivating native plants that were disappearing, which she then replanted in the wild with Cail.

'And what about whales, musk deer, beavers and civets? Is it true that parts of those animals are used to make perfume?'

Elena chose her words carefully. 'I could say yes . . . but that wouldn't be entirely true. Ambergris is a spontaneous secretion produced by sperm whales. It's very rare. As for other animal products, nobody uses them any more.'

'Really?'

'Yes. Apart from the fact that it's prohibited by law, all the perfumiers I've worked with replaced them years ago with synthetic substances that are more acceptable from all points of view.'

'So you don't make perfumes with those ingredients?'

'For me, perfume is about well-being, about respect for nature. Of course, that means I have to work with fewer essences, but that's fine. I believe that every perfumier should take an ethical stance on this. Extracting natural substances can have a huge impact on the environment, too. Sandalwood, for example, is now a very precious substance; it's practically on the verge of extinction. And it takes tons of water to produce just a litre of bergamot essential oil. In these cases, a product made by a chemical laboratory is an excellent alternative. It's best to dispel the myth that natural equals good and synthetic equals bad. All the choices we make should be as well informed as possible.'

Sophie listened attentively to Elena's explanations, the colour of her eyes, such a dark blue they seemed almost black, giving an added intensity to her gaze. She was blonde, like her mother, with a pale complexion. Cail, however, had inherited his features from his father, who, with a certain pride, still sported a lion's mane of chestnut-brown hair, with just a fleck of white at the temples. He was tall and well-built, like his son, and just then the two were having an animated discussion in front of the huge stone fireplace in the dining room. Elizabeth glanced over at them from time to time as she set the table. Elena couldn't hear what they were saying, but she was watching them with growing concern.

'They always do this,' Sophie told her. 'My dad loves flexing his muscles, but with Cail around there's not much he can do. I've never met such a stubborn man.'

Elena smiled, but she was still worried. What if she was the reason they were arguing?

Sophie seemed to read her mind, and gave her a nudge of encouragement. 'Dad's so contrary. You know he'll disagree with everything Cail says,' she went on, pouring a glass of wine that smelled of blackberries. 'Then, as soon as my brother's back is turned, all he does is brag about his success, his theories. "Cail says this, Cail says that." Do you know that in Paris, at the start of June, there's going to be a competition for new roses at the Parc de Bagatelle?'

Elena nodded.

'We're entering a special rose. Dad's really happy with the work Cail has done. He thinks Cail's rose will win – actually, he's sure it will. But he'll still argue with him about it, come up with other options that Cail just rejects. He's already decided what he's going to show. A new rose, a red rose.'

Elena knew; Cail had often talked to her about the competition. It was one of the most important dates of the season. They were going to go together, and she couldn't wait.

At that moment he caught her eye, smiled at her and raised his glass in her direction.

'Cail doesn't seem bothered by the argument,' she commented.

Sophie looked at her, puzzled. 'Why would he be? He's having a whale of a time. Ever since he grew as tall as our dad, when he was about thirteen, fourteen, he's done nothing but hold his own. I used to enjoy watching them argue. You know, Elena, it couldn't have been any other way, our dad's such a strong character.'

Her grandmother was, too, but Elena, like her mother, had always tried to avoid confrontation. Susanna had even left to seek her own path, casting aside anything that could get in her way.

And Elena? Well, she, too, could be pretty stubborn when she wanted to be. Didn't she refuse to follow Lucia's teachings just to prove she had the right to choose? And hadn't she tried to marry a man she didn't love and who, thank God, had cheated on her and got caught? She sniggered. Where had that thought come from? Thank God that she'd caught him at it with Alessia? The betrayal had taken her by surprise, throwing everything into disarray. But in the end, life really was all about perspective. Now she was glad it had happened. It seemed almost absurd, but it was the truth. Matteo's infidelity had triggered a chain reaction that had brought her into Cail's arms and given her a new life, a new Elena.

For the first time in a long time, she could make sense of so many things: she had ambitions, a plan, goals. She looked over at Cail, who was still talking to his father. Sparring. It really was wonderful; she was a lucky woman.

She just had to wait until the baby was born to be absolutely certain.

★　★　★

'Are you sure this is the castle?'

Elena was still looking at the majestic building that stood proudly on top of a low hill, between a village and a beautiful green valley. They'd set off early, leaving La Damascena at dawn. Cail called in to see a customer on the way, then they arrived at the village of Lourmarin.

'No, but there are a couple of things that made me think it might be.'

Elena carried on gazing at the castle, which still seemed too modern. 'I don't know – look at the towers, and then down there. Doesn't it look . . . well, new?' she said, pointing at one wing of the building.

Cail stared at her. 'New? Not if we assume it was seriously damaged during the French Revolution. This part might have been restored more recently.'

Yes, that was possible. Elena looked around, trying to find details that would bring her back to the diary, to what Beatrice had written. They were in the village now, the sun reflecting off the bright stone of the houses and medieval turrets, part of whose walls had been incorporated into the subsequent constructions. Tourists wandered around the narrow streets, where lush ivy climbed the walls. All in all, Lourmarin wasn't much different from the other hundreds of small Provençal villages. Solid structures made of stone and seasoned wood, squares with shops selling local fabrics in red and turquoise, essences and perfumes bearing the label 'natural', bunches of dried lavender and other herbs. Then all the cafés and restaurants where people stopped to try local dishes. But there was also something special about Lourmarin, something soothing. It was truly lovely, with a quiet beauty that came from its simplicity.

'Everything will be different nowadays,' Cail said.

'Yes, it's all very pretty, but I can't find anything that reminds me of the descriptions in the diary.'

He pointed to the castle and slowed down, so that Elena didn't wear herself out trying to keep up with him. The effort was starting to show on her face.

'I feel a bit tired,' he said, stretching. 'How about we have a rest?'

'Rubbish!' Elena exclaimed. 'Shut up and keep walking. I'll tell you when I'm too tired to carry on.'

Cail tutted, then brought the hand he was holding to his lips.

'Now why don't you tell me what convinced you that this might be the castle?' she continued.

'Remember that I told you I'd been here before? I've visited a lot of villages in Provence – my history teacher had a real passion for castles. And there are certain aspects of this castle in Lourmarin that seem very similar to what Beatrice described.'

'What do you mean, exactly?' Elena asked.

There was no need for him to reply, for as soon as the towers and keep appeared, she saw the gargoyle.

'I always thought she was talking about a lion, but I was wrong,' she whispered with her eyes fixed on the sculpture adorning the polygonal tower. 'It's more like a wolf.'

'She doesn't say exactly what animal it was, but the diary mentions some sort of mane. And the wolf is the symbol of the Lords of Lourmarin.'

Elena kept staring thoughtfully at the sculpture, her head tilted back. 'It does seem like a significant detail. But I don't think we can base our theory on it. After all, gargoyles were one of the most popular decorations of the time.'

'It was functional, too,' Cail added.

Elena looked at him, puzzled. 'You know, I've never really understood that. They have them at Notre-Dame, too. But it doesn't seem as if they actually drain water. They seem more like stone guardians.'

They carried on looking at the sculpture for a few minutes but there was no real way of knowing whether it was a lion or the symbol of a wolf. Cail pointed out the entrance. 'Come on, let's go inside.'

They went up the stairs, in through the main doors, and found themselves in an internal courtyard, with a pond covered in water lilies. At one end stood a statue of a woman who seemed to be resting. 'I don't remember her,' Elena said, referring to the diary.

'Maybe she hadn't been sculpted yet. She might be from after Beatrice's time.'

He had a point. Who knew what had happened since then. Time distorts and hides so many things.

They kept on looking around, moving from the flowerbeds to the open-air market where men and women in medieval costume were showing typical local products to tourists. Once they were inside the castle, however, everything changed. The air was dense, humid. Centuries of footprints had worn away the steps of the magnificent spiral staircase.

There was no need for words. Elena and Cail exchanged a smile and set off on the visit. She did recognize that splendid staircase. She wondered whether it was the same one the castle's owner took when he visited Beatrice in her room, at the top of the tower.

They moved through one room after another, seeing magnificent furniture, extraordinary antiques – but every-thing dated from later than the early 1600s, when Beatrice would have been resident there.

'I think it's that time . . . you know, when you say you feel tired and I nod and tell you to have a rest,' Elena whispered.

They separated from the group of visitors and Cail took her into a small drawing room. They sat down by the window, on a sort of stone bench carved into the thick wall. 'It's not very comfortable, but you can see the whole valley,' Cail said. But Elena wasn't listening. She was staring into a corner of the room that was sectioned off by a pretty, decorated screen.

Cail carried on talking, reading out the history of the castle from a book they'd bought when they arrived. ' "Built in the fifteenth century by Foulques D'Agoult on the ruins of a previous fortress, the château had many owners; at the end of the sixteenth century it passed to the Créqui-Lesdiguières family . . ." There you go, I reckon that's the period we're most interested in. It could be him, Charles I of Blanchefort. Listen, it says here he married the daughter of Duke François de Bonne and inherited the Duke's estate. But . . . damn! Everything in the castle was lost. They only saved a few pieces of furniture that were hidden in a cellar . . . Elena, are you listening to me?'

She pointed mutely at the screen. Cail noticed that her finger was trembling. 'What's wrong?' he said.

Elena stood up, quickly followed by Cail, and went over to the screen. 'Look,' she whispered. 'It's like my grandmother's.'

She edged closer, scanning through the images. Cail walked around it, checking the wooden frame, then he focused on the scene it depicted.

A knight and a lady were dancing in a garden. On the next panel, he was leading her under an arch of roses. There were three clearly stylized white roses. On a third panel, the woman was leaning over a workbench, and in front of her was an alembic.

'It's a distiller – look!'

Cail came closer and nodded. After she'd stared at the image for a few minutes, Elena went round to the other side of the screen and kept following the production of the perfume – because that's what it was. Roses: three, white. Water and oil. Citrus: lemon and orange. Then gardenia – no, impossible – it must be iris.

Elena took a long look at the first panel, then she moved on. Now the woman in the painting was mixing the essences and pouring them into three vials. Elena hurried to the final panel. And it left her speechless.

'This is the formula, Cail. Do you see?' she said, grabbing him by the arm. 'Beatrice set out the formula on this screen. Look, it's not a painting, it's a tapestry!'

Cail looked again at the images. 'You're right.' He walked around it: front and back, then again from the beginning. 'So, now you know what's in the mysterious perfume?'

Elena shook her head. 'No, this is only part of the recipe. Beatrice formulated the perfume exactly as we do today: she didn't simply combine essences, she thought about it. Rose, citrus, iris . . . I've got no idea how many drops, maybe just three, maybe thirty. I'll have to try,' she said. 'Then she added water – if that is, in fact, water – and waited three moons. Right?'

'Yes, there are three moons in that sky. What makes you say this is just part of it?'

Elena kept on gazing at the screen. 'There should be other ingredients . . . and in Florence, there's a very similar screen in my grandmother's workshop. The structure is identical, but the design is different, although it's in the same style.'

'You think it's got something to do with this one?'

'I'm not sure . . . They were very common items of furniture in those days.' But she hoped so, she really hoped so. There was a good chance. Even if she hadn't determined the formula, maybe the tapestry in Florence would hold some clues. So, two screens: one in the castle where Beatrice had stayed, all those centuries ago, and one where she lived. Yes, there was such a thing as a coincidence, but Elena was convinced that there was a link between the two. Perhaps one was the key to the other?

'If the other piece of the formula really is in Florence, the Rossinis had it under their noses all these years. That's crazy, don't you think?' she mused.

'It depends what it shows. Without this one,' Cail said, pointing towards the screen, 'how would you have known that it was part of a formula? Without both the tapestries, no one could have known.'

'It's a truly ridiculous way of recording a perfume composition.'

'Not that ridiculous, if you want to keep it hidden.' He pulled out the camera he'd used to immortalize the gargoyle and started to take photos.

They didn't leave Lourmarin until the evening, spending the rest of the day looking for other signs of Beatrice's existence, but apart from the screen and the gargoyle with a wolf's head, they didn't find anything else significant.

Though perhaps it was a sign that there were so many surnames of Italian origin amongst the village population. Apparently, there had been mass immigration from Piedmont under the first Lord of Lourmarin, and the Italian settlement had then been boosted by a skilled workforce of silkworm-breeders. The migration encouraged by the first de Medici

Queen, Catherine, continued until the second Italian Queen of France, Marie.

Cail and Elena had discovered that almost by chance as they read the guidebook. Then they'd asked in the restaurant where they had lunch, Le Moulin – with two Michelin stars, no less.

They arrived back at La Damascena exhausted. Cail had another meeting the following morning, then in the afternoon they were going back to Paris.

Elizabeth and Angus spent a lot of time with Elena. They were both dying to ask about the baby, but they held back. And she was glad they did, because she wouldn't have known what to tell them. Of course, she could tell them the truth: that the baby was just hers. But there was too much at stake. She'd cleared up some of their issues, but not all. Cail was always at the forefront of her mind, but she still didn't feel ready to take things any further, and she knew that he wasn't ready either. The strange compromise they'd reached together was their business and no one else's. Sooner or later, things would move on. Or Elena hoped they would . . . with all her heart.

Avignon was exactly as Elena remembered it: full of charm, understated and refined. The high-walled Papal Palace still took her breath away with the grandeur of its battlements and pointed towers.

Cail drove Elena to the gardens. Flowers, plants and swans – an incredible number of swans gliding peacefully along the streams that ran amongst the fragrant greenery. They took a long walk, had lunch on a restaurant terrace, then headed back to the airport.

While they were waiting, Elena called Monique. She couldn't wait to tell her about the screen and the possibility that it might reveal part of the formula. Her ancestor had been very imaginative in handing down the Perfect Perfume. She spoke to Monique for a few minutes, giving her a brief update, then she turned to Cail and said, 'Do you want to go out for dinner? Monie's just been promoted, and she's taking us to the Lido de Paris to celebrate.'

He raised an eyebrow. 'Have they made her Vice-President or something?'

Elena laughed. 'Hah! So we'll go?'

'Aren't you too tired?'

'Did you hear what I said? The Lido de Paris on the Champs-Élysées!' she repeated, enunciating each syllable carefully.

'*Oui, ma belle,*' Cail replied.

'We're coming!' she almost shrieked. And the two women went on talking for a while. By the end of the call Elena was feeling decidedly happy. 'Monie says hi,' she told Cail, who was still reading though the various leaflets he'd picked up in Lourmarin.

'How is she?'

'Same as usual. That Jacques . . . Well, it's probably better if I don't say anything,' she decided. 'Anyway, she says she can't wait to hear all about our trip. You know, when we were little we were always speculating about Beatrice and her Perfect Perfume. It almost doesn't seem real that the formula could be so simple. At least the top notes. I can't speak for the rest yet.'

'And what if it's the second screen that holds the secret?'

22

Ylang-ylang: expression. Warm and feminine, tropical and
sweet.
The fragrance enables us to overcome disappointment and
offence.
Releases hidden feelings and helps us to express the poetry
in our souls.

The Lido de Paris. Monique had decided tonight would be
different. She was sick of staying at home; that kind of life
wasn't for her. *Merde!* She almost didn't recognize herself.

While she was getting dressed, she listened to Apocalyptica's
first version of 'Hope'. Yes, she could certainly use some of
that. She started to dance in her bare feet, letting the sound
of hard rock penetrate to her core, and a moment later, when
it was suddenly replaced by a sweet melody, she thought she
actually felt better. Soaring, violent chords echoed in her heart
and became a slow, harmonious melody, moving her to tears.
Wasn't that what life was like?

No, lately hers wasn't.

She felt a familiar knot, one that had been crushing her throat for a while now, sometimes even preventing her from breathing. But she refused to give in to the unpleasant sensation.

'You don't like it? Then stop whining and do something about it,' Jasmine had told her in no uncertain terms, the last time she'd visited Grasse. Her mother was a very pragmatic woman. And she was completely right! Monie knew she should change the things she didn't like. Jacques hated her going out without him. In reality, especially recently, all they did was stay at home, in bed. Their relationship had been reduced to sex, nothing more. It was good – no, it was fantastic, amazing. But that was it. Every time they tried to discuss anything, they ended up arguing, so they'd gradually stopped talking and met in the only place they actually seemed to understand one another. But afterwards . . . afterwards she felt sad, so full of resentment. And she'd had enough.

Tonight she was going out as a single girl, while her friends were now a couple. True, it wasn't the perfect time for Elena to be getting involved in a relationship, but the pregnancy was quite far along now. The wait was coming to an end. Soon Monique would become an honorary aunt, Elena a mum – and who knew how Cail would act? She sincerely hoped that for once, things would turn out a little bit like they do in fairy tales.

That night, Monique wore an indecently short, sparkling black Dolce & Gabbana dress. Just two silk straps, a scrap of material and an enormous number of glimmering beads. High heels, curled hair, and a touch of her new perfume. Le Notre was excited about this creation. She couldn't take all the credit, of course. Ilya Rudenski, the new *maître parfumeur*, had come up with the fragrance, while she had simply guided the variation of the perfume towards simpler, more popular tastes.

It had been very interesting working with Ilya. The man was a genius: the perfume was impressive, and almost entirely synthetic. It had to be, to give it that intensity and durability. The imagination, the vision that Ilya had shown, had convinced everyone. The perfume was completed by a few natural essences, which gave it body and a retro charm.

Elena would have been horrified by the composition. But Monique wasn't interested in the backstory of a perfume. She was only ever interested in the final scent, not what went into it. She loved to change her scent, depending on her mood. For her, perfume was like a dress: one today, another tomorrow.

Thinking about clothes, she decided to take something with her. She would happily bet that Elena didn't have anything to wear. That woman was hopeless when it came to fashion.

She finished getting ready: a dash of lipstick, a light jacket and one last look in the mirror.

'Too bad, Jacques!' she said. 'When you get back from London I'm going to tell you just how much fun I had.'

Elena unpacked, watered the plants and had a little chat with them. Then she started to panic. There was nothing in her wardrobe that could possibly be suitable for an elegant night at a place like the Lido. Once she'd rejected every single dress she owned, she phoned Monique.

'I can't come, I've got nothing to wear!'

'I'm on my way. And I'm bringing a couple of things for you. So take a deep breath, have a long hot shower and put your hair up. I'll take care of everything, OK?' She hung up immediately, before Elena could object. She was going out tonight, whatever it took.

Elena scowled at her mobile. Then muttering something about how stick insects would never understand whales in a million years, she took a long bath, tied her hair back in a low bun, leaving a couple of loose strands either side of her face, and put on mascara and a lick of eyeliner.

'Come up,' she yelled as soon as she heard Monique's voice calling her from downstairs.

Monique handed over a coat hanger with a couple of dresses on it. Elena was in a filthy mood, and the banana-yellow dressing gown she was wearing wasn't making things any better.

'See if you like one of these dresses. They're floaty, and blue is so slimming.' Monique looked her friend up and down. 'You look really well, *chérie* – this holiday's taken years off you. So, what's new?' she asked, giving her a wink.

Elena pointed at her protruding stomach. 'Well, I've put on two pounds for starters. But the real news is that we've probably found out where Beatrice stayed during her months in France – *and* who the man was who broke her heart!'

Monique was dying to ask her more about the discovery, but it was clear Elena was ready to explode.

'I'm so huge,' she moaned. 'I don't even know if I can get these on.'

'Don't worry,' Monique said soothingly. 'I'm sure you'll surprise yourself. Have you got a pair of high heels?'

Elena took the dresses, retreated into the bathroom and half-closed the door.

'Yes,' she called. 'All the ones you brought me. How you manage to walk in those damn things I will never know.'

'Remember this moment when it's my turn and I make you want to strangle me,' Monie muttered to herself.

A couple of minutes later, Elena emerged from the bathroom.

'Wow! You look great!' From the hold-all she had brought with her, Monique produced a matching clutch bag and handed it to Elena.

Just then, Cail joined them. He went over to Elena and spun her around. 'You look wonderful,' he whispered, before kissing her on the lips.

'If you two have quite finished smooching, it's time we got going. And don't think I've got any intention of playing gooseberry. I want to know all the details of what you found out.'

In the taxi on the way to dinner, the couple gave Monique the low-down. The knight, most likely, was Charles I of Blanchefort. With the help of Beatrice's perfume, Charles had acquired everything he ever wanted, from his bride to his valuable possessions – including the dukedom.

'How could a simple perfume have so much power?' Monique wondered.

'In general, in those days, perfumes masked bad smells,' Elena reminded them. 'Poor hygiene was rife. Think of the difference a slight scent of roses, neroli, or citrus and iris would have made. The middle notes are quite clear, but there's no indication of the base notes at all. Beatrice left the mixture to mature for three months – I think she used alcohol and water – and I'm afraid the final fixative is some kind of animal musk. I can't come up with anything else that would explain the effect it had on the young lady of Lourmarin.'

'Ambergris?' Monique suggested.

'I don't know . . . it could be. As soon as I get back to

Florence, I want to take a good look at the screen – you know, the one in the workshop.'

'You mean that's where Beatrice wrote the formula?'

Elena shrugged her shoulders. 'I'm not sure, but there's a good chance.'

'God, this is huge! When are we leaving?' Monique asked. 'Because, I mean – imagine if it's true. An ancient perfume formula from the seventeenth century illustrated on a screen. It would be a massive hit, and I don't mean the perfume, I mean the story.'

Cail frowned. 'After the baby's born, we'll all go together, OK? Look, we're nearly there.' He pointed at the brightly lit area with people milling around on the pavement.

There was no way of continuing the conversation right now; they got out of the taxi and went up to the doors. The Lido de Paris was busy that night; the show always drew a huge crowd of tourists. Monique had been there often. At the beginning of their relationship, Jacques had taken her there all the time. She loved the place – she really enjoyed the shows and the atmosphere. The dancers were quite extraordinary.

While Monique went to collect the tickets, Cail had to go back and find Elena who was still standing there, staring at everything like a little girl. If the outside of the building was luxurious and fascinating, the inside looked like a film set. Blue and gold were the dominant colours: a grand arcade led to the dining rooms.

Cail helped Elena take off her coat and took it to the cloakroom. Monique was about to rejoin her friends, who had gone on ahead, when she accidentally bumped into someone.

'Oops – sorry!' she said pleasantly.

348

'Watch where you're going, will you!' the woman snarled, smoothing out the wrinkles in her dress.

Monique looked up and met the furious gaze of a very young, very pretty girl. 'Actually, it's *you* who should watch out for *me*. It's not as if you have right of way,' she replied frostily. Then she recognized the girl, and her heart skipped a beat.

'What's going on?'

It was bound to happen sooner or later. That was all Monique could think as Jacques walked over to join his fiancée.

'This clumsy idiot walked into me and made me drop my bag,' the girl whined. For a second, Monique toyed with the idea of raising her hand and teaching the little cow a lesson. Meanwhile, Jacques stood, frozen, between the two women.

Monique was seething with rage. So many lies! 'Unavoidable commitments relating to the management of the new Narcissus headquarters.' What a bastard. She would have liked to give each of them a slap.

Jacques picked up the handbag from the floor and passed it to the girl, who continued to insult Monique. No greeting, not even a glance. When Monique realized he was pretending not to know her, she felt the blood drain out of her body, taking with it all the warmth, happiness and good humour she'd been feeling just seconds before.

In the background, the tempo of the music had increased. Jacques's fiancée was still whinging and he was trying to stem the tide of words.

Monique felt sick. Sickened by herself and by that silly little girl who thought she was Queen of the World. But wasn't that how she felt about herself, too, when she and Jacques were together? Queen of a lie, an illusion; queen of a handful of dust that slipped through her fingers as soon as she opened her fist.

Finally, Jacques looked at her. He was pale, his expression impenetrable. 'We're leaving,' he said tersely to the girl. 'I've had enough of your tantrums.'

Monique watched the couple until they disappeared from view. Then she looked for Elena and Cail. They were about fifteen feet away, standing quite still, watching. She noticed that they were holding hands, Cail towering over Elena, as if he wanted to protect her.

That was the way it was supposed to be, Monique thought. And it wasn't the knowledge that they'd witnessed the ugly encounter that made her decide to leave; it was the deep compassion on their faces. For a moment she saw things through their eyes, and she felt a profound shame.

When Elena took a step forward, Monique shook her head and hastened out into the night, clutching a tiny handbag; at that moment it seemed as if it was all that remained of her life.

I'm not home, leave a message and I'll call you back.

Elena listened to Monique's answerphone message for the umpteenth time and waited for the beep before saying, 'Call me or I swear I'll come round there. Actually, no – I'll phone your mum and tell her everything. I mean it!'

She put down the receiver, slamming it with more force than was really necessary. Aurore, who was arranging a pyramid of perfumed soaps, cast her a puzzled glance then quickly got back to work. Elena had decided to take the girl on for a few hours a week. Since that night at the Lido, Monique had all but disappeared, not answering the telephone other than to say she was OK. Those two syllables were all Elena could get out of her. She missed her friend desperately; she was worried about her and also felt very lonely without her.

During the day, Cail was out at work. He'd moved some of his plants to a greenhouse outside the city, so they could grow in the best possible conditions. There wasn't enough space left on the terrace in the Marais. The Bagatelle competition was coming up, and everything had to be perfect for it. In the evening, when he got home, he was so tired he often fell asleep on the sofa while they were talking. When he did so, Elena would cover him with a blanket before she went downstairs to bed. The baby was very active these days, kicking with an enthusiasm that sometimes made her feel quite uneasy.

Damn! She nervously rearranged the objects on the counter, then put them back where they started. It was unfair of her to be angry with Monique and Cail, and she knew that. But she just couldn't help it. She really was in a bad mood these days.

Cail was making regular exhausting journeys just to come back and sleep in Paris. Elena was aware that he was only doing it to make sure she wasn't on her own. But that didn't mean that she missed him any the less. Sometimes, it felt as if both her friends had abandoned her. First Monique, now Cail. Work, work, work. And who was thinking about her? No one, that's who!

She knew it wasn't true, of course. When her bad moods gave her a moment's peace, Elena admitted to herself how lucky she was. But then all it took was one glance at herself in the mirror, and she was full of despair again. Her back pain wasn't letting up either and, what's more, it was increasingly likely that if they didn't widen the doorways soon, there was no way in hell she was going to get through them.

That afternoon, Elena was completely exhausted. She'd had a long and tiring day. Aurore hadn't said a word the whole time. On several occasions, she'd caught the girl staring longingly at the perfumier's organ she kept in one corner of the shop. It was a gift from Cail, who'd found it in a terrible condition at a street market and restored it. At first, she'd struggled to find the right kind of tiny essence bottles to suit its nineteenth-century style, but eventually she had, and now this piece of furniture was amongst Absolue's main attractions. It was what she showed the clients when she made customized perfumes. 'Why not?' Elena decided. The next day, she would let the girl make her first whole perfume.

She tried calling Monique again, and this time she left a furious message. She'd managed to find out from Jasmine that Monique had split up with Jacques, for good. Then, on one of their phone calls – more silence than talking – Monique had told her mother that she needed a change of scene. Elena was desperately worried. How was Monique going to get through this difficult period without her friends or her family?

She wondered what might help, but nothing came to mind. Besides, she had something else to worry about: she couldn't manage Absolue by herself, not now the birth was so close and Cail was getting busier at work. She would have to close the shop – a terrifying thought.

She sat on one of the shop sofas and put her head in her hands. Then she heard the bell ring and pulled herself together.

'Is everything all right, dear?' Geneviève Binoche walked over to her with a big smile. Since the first time she'd come looking for her, the writer had become a regular visitor at the perfumery.

'Yes, yes. Just a bit tired. How are you?'

'I'm well,' the woman replied, settling herself down next to Elena. 'I wanted to give you some good news.'

'I could really do with some,' Elena told her.

'Let's see if this cheers you up. So . . . my editor likes the idea of the perfume of Notre-Dame, and wants to give me the money to get it made. I don't need to tell you how incredible it would be to compose it on the day of the launch. Imagine the scene: you, my dear, picking out the essences one by one, and, while you measure them, telling the audience what inspired you. The grandeur of the cathedral; the cold calculation of people who give up love for wealth and power. It will be a resounding success, not to mention the good it will do for Absolue's reputation.'

'You're asking me to make the perfume?' Elena enquired.

'Of course! We've always talked about it as a possibility, and after the unfortunate incident with Narcissus I thought about scrapping the whole idea, but that would be a real shame. Elena, I have every confidence in you. I'm sure you can make this perfume.'

Elena smiled at her. 'It would be wonderful.' But her mind had already started to drift in another direction.

It wasn't the desire for success that made her thoughts turn to the formula for the Perfect Perfume. It was the similarity between what had happened to the characters in Victor Hugo's famous novel and to her ancestor, Beatrice. Phoebus, the man Esmeralda loved, rejected her so he could marry the rich Fleur-de-Lys. Charles de Blanchefort did exactly the same thing to Beatrice.

The Rossinis' Perfect Perfume had returned to her life, Elena realized with a jolt. And who better than her ancestor to express the grief of an undervalued, discarded love that was unable to compete with a man's desire for power and wealth?

353

The Perfect Perfume could be the perfume of Notre-Dame!

Beatrice had known from the start that there was no hope for her love. The knight who commissioned the perfume had already told her it was for his future wife: a rich noblewoman of high birth who was set to change his future. His relationship with Beatrice was just a bit of fun. Elena felt a lump in her throat – for Esmeralda, for Beatrice, and also for Monie. Centuries might have passed, but men and women were still making the same mistakes.

She sighed and looked thoughtful, while Geneviève waited patiently, allowing her time to think things through. She had half the formula, Elena said to herself, and she was willing to bet the rest was on the twin screen in Florence. She'd need to adapt the recipe to suit the cathedral, but it was do-able.

'How long do we have until your book launch?' she asked Geneviève.

'It's in September.'

They were already approaching May. Beatrice had left the mixture to macerate for three months. The baby would be born at the beginning of June. June was also the time of the prize-giving for Cail's rose, to which he had dedicated his body and soul.

Elena went over it again and again, but even if there were three of her, there still wouldn't be enough time. In the end she sadly shook her head. 'I'm afraid it can't be done.'

Geneviève's face fell. 'That's a real shame, my dear. I would have liked you to be the one to handle it all. It will be difficult to find someone else to make the perfume. It really meant a lot to me.'

'We just don't have enough time, that's the problem,' Elena explained. 'You see, the perfume needs to mature, and in order to compose it, I need to go back to Florence. At the moment I can't leave Absolue. Could it wait a little bit longer?'

Madame Binoche stood up, looking thoughtful. 'I don't know. I could try,' she said. 'I'll speak to my editor – she's trying to speed things up.'

Elena hoped some compromise could be arranged. Her desire to compose the perfume was growing stronger by the minute.

'Think about it, my dear,' Geneviève went on. 'There's a very famous house lined up to buy it and distribute it. They're talking about a lot of money, and naturally you would be named as the creator of the essence.'

She would love to do it. Elena was sure Beatrice's perfume would be perfect for Notre-Dame. But she had no idea how to fit it all in.

'Thank you for understanding,' she said.

Geneviève gave her a gentle hug and told her she'd call her for her final decision.

It was Cail who had first played her Ludovico Einaudi's piano music. He put it on while they were looking at the stars. Elena liked to lie back in the rocking chair, wrapped in a blanket, while he tinkered with the telescope. These were moments of total relaxation; few words and real contemplation. And so many thoughts. 'Nuvole Bianche' – 'White Clouds' – was her favourite piece. Cail had given her some long compilations on CD, and she had started to put them on while she was working. It had become a habit now.

'Don't you get bored of it?' Aurore asked as the notes of the piano began almost unnoticed, rising in a crescendo to come back down and pick up the same swirling rhythm before subsiding again. This music was a background. For happy

355

thoughts, sad thoughts, for people who had had enough of their problems, but more than anything, Elena thought, it was the perfect companion because they both liked it, she and Cail.

'It helps me concentrate ... It's like a stream to rest my thoughts on; it softens the bumps. And besides, it's soothing. When I was little and composing my first perfumes, I couldn't control the essences – I was under their power. I saw them in the form of colours; I was afraid of them, I loved them; whenever I smelled them, the emotions I felt were so intense they made me euphoric and upset at the same time. Music like this would have been a great help.'

'That's amazing!' Aurore was awed.

Elena gave a half-smile. 'I didn't think so at the time. Perfumes weren't always something I wanted. For a long time I detested them. Then they became a necessity, a duty. It's only recently that I rediscovered them for what they really are, and they became a source of joy and happiness again.'

Aurore didn't understand. 'How could you ever hate perfume?'

'Good question. Maybe one day I'll tell you. But for now, let's get on. So, you're not wearing perfume today, right?'

'No, you told me not to.'

'Good. Let's move on. First thing: the essences ... we've got those. They're the ones in the aluminium bottles.' She pointed them out one by one, then she froze.

The scene was like *déjà-vu*. An image flashed into her mind, jostling its way through her memories. Herself as a little girl and her grandmother showing her the essences in exactly the same way, making the same gestures as she was now. Elena felt a deep sense of belonging and loss at the same time. Suddenly, she felt terribly alone. She desperately missed Lucia. She missed her grandmother's presence, the way she handled everything – she even missed her silences.

Then Elena came to her senses and realized that Aurore was asking her something. The image gradually faded: the Rossinis' laboratory disappeared and became her bright workspace in the Marais once more. But Elena had learned something important in the last few moments: that, despite the acute sense of nostalgia she was feeling for her grandmother, there was no longer any sadness in her. She was celebrating Lucia Rossini with the gestures that had once belonged to her grandmother and were now hers, passing on the knowledge she'd learned, teaching someone who would also make good use of it one day.

'Yes, yes, you told me that already. Then what? What comes next?'

There was a clear impatience in Aurore's voice. Elena almost wanted to laugh: the girl was as twitchy and eager as an athlete on the starting-line. Setting aside her memories and feelings, Elena focused on the work they were about to do.

'Dropper, *mouillettes*, cylinder to put our composition in, alcohol, paper filters. We've got everything we need. But today I thought we wouldn't make just any perfume: this one will be *your* perfume.'

'I don't understand,' Aurore said quietly.

Elena smiled. 'This perfume will belong to you – it will be Aurore's perfume. You'll make it according to the process we use to create a perfume of the soul – or "a customized perfume", as the customers would have it.'

'Seriously?' Aurore was going to make her first perfume, and she was going to make it by herself! She still couldn't believe it.

The girl's face revealed the utmost concentration. Elena

would bet Aurore was already imagining how to mix the various essences, and decided she'd better give her a quick explanation before she got carried away by her artistic streak.

'Perfume is emotion – we agree on that. But it is also objective. Perfume has a structure: it comes from a framework, it follows a route, and we have to bear that in mind. But almost immediately, the perfume becomes *subjective*, because it stirs something in the person smelling it. A customized perfume represents us entirely, more than anything else: we like it, it comes from us. It's a way we communicate with others – with anyone, actually; it's not limited to people we know.'

'When you talk like that I could listen to you for hours,' Aurore whispered.

They exchanged a smile, and the lesson continued.

'For it to truly represent us, a customized perfume has to say something about us. Who are we? What do we want? What do we like? What do we *not* like? We can outline the concepts, then use them to create the formula. The more clearly we can establish what our customer's perfume should represent, the easier it is to find it. In general, there are three types of people who ask for a personalized perfume. Firstly, people who want a fragrance that brings joy, well-being and happiness with every breath. Secondly, those who want the perfume to identify them: it's unique, it belongs to them, distinguishes them from the rest of the world. Finally, those who see customized perfume as something glamorous, an expression of sophistication as opposed to standardized perfume, which has lost its identity.'

Elena paused; now came the difficult part, and she wanted the girl to really grasp the various mechanisms involved in the process. 'To really understand what a customer likes and what they don't like, we have to start with the five senses: visual colours, tactile sensations, sounds, music, what they like about food, flavours, and of course, smells, bearing in mind which perfumes they've worn and why they bought them. In short, a full sensory identikit. And last but not least, you need to take into account the personality of the client, and you do that by creating a rapport: talking to them, exchanging emails, making some personal contact. These are the essential things you have to know.'

'Everything looks different when you say it like that.'

'Exactly. Perfume isn't just something you put on – it's a wonderful, complex world of its own, a symbol.' She looked at Aurore. 'When the overall picture of who the customer is becomes clearer, the perfume should interpret it, transform it into smells. So then you choose the base notes; these form the backbone of the perfume. From there, you can make a few more suggestions, from which the customer can choose. It will still be a draft at this stage, though, to be corrected on the basis of its master's feelings.'

'The perfume's master ... wow. So I could become the master of the perfume we're going to make,' Aurore said.

'Not you *could*, you *will*.' Elena didn't say anything for a moment; she wanted to make sure the girl understood. 'Now, let's get started. First question: who is Aurore?'

Aurore laughed nervously, then the smile vanished from her lips and a look of real bewilderment appeared on her face. Elena grinned at her and winked. 'OK, let's start with an easy one. What do you hate?'

'People shouting, cooked vegetables, snobs who think they rule the world, private schools, pink, people who wear fur.' After this list, Aurore seemed to relax.

'What do you like?'

'Blue, soft fabric, chocolate, people who smile at stupid stuff, World Music, strawberry ice cream, my mum and dad's perfume. I try to mix them but it doesn't work properly, but I can't just wear one. One of them might be upset.'

Elena nodded. 'I understand. But by combining them you run the risk of knocking out anyone who gets too close.'

Aurore's eyes widened, then she realized Elena was just winding her up. They both laughed, clearing some of the tension in the air.

'OK, I think you're pretty clear on the concept. Now I'd tell you to start from an idea, which will be our brief. What should your perfume mean?'

Aurore gave it some thought, as she played with the hem of her jumper.

'I'd like it to mean change. For there to be flowers, light clothes, the warmth of the sun on your skin and the light you see in May, when the sky is clear.'

'That sounds like a description of spring,' Elena replied.

'Yes. I've always liked spring.'

'OK, so what do you think about starting with flowers? They could be the top notes. Then we need to go deeper into the concept, choosing the middle and then the base notes. The soul of the perfume.'

They started to select the essences: lime wood, lily of the valley, angelica, and then other, more delicate fragrances, reminiscent of a fresh, bright Parisian spring. Arranging them on the table, they sniffed them, passed the vials around, and set aside the ones that weren't suitable. In the end they were left with just the essences they were going to use. Every time they added a new drop, letting it slip inside the tiny filters, they noted everything down on a pad, sniffed the perfume on a *mouillette* and decided whether or not to increase the dose.

It took all night, but in the end, Aurore's spring bloomed in the graduated cylinder. The perfume would have to rest for a few weeks, for the alcohol to dissolve all the molecules. Only then would they smell it again and, if need be, correct anything the girl wanted to change.

'I'm so happy. This perfume means a lot to me.' Aurore was standing in the doorway of Absolue, but showed no signs of leaving.

Elena knew exactly how she felt. Finding a perfume, knowing it was right, smelling it and experiencing it was an incredible feeling. Creating something was always accompanied by a sense of joy.

'Me, too. You know, I'm really impressed by your intuition, by the way you chose the essences. You showed real skill and extraordinary sensitivity. I think it's time for you to think properly about continuing your studies in the subject. You would make a great fragrance designer.'

Aurore's face lit up. 'Next time can I make a perfume for my mum?'

Elena nodded. 'Of course. Next time you can make a perfume for Eloise.'

23

Tuberose: change. White, intense, sweet and seductive.
The fragrance of audacity and awareness.
Stimulates creativity, evokes the power of change.

'I'm going away.'

'What do you mean?' They were sitting around Elena's kitchen table. Monique had arrived first thing that morning, as soon as Absolue opened. Elena had taken one look at her friend and, realizing how upset she was, she'd pulled down the shutters and brought her inside.

'Le Notre needs someone in the New York branch. I volunteered.'

Elena gripped the cup she had in her hand. The aroma of tea was helping to absorb the shock. 'What about Absolue?'

'You know as well as I do that it's much more yours than it is mine,' Monique replied after a long pause. 'And let's be honest, *chérie*, natural perfume is your field. You have a God-given gift: incredible intuition, the magic touch – call it

362

what you want. But I don't belong here. I need stability, and for me to get real results I have to use synthetic molecules.'

It was true, everything Monie was saying was completely true. Elena had heard this conversation ever since she was a child. Her mother and grandmother had done nothing but argue about it, and neither of them would change their stance: one natural, the other synthetic. As for her, she'd chosen niche perfumery because she didn't want to have to compete with others and because she had a feeling for essences. It had been a rational and conscious choice. But it wasn't an easy job.

'How will you get by? You invested nearly everything you'd put aside in Absolue. I've got a bit, but—' Monique interrupted her with a firm hand gesture.

'Don't even think about it. You need that money for the baby. I already feel awful, knowing that I probably won't be here when he or she is born.' Monique was so overcome, so sad that Elena couldn't find the words to reply.

'I'm so sorry things have turned out like this.'

Monique pulled her hair back and tied it up. She'd straightened it that day and it came down to her waist. The cobalt-blue dress she was wearing suited her perfectly. She looked beautiful, as always, but she'd lost that self-assured edge that made her so special. Despite her stunning appearance, there was real despair in her eyes.

'Do you want to talk about it?' Elena asked.

Monique shook her head. 'I'll get over it. But I need to leave if I want to get my strength back. Jacques knows me too well: he knows how to trick me, how to say the right things. I didn't sleep a wink last night, I started dreaming about the two of us ... How he would say it was all just a misunderstanding, how he'd convince me *I* was the one he really loved. And when I came to see that, even after everything he's done

363

to me, I still wanted him back in my life – I felt sick. I actually threw up. Then I knew I had to put as much distance as possible between us.

'I have to do it now, Elena, before I lose this last scrap of pride, before he destroys it, along with whatever is left of my soul. I don't know who I am any more – I don't know anything any more!' Her lips were trembling so much she couldn't get the words out.

'*Chérie*,' Elena whispered, trying to comfort her friend.

Monique wiped a finger over her eyes, dabbing them to make sure her make-up didn't run. She took a few breaths, and smiled. 'I feel completely pathetic, I swear, feeling so sorry for myself. Now I understand Beatrice. In the end she went away to find herself.'

The two friends cried together, cursed and devised all sorts of torture they'd like to inflict on Jacques and his fiancée with all her wealth and titles.

'She's the daughter of Dessay, one of the biggest perfume-exporters in the world,' Monie explained. 'I never stood a chance. But you know what? In the end, I don't think he's even worth it.'

That wasn't true, and they both knew it. Right now, all Monie could do was wallow in her suffering and the belief that fate would somehow deal Jacques an appropriate punishment. This heartbreak was a phase, that's all: anyone who's had their feelings trampled on gets over it sooner or later. Eventually, there would be an afterwards . . . there always was. And then, all being well, Jacques would just be a regret, a poignant wish that things had gone differently. Life would go on.

Monique could rely on her work, Elena thought as she kissed her friend goodbye. A prestigious, interesting job in an exclusive, almost elite atmosphere. She would be successful, Elena was sure of that. And perhaps she'd meet someone who could love her for who she was. At least, that's what Elena hoped. Secretly she knew that, whatever the future held, the love Monique had once felt for Jacques would still be there somewhere, deep in her soul; it would never disappear entirely.

Moving to New York . . . Elena couldn't imagine it. It was so far away, so different; another continent. Monique would surely miss Paris. And even if she had asked for an advance on her salary, she couldn't manage without money, alone in New York. She needed cash.

Elena thought it over again and again. And her thoughts focused on one thing: Madame Binoche and Beatrice's formula. In a month or two, it would be impossible for Elena to make the trip to Florence. It all depended on the baby, on her health, on her documents for travelling abroad.

What if she went straight away? The thought sprang into her mind like one of those crazy notions that you usually dismiss out of hand. But not this time. Elena hurried downstairs and turned on the computer. She went to the website of Charles de Gaulle airport and checked the daily flights to Florence. There were still seats available, although it would cost a fortune. She checked the clock again. The flight left in the afternoon. If she wanted to get there in time, she'd have to get a move on.

She chose a travel agency, entered her details to make the booking, declared she was thirty-four weeks' pregnant, hesitated for a few seconds – and then hit SEND. Leaving so suddenly, without telling anyone . . . it was insane, it made no sense.

But then Monique's face appeared in her mind and Elena

knew it was the right thing to do. She couldn't stop to think. If she did, she'd never leave. And she had to go now, immediately.

Fortunately the airport was less than an hour from the Marais by taxi. It would take her another couple of hours to get to Florence. She wouldn't need long there – a day, maybe two. Then she'd be able to compose the perfume back here, in Paris.

Elena hurried into her bedroom, threw a couple of dresses, her medicines and vitamins into a suitcase, then she called Aurore.

'Can you look after the shop until I get back?'

'Yes, of course. When? I'll tell my mum. She'll be happy to help, too.'

'Now, right away. I'm going to Florence.'

'Wow. In that case, I'm on my way now,' Aurore promised.

'OK, thank you. I'll be away for a couple of days at most,' Elena said breathlessly. She finished arranging things with Aurore, told her where to find the keys and ran her through the system for opening and locking the doors. And anyway, she'd have her mobile with her all the time: they could get in touch if anything came up.

She called a taxi and, as she went downstairs, decided she'd phone Cail from the airport. Something told her he wasn't going to be best pleased about the decision she'd just made. She quickly pushed that thought to the back of her mind. One thing at a time, or she was going to go crazy.

Two hours later at the airport, Elena was starving. The plane to Florence didn't leave for another half an hour and, as if that weren't enough, she hadn't been able to get through to Cail.

She checked her documents and the tickets she'd printed

out again. The cost of them was enough to make her pass out. But it would be worth it, she could feel it. She put her head back, resting it against the wall. She was tired, and the baby had done nothing but wriggle around the entire trip. She closed her eyes for a moment, waiting for them to call her flight.

'There we go,' she said, struggling to get up. She checked the telephone for the thousandth time, hoping that Cail had got her message, but his mobile was still unreachable.

'*Merde, merde, merde*,' she cursed. Then she went over to the stewardess who was waiting at the boarding gate.

'Are you feeling all right?' the woman asked.

Elena forced a smile. 'I've still quite a long way to go, don't worry.'

The woman smiled politely. 'Yes, I see your ticket has the due date on it – tenth of June, right? But I'm afraid you also need a doctor's note.'

Elena's eyes widened. 'The declaration isn't enough?' she asked, alarmed.

The stewardess shook her head. 'A certificate would be better. The baby might decide to be born early and as you know, on a plane we're not exactly equipped.'

'But the flight is leaving,' Elena stammered, getting upset. 'I absolutely have to go to Florence, please! It's really important.'

The stewardess looked at the documents again. 'I suppose, under the circumstances, the information on the ticket might do,' she said after a few seconds, eyeing the queue that was starting to form behind Elena. 'OK,' she said eventually. 'Go on, and have a good trip. But bear in mind that after thirty-six weeks, no airline will let you fly.'

'Of course,' Elena replied with a relieved smile. She took

the documents the stewardess was holding out to her and hurried past. Thank goodness she'd bought a return ticket, she thought. And as for her due date: well, she hadn't exactly lied, she'd just taken into account the fact that first babies are usually born a little late. Where had she read that?

'Everything will be fine,' she found herself whispering. She ignored the shiver running down her spine, and carried on walking. She wasn't in pain, she was healthy and she had a mountain of things to do. One day – she just needed one day. She would find the formula, pick up a couple of things from her grandmother's laboratory, and come back to Paris. What could possibly go wrong?

Cail took the SIM card from what was left of his mobile phone and put it into the new phone he'd just bought. It was only a stupid accident, but it was one he could have done without. When he'd left Elena that morning, she had seemed fine, talking happily about Aurore and how the girl had made her first perfume.

Cail entered his PIN and the smartphone started to vibrate. Ten missed calls. He felt a knot in his stomach. Elena! The baby. Of course it had come the minute he wasn't there. He called her back, getting the number wrong, as he couldn't find it stored anywhere. He waited with his heart in his mouth.

The person you have called is not available. He swore and tried again. Then he ran to the car. As he made his way into the traffic he called Elena's gynaecologist. She would be able to tell him where they'd taken her. Paris was barely an hour away by car, he just had to hurry. After a couple of attempts, the doctor answered – but she didn't know anything about her patient.

'I can assure you she's not in labour. She has a code, so even if she were taken to another hospital I would have heard. Don't worry, your wife is fine.'

'Thank you,' Cail said. But he wasn't convinced; he wouldn't be until he'd heard it directly from Elena, and if he could confirm it for himself in person, even better. He tried calling her again, but her telephone was still switched off.

As he drove back into the city, taking every shortcut he knew and committing a considerable number of traffic offences, Cail cleared his mind of any thoughts. He was almost in the Marais when the phone rang. He stopped the car and answered.

'Cail, at last.'

'Thank God.' When he heard Elena's voice, Cail's heart-beat returned to a normal rhythm. 'I'm nearly home, darling. Are you all right? I'll be with you in ten minutes.'

'Um . . . that's actually what I wanted to talk to you about. I'm not in Paris.'

Cail thought he had misheard. 'Say again? Tell me Monique is with you. It's not wise to travel in your condition, Elena, you know that. The baby might be born early.'

Another silence. Then Elena cleared her throat.

'Cail, a couple of things happened. I'm in Florence.'

It was like a punch in the face. Cail drew the phone away from his ear and held it there for a few seconds.

'Are you there? Look, it all happened this morning. Monique's leaving, she's moving to New York. And Madame Binoche asked me to make the perfume again, remember? I told you about it. If I find Beatrice's formula, I can correct it and adapt it to Notre-Dame. I'd have the money to pay back Monique, and then . . . you know, Cail, I really want to make this perfume.'

Silence. Cail had never felt as alone as he did in that moment.

'And you didn't think to wait for me.' It wasn't a question but a bitter observation.

'There wasn't time. I kept calling you, but I couldn't get through.'

'I dropped my phone. One of the guys at work ran over it with the tractor,' he said in a monotone voice.

'Right,' Elena said. 'Are you OK? You sound angry.'

Cail took a breath and asked himself the same question. 'In your opinion, how should I feel when I find out you've gone off like this? You had no qualms about making the decision on your own. You didn't want my opinion because you knew I would have disagreed. You just didn't care.'

'Listen, we'll talk about this properly when I get back, OK? I'll explain everything,' replied Elena, who was beginning to lose her temper.

'There's nothing to explain. You've made no commitment to me. I haven't got any rights, I'm not even the father of your child. And you've just reminded me of that.'

Oh God. He really was angry, Elena thought.

'That's rubbish, Cail, as well you know. I'll be back tomorrow and we'll talk about it then.'

But Cail didn't think so. Suddenly he was faced with the reality of the situation they were in, and he could see it for what it really was, acknowledging everything with ruthless clarity. He gripped the phone in his hand, staring into the distance, at some indefinable point.

'No, Elena, it's too late for that. I . . . Take care of yourself.' He ended the call and sat holding his phone, his eyes fixed on the Seine flowing nearby, as dark and heavy as his soul.

When Elena called back, Cail turned off his mobile. He

had no desire to talk to her, nor to hear her voice. He couldn't bear the feeling of having a door slammed in his face again. God, he hadn't seen her for just a few hours and he already missed her like crazy. After a few minutes, he restarted the engine and screeched his way back into the flow of traffic.

The taxi dropped her right at the door of her grandmother's house.

'They say it's good to walk in your condition, but you know, I actually think the less exertion, the better,' the driver told her, helping her with the suitcase. 'Sure everything's all right?'

Not really. 'Yes, thank you,' Elena lied politely, then she paid her fare, said goodbye to the taxi driver, and closed the door behind her. There it was. The perfume of the house wrapped itself around her in a welcoming embrace. Elena went inside and collapsed on to the sofa. Silence. Everything there seemed to be sleeping, as though she'd arrived at night. She looked around and it felt as if she'd left the place just yesterday. The baby kicked and she put her hands over her face. A lifetime had passed since she'd left Florence: a whole lifetime.

Elena stood up, looked for the main switch and turned on the lights. She had a lot to do and she didn't want to waste a minute. She was upset that Cail had taken it so badly, desperate to see him again, to explain her reasons. Monique needed the money and Elena wanted to create this perfume. She felt compelled to do it. In fact, she *needed* to do it, end of story.

First of all, the screen; then everything else, she thought. She crossed the hallway and went into the workshop. There it was. She walked over to the corner where it stood and turned

371

on the lamp. A shiver ran down her spine. It was the same as the one in Lourmarin, there was no doubt. Even the frame seemed to be the same: simple, linear, almost as though it had been especially made to hold the screen. She imagined Beatrice leaning over the fabric, and it brought a lump to her throat.

She looked and saw a lady on a horse: she was on a journey. Alone. The knight was a long way off, behind her, and next to him rode another lady, dressed in finery.

'The wife,' Elena whispered. She kept following the design, but that was the motif for one whole side of the screen.

'Where did you put it?' she mumbled, baffled.

Then she went round the other side. A small deer and a forest. Trees, a stream, a necklace that could be gold, or ... amber. Water, the moon. And a vial.

Elena took out the notebook she had in her bag and went back to inspecting the screen from top to bottom. As she observed every detail, she tried to picture herself inside the scene. After all, she'd seen these places, and even though they'd changed over time, they were still essentially the same, weren't they? The forest below the castle came to life in her mind. The air filled with perfumes; it had rained recently – a stream had formed and was gurgling over the stones. Elena heard the knights calling and looked up. The sky was blue and clear, hawks were flying overhead. They were celebrating the nobles' wedding. Jubilant shouts and cheers echoed through the valley.

Beatrice spurred on her horse. She'd waited until the last possible moment, before realizing there would be no place for her there: she didn't want to feel how much joy there was at the wedding celebrations; she didn't want to watch him kiss his wife. He'd given her an escort for the journey. And he'd broken her heart.

A deer and three trees. Oak. They were oak trees. Beatrice had used animal musk and oak moss to make the perfume, and ambergris, all typical ingredients for that time. The symbolic necklace played on the double meaning of amber.

Elena came back to reality, observing and searching – and eventually, she had a firm idea of what went into the perfume. She wrote down the formula and closed her eyes. It was so simple, so commonplace; that couldn't be it, she thought. Her mind went back to the screen she'd seen in France. Lemon or hesperidium, she hadn't quite worked that out yet. Then rose, iris, jasmine, wood, musk, amber. Water, oil. A path, a walk through a garden – it was all there.

It wasn't possible, she thought. This was a very simple formula that even Aurore could have figured out by herself if she had the right ingredients. At this point, the only thing that made Beatrice's perfume special was the use of musk, an animal component which had since been banned on ethical grounds and replaced by synthetic molecules.

Her mother was right to believe that this perfume could have had a certain importance in the 1600s, but not in their time. So why had all the Rossini women sought it out with such intensity?

Even her grandmother, who was so rational and pragmatic, had dedicated her entire life to finding the Perfect Perfume. But however good it was – and it was – the formula Elena had in her hand didn't have the power to ignite a woman's love and passion; it had nothing that could influence her will.

Elena could smell it in her mind: it was one of those things she'd always been able to do, get an idea of the perfume simply from reading the formula. And she didn't understand.

She went down to the basement, notepad in hand, turned on the lights and entered the study. Now that she knew the ingredients, she wanted to try combining them.

The essences were in a wooden box, she remembered it well. The last time she'd looked inside she'd had to throw out a fair few. But she hadn't checked the musks, or the amber. She knelt on the floor and picked out a few of the metal bottles, but the moment she opened them, her hopes vanished. Rancid, off. All for the bin. A sigh, a flash of anger. Her disappointment was huge. She had the formula and she couldn't make it.

She dragged herself into a chair while the baby kicked around. The Perfect Perfume handed down through whole generations of Rossinis was the story of an ill-fated love, reminding her of what was really weighing on her heart: Cail, his words, the disillusion, the pain in his voice when he said them. She hoped she hadn't made a terrible mistake and ruined everything.

'Are you sure you don't want to leave John with me? It won't be any trouble to look after him.' Ben was watching Cail fill his rucksack and he didn't know what to do.

'I'm not sure how long I'll be away, so it's better if John comes with me.' Cail's voice was hard; his face looked hollow.

Ben was dying to ask what had happened.

'Shit, Cail, you can't just disappear like this. Elena doesn't deserve that. Did you have a row? Right, so talk about it and make up. What can possibly have happened? There's always a way to fix things.'

Cail didn't answer. He rarely did now. He fastened his

rucksack, threw it over his back and walked out of the bedroom. 'Lock the door,' he said.

That was the only reply Ben was going to get.

Elena had woken up early that morning, and packed her suitcase with the diaries she planned to use to reproduce some vintage fragrances, as well as a few objects that would look good in Absolue, and a container full of amber that she had found. She had no idea whether she'd be able to use it, or whether she'd have to make do with an equivalent molecule, but she was bringing it with her anyway. She was sitting in the kitchen, like she had thousands of times in her childhood, holding a cup of tea in her hands. On the walls, in between the furniture, was a collection of china. They were plates her grandmother used only on special occasions.

Memories came flooding back, carried along on the perfume of the house. It was a piece of her family history, that collection of china. Her grandmother used the crystal glasses and silver cutlery, too. One of the Rossini women had bought them. Another had ordered a set of Venetian glasses, complete with carafes and bottles. The plates, though, were French, from the end of the seventeenth century.

Elena was surprised to find herself thinking that she would like to tell her child how each of her ancestors had contributed to this little legacy that told their story, about what they loved, their deeply rooted tradition, their taste for beautiful things. Because they really were beautiful, those plates. As was the furniture, the screen, the objects that, over the course of the centuries, had been collected and kept for whoever came along next.

Family. The word stretched out in her mind and gathered force while she went on remembering. She'd never cared about those things before. So why did she feel like crying now?

She dried her face, sighed and decided to stop trying to find any sense in her thoughts. She was tired and bitterly disappointed.

'Beatrice's perfume doesn't exist,' she said aloud. 'It's just the projection of a desire – mine, my grandmother's, and whoever came before her. The Perfect Perfume is nothing but a pile of hopes and illusions. We're the ones who gave it that power; the ones who thought it was special.'

She must stop talking to herself, and to objects. It was embarrassing. It was what people did when they didn't have anyone else to talk to. Whereas she had the baby; she talked to it all the time, didn't she? And besides, there were plenty of people around her. Maybe not right at that moment, but there were normally. Aurore, for example, was the person who listened to her most, and in some way reminded her of herself. They had so much in common.

Just then, Elena remembered the perfume Eloise had bought for Aurore. She clasped her hands around the tea cup, then she put it down and stood up. Quickly, she made her way to her grandmother's room. There it was, the trunk, in its usual spot. She opened it and stared at the contents. A neat stack of diaries, documents, little bags filled with essences, photographs faded by time, and a few pieces of cheap jewellery. Elena frowned. This was where her grandmother had kept the perfume Susanna had made as a gift for Elena's sixteenth birthday; she was sure she had, because she'd watched her put it in there.

'I don't want it, I don't know what I'm supposed to do with it! It will be foul. Actually, I bet it was Maurice who made it. He probably put a drop of poison in there, too,' Elena had yelled.

376

Lucia had compressed her lips into a thin line and flared her nostrils. She was truly angry. 'When someone offers you their hand, Elena, you'd do well to accept it. It's called mercy, you know. Do you really think you won't make mistakes in life? I'm sorry to disappoint you, my girl, but there is no such paragon of perfection, except in some people's arrogant minds, and you're not arrogant, are you?'

Elena had obstinately refused to reply. She didn't want that perfume – and she didn't want her mother any more either, she thought angrily.

'One day you'll understand that there are many, many things to take into account, little one.'

'Throw it away. I don't want her perfume, I don't want anything from her,' Elena screamed in temper before she ran out of the room. But when she reached the door, she stopped, her heart in her mouth. What if her grandmother really did throw it away? She went back then, determined to pick up the package Susanna had sent her. But Lucia still had it in her hands, looking deeply sad. Elena followed her as she went upstairs to her bedroom and put it into her trunk, the one she kept locked.

It had been so long since then, how could it possibly still be so painful to remember that scene? She hadn't behaved well, Elena knew. She had been mean. It occurred to her that for all these years, she'd been hiding the shame for her own contemptuous gesture behind her anger towards Susanna. In the end, she'd made her mother the scapegoat for everything.

The perfume had to be there, she thought. Now she did want it. She wanted to smell it.

With her heart racing, she moved things around, all the letters and papers her grandmother had kept. Then she saw it.

The box was exactly as it had been, back when she'd been given it, all those years ago. Taking a couple of deep breaths to gather her courage, Elena opened the box carefully. In the morning light, the glass bottle glinted in her hand. The liquid swayed; it was a soft, pastel pink. She loved that colour. Could her mother have remembered? She was deeply moved at the thought.

She would bring it with her, Elena decided. In spite of everything she didn't feel up to opening it now, but she would take it to Paris.

She went back into the hall and picked up her mobile phone. There was no need to check if Cail had called back. Elena knew he wouldn't forgive her that easily.

'There is no way you're dumping me like this,' she said aloud.

Paris was bathed in light. The plane landed on time. Elena had done nothing but watch the bright, clear sky.

She couldn't wait to get to work. She had decided she was still going to compose the perfume, regardless of Beatrice's formula. The perfumier's organ was full of the essences she needed, and thanks to Monique, she also had a sizeable collection of chemical substances. This time, she would make an exception. To compose the perfume of Notre-Dame she needed to use a lot of substances in order to keep the formula as stable as possible. She couldn't allow herself to slip into the vagaries of essences; the perfume had to be easy to reproduce.

She would adapt, she told herself. After all, it wasn't every day you got to compose the perfume of a novel. Geneviève would have her perfume, whatever it took.

On her way home, she came to a decision: she would deal

with one thing at a time. Most importantly, she had some unfinished business with a man.

'Thank you,' she said to the taxi driver, as she paid the fare and went into Absolue.

'Hi, Elena, I wasn't expecting you this early. You should have let us know – Mum would have come to pick you up,' Aurore told her.

'It's better this way. So, is everything OK?'

The girl nodded. 'Yes, perfect. I've sold a couple of creams, a few soaps. Then a man came in, said he needs to talk to you about his wife for a customized perfume.'

Elena stared at her blankly, then she remembered. 'That must be Marc Leroy. Heavens, I thought he'd changed his mind.' She was glad he'd come back, very glad indeed. 'Can you stay for the rest of the day? I've got a couple of things to do, so I still need you.'

Aurore smiled. 'You bet! I love it here. People look at you differently when you're behind a counter.'

'It's all about perspective,' Elena told her, dragging the suitcase behind the wall Cail had built to separate Absolue from the part of the shop that led into Elena's apartment.

'See you later,' she called to Aurore and went out into the hallway. She climbed the stairs to Cail's apartment and knocked.

After a few minutes she decided to try the door, but it was locked. So she went back downstairs, out into the courtyard and headed for the building opposite. A minute later she was knocking at Ben's door.

'Hello,' she said when he opened the door.

'Elena, what a nice surprise. Come in, please.'

But she stayed in the doorway, concerned by the way Ben was looking at her. She was all too familiar with pity, and she

379

could see it in Ben's eyes now. Her heart started to beat unevenly.

'Do you happen to know where Cail is?' she asked in a small voice. 'He's not answering his phone and he's not at home.'

Ben shot her a brief glance, then stepped back. 'Come on, come in. Colette's here too. Sweetheart, can you join us? Elena's here,' he called, turning around.

'I'm here, won't be a minute.' It seemed as if they were expecting her, Elena thought with another twinge of concern.

'Thanks, but I can't stay. Sorry if I've disturbed you. I'll try looking for Cail later.'

'Wait . . . he's not there. He left.'

Elena took a step back and shook her head. 'What do you mean?' she asked in shock. 'What about John? Is he with you?'

Ben shook his head. 'Cail took John with him. I've got no idea when he'll be back.'

Or if he ever will. The phrase hung in the air between them.

'I'm really sorry, Elena. If there's anything we can do . . .' Colette murmured.

'It's fine,' she replied, trying to sound cheery. 'He probably forgot to tell me. I'm sure he'll call soon to let me know where he is.'

'Like you say, that's bound to be it.'

Elena forced a smile. 'Yup.' She turned around and for a moment the world went black. She stumbled, but recovered quickly. She'd handled worse, she thought dizzily; she could deal with this.

'Are you all right?' Ben asked, running after her.

'Perfect. Everything's fine – I just tripped. Don't worry.'

As she crossed the courtyard on her way back home, she quite clearly heard Ben say a couple of swear words. She was feeling rotten. Her head was full of cotton wool. Sounds were distorted, and the pain of grief reached all the way down to her stomach.

She went slowly back into the apartment and dragged herself up the steps. Once she was upstairs, she went into the bathroom, took a long shower and then changed into clean clothes. She put on the white coat she wore when she was working, picked up the notepad and went into the laboratory, trying to ignore the images that were forming in her mind: Cail as he set up the distiller, Cail smiling at her, Cail kissing her.

'Enough!' she chastised herself. She had a perfume to make. She had to try to concentrate, she had to learn to manage her own life, once and for all.

Elena sat down in front of the essence droppers: this perfumier's organ wasn't wooden like the little one she had downstairs, the one Cail had given her. Monique had bought this one; it was modern, aluminium. But she still liked it. Actually, the only thing she had changed was the layout: the bottles of essences were arranged in fragrance families, the way Lucia had taught her, not alphabetically. Citruses, florals, *fougères*, *chypres*, *boisés*, orientals, and lastly *cuirs*.

She selected the essences she needed and, one by one, she put them on a tray. Then she started preparing herself to compose the perfume. It took several attempts, but in the end she managed to establish some order in the confusion of her thoughts and feelings. The world around her disappeared . . .

She had to make two perfumes: Beatrice and Notre-Dame. Two very special perfumes. The first would form the basis for the second. She knew that was the right path to take. It had to be, because she was staking everything on this. Beatrice would give life to Notre-Dame.

She set out the essences in front of her, looked at them, imagined them together, closed her eyes and composed her ancestor's perfume in her mind. Then, and only when she was absolutely convinced of the result, she began. Carefully, she counted the drops of each essential oil: lemon, iris, jasmine, rose, amber, oak moss. She watched them slide across the surface of the tiny funnel and breathed in their aroma. Each step was important – it was critical, in fact. She recorded everything in her notebook, meticulously. Once the mixture was finished, she stopped, waited a moment for it to settle . . . then she sniffed.

This was the perfume Beatrice had created for a lady centuries before. A perfume that, for her ancestor, had been both a beginning and an end.

She wiped away a tear with the palm of her hand and then, holding her breath, she poured the perfume into a little bottle. She would have to let it rest for a few hours and then she could smell it again. At this point she stood up and left the laboratory, badly in need of a cup of tea.

When she came back, she smelled the perfume again, checked the formula she'd written in her notebook, and nodded in satisfaction. A whirlwind of emotions seized her: longing, passion, tenderness. Closing her eyes, she sat down and savoured every single layer of the perfume, letting it slide over her skin and penetrate deep into her soul. It was meaningful, seductive, it stirred up deep emotions. But what she felt inside at this moment was longing – it was the pain of abandonment.

Hours went by. Elena spent the whole time waiting until

the perfume molecules had dissolved sufficiently to give her a hint of what the result would be. Her faith in her own abilities had taken a knock.

She was confused – but the perfume was helping. One after another, the essences combined, even the synthetic ones that invigorated and brightened the mixture. She'd used them, in the end, because some of the ingredients Beatrice had employed no longer existed. She had had no choice – but she didn't regret it: the perfume was good, it was more than good. This was Beatrice's perfume. The one that had sealed the fate of the Rossini family. She gave it another sniff and it was like an explosion of flowers. Rose petals everywhere, a floral middle, laughter, playing by a fountain, in the sunshine, in a citrus grove, beneath a warm breeze and the heady tang of lemons. Then the evening: humid, dark, animal. Suddenly, captivating wood and a field of silver, under the pale moonlight. Jasmine, iris. Love, but not the sweet kind, no whispers, no heart-felt confessions. Then a sudden flicker, sensual, almost mesmerizing. A dense, heart-wrenching, painful story.

Elena wiped away her tears again. She was exhausted, she didn't have an ounce of energy left in her. But she had to carry on. She had to keep going. Beatrice's perfume was her starting-point, but she still had to find the mystique of Notre-Dame Cathedral, its magic, the centuries of history. That union would then give life to a new perfume: the perfume of Victor Hugo's *Notre-Dame de Paris*.

She placed one of the two vials containing her ancestor's perfume in a locker, in the dark. In her mind, she could hear her grandmother's words, recounting to her the steps she had to follow for this next creation. Starting from a base and then having to rediscover the path of the perfume wouldn't be simple, but she could do it, she knew she could: she could feel it.

Bracing herself, she transferred the contents of the second vial into a graduated cylinder and closed her eyes for a moment, searching her soul for the right direction to take. Then she added a drop of incense to the mixture. She gave it a sniff and kept going until she was suitably convinced. Then came vetiver, because she wanted water and humidity. Once she'd found it, she added another drop of myrrh.

She worked tirelessly, almost feverishly, testing and then testing again. Finally, she stopped. She gave it another sniff and nodded. That was it, in her hands: she'd found it.

When she went downstairs, the perfume of *Notre-Dame de Paris* was ready. She just had to leave it to rest. The process demanded that she would have to smell it again and correct it if needed. But she knew that wouldn't be necessary.

Aurore had gone. She'd closed the shop and left a note. It was the school holidays, she'd be back the following day. Elena stared at the scrap of paper, the neat handwriting with clear, definite letters, and that stylized flower instead of a full stop. She put it in her pocket, then she went over to the telephone.

'Madame Binoche? It's Elena Rossini. The Notre-Dame perfume is ready. Yes, thank you. Come whenever you like. I'll show you the first sample, and from there we can start working on the final version.'

She hung up, went back upstairs, lay down on the bed, still fully dressed, and immediately fell into a deep sleep.

24

Neroli: marital love. Derived from orange blossom, this is the
   heavenly essence of flower petals.
The fragrance of peace.
Evokes positive feelings. Opens the way to love.

If Elena had thought that Geneviève Binoche would stop
coming to see her once she had her perfume, she was sorely
mistaken. The writer had been utterly bewitched by it. She
told Elena it was the perfect perfume – *her* Perfect Perfume.
And she continued to visit regularly – and even though Elena
didn't feel much like going out, or talking, Geneviève hadn't
lost heart. That night she'd even taken Elena out shopping
with her.

The Lafayette department store was crowded, as usual, and
had the most beautiful things on sale. Geneviève had decided
that would be the first stop on their expedition.

'I've never been shopping for baby clothes. I never had any
children, and nor did Adeline. My brother died before he

could become a father and my sister-in-law is one of those hard-to-please women. At least, that's what she told me once when we had a heart-to-heart. I pointed out that she was still young and could start a new life. Adeline came back with the argument that she'd never find another man like Jasper. Isn't that romantic?'

Given that he died just a year after they were married, there wasn't really anything romantic about it – but everyone sees things their own way, Elena thought. She knew that Madame Binoche was trying to be kind with her constant chatter, but she struggled to express her gratitude. It seemed like an entire lifetime since she got back from Florence, instead of just a couple of weeks. Cail had disappeared from her life and it was an effort to engage with anything any more. She saw everything at a distance. The only thing that hadn't changed was the instinctive attachment she felt to the baby. In fact, it was the baby who helped her get up in the morning and live from one moment to the next.

'Thank you,' she said mechanically. 'I suppose I should pack a hospital bag.'

Dr Rochelle had suggested she get everything ready, now that the pregnancy was in its final stages.

'I was supposed to come shopping with Cail,' Elena whispered to Geneviève. She didn't have the strength to go on with the conversation. She let it go, like she did every time it got too difficult to hold on to a thought.

'But we ladies are so much more practical about these things, my dear.'

Fortunately, Geneviève was blessed with formidable intuition and had immediately grasped the nettle: a day of intense shopping was exactly what was called for.

They reached the department for newborns, and it was like

walking into a sweet shop. Everything was in pastel colours, from the walls to the furniture. Dolls, toy trains, teddy bears in all shapes and sizes. And the scent of talc and vanilla. Madame Binoche started pointing out Babygros and outfits that would suit both boys and girls. Then she moved on to stronger colours and finally to pink and blue.

'If you ask me, babies should be dressed in all the colours of the rainbow. It's not fair that they get stuck with one colour that defines them. It's discrimination,' she announced, casting a critical eye over the whole themed display.

Elena nodded from time to time. She was looking at the little outfits and putting the ones she liked best into the trolley. Jasmine had advised her not to buy too much – babies got bigger by the minute – but Elena didn't want her child to go without anything. So the trolley ended up brimming with baby products: socks with duck and pig noses on; romper suits in red, pink and light blue; tiny shirts; anything she liked the look of, she bought. She had no idea whether her baby was going to be a boy or a girl, so she decided to pick out some tiny little dresses, too.

Money was no problem: the sum she'd been paid for the Notre-Dame perfume had more than covered Monique's share in Absolue and given Elena a huge advance for her next project. Absolue wasn't going to sell just perfumes of the soul, but a whole range that paid homage to the women in her family.

'What do you think of this pram?' Geneviève asked.

'I don't know. It's too dark.'

'Don't you like the colour?'

No, she didn't like it. She wanted yellow for her little one, the colour of the sun, or maybe even light blue like the sky.

'I want something brighter, like a turquoise.'

Geneviève looked around, then pointed a finger. 'Over there. Aren't they beautiful?'

Slowly, Elena followed her. By this point she had to be careful getting around. If she made any sudden moves, the baby got anxious and started kicking. She'd see her child soon, and knowing that helped her to keep going without Cail.

Elena was an expert in abandonment, but the chasm in the middle of her chest was something she'd never felt before. It was sheer emptiness. It was the essence of nothing. It only took a moment to get lost inside herself; that's why she was keeping busy any way she could. So she didn't have to think, so she didn't get lost in the emptiness.

The pram was a gift from Geneviève. Elena didn't know what to say; they'd all been so kind to her that sometimes she felt like curling up in a corner and sobbing. She forced out a thank you and a smile, and carried on.

She had to keep reminding herself to breathe, that was important: one breath, then another. One step forward, then another.

They moved on to choosing bedding, blankets, tiny pyjamas. Then dummies, bonnets, bottles and teats. They'd bought a huge amount and Elena started to worry about how they were going to transport it all, when the assistant handed her a business card.

'You just have to give us a call, *madame*,' she said with a broad smile. 'As soon as the baby's born, we'll make sure everything is delivered to you. Transport, assembly – we'll take care of all that. You don't need to worry about a thing.'

Relief. Another thank you. She seemed to have done nothing but thank people lately. They all expected her to be full of joy and smiles. She paid for the shopping and dragged herself through another day.

She just had to be patient until the birth; the rest would take care of itself. The baby was the only thing that really mattered; and there was Absolue. Elena repeated that to herself several times a day, and sometimes it worked. Sometimes it was enough.

During the day, she managed to handle everything quite well. Aurore rushed back from school to give her a hand, and Eloise came round whenever she could. So did Ben. Colette also came over regularly; she cooked lunch and dinner and separated individual portions into little containers to go in the freezer. All Elena had to do was pop one in the microwave and that was it. Her friends never left her on her own, not even for a moment.

The next day, Elena received an invitation. Monsieur Lagose and Babette Dufour had just left. Things between them seemed to have settled down, but they were still bickering. It couldn't be that bad, given the way they smiled at one another during their arguments. While she'd been pleased to see them together at first, now their happiness was another thing that made her eyes sting and brought a lump to her throat.

'Here's some post for you. It looks like an invitation,' Adeline said, looking at the thick ivory envelope. She'd called in to say hello and decided to stay.

Elena looked up from the records she was updating and gave her a distracted look. 'Could you open it?'

'Of course,' Adeline said. 'Did you enter a competition?'

Elena frowned. 'No, no competitions.'

'But here it says you need to claim your prize.'

'It must be a mistake,' Elena said, turning her attention back to the books.

'It's got the foundation's logo on it: *Paris-Bagatelle*

389

International New Rose Contest. I've heard about that. It's a very important event, held in the most beautiful gardens in Paris. And it says the winner is the Floribunda Hélène.'

Silence, confusion. Then: 'Let me see,' Elena murmured, stretching out her hand. That was Cail's contest, for the rose he'd created. She knew because they were supposed to go together.

Adeline handed her the letter and Elena read it from start to finish, several times.

'I don't understand,' she said quietly.

'Are you sure? Is there someone you know who might have wanted to surprise you?'

Yes, there was: Cail. But he'd made it clear he didn't want to see her or speak to her. So it couldn't be from him.

'It's for Saturday,' she said. 'I've got nothing to wear.'

What a stupid thing to worry about, she thought. Cail had sent her an invitation weeks after he'd practically disappeared out of her life, and the first thing she could think of was that she didn't have anything to wear.

'I know a wonderful shop. We can go as soon as Aurore gets here, what do you say?'

Elena closed her fingers around the card. 'I don't know. I don't think I'll be going.'

She put the invitation on the counter and went back to checking the books. Adeline didn't say anything. She just gave her a gentle look from behind her half-moon glasses. Elena could feel the weight of that patient gaze on her. She tried to ignore her, then she decided to look up.

'It's Cail.' She paused. 'But he won't even answer my calls, so why would I go there?'

'To give him a piece of your mind?'

Oh yes, she would love to do that. There were one or two

things she was dying to say to him. 'It's complicated.'

'If it wasn't, it wouldn't be worth wasting your time for, would it?'

'I kept him at a distance, you know, because of the baby. I wanted to be sure the three of us stood a chance. Because I'm not on my own, Adeline. I have a child. Or rather, I will have one very soon, and he or she will be part of my life for ever. I would never give up my baby, *ever*, not for anyone.'

She didn't know how she'd gone from whispering to shouting. Adeline went over to her and stroked her hand.

'Calm down, Elena. Your baby can sense everything, and right now it will be wondering why its mummy is so upset.'

Elena pulled herself together almost straight away. 'I'm sorry,' she said. 'It's a bit of a difficult time.' She made an effort to smile. 'I lost control. Please forgive me, Adeline. You must think I'm crazy.'

'Sweetheart, you're pregnant, you've had a big row with your boyfriend. It wouldn't be normal if you weren't at least a bit upset. You're hardly made of stone now, are you? Right. So, dry your face. Good, that's it.'

Elena was shaking. The words had poured out like a river, urged on by the spectre of the past: Maurice. Her stepfather had hated her with a vengeance because she was someone else's daughter. She was never going to put her own child in a situation like that. She'd much rather bring her child up all on her own.

'I . . . Life was quite hard when I was little,' she said in a small voice. 'I have to be sure the baby will be loved and protected. I should have talked it through properly with Cail, but I never did. I was stupid to go back to Florence without even consulting him. I could have waited, included him in my decision.'

Adeline smiled at her. 'I haven't got the faintest idea what you're talking about. I don't know what happened, but I did get to meet Cail. And apart from being a fine young man, his eyes are right.'

'His eyes?'

'Yes, his eyes. Several things can reveal a man's character. Apart from his behaviour, obviously, it's his look that tells you what he's really like. Cail's face lights up when he looks at you. And he's always by your side. I've watched him quite carefully. One of the advantages of being a little old lady, and already off the market, is that you can stare at anyone you like without worrying that they might take it the wrong way.' Adeline also had her doubts about Cail having abandoned Elena without a second thought. She was certain she'd seen him a couple of times around Absolue.

'And what if he decided it wasn't worth it? Let's look at things for what they are: I'm pregnant by my ex, and I want this baby. What kind of man would take on a situation like that?'

'Come on, Elena!' Adeline exclaimed. 'It's not as if he's a lion who wants to do away with your cubs, he's just a man.' She smiled encouragingly. 'What really counts are the facts. Did he invite you to the prize-giving? Yes. Has he bred a rose and named it after you? Yes. What more proof do you need? The question you should really be answering here is: what do you want?'

There it was. She'd gone round in so many circles, but that was the crux of the matter. There was no doubt that she loved Cail. She'd been crazy about him for so long. But she was also intelligent enough to know that love wasn't enough.

'I'm so angry, Adeline. In fact, I'm furious. He showed me what it could be like, he loved me for who I was. I felt like myself when I was with him, and then . . . I'm not sure I can go through that again. It hurts so much. At night, I wake up thinking it's all just a dream. Once I went up to his apartment because I thought I'd heard him come back, but I was wrong.' Her voice was like steel wire, thin and sharp. Every word stung her throat.

'If you don't get to the bottom of this thing, if you don't sort it out, you'll never be free of it. I know it's really none of my business,' Adeline said, 'but I would go, if only to say good-bye. You know, properly, face to face.'

Goodbye. For good. Elena thought about it, then gave a shuddering sigh. Yes, in the end, that was the one thing she could do.

Despite everyone offering to accompany her to the prize-giving for the new rose at Château de Bagatelle, Elena had decided to go alone. The château's grounds were an expanse of bright green, dotted with rosebushes boasting flowers of all shapes, sizes and colours. The avenues were divided by dozens of neatly ordered flowerbeds, reminiscent of an Italian garden. In the middle, roses of all hues: from the most delicate shades of yellow and pink to bold, vivid reds, dark garnet reds and pure white blooms with iridescent petals, fleshy or thin as the finest organza.

Elena had taken a walk around, but then she had to sit down. She was tired, and afraid. Once her anger had subsided, she had been left with a deep sense of desolation. She wanted Cail to hold her; she wanted things to go back to the way they were before.

She closed her eyes for a moment and let the sun warm her face. Slowly, the smell drifting through the air seeped into her thoughts and calmed her down. When she stood up to walk inside to where the prize-giving was to be held, she felt better.

Cail took care to make sure he was never seen. His anger about the trip to Florence had passed and only the emptiness remained.

He couldn't leave her. He'd stayed in Paris and gone back to the Marais at least once a day to check she was all right. He missed her terribly – her and all her crazy ideas. Jumping on the first plane and going off to Florence, while heavily pregnant! Another stunt like that would kill him, Cail thought.

There she was; he finally managed to spot her and moved carefully over to get a better look. She seemed so sad, so desolate. He had to force himself to hold back. He needed to wait for the right moment: he needed to be sure Elena would understand before he spoke to her.

She was beautiful. She always had been, in a serene way. And that beauty, of which she was almost unaware, along with her voice and her sweet ways, had bewitched him from the start. But now, as she walked along, with her black dress and her plaited hair, it was as if he was seeing her for the very first time.

Cail stayed out of the way. He didn't want Elena to see him, not yet. But he wouldn't have missed this moment for anything in the world: his tribute to her.

'Madame Elena Rossini will collect the prize for Floribunda Hélène. Bred by Caillen McLean of McLean Roses.'

Now that the moment had come, Cail felt incredibly nervous. Elena stood up and slowly, to the audience's applause, took to the stage and thanked the presenter.

'We've been lucky enough to see a lot of McLean creations.

I must say, however, that Hélène is one of my favourites. Its perfume is without doubt one of its strengths. Fruity, intense, drifting along on spicy notes. An excellent contrast. Each bunch consists of a dozen chalice-shaped buds, opening out into a remarkable bouquet. And the colour, that deep red with a heart of gold, deserves a mention for its purity, its intensity. Yes, this is undoubtedly one of the most important roses of the season.'

Elena had listened patiently and had formed an idea of what the rose might be like.

'Could I see it?'

Her question surprised the presenter, who recovered immediately. After signalling to a colleague, he gave her a broad grin. 'But of course.'

Cail had reached the door when he realized what was happening. Lowering his head, he quickly regained his seat. He wanted to see her, he wanted to remember the look on her face for ever. And he'd go and talk to her tomorrow, for he couldn't bear for things between them to end like that.

Life was funny. He'd known Juliette for ever – they'd grown up together and it felt natural to think about starting a family with her. Then there was the accident. And all he could do was piece together what was left of his own existence. A few seconds, and that dream of the future was all over.

With Elena, though, he'd chosen her, desired her, wanted her more than anything. He'd carefully planned out every little detail of their relationship, so that nothing could go wrong. And she had proven it was all just an illusion. He had no power to decide anything; all he could do was stand and watch. Just like he had done in the past.

This profound sense of powerlessness was something Cail couldn't come to terms with. It was as if his whole life and their relationship had been one big house of cards, a pile of leaves ready to fly away in the first gust of wind.

Now Elena was saying thank you; she was hugging the plaque she'd just been given close to her chest and smiling at the audience.

Then their eyes met. Without shifting her gaze, she walked down the stairs towards him.

Come to me, Cail willed silently.

Suddenly, Elena put a hand on her stomach and stopped. She took a deep breath, then exhaled – but the sensation that gripped her showed no sign of easing; in fact, it got stronger. There was a sharp pain in her stomach and she felt something happen.

My waters broke, she thought, incredulous.

'Cail!' she screamed with all the breath she could muster. Cail felt the blood run cold in his veins. He pushed his way through the crowd, to Elena. He only needed to look at her to realize it was time.

'Don't worry, my love. Everything's OK. It's all going to be fine.'

'No, it's not fine. You left, and the baby has decided to come now. Right now. I haven't even got my bag with me. The doctor told me to take it to the hospital with me. Why wouldn't you listen? You promised me, and I believed you. I found Beatrice's formula, I wanted to tell you. I wanted to tell you, but you weren't there.'

Cail took her face in his hands. 'Look at me, Elena. Listen to me. I'm going to take you to the hospital now. I'll go in with you, I'll be there with you.'

'Don't leave me. Don't you ever do that again.' It was just a whisper, but Cail heard it loud and clear, and it went straight to his heart. He didn't reply, but he did kiss her. Right there, in front of everyone. Then he took her in his arms.

'I've got the car outside. Take my mobile out of my pocket,' he ordered his sister Sophie who, intrigued by all the commotion, had made her way through the group of people surrounding them.

'Elena, sweetheart, are you all right?' she asked, getting closer.

'She's gone into labour. Sophie, call the hospital, the number's saved. Tell them we're on our way,' Cail said.

Elena was too frightened to object, or do anything other than cling on to Cail. But once they were in the car, while he was driving to the hospital, the words she'd imagined saying came out of their own accord.

'Why didn't you answer the telephone? Why didn't you talk to me?'

'There was nothing to say, Elena. It was my fault, I just misunderstood. I've already told you.' This wasn't the time to straighten things out. Climbing through the gears, Cail switched lanes.

'You told me you would love me, regardless. That it didn't matter what I did, or how I acted. You promised me and I trusted you. You deceived me, Caillen, you lied to me!'

'Later, we'll talk about it later. Try to stay calm now.'

Elena wanted to respond, she needed to, but she couldn't. A pain had gripped her and made it hard to breathe. Cail put the accelerator to the floor. And then there was no time for anything else.

The gynaecologist didn't want to let Cail into the delivery room, but eventually she relented. He stayed with Elena the whole time, holding her hand, even when the labour became complicated. The only time he wasn't with her was while they carried out an emergency caesarean. But he stayed glued to the window of the operating theatre, just a few metres away from her.

Nothing and no one could have kept him from Elena. Not while he was still breathing or conscious, despite the bright dots that swirled in front of his eyes on a few occasions.

'It's all going to be fine,' he kept saying out loud.

When the first cry pierced through the silence, Cail's heart stopped.

'It's a girl! Welcome to the world, little one,' the gynaecologist said, holding her up and handing her to the nurse, who quickly wrapped her in a cloth.

Cail was desperate to get back into the room. A nurse opened the door and helped him put on a mask and gown. Then she let him go in, and Cail gently took Elena's hand. Groggy from the anaesthetic, she'd lost consciousness for a moment. He kept his eyes fixed firmly on the bundle wriggling in the doctor's arms, on the activities of the nurse and paediatrician.

'What's happening?' His voice came out choked. Elena wouldn't survive if anything happened to her baby.

'Nothing, don't worry. We're just sucking out the liquid this little lady swallowed and then you can see your daughter. I have to tell you, she's a cutie,' the paediatrician said, setting the baby down on the weighing scales. Her cries and her movements grew stronger.

Cail craned his neck and caught sight of a little fist, angrily punching the air.

A girl. Elena had a girl. The emotion suddenly burned his throat and clouded his eyes.

'There we go, she's nearly ready,' the nurse went on.

But he couldn't see anything. Then they put her in his

arms. It was very difficult to hold her without letting go of Elena's hand, but Caillen McLean was a man who knew how to improvise: he found a way to do both.

'She's tiny. My God, she's so tiny,' he said, terrified. 'Are you sure she's all right?'

'Don't worry, your baby is perfectly healthy. Seven pounds and completely normal.'

But Cail had stopped listening. Now he was looking at the child, who was staring right back at him. She'd stopped crying but she was still waving her little hands around. One caught his gown; the tiny fingers instinctively closed around the material and held on tight. Elena did the same thing. The block of ice lodged in him for so long melted away in a sudden burst of warmth.

'Hello, my darling,' he smiled tenderly. Slowly and very carefully, he rested his lips on the baby's tiny head, still holding her tight. 'You're beautiful, you're just like your mummy.'

Elena had always dreaded this moment; she'd been waiting for it with trepidation. But when she looked at Cail, she realized she'd been a fool not to trust her own heart. He carried on talking to the baby, smiling at her, and wouldn't let her go. He would never let her go.

'Is she OK?' she murmured.

Cail turned and smiled at her, then he leaned down and kissed her gently. 'She's gorgeous,' he whispered. Elena noticed the salty taste of tears on his lips and smiled back. Then she gazed at her daughter. The little girl looked sullen, as though she were frowning, and was red, wrinkled, and completely bald – but Cail thought she was beautiful. Now Elena knew he was the right man.

'Do you want to give her to me?' She needed to touch her, to smell her. Her daughter. Her little girl.

Cail held the baby up to Elena's face.

'Hello, little one,' she said. Softly, she stroked her nose, traced the outline of her profile, the contours of her tiny face.

'She hasn't got a single hair,' she murmured.

'Well, it'll grow,' Cail replied. 'She hasn't got any eyebrows either. Isn't she perfect?'

By way of a response, the baby yawned and closed her eyes.

Elena kissed her, held her close to her chest, and was overcome by a joy she'd never felt before. As she cradled her, the thought that she had her daughter in her arms pushed its way through the tangled knot of emotions that was her soul, until everything else disappeared. Until there was only herself and her baby – the child's weight, her warm breath, the soft, delicate perfume rising from her skin. And she knew that the moment marked a clear boundary between what she, Elena Rossini, had been before, and what she had now become.

Cail refused to leave Elena except when the doctors came round to examine her; when they had finished, he went straight back to her side. And although he made an exception at night, in the daytime nothing could keep him away.

Then he started to act strangely, standing over the crib and casting silent glances at Elena.

'I need to tell you something,' he blurted out finally.

'Would you mind telling me over here, sitting next to me?'

But he didn't move from the crib.

'OK,' Elena said. 'Pick her up, but she'll get used to it, and then you'll always have to do it, even when she gets bigger and weighs a ton.' Cail beamed happily at the thought. Then, very carefully, he picked up the baby and settled her in his arms before going to sit down next to Elena.

'Were you being serious before?' he wanted to know.

'Before when?' Elena replied, confused.

He sighed. 'About me picking her up.'

'Why shouldn't I?' she asked, perplexed.

He didn't reply, but looked down, focusing on the little girl.

'Look, Cail, my brain cells are shrinking. Don't worry, they'll go back to normal as soon as I stop breastfeeding. Apparently it's nature's way of stopping new mothers from worrying about too many things at once. The point is, I haven't got the slightest chance of understanding what you're saying unless you spell it out loud and clear.'

Cail took a deep breath, then said in a rush: 'I signed the papers. You know, the ones for the father.'

'You . . . what?' Elena was speechless.

'Everyone here thinks I'm the father – Dr Rochelle thought so, too. It's even written in your notes,' Cail hurriedly explained.

Elena took time to think it through. Then she looked at Cail and asked, 'Is that why you did it? Because everyone thinks she's your child?' The question was clear and direct.

'No, it wasn't because of that. I . . . I don't know how to explain it, Elena. There are lots of things we need to talk about. There are things you don't know. It's all very complicated. But you see, I love you . . . I love you,' he said softly.

Elena took a moment to digest what he'd just said. She wanted to cry, to laugh, to hug him. Instead she asked another question. 'So, is that why you want to say she's yours, because you love me?'

401

'No,' Cail said. 'It's not that. I just feel that she's mine. She's the child of my love for you.' He paused. 'That's why I wrote my name as her father on those forms.'

She was powerless, Elena thought. This man knew the way to her heart.

'Why are you crying?' he asked now, still holding the little girl protectively in his arms.

Elena glared at him. 'There are such things as tears of joy, would you believe.'

His eyes lit up with delight. He bent his head and kissed the baby, who was still sleeping peacefully. Then he stood up and put her back in the crib.

'I think we missed a step,' he said, turning back to Elena.

'We've got some catching up to do, then,' she said through her tears.

'Yes, I think we have.'

His lips brushed hers, then he kissed her deeply. He told her how he felt, what it had been like in the weeks he'd stayed away . . . then he held her and kissed her again. Now everything was clear between them. Now they were just a man, a woman . . . and their child.

'I'd like to call her Beatrice,' Elena told him. 'She'll be happy, she'll be loved, she'll have a brilliant future. And then . . .' She reached for Cail's hand. 'Do you think Elizabeth would mind if we named her after her, too?'

Cail felt his heart leap. His mother would be over the moon. 'You can ask her yourself,' he replied. 'She'll be here in a minute. Sophie sent me a message earlier. My dad's coming, too. Do you mind?'

Elena grabbed hold of his jumper with both hands and, pulling him towards her, she kissed him with all of her heart. She'd done enough crying, and now she couldn't wait to get out of the hospital. She was in a hurry – a hurry to start living.

In the days Elena had to stay in hospital, the two of them talked endlessly. Cail told her about Juliette and her death. How he'd been captivated by her bravery and her carefree ways. He'd followed her, indulged her, and loved her without question, as if there were no tomorrow. In the end, it had cost him dearly, and it had cost Juliette, too; she had died because he never knew how to say no to her.

It wasn't easy to explain. There were things he struggled to understand himself. But a deep sense of guilt and remorse had tormented him all these years, as had the despair that wouldn't go away, the questions that nagged at him, the uncertainty; not knowing whether there was any way he could have avoided the accident. He was young when it happened, and he'd carried that pain in his soul, stopping him from moving on. Until Elena came along and changed everything.

Now there was a new life sketched out in front of him, one that had nothing to do with the past. Elena wasn't Juliette, and he wasn't the same man as he had been, back then.

There was no sense in digging up the past, and he didn't want to. So he'd decided to look forward, leaving everything behind. Now the time had come to smile, to live, to love.

At first, Elena was upset that he hadn't told her about Juliette earlier; then she had to admit to herself that she wasn't being fair. After all, she hadn't been completely honest either. She started to reflect on what Cail had said and little by little she understood why he had run away from their relationship.

The past was water under the bridge. All that mattered was the future. Their future.

That was when Elena realized she had a family. A real family. The sense of belonging was intense and comforting.

People were constantly coming and going: Geneviève Binoche and Adeline, Monsieur Lagose and Babette, Ben, Colette and Eloise. Aurore couldn't tear herself away from the crib and was already imagining the perfumes she could make for little Beatrice. Then Monique's parents arrived with her brother and sisters. Elena talked to Jasmine for a while, in private. Apparently Susanna had been to see her. They'd had a long chat, mostly about Elena.

Despite the bitterness she had always felt every time she thought about her mother, Elena discovered that she no longer felt the acute pain that had always accompanied her memories.

Monique called her on the telephone every day from New York. Elena was very pleased to hear her sounding happier. Perhaps it had something to do with the *maître parfumeur* she'd been working with recently, who went by the exotic name of Ilya. He'd asked her out a couple of times. Elena didn't know whether Monique was interested, but she was sure of one thing. Love brings joy. Pain and despair are something else.

At some point, you have to remove whatever it is that is poisoning your soul. It's a matter of survival. She hoped that one day, Monique would be able to forget Jacques Montier and look forward, to the horizon, illuminated every day by the sunrise, bringing with it hope and life.

Epilogue

*Inula: confidence. Precious perfume, golden like its flowers that
    welcome the sun.
The fragrance accompanies inner growth, reassures and helps
    to express the feelings in our hearts.
Banishes all kinds of fear.*

They had decided to live in Cail's apartment. The room next to
his had been transformed into a nursery for little Beatrice. Cail
had painted it turquoise and yellow, and covered one wall with
dozens of stars that glowed in the dark. They placed the crib in
the middle, surrounded by white furniture; everything bright
and welcoming.

Cail had replaced his own bed with a new double. It was
there when Elena came out of hospital, ready to welcome her.
At first they simply slept together, knowing they could reach
out and hold one another in the night. But soon their movements revealed a need that had deepened over time and become
a longing. There was no reason to stop, now. Skin on skin,

breathing together, possession and fulfilment; all the things they had thought they understood, they rediscovered together, as their world took shape and they lost themselves in each other.

Elena loved that bed, especially when they stayed there for hours, in each other's arms, making up for lost time, or the nights she spent watching over Bea.

Happiness had tiptoed gently into their lives and taken over, making everything look different. All they had done wrong seemed like a distant memory that not even perfume could evoke. Elena could now contemplate things that, not so long ago, had been unthinkable.

That morning, Elena woke up early. She'd opened her eyes and noticed how the sunrise lit up their bedroom. Cail was beside her; she could sense his warmth, his smell, the murmur of his nonsense talk with the baby sitting on his chest.

'Good morning, my love,' he said, realizing she was awake.

Elena kissed his chest, nibbled at Bea's foot, making her squeal with delight, and after a long yawn got up and went into the kitchen. 'Do you want some tea?' she asked.

'Yes, please,' Cail replied.

Elena opened the windows, lit the gas under the kettle and then prepared the coffee pot for herself. The sounds of everyday life drifted in from the street: Paris was already bustling. That morning she had a few important appointments, two for customized perfumes, and then she had to meet the representative from a consortium of small, niche perfumeries that wanted to sell some of her all-natural creations. Now that Aurore was at the ISIPCA in Versailles, she had less free time. Fortunately, Adeline was around to lend a hand. Cail was a great help, too. That morning he would stay with Beatrice and take her to the gardens.

Suddenly a gust of wind lifted up the curtains, blowing into the kitchen and diffusing the aroma of hot coffee. The tea was already sitting in Cail's cup. John wagged his tail. Elena smiled at him and filled his bowl. He waited for her to stroke him before he got any closer. She still found it difficult to touch him, but with a little determination, she was getting there. That same determination which had enabled her to do so many things.

She poured the coffee into her cup, careful not to splash the postcard that had arrived the day before. Jean-Baptiste Lagose was on holiday with Babette, and from his postcards, it seemed that everything was going swimmingly. Elena thought back to when they'd called in to say goodbye before they left. She could tell they were really excited. She smiled to herself and put honey into both cups. Everything was ready. She was about to call Cail when a little turquoise box sitting on the sideboard caught her eye. It was the perfume Susanna had made for her all those years ago, and which Elena had brought back from Florence. She'd left it there, where she could see it, thinking that one day, when she was ready, she would open it.

She set the cups down on a tray and put some biscuits out on a saucer. But her eye kept returning to the little box and its contents. She stared at it for a moment, before opening it carefully and taking out the bottle. It weighed nothing, she thought, holding it in her hand. For a moment she was tempted to place it back in the box, to put it off again. Now that life was so good, what did this perfume matter?

She closed her eyes. When she opened them, she slowly unscrewed the lid and brought the bottle to her nose.

The first blast took her breath away. It was strong and pungent. Could it have gone off? But that wasn't possible; it had been kept sealed and safe. She drew the perfume away from her nose and decided to put it on her skin. A couple of drops on her wrist . . . and she waited.

One by one, the molecules that made up the top notes rose

up, warmed by the heat of her skin. Strong and pungent again. Like the hostile relationship Elena had had with her mother. But soon there was a floral explosion and a burst of vanilla. The heart of the perfume, evoking a lullaby hidden in the depths of her memory. How did that refrain go?

'*Lullaby and good night, thy mother's delight . . .*'

Then it became more stable, warm and welcoming – like an embrace. It was beautiful. And it was one of the most wonderful fragrances that Elena had ever smelled.

In the end, she recognized it. A gentle shiver ran all the way through her. Surely she must be mistaken? But she wasn't. She knew exactly what this was.

This was the perfume she'd made for her mother when she was just a little girl. Only there was something new, something different about it. Elena soon realized what it was. Susanna had kept the perfume and she'd finished it. Now it was perfect. It was her Perfect Perfume.

She smelled it again and rose filtered through the other notes; then came vanilla – and in that floral middle, Elena found the meaning in the message. It was her mother's answer: it was her embrace, it was her love for her. Delicate and then intense; bitter, yet there was a hint of sweetness; warm and enchanting. It was the perfume of life, it was the perfume of happiness.

She stood still, breathing it in slowly with her eyes closed, immersed in the magic. Then she opened them again. The time had come.

With Cail still talking to Beatrice, and the baby responding in her own way, Elena took her mobile phone out of her bag, sat down on a chair and dialled the number. She waited patiently, her heart pounding, counting the rings.

'Hello?'

'Hello, Mum. It's me, Elena.'

The Ways of Perfume

Floral Perfumes

Angelica: self-knowledge. Angels' grass, a captivatingly sweet, honeyed perfume. The fragrance awakens the hidden essence of everything. Promotes self-awareness. A remedy for all ills.

Calendula: bravery. Sun-loving flower with a delightful, comforting perfume. The fragrance soothes and refreshes. Frees the mind of bad thoughts.

Chamomile: serenity. Warm and intensely floral. The fragrance of calm. Aids clarity of thought and fights restlessness.

Frangipani: unparalleled charm. Extracted from the plumeria flower and intensely floral. The fragrance of blossoming femininity opening itself up to life. Bold and voluptuous.

Geranium: intensity. Resembles the perfume of a rose without its subtlety. The fragrance symbolizes beauty, posture and humility. The ultimate feminine flower.

Helichrysum: understanding. Sweet as honey and bitter as a sleepless dawn. An intense perfume. The fragrance of kindness; to be used sparingly, blended with delicate scents like rose that can take on its qualities. Unites heart and mind, passion and reason. Evokes compassion.

Inula: confidence. Precious perfume, golden like its flowers that welcome the sun. The fragrance accompanies inner growth, reassures, and helps to express the feelings in our hearts. Banishes all kinds of fear.

Iris: trust. Precious and essential, like water, air, earth and fire. The fragrance is bright and intense. Relieves tension and renews faith in the soul.

Jasmine: sensuality. Flower of the night, it only gives off its perfume at sunrise and sunset. The fragrance is heady and warm. It evokes a magical world, blurs boundaries, bestows well-being and happiness. The real pleasure is hidden in its small white petals: picking it is just the beginning.

Lavender: relaxation. Intense and sweet; herbal with balsamic undertones. The complex fragrance seduces and bewitches. Refreshes and purifies the spirit; relieves exhaustion, fear and anxiety.

Magnolia: truth. One look is not enough: our eyes rarely perceive what hides behind appearances. An intense, brilliant scent. The fragrance illuminates the mind by promoting inner knowledge and releasing the energy required to face secrets and lies – things that seem true, but rarely are.

Mimosa: happiness. Intensely floral. The fragrance of mimosa flowers gives joy and vitality. Relieves sadness, encourages dialogue.

Narcissus: desire. Intensely sensual and intoxicating. The fragrance of pleasure and sexuality.

Neroli: marital love. Derived from orange blossom, this is the heavenly essence of flower petals. The fragrance of peace. Evokes positive feelings. Opens the way to love.

Rock Rose: good cheer. Lovely and delicate, like a tiny pink rose. The fragrance is intense, enveloping. Its spicy heat can melt frosty souls, invoking the ability to smile and love.

Rose: love. A difficult essence to obtain. Sweet and light. The fragrance symbolizes feelings and emotions. Encourages personal initiative and the arts.

Scotch broom: courage. As rich as the colour of its flowers, it is fresh and heady, with exciting floral notes. The fragrance announces the spring, the transition from old to new. Helps us not to lose heart.

Tuberose: change. White, intense, sweet and seductive. The fragrance of audacity and awareness. Stimulates creativity, evokes the power of change.

Verbena: good humour. Warm and enveloping. The fragrance invokes cheer and happiness. Encourages us to socialize.

Violet: elegance and discretion. Sweet, delicate. The fragrance of femininity. Soothes and invigorates.

Yarrow: inner balance. The scent of heaven and earth together. The fragrance is aromatic and resinous. Promotes harmony where conflict reigns, inspires clarity and stimulates the spirit.

Ylang-ylang: expression. Warm and feminine, tropical and sweet. The fragrance enables us to overcome disappointment and offence. Releases hidden feelings and helps us to express the poetry in our souls.

Fruit, Berry and Herb Perfumes

Basil: happiness. Regal perfume, deeply aromatic, fresh and spicy. Lifts the mind and spirit, freeing the heart of melancholy.

Bergamot: hope. Lively, scintillating. The fragrance gives energy and agility when all expectations have withered under the weight of monotony. Lights the way and helps us see alternatives.

Black pepper: perseverance. Warm and stimulating, the 'King of Spices'. The fragrance awakens the senses, promotes inner strength. Teaches us that when it seems there is nowhere to go, we've just lost our way.

Cardamom: attraction. Enveloping, sweet and slightly spicy. The fragrance of Eros. Stimulates the spirit and encourages sharing.

Cinnamon: seduction. A full-bodied, sensual and intensely feminine perfume. The fragrance is exotic and spicy. Passionate and warm like the sun in the faraway lands where it is grown.

Citronella: enthusiasm. Stimulating and intense. The fragrance is aromatic, lemony. It channels energy.

Cloves: sweetness. Intensely spicy, sweet and aromatic. The fragrance of affection. Helps to bear the pain of waiting, easing transition.

Cumin: passion. Deeply mysterious. The fragrance is delicate, yet warm and enveloping. Inspires openness, strengthens Eros.

Fennel: fortitude. Banishes negative thoughts. The fragrance is pleasant and aromatic. It relieves fear and doubt, helping us face difficult situations.

Hay: calmness. Ancient, ancestral, akin to fire, sea and earth. The fragrance is etched deep in the ancient spirit we all possess. Evokes tranquillity.

Hyssop: purity. The sweet, fresh scent of a new dawn. The fragrance retains the carefree lightness of morning. Stimulates concentration, clarifies ideas and, like all ritual herbs, promotes meditation.

Juniper: zeal. Intense and balsamic. The fragrance neutralizes negativity, brightens the mood, banishes problems and fears. Purifies the environment and the soul.

Lemon: rationality. The scent of reason. Intense, fresh, enveloping. The fragrance eliminates excess, inspires reflection and moderates instability. Banishes darkness weighing on the soul.

Mandarin: good fortune. Delicate, sparkling and fresh. The fragrance takes us back to the innocence of childhood. Lifts the spirits.

Marjoram: consolation. Combats pain. The fragrance is sooth-ing and comforting. Banishes the fear of loneliness, strengthens the spirit and eases the pain of loss.

Melissa: comfort. The fragrance brings relief and dispels fear of the unknown. Helps to overcome sorrow, inspires self-awareness.

Mint: creativity. Fresh and invigorating. The fragrance gathers and clarifies ideas. Stimulates the imagination, subdues arrogance and improves judgement.

Nutmeg: determination. Deep and spicy. The fragrance inspires decisiveness. Gives courage and spurs action.

Orange: joy. The golden apple of the citrus grove, it thrives on sunshine and preserves its light and heat. The precious oil is concentrated in the rind. The fragrance combats sadness.

Rosemary: care. Dew of the sea, it protects and heartens. The fragrance gives courage, invoking fortitude. Inspires insight and clarity.

Sage: wisdom. Fresh, sweet aroma. The fragrance dispels doubt. Instills common sense, sharpens the senses and memory.

Thyme: clarity. Energizing, invigorating. The fragrance dispels confusion and opens the mind to logic. Deciphers the uncertainty of dreams. Restores mental stability.

Tonka, fava: generosity. A warm, sweet perfume with the happiness of a ray of sunshine. The fragrance soothes even the most troubled soul. Encourages softness and sharing.

Vanilla: protection. The warm, sweet perfume of childhood. The fragrance gives comfort, boosts mood and relieves tension. Goes well with leather. A few drops combine to direct affairs of the heart.

Wood, Resin and Leaf Perfumes

Benzoin: composure. A dark resin with a thick and intense balsamic essence. The fragrance relieves anxiety and stress. It enables spiritual energy to grow in strength and is the ideal preparation for meditation.

Birch: well-being. Intense, aromatic perfume. The fragrance is enveloping and therapeutic. Frees the mind from the burden of pain, releases the spirit, aids physical and mental recovery.

Camphor: decisiveness. Strong and deeply balsamic. The fragrance of courage and determination. Strengthens the will.

Cedar: reflection. Extracted from the wood, this is one of the oldest known essences. The fragrance strengthens and guards the spirit. Helps maintain clarity, balance, and a sense of proportion. Encourages profound observation.

Cypress: support. Pleasant, mild, aromatic. The fragrance of its wood refreshes, relaxes and chases away worries. Helps with any form of change, strengthens the soul and prepares us to face even the most arduous trials.

Elemi: awareness. Pungent and aromatic. The fragrance rebalances, instills peace. Brings to light our deepest fears. Dispels delusions and restores reality.

Eucalyptus: positivity. A purifying, intense plant fragrance. Dispels negativity. Stimulates deep breathing, restores reason.

Galbanum: harmony. An intensely spicy, plant fragrance; the scent of nature and the forest. Calms anger.

Incense: reflection. A unique, fresh and sweetly camphorous scent. The fragrance slows breathing, inducing a calm and serene state and invoking deep spirituality. Prepares us for meditation and prayer.

Myrrh: security. More earthy and 'concrete' than incense. The fragrance is strong, balanced and unambiguous. Represents the link between spirit and reality.

Myrtle: forgiveness. Beautiful, magical, evergreen. Intense and deeply aromatic. The fragrance of serenity, the very essence of the soul. Soothes the spirit, relieves anger and resentment.

Oak moss: lightness of heart. Intense, penetrating, ancestral. The fragrance of perseverance and strength. Drives away thoughts of our own mistakes. Lessens nostalgia for what might have been.

Opoponax or sweet myrrh: optimism. Delicate, balsamic, intensely floral. This is the fragrance of serenity.

Patchouli: mystery. Sensual and exotic. The heady fragrance of life. Encourages decisiveness.

Petit-grain: concentration. Extracted from precious orange leaves, this fragrance awakens the spirit. Clears the mind; helps to make important decisions.

Pine: determination. Solid and tenacious, this tree of fortitude does not bend or break. Its fragrance is balsamic, aromatic. Instills courage, boosts self-confidence.

Rosewood: movement. Sweet and fruity with a hint of spice, obtained from tropical trees. The fragrance of trust and serenity. Evokes the sweet pain of longing and hope.

Sandalwood: temptation. Powerful, mysterious and fascinating. The fragrance of Eros. Extremely complex: sharpens the senses, opens the heart and restores feelings.

Vetiver: resistance. Fresh, moist, green. This is the heavy, complex fragrance of the earth. Tenacious, invincible, it gives strength, encourages openness towards others, and self-forgiveness.

Perfumes of Animal Origin

Ambergris: beauty. The oldest of perfumes, sweet and seductive, adored by women. The fragrance is transported by the sea and deposited on beaches like a precious gift, after which it still retains its profound, mysterious charm. Evokes the awakening of femininity, elegance . . . and the heat of a summer's night.

Beeswax: elegance. Warm and delicate. The fragrance of wax harnesses the power of nature, flowers and pollen.

Leather: strength. Animal, intense, full of character. The fragrance of primordial energy and masculine strength.

Author's Note

I've always loved perfumes, but at a certain point in my life they took on a much greater significance for me. When your livelihood depends on flowers that bloom and provide nectar for the bees you keep, your perception of nature changes. Flowers, and their perfume, herald both the days and the months, as well as dividing them according to the different harvests. It was when I started to truly notice the smells of the world around me that the idea of a novel was born.

But talking about perfume isn't easy. Smells and scents are very difficult to portray on the page – if it's even possible at all. But it has been done superbly by two young Italian perfumers, Marika Vecchiattini and Caterina Roncati, fragrance designers at *Farmacia del Castello* in Genoa. In their *Profumificio* they both create customized perfumes – perfumes of the soul.

One day, having spoken to them about my book, they sent me three of their creations: a perfume for Beatrice, one for Aurore and a wonderful perfume for Elena. I was amazed. Not only had they been kind and patient enough to answer my questions, throwing open the doors to a world I'd just discovered, but from my descriptions alone they had created perfumes for my characters. Anyone who wants to smell the three fragrances can do so at the *Profumificio del Castello*.

Marika also wrote the essay *The Secret Language of Perfume*, which was invaluable to me when I was writing the novel, as was her blog '*Bergamotto e Benzoino*': one long journey of the senses, full of magical, professional tips. And this is how I discovered a different kind of perfume industry to the glamourous one we know so well: artisan, niche perfumery. I have Marika and Caterina to thank for all of this.

Finally, I would like to say that, even though it uses real settings, *The Secret Ways of Perfume* is a work of fiction, and uses the poetic licence of storytelling. Measurements in grams, with precision scales, have long replaced drops. Beatrice Rossini and her descendants, Caillen McLean and his magnificent roses, Absolue, Narcissus and La Fougérie are all fruits of my imagination, as is the famous work by Giulia Rossini. So, if you were to look for Enchanted Garden in the Osmothèque in Paris, alas you wouldn't find it, because it exists only in this novel.

Acknowledgements

Thank you to my family for supporting me, accepting me, and loving me for who I am. Thank you to my husband for keeping my life and our children's lives going while I write, and especially for making sure that I eat properly.

Thank you to Silvia Zucca for being my friend, for lending me her perfume books, and for telling me about Marika Vecchiattini and introducing us. Thank you to Anna for always being there, Andreina for cheering me up, Lory for being so sweet, and Eleonora for making me laugh. Thank you to Antonella for keeping me going when I lost faith, and for celebrating every victory with me. A huge thank you to Garzanti for choosing me, to the staff who looked after my novel, to my editor Elisabetta Migliavada for whom there are simply not enough words. And finally, thank you to the agency that represents me. To Laura Ceccacci who believed in me from the beginning, who is so much more than a friend, and to whom I am profoundly grateful. To Anna Chiatto, who welcomed me with a beautiful smile, and to Kylee Doust who opened the doors to a new world.

Thank you.

A Conversation with Cristina Caboni

Where did you find the inspiration to write *The Secret Ways of Perfume*?

From my own experience. I live in the countryside, surrounded by all kinds of plants and flowers – and I'm a beekeeper, which is more than a job for me, it's a lifestyle. My world is full of perfumes. Keeping bees means you live very closely with nature. Their wellbeing is essential, so I learned to watch them, study their work, adapt to their habits. When flowers mature and start to secrete the nectar the bees feed on, the air is filled with perfumes. That's when harvesting starts. Over time, I've learned to recognize the different nuances of how flowers communicate with the bees. While this knowledge came gradually, it has ended up being quite extensive. I started to pay attention, to smell everything, and I understood that perfume is a language, a subtle and immediate means of communication. It wasn't a discovery, though – you can't discover something that has always existed. I just saw what was already there, available, before my eyes. I had a sense of loss for the things I hadn't known and I was so fascinated by this world – that I'd unwittingly neglected for so long – that I felt I had to share it with everyone. But how could I tell such a complicated story? Only a perfumier could do it. A woman capable of great feelings, delicate sensitivity. The descendant of an ancient family that passed down their knowledge from mother to daughter. I was sure she would know how to describe this world of perfumes and smells, carefully weighing words and concepts, communicating emotions. That was when I saw a little girl, and her grandmother. They were the right people; they would be able to convey the importance of perfume.

Perfume is the way, it tells a story, and it is a language to communicate our emotions: this is what Elena's grandmother tells her. Does perfume have these powers for you, too?

I'm certain it does. Smells are primal: they warn us, they fascinate us, some of them disgust us. Perfumes reach deep inside us and crystallize our emotions. Some of them bring back moments from our past, evoking the feelings we had. Just one smell – the perfume in the air on a particular day – and our memory springs into action. Perfumes cheer us up, so a couple of drops of our favourite perfume can turn a dull day into something special. They can also be comforting, like the smell of bread or biscuits fresh from the oven, vanilla, or washing powder.

How did you discover the meaning of perfumes?

When the idea for the novel was taking shape, I began to take an interest in artisan perfumery, in fragrances for people who want a unique perfume. It was a very intriguing concept: that of an individual essence, made to measure like a suit. And I wondered why I adored certain smells, felt indifferent towards others, and some I just couldn't stand. So I started to research as much as I could to do with perfume and I discovered that each smell has its own message, and each perfume elicits a reaction from the person who smells it or wears it. For example, some fragrances are therapeutic, they help us through difficult situations, some make us feel more secure, others might be the touch that livens up an important date or makes a special night unforgettable.

The book contains several formulas for creating perfumes, from the ancient to the modern. Where does this passion come from?

It comes from the pleasure I take in smelling them, and from my endless curiosity for perfumes. I wanted to know about every mechanism, every step required in the creation of a perfume. And discovering that the process hasn't really changed over the centuries was illuminating. Of course the essences are different now to the ones used in the past, and everything is properly regulated, but the process itself isn't so very different to what the original master perfumiers were doing. What is different today is the concept, the idea, or, as they call it, the brief. Now perfume tells a story: it starts with the top notes, the first ones you smell, then the middle, and finally the real weight of the perfume: the base notes.

Elena has a special talent for understanding people and trying to help them using perfume. But at one

point in her life she rejects it because it's linked to memories that are too painful for her. Do you think your past and your own experiences can make you forget who you really are?

A deep disappointment, especially when you're very young like Elena, can trigger a sort of resistance to the thing that caused the pain. We often turn to something else, something we can rationally approve. I think we lose ourselves a lot, but I don't believe it's a real rejection, rather the search for an acceptable alternative. But taking a path that isn't really yours only works up to a point. Deceiving yourself won't make you happy. We are heart and soul and roots, it's not enough to be rational. We live in a society that focuses on appearance at the expense of substance, and our standards distance us from our own individuality, which is actually our greatest asset. The most wonderful thing that can happen to a person is for them to be themselves. Finding yourself, knowing yourself and accepting yourself is a good start to being happy.

When she was still very young, Elena had to learn that even a mother can make the wrong choices. And only when she is about to have a child herself does she come to understand her own mother and perhaps to forgive her – because being a mother is the most diffi-cult job in the world. You have three children – do you think that's true?

I think that's a universal concept. It's easy for us all to be harsh judges, but when we have to deal with a new role, when we stop watching and start doing, everything changes. Being a mother is complicated. So being a good mother is very difficult. You have to think of everything, be there all the time – and often that's impossible. I think a lot of generational rifts have been bridged and healed by that change of role from daughter to mother. This happens to Elena, who finally begins to understand her own mother when she faces difficulties she could never have imagined before. At a certain point in her life, Elena finds herself going through a difficult pregnancy, alone, exactly like Susanna – what could be more enlightening?

The first time Elena meets Cail, she can tell that he's a sensitive man with a troubled heart from his perfume only, which 'smells like roses and rain'. Perhaps she also recognizes some of her own suffering in him. Two lonely souls who meet and discover new ways of making peace with themselves so that they can open up to each other . . . Is that what love means to you?

The thing that first unites Elena and Cail is instinct, something magical and illogical. They both feel the need to look at one another, to be close to one another, to find moments of happiness. It's not something you can explain, it's entirely irrational: a meeting of kindred spirits, a mutual affection and desire. That mystery is what love means to me. Love has the power to change anything – it is essentially the most powerful driving force that exists. Love makes us consider things that were inconceivable before. And a change of perspective can help us to understand others and accept ourselves.

Another of the novel's protagonists is Paris. The *Ville Lumière*, with its characteristic winding streets, its

stunning monuments, its magical atmosphere. When did you fall in love with this city?

I visited France years ago. The whole country made an unforgettable impression on me: the dazzlingly bright sky, the perfume, the friendly, smiling people, the magnificent castles, the countryside lined with long rows of flowers. And Paris is the symbol of France. A city full of charm, history, art and genius. It's synonymous with wonder and romance . . . and perfume. Everything about it inspired me: the places; the sophisticated, musical cadence of the accent; the way a cosmopolitan city takes life with a smile. I couldn't have chosen any other setting for my novel.

There is a lot of nature in the book: blooming lavender fields, gardens full of roses, even the markets brimming with flowers and plants. How important is nature and the outdoors to you?

'Important' might not be the right word. For me the outdoors is fundamental. It couldn't be any other way, given that my work takes me into the countryside, looking for flowers for my bees. But I think nature has always been part of me. I grew up in the countryside, and my grandparents there played an important role in my upbringing. They taught me to watch and listen. Then there's my other great passion that brings me close to nature: roses. I love them! And I share that beautifully scented joy with my mother. We have so many, from the biggest, most captivating blooms to the simplest, most delicate buds. We have historic, ancient and modern roses. Smelling the perfume of English roses, for example, is an unforgettable experience.

What's your favourite perfume?

My house is surrounded by citrus gardens, and in May everything turns the bright green of new leaves and the white of the flowers. In those few weeks, the air is full of perfume. It's fruity, intense and heady, or dare I say hypnotic: the perfume of orange blossom, my favourite perfume. It reminds me of my childhood, the desserts the women in my family used to make when I was little, playing games and running under the trees. Whenever I smell it, I'm enchanted and I feel good, I feel happy.

Are you working on a new novel yet?

Yes. It's a novel about deep emotions, the story of a family, a secret and a passion that helps the protagonist see her life in a new way. Women are always a great source of inspiration for me: they never give up, and despite their difficulties, they always manage to face life with a smile.

Do you love talking about your favourite books?

From big tearjerkers to unforgettable love stories, to family dramas and feel-good chick lit, to something clever and thought-provoking, discover the very best **new fiction** around – and find your **next favourite read**.

See **new covers** before anyone else, and read **exclusive extracts** from the books everybody's talking about.

With plenty of **chat, gossip and news** about **the authors and stories you love**, you'll never be stuck for what to read next.

And with our **weekly giveaways**, you can **win** the latest laugh-out-loud romantic comedy or heart-breaking book club read before they hit the shops.

Curl up with another good book today.

Join the conversation at
www.facebook.com/ThePageTurners
And sign up to our free newsletter on
www.transworldbooks.co.uk